SOJOURNERS and SUNDOGS

SOJOURNERS and SUNDOGS

First Nations Fiction

LEE MARACLE

PRESS GANG PUBLISHERS
VANCOUVER

SOJOURNERS and SUNDOGS

Press Gang Publishers acknowledges the ongoing support of The Canada Council; the
British Columbia Ministry of Small Business, Tourism and Culture through the BC Arts
Council; and the Government of Canada through the Book Publishing Industry
Development Program (BPIDP).

This book was previously published in two separate editions: *Sundogs: A Novel* (Theytus
Books, 1992) and *Sojourner's Truth and Other Stories* (Press Gang Publishers, 1990).

This book is a work of fiction. Names, characters, places, and incidents are products of
the author's imagination or are used fictitiously. Any resemblance to actual events,
locales, or persons, living or dead, is entirely coincidental.

Cover design by Val Speidel.
Cover art: "Wolf Brothers" by Susan Point.
Author photo by Columpa Bobb.
Printed and bound in Canada.

CANADIAN CATALOGUING IN PUBLICATION DATA
    Maracle, Lee, 1950-
    Sojourners and Sundogs
    ISBN 0-88974-061-5
    I. Title.
    PS8576.A6175S59 1999   C813'.54   C99-911162-0
    PR9199.3.M37S59 1999

PRESS GANG PUBLISHERS
P.O. Box 5238, Station B
Victoria, British Columbia
Canada   V8R 6N4

In the United States:
PRESS GANG PUBLISHERS
1436 W. Randolph Street
Chicago, Illinois
USA   60607

00 01 02 03 • 5 4 3 2 1

I would like to thank the original editors and publishers of *Sundogs* (Theytus Books) and *Sojourner's Truth and Other Stories* (Press Gang Publishers) for their work and support. I would also like to acknowledge my children for their continued support of my work. I now need to add my granddaughters to my list of supporters.

Sojourners and Sundogs is dedicated to those youth running at the new millennia from a place firmly rooted in culture and all those children I helped raise who remember their teenage years without crying.

This book is also dedicated to those youth suffering from HIV/AIDS. My family and particularly my children have been touched by death from this epidemic which crosses race, class and gender lines. Our youth are burdened with the inherited hurt of five hundred years of oppression. To also have to carry this epidemic into the new millennium is unbearable. I can't imagine what it is like to be young and finally see freedom around the corner only to have that threatened by a "new" epidemic.

SOJOURNERS and SUNDOGS

Foreword

Lee Maracle is unforgettable. You will meet her here in these pages as you read these amazing stories of survival and wit, a reclamation of a manner of thinking after years of forced colonization of her peoples. She veers straight for the most tender place of the conflict and stays there. And like those whose actions we owe our lives to—those who kept walking on the trails of tears, those who fought when there seemed to be nothing left—she keeps her head and heart about her, and stands there despite the debris of war, and confronts this wound called North America and sings. She is an original warrior, the consciousness of an age.

I cannot think of Lee Maracle without remembering the kitchen in her flat where we gathered some years ago after a reading by indigenous peoples at an international conference in Vancouver. There was hot coffee, warm fresh-baked bannock, a table around which we sat, a group of native writers gathered with the children and the neighbours, sharing.

We were all hungry for stories and songs that affirmed our place here and marked the boundaries of loss and hope, for the sustenance of spirit that would give us strength to keep moving, despite Wounded Knee, despite the Oka that was to come. That night we were fed by Lee's hospitality of house, food and most of all, spirit. And that's the life you will find here in this collection.

These aren't just stories. They carry old spirits, as do many of the stories and songs that have enabled us to arrive here together. I think of how a particular mountain, turn in a river or a line of coast can embody a story, a song, and in so doing can be a marker for a people, instructing them on how they came to be in that place, their relationship to it and how they will continue. To sing, to speak, is to solidify, acknowledge and honour the connection. During the court case for the Gitskan-Wet'suwet'en land claims litigation, Mary Johnson, one of the Elders, asked to sing a song — an adaawk — in court. An adaawk is an oral history that carries stories, the spirit of the people. It would give evidence as to the prior title of their land claims as an indigenous nation. It was crucial evidence to the case. She was begrudgingly allowed to sing, but the evidence was disallowed because the judge saw singing in the courtroom as inconvenient and ridiculous, and as having no merit. Oral traditions were not reliable, said the judge, though he allowed the testimony of a non-Indian resident of the area to be taken as the truth and accepted as evidence.

I consider Maracle's stories to be markers of a time and place in which native peoples in North America began to redefine and reclaim their names, their place in the world after a terrible holocaust.

The novel *Sundogs* is the coming-of-age story of a young native woman growing up when the world appears to be coming apart. Maybe the world is always at the edge of destruction. But this is a particular world, and concerns a girl of questions who seeks to become a woman of answers. Her questions may be universal, but the answers will have the shape of the city, the road along which her family travelled to that city, and the shape and stories of the land and people from which they arrived. They will be found in that ongoing conversation that is both inside and outside, as Maracle says, the conversation that characterizes the form of this novel.

Sojourner's Truth and Other Stories is still fresh, raw and wise. These are stories given birth to in the spirit of Sojourner Truth, an African-American slave woman who stood up when many had been stooped over with shame, and gave voice to generations of women who had been disregarded due to race and other forms of repression. "And ain't I a woman?" still echoes to the end of the 20th century where Lee Maracle's characters stand up despite all manner of obstacles in a colonized world. The story "Who's Political Here?" is a classic. I love the bravado here, the wit and revelation. This is a story of a woman coming into her own power, and as such it tells of a journey that characterizes all of Lee Maracle's work. You cannot separate the writing from the history of the people. Just as the inside is also the outside, the struggle of one woman embodies the struggle of the nation.

Maracle's writing came of age during the uprisings of our nations and continues to translate the consciousness of our communities. Her work is moral, harbouring an ethic that will invariably lead you back to the heart. She does not close her eyes, her ears, but speaks no matter what the cost. She will ask that you participate, voice the many questions that will inevitably surface, and take part in the mystery of the answer as you continue a journey that began for all of us between the legs of a woman.

These stories will last because those who follow us will look again to our words, our songs, to gain evidence, to know who they are and where they came from. I've often thought of our poems and stories as force fields, as houses for spirits who construct them so they will always be with us, to protect us, to guide us. Lee Maracle's stories will show us to be compassionate, original, funny-as-hell, failed, sometimes wise, sometimes foolish and utterly human.

I look forward to the next story, the next song Maracle will sing.

— *Joy Harjo*

Preface to the New Edition

The birth of *Sundogs* was an inadvertent happy accident inspired by a student of mine many years ago, while *Sojourner's Truth* is a collection of stories I wrestled with for some 18 years. Short story for Salish people is an old medium, not necessarily in the written form, but it is a very old oral tradition. The novel is fairly new. The only form comparable to a novel in the history of our storytelling is our origin story, which can go on for hours and hours depending on how many members of creation receive attention in the telling. Binding *Sojourner's* to *Sundogs* is like putting an old grandma and her grandchild together in a photograph, and it's so fitting.

In the preface to *Sojourner's Truth*, I stated that in some of the stories the reader becomes the trickster. This sparked literary criticism from some learned corners, making various complaints which I won't list. These critics all had the following in common: they defined "trickster" for me. Attempting this they provided me with a source of much amusement.

In many of these stories and in parts of *Sundogs*, Raven calls you forth to jump into her jogging shoes, or put on an old slouch hat and try to see the world through some other angle. Being Raven can be a difficult task for Europeans, because being is not about definition or theory. Defining and naming things is an external world phenomenon. It takes place outside the self while being takes place inside the self. The journey from outside the self to inside is sometimes a long one.

All of my stories are "internal world" stories. My Raven, my transformer, is the catalyst for internal transformation. This is because my stories are woman-centred stories. In the past, all Salish stories were gender specific, whereas all anthropological discourse concerning "Raven" in the non-Native world is male-based. So, for someone to hand me a Salish male definition to work with is amusing. If I choose, I am entitled to pick up any knowledge from the Salish world, including male knowledge, because we are a freedom-loving people. But I am also free not to pick up that knowledge; see "Black Robes" from *I Am Woman*. Of course, the world is free to critique my work from its patriarchal position, and I am free to find this amusing.

All of my characters live within both a condition and themselves. In the course of any story both the character and the condition are "being". What you see is the journey from the outside to the internal world. You see impact on being, then you see being's response. Raven calls upon the listener/reader to see yourself in this story and respond to creation, to "being".

You see, my Raven is female and no anthropologist ever heard a woman's Raven story.

So, no one outside of our people would really know how particular the meaning is of a woman "trickster". In fact even among our people few of us know.

We, as Native women, are in the process of rediscovering and reclaiming our separate body of knowledge. I have felt the burden of having to drive through darkened tunnels of memory and magic to reclaim the internal world of women. The Native women who know me understand I have a very firm grip on our feminist sense of Raven, the transformer, trickster, clown. We know that the process of transformation in the external world begins with the transformation of the internal. We know that the transformation of the internal world requires a clear picture of the external conditions of that world and our relationship to it.

Enough. I wish the readers luck and enjoyment.

— *Lee Maracle, 1999*

Part One:

SUNDOGS: A NOVEL

SUNDOGS

It's Tuesday, not a very busy day. The cars on the road in front of my bedroom window drone lazily in the direction of their homes. The parking lane on the roadside is filling up. This is the East End of Vancouver, so few of any of the residents here have personal garages to park their cars in. Just a few short years ago the city put "Parking For Residents Only" signs up all over the place. It helps, but invariably one or two of the residents end up driving up and down the street looking for a space to put their car to sleep in. No one seems to call the towing company — at least I have never seen a tow truck on our street. Most of the people just park a little farther away. The houses here are built side by side with skinny walkways between them. There is barely five feet between us and both neighbours.

I shouldn't be thinking about the crowding here in the East End. I have a sociology paper to do. I wonder if anyone has bothered to survey the social implications of growing up here in the East End as opposed to some Yuppie neighbourhood, like False Creek. This thought brings me around to my paper. It is not about density; it's about Marriage and Divorce in Khatsalano's community, which was once located at False Creek but is now integrated with a local North Vancouver reserve. I'm at the wrap-up stage. All my notes are piled neatly in little card files in front of me. My typewriter is all wired up and ready to go. I am not a procrastinator, but something keeps me hesitating.

It's the first line. I always seem to have trouble grabbing the first line. I look about my room hoping something in my corner of the world will deliver up the first line. The desk I work at is old, but not respectably old. It doesn't qualify as an antique. It's just rickety. A single bed graces one corner and an old chiffarobe hides all my clothes. I am not into the poster culture of some of my friends so there isn't much hanging on the walls. Just a piece of art work from one of my nieces — a water colour. It's a painting of what she imagines Khatsalano's village to look like, and layered over it is a bunch of apartment buildings. It's kind of neat. Khatsalano's village is actually a line drawing, while the new apartments that crowd the old location are superimposed on the village in water colour. Otherwise, it is a pretty barren room. I think about the words "pretty barren" and wonder why we string two things together that are so opposite by themselves in order to emphasize the negative. It doesn't make much sense. Nothing to do with the sociology of Relocation and its effect on Marriage and Divorce among Khatsalano's villagers, so I stare back at my notes:

Khatsalano and his fellow villagers were loaded onto a barge and shipped out to sea ... I didn't write the date down, but it doesn't matter for sociology. It is the anomie of relocation and its effect on marriage I am after. My mind kicks into gear; the first line rolls out — and is stopped dead by a familiar sound that scatters my thoughts. For Pete's sake, who is she talking to? I can hear my mother's voice, clear as a bell.

"Oh sure, and if you cut off your head, you'll end your headache too. Cutbacks. That'll fix things." I know the rest of the story. It must be six o'clock. It's my mother arguing with the six o'clock news again. It's embarrassing. Some little piece of me wants to give her a break. I even argue with myself that someone could be out there in our living room listening to the news with her. It could be that she is actually talking to another human being. No. Don't bother going to look. I try to sit still and get back to my essay. I squirm, tense up. I can't do it. I have to look.

I have no idea why I am doing this, but I sneak downstairs through the kitchen to the living-dining room. This house was built in the early fifties, when L-shaped living-dining rooms were in style and kitchens were still good sized. It takes me a minute or two to get there. By the time I arrive to peek around the corner my mom is mad as can be. She turns to look at me; she's not the least bit embarrassed; then she lectures me about the stupidity of the voters who "chose this fool to lead them." I have grave doubts about the brilliance of arguing with the Premier via TV, but I don't say anything. I can't admit that secretly I admire her sense of logic, even to myself.

Her evening ritual disturbs my writing. I want to say something but I bite it back. It would offend her. She looks pretty mad. I don't want to turn her rage at the Premier onto me. Besides, the news only lasts an hour, and half of that is sports. I don't mind the interruption that much, but deadlines for essays are beginning to weigh on me. I would like to get her off the subject of the voters and the Premier, though. She isn't young, my mother, and her blood pressure continues to be a problem, especially since she doesn't follow her doctor's advice about diet and relaxation. Stress enlivens her and she fails to relate it to her blood pressure problem.

Her face is reddening. I ask her if she has taken her pills. Behind the question is a small hope that this will throw her off track. It doesn't. She turns the question into another slice of anger at the Premier and his new policy. Welfare cutbacks. I am more than aware of how many of us are on welfare in this city. I just don't feel the same about it as my mom. It shames me some to hear the statistics about us in class. The shame burns holes in whatever sympathy I may have for Indians; it's not like that for my mom, though.

"Pills? I have had enough bitter pills today, thank you. Did you hear him?" She shakes her dustpan at the TV.

"No," I mumble. How could I? She was complaining to the TV the whole time he was speaking. I wonder how the heck she heard him. She starts in again and I stop listening and try to find something else that might twist the conversation in a new direction. Her hands are shaking. Underneath her anger is some other feeling I try not to think about. It's in her eyes. That dull look she gets when she is trying to cover up sadness and anger. I can't get past this, can't break through wondering why she is so sad about people she has never met. No one in our family is on welfare. How Momma could get so upset over welfare cutbacks is beyond me.

"It's almost Christmas ... Christmas, and the rest of those toadies just sit on their thumbs while ... " I can't repeat the rest, but it's very colourful. Let her blow off steam. She'll settle down eventually. I withdraw emotionally and let her words drift into the dead file in my mind without feeling them. This helps to keep my blood pressure down. It takes a lot of years of schooling to numb out like this. Momma knows a lot, but she didn't attend much school. She can't be numb about anything. She shed tears for that guy, Martin Luther King, when he died, and everything and everyone else who suffered too.

She turns to me and waves her broom in my face. She misses. She is Native enough to feel everything she thinks and hears, but French enough to get wild about it. "Get command," I tell myself. It doesn't occur to me that she might instill some feeling about the government's new policy in me. She stops to take a breath and I move.

"Why don't we eat out tonight?" This is lame. Neither of us can afford to eat out and a change of scenery would not have changed her mind anyway. I had to try.

"I'm not hungry." The snap comes back into her black eyes. Momma's eyes change colour with her moods. Angry, they are deep black and without sparkle. Peaceful, they are dark brown and snappy. Fortunately, her anger is quickly spent. The sparkle returns and her eyes lighten. "Don't you have work to do?" Where has she been? How can anyone work while she is warring with the television? I mumble "yes" and turn to leave. I am almost out the door without getting her in a new rage over the Premier and government policy when she asks me what I am working on.

"A sociology essay." Stupid me. I should have lied and said biology. Too late now.

"What's that?" I have to duck and dodge.

"Sociology or essay?" Not a very good duck or dodge but it's the best I could come up with.

"Whichever." She is picking crayons up off the floor and herding little bits of scrap paper into the box in the corner of the living room. She piles them up neatly. She seems calm now. It is I who am upset. It dawns on me that this is Tuesday. My nieces and nephews haven't been here for two days. She usually tidies up after them right away. What was she doing on Monday, or Sunday night for that matter?

"Were the kids here yesterday?" It slips out.

"No," she answers flatly. I think I see her pause before she puts the last bit of scrap paper into the box. She spins around and mumbles something about how I better finish my essay, then retreats to the kitchen. I hesitate, confused. I am grateful for the change of subject and suspicious of Momma's strange behaviour too. I never knew her to let go of a question this easily.

I can hear her rooting about the kitchen, banging the pots and pans. I look about the living room. Everything seems normal. The sofa is squatted there, heavy, deep red and velvet. It's aged now, the arms have worn smooth of their velvet. The little TV sits on an old crate, still delivering the news. Sports is on now. A coffee table lingers in front of the couch waiting for the weekend round of children to arrive. Underneath the coffee table is the crayon box. Now that some of my nieces and nephews are older, oil pastels, ink pens, and charcoal also fill the box. Otherwise nothing is different.

The dining room is the same as usual. Neater maybe. No old

papers on the table. There is a vase of fresh flowers sitting in the middle of it. It isn't spring. Why the flowers?

"Where did the flowers come from?" I ask.

"If you came home once in a while you'd know," she answers, arching her eyebrows and squinting her eyes. I hate this. Guilt is the klutsiest of all human emotions. I want to tell her how coercive this is and at the same time I wish I hadn't gotten curious about the flowers. I am twenty years old and still have to report my whereabouts to Momma and seek permission to be anywhere but home after school. Permanently grounded, I have never enjoyed the freedom other kids have had. When I was young she punished me. These day she keeps me tied to the house by guilting me. I am about to scream when the phone rings.

"Oh, hello Dearie." It is my sister one up on me. She is "Dearie." We are all nicknamed, "Dearie," "Darling," etc. Momma fancies we enjoy these names. She mixes up our christian names on those occasions when she tries to use them, but she never forgets who is "Dearie" and who is "Darling." It doesn't bother the others. They are all much older than me. Rita is "Dearie" and thirty with three "Dearies" of her own. She is about to have a fourth child. I ignore this child. I did enough baby-sitting during my teenage years to know that another niece or nephew means work for me. Work I don't like.

"You're at the hospital? Isn't this too early? … Tell you what, just put your knees up. Have you a pillow under your hips? … No … What is wrong with those people? … Tell them to give you a pillow, put it under your hips … What? … They're going to go ahead. But you're three weeks early … Don't do anything. I'll be right there. Don't worry, Dearie. I'm on my way."

I am sure that even passive Rita didn't feel she needed this, but I am grateful. Now I might get the damned essay done. Not nice. The least I should do is worry about my sister and her premature birth. To tell the truth, I don't even feel guilty about not worrying. I have nearly a dozen nieces and nephews. I had to baby-sit each weekend for half of them and can't get up any sympathy for my brothers or sisters anymore over them. Not one of my brothers or sisters ever asked me about another child but they all thought I would be delighted to go another round of baby-sitting when the time came.

"Get your coat. We're going to the hospital," and Momma swings into her coat. She rummages about the hall closet trying to find two shoes that match. I always want to chuckle when she jumps into her coat like she is on some dangerous mission. Momma is prideful and fancies she looks elegant. I don't believe she has ever paid attention to the styles of the day. She shops at second-hand stores and buys only the cheapest things there. She never bothers matching what she buys. She ends up with the loudest checks, plaids and flowered designs in the store. Dressed, she looks like a wild array of colour and patterns. She is wearing her houndstooth car coat over plaid pants and a flowered shirt as though she were a fashion model who just stepped off the cover of *Vogue* magazine. I think about this while I dread going to the hospital.

"I'll drive," I say to her. I don't need the kind of ride to town she likes to have when she drives. She learned late. My elder brothers and sisters excuse her. Late or no, there are some things drivers shouldn't do. One is getting out of the car in the middle of the road when the light is green to curse at someone. We can't get two blocks down the road without Momma leaning out the window and calling someone an idiot or some other more colourful name. She doesn't answer — selective hearing.

I rummage around in the hall closet for my own shoes and coat and follow her out the door. When am I going to find the courage to quietly say to her, "No, I am not going"?

By the time I am dressed, she is stamping her feet and telling me to hurry. I don't bother paying attention. My mind is already wandering off down memory lane. Momma has no sense of propriety. I was about six the last time she wore high-heeled shoes. We were turning onto the old bridge heading up the ramparts when

Momma took a swing at Rudy, who was fighting with Rita. Rudy ducked. Momma missed. Her coattail was caught in the car door so she couldn't get a good swing at him. The high-heeled shoe she wasn't wearing fell out. She put the car into reverse and backed up the wrong way, opened the passenger door and told Rita to pick up the shoe while she slowed the car down. Rita scooped up the shoe. The driver behind her was mad. He nearly rear-ended her. He yelled, she stopped the car and said something really nasty to him, then took off again. I choke back the laughter at the old image. Just before we get to the car she hands me the keys.

"Here, you drive," she says and a sigh escapes me. On the way, I listen to her ramble on about doctors, how little they know and how much better the old midwife system was and how the criminalization of midwifery was aimed at us. I want to believe my Momma is sane, but she has a way of leaving out whole paragraphs when she condemns these people and the verdicts she hands out lack evidence. I have no idea what medical school courses look like but they must teach some notions about childbirth there.

"Genocide. Pure and simple ... They knew." I want relief. Relief from always considering every law, custom and practice of these people as some sort of anti-Native genocidal plot. My mother, I muse, thrives on the plottiness of these people. Without their plottiness, she would have no reason to get up every day. Without their wickedness, she would have very little reason for being. What a rotten thing to say about my mother. Just then she leans out the window and curses some driver blocking our way.

"Get a move on buddy — we're busy." He would, but whacking the woman pushing the baby buggy doesn't appeal to him. She is a young white woman, the kind of white woman my mom never looks at, petite, pretty normal and with a baby buggy. The guy in front gives her the finger. Wrong move, buddy. She is out of the car and punching his car, calling him names.

"Momma. Get back in this car. We'll be late." Thank Christ he didn't bother getting out. She comes back mumbling.

"Damned fool. Probably voted for that other idiot." The door shuts; I pray she doesn't continue, but she does. "These people stick together, doctors, politicians and their voters." I feel fed up coming on. I fail to see how that driver and his concern for the girl and the baby could possibly be connected to the general conspiracy of genocide, my sister having a baby too soon and the Premier cutting back on welfare. I don't say anything, though. I know my mother would present a picture I might believe about their general trickery, so I sit and fume. We hit a whole series of red lights.

"Isn't that just like it. Every light red. I knew we should have left home earlier to see her. Serves us right. Got no business sitting at home doing nothing when she is so close to her time." I figure I can bite onto this one without re-conjuring images of genocidal theory.

"How were we to know, Momma?"

"You sound just like them," she snaps. I grip the wheel. I can feel my face change. My eyes narrow and my brow is crowding them. My lips tighten. It's going to take a minute or two to get myself under control. "At one time, pregnant women were watched over night and day. Now they are left alone as though having a baby were as simple as going shopping. Rita's in trouble and you could care less." I am fed up. A groan nearly escapes. She carries on. "They got our kids so filled with their junk, they don't know shit from sugar anymore." I don't know what's the matter with me today. I should know by now that nothing in this world is simple for us. Everything is connected to some sort of injustice in my mom's mind. My insides rage. At home, I am not Indian enough and at school I am much too Indian. The tension wire inside is stretched thin. A few more words and it will snap.

"Look, look. There it is." A hospital is hard to miss, Momma. I see it. It's the damned Premier. If he hadn't gotten on TV with his new policies, this would not be happening. Careful girl, you're beginning to buy into the genocide conspiracy. I can't stop. She's right as rain. All my misery, and my mother's, is being orchestrated

by a premiere idiot. I look out the window at the other drivers —
the voters, I hiss. I'll bet you did vote for him too. Blood. Genetics.
I can feel myself get out of the car and march into the hospital full
of the same grim determination and missionary zeal as my mom.
We're here to save my sister. The Premier dances in my head like a
puppet. I give him what for. I get so caught up in my daydream I
stumble on my sister, nearly knocking her off her bed. She moans.

"Oh, I didn't know you were coming," and she emphasizes "you"
in a way that makes me cringe. I deserve the shot. I have never
gone to the hospital for any of the babies born in our family. Cultural genocide — not my fault.

"How are we?" We aren't doing well. Rita is in labour — pain
really. And Momma and I are still a little mad, but then she knows
how *we* are. She wants to know about Rita, so I don't bother answering.

"I'm ready. It's too late to stop it now." Rita's long hair is spread
out all over the pillow, sticky and wet looking. The waves in it are
tighter than usual. Her hair is not black, not even dark brown. In
fact, it's almost the same colour as her skin, honey amber. She is
suppressing pain and it shows on her face. On the surface it looks
calm, but it is a calm veiling the pain and agitation she feels. Why
women do this when they are having babies is beyond me. They
must all think that hollering around during birth is shameful. It's
funny that screaming and hollering after whacking your shin is
OK but expressing pain during birth isn't. It makes no sense to me.
She lets go a funny pinched grin.

"You should've called earlier," Momma scolds gently, burying
her earlier feelings of guilt.

"I called as soon as it started. No warning, bingo, and there it
was." Rita chuckles. It's a laugh pressed out between contractions.
Sounds more like a squeaky grunt.

"Where is Bill?" Momma's tone is laced with accusation. Rita
doesn't seem to notice it. She answers flatly.

"He went to the bathroom."

"Is he going in with you?" Momma purses her lips and nods in the general direction of the bathroom. I wish she hadn't asked this. Rita might answer yes, which would put Momma on another cultural genocide roll. She still thinks birthing is the private sanctuary of women. The whole idea of men watching their wives give birth is intended to discourage couples from having more children as far as she is concerned. She has this clear line drawn between what is men's business and what is women's. Any crossing over, back and forth, is going to disturb the natural order of things and she doesn't like it.

"No. He has the flu." Good.

"Mnhmh," this sounds like an accusation. His "flu" is likely caused by Pilsner and not a virus. I pray Momma says nothing. I have two sisters and two brothers — all married. If my mom may be believed, her children can't tell the difference between ham and eggs and steak and caviar, because not one of their spouses is good enough for Momma's children. Rita doesn't answer. She doesn't seem to notice the gravel in Momma's tone. Is it me? Did I hear or imagine the tone in my mother's voice?

"You wait here, Sweetie. I'm going to get us a cup of coffee." She turns to Rita, "Would you like one too?"

"Sure. That should sharpen our nerves," I answer for both of us. My words grate across the same sort of sand that lives in my mother's mouth. She scurries off unaware.

"Been a bad day?" My sister's voice cuts through before I have a chance to guilt myself.

"The six o'clock news. Other than the genocide plot, everything is fine." Rita holds her belly, which is now twisting itself into some shape I never imagined, and laughs, or tries to. I don't get the joke. 'Course by now I feel like I will never laugh again.

"Honey. It's such a long story. Our mothers have trekked through one wilderness after another without let-up. Try to ... " She rolls forward, grunts, then carries on, "understand. There you are at the bottom of the hill watching Mom grumble through the rest of her journey home and it all just seems too much." I am not sure why Rita said "our mothers." We have the same mother. And the "journey home" confuses me more. If she means the place other folks call heaven then it isn't any place I can imagine. I don't say this to Rita; instead, I just watch her. I am sorry I never watched the birthing process before. There is some humour in this bit of work half the world volunteers for. Irony, I suppose. There you are on a gurney, grunting and sweating away, your body is being ripped open and you're talking as though nothing unusual is going on. I want to tell her to be quiet and concentrate on her work.

Rita is smaller than I, shorter and thinner. She looks so delicate, frail even now. Her mouth is open and she is breathing in short raspy breaths. My heart aches for her. Why women do this is beyond me. Her thick eyebrows arch unevenly and she closes her eyes. "Soon, oh soon," leaks from her mouth, all breathy and full of hope. My hand reaches out to touch hers. She opens her eyes and smiles. The pain subsides. She carries on trying to explain Momma's raging around. She has a way of talking in riddles. I hear the words but they don't stick so easily in my mind. It sounds like poetry that I have to turn over and over before I can figure it out. I chose sociology as my major because I hate literary confusion. I look at her face intently. It isn't much older than mine but there are tracks on it, telltale lines of age. Ten years of another world are etched on her face. I feel jealous of Momma. She knows the stories behind each track and how Rita earned them. I don't know Rita very well.

"How is it to be married?" Where did this come from? It isn't what I was thinking about.

"Not a bit of what it's cracked up to be." Sharp and crisp, Momma's voice jumps out from behind me before I hear the shuffle of her feet. "You finish school before you think about marriage." She leans over Rita's bed and whispers, "Beats being single though, doesn't it?" and she winks. Rita shrieks, "Noo ... Momma, you aren't?" I don't get it. "I am ... thinking anyway."

" ... Noo ... " and Rita giggles in the middle of a major con-traction, then grunts and laughs and Momma says, "Darned fool ... I must be ... he must be." Rita doubles over again with pain and chuckles out "no's" and grunts by turns while my mother gets lost in a series of darned fools. I stand there stupidly, wondering what the heck they are talking about. Finally, the doctor shows up. We have to leave. Bill is hot on the heels of the doctor. He gets to stay.

"What was that all about?" I ask before we are quite out the door. Momma doesn't answer. She digs around in her purse while we walk down the dimly lit hospital hall to the waiting room at the end.

"I hope everything goes well," she says as she grabs her rosary of purple crystals and retreats to her Catholic prayers. Momma is not a devout Catholic. She does this only when she is forced to rely on white folks and when she is in public; otherwise she counts on her indigenous sense of the sacred — something I know little about. Convenient. Running around burning sweet grass or sage in a hospital wouldn't go over well. Still I am annoyed by the ro-sary. I want to know what they were talking about back in the room. I think about it for a while. For Pete's sake. She's thinking about marrying that old fool Johnny. Why, he's old — fat too. It doesn't occur to me that my mother is reasonably old too.

Momma's "hail Mary full of grace" slides out from under her bowed head. The soft resonance of her voice clashes with the stiff-ness of the hospital. Pale green halls stretch out empty but for the nurses who click by every now and then. A red light goes on over the archway above the nursing station and a nurse comes out and heads in the direction of Rita's room. This one wears rubber-soled shoes. They squeak. She jingles her keys as she walks by. She doesn't look at us. I am thinking about Momma getting married and the lonely hours Rita will have to spend here. Five days of rest among strangers in a boring room with an odd smell to it, poor Rita. Momma is sixty for Gawd's sake. Five days of having to tell strange white women intimate things ... what does Momma mean "beats being single" and winking seductively at Rita? ... five days of dull foreign food ... Momma's prayers annoy me more now ... I want to remind her that her Pope thinks lust is a sin, that Rita would not be in this mess if he weren't so down on abortion, but she would probably argue the wisdom of both those remarks. What in the world does she need to get married for — have another baby? I shudder at the thought. Rita is busy having enough for all of us. Just then, Bill backs into the room, makes a crazy circle, then faces us. He looks lost. He tells us they threw him out. He sounds like he is sorry to have left Rita so soon.

"Flu is a no-no in delivery," he says, grinning sheepishly. Thanks, Bill. We knew that.

"This isn't like the last one," he offers, his voice rich with worry. Great thought, Bill. Glad you could come by and depress us. "Something is different. Can't put my finger on it." Spare us. "If anything goes wrong, I'll never forgive myself." Too bad you didn't think of that on party night. What has gotten into me? Bill is a nice man for a Catholic. *Shut up, Marianne.* OK. I don't think I do well under pressure. Something could go wrong. Everything could. Mother could marry her cribbage partner, Rita could have twins and I may never get the damned rocks out of my personality. Bill paces. Momma has finished her rosary. She looks ready to talk.

"Don't worry, Bill, everything is going to be fine. Marianne, call the others." Grief. I forgot. Lacey, Rudy and Joseph don't know we're here. I dash for the phones and call them all. Each in turn is as excited and happy about Rita's birthing as Momma is and I wonder if anyone in our family has any sense at all. Their joy is nearly contagious, though, and by the time I am back in the waiting room my icy cynicism has melted somewhat.

There isn't much to do in a hospital waiting room but wait. I look up and down the hall and try to find something to catch my attention. The hall walls are bare except for the odd fire alarm and extinguisher. The ceiling lights are few and far between, dim and all the same. There are a few ancient magazines on the coffee table in front of the row of uncomfortable chairs in the waiting room, all of which I have read. Not even the pictures on the fronts of them look interesting. The nurses have become familiar. There goes the key rattler, followed by the clicker. I hope the others come soon. The rattler is about forty and handsome looking. She isn't fat, but her breasts and hips have expanded some over time and her face has a forty-year-old calm to it, like my sister Lacey's face. The squeaker is young, slender — edgy looking. She looks like she thinks nursing is serious. The key rattler takes her skills for granted. They pass in front of us every so often. Monotony is huge here. Wait, imagine the nurses, dream their personal lives into being, character them up, re-create them, play with their lives and wait. Both women are wearing gold wedding bands. I think about sociology and divorce, the subject of my next paper. Why, I don't know. The wedding bands remind me of our last lecture. Half the women in this country will likely divorce and remarry at least once. Of those, most will live below the poverty line until their kids grow up. So much for the institution of free-choice marriage. Maybe the edginess of the young one has something to do with the state of her marriage. *What a thought, Marianne.* One of these days I will learn to mind my own business.

"What the hell does it take to deliver a baby anyway?" I know the answer but I ask it anyway. I fill my head with all sorts of questions, trying to get my mind off marriage. It keeps bringing me back to Momma and her old fool. Where did she find the time? How do old people romance anyway? Images of them snuggled up in their old beat-up car, necking up a storm, almost make me laugh, then turn to disgust. I look over at Momma and Bill. They are both seated in the corner trying to look peaceful. Momma's hands still clutch the rosary beads. Her almost pudgy fingers are holding the beads too tightly. Memories of her hands tug at me.

It has been a while since they were used to take a swing at any of us. Momma never spanked us the way some folks do. Had this habit of letting go a quick punch if she caught you doing something you weren't supposed to. She'd see you at the cookie jar stealing cookies, haul you off the counter, jab you a good one in the arm and carry on like nothing happened. She never bawled you out, either, but you knew, don't do that again. Her hands and arms were strong then. In memory, it looks kind of funny. There'd be Rita and Rudy bickering away and Momma sneaks up on them, jab, jab, "finish the dishes," in a sweet sing-song voice. I have never seen her hands do anything but work and whack. I try to imagine them touching Johnny romantically. The picture fades before a clear image comes up.

I stare at her face. She doesn't look old. The lines around her eyes are deep but the rest of her skin is smooth. Her eyes aren't as big as they were when she was young, but they are still thickly lashed and full of life. She must have been a beauty when she was young — Johnny probably thinks she is a beauty. Her brown, silvering hair is short, wild and wavy and her skin is lighter than the rest of us. The lightness of her skin sharpens the dramatic darkness of her eyes, especially if she is laughing. It's possible, this romance, and I wonder when it becomes impossible. *Never, silly, some old people stay married all their lives.* Funny, it never occurred to me that Momma might have been lonely all these years, and now I wonder why she waited so long before getting tangled up with a man.

Bill meanwhile is working himself into a frenzy. He has been jumping up out of his chair and sitting down, jumping up again, mumbling that something must have gone wrong. It shouldn't take so long. Momma ignores him. Her hands fidget with the beads but her face is calm. Her brows rise slightly every time Bill jumps up, otherwise nothing changes. I don't know Momma well enough to be able to tell if she is worried; her face says no, but her hands say yes. The arch of her brow also leans towards doubt about Rita's safe delivery. Only Lacey inherited the clean thin lines of Momma's brows; the rest of us have thick, tipi-shaped eyebrows like our dad. Women spend hours plucking out their hair to have the eyebrows Momma and Lacey were born with. Both of them take them for granted. I am beginning to see why Ol' Johnny chased Momma around the mulberry bush. Bill is sweating and the area around his armpits is wet by the time the doctor arrives.

"It's all over," and we gasp. Dr. Neely's bedside manner wants for some cultural polish from our side of the bed. "All over" means death for us. "Twins," he blurts out. Momma and Bill jump for joy. Twins. Just what Rita needed.

It has been about two years since I baby-sat any of my nieces and nephews. Who looks after them now when she goes out? When the kids come over on weekends Rita is always with them. I take another look at Bill. His shoes are worn thin and his pants are ragged. They must be having a hard time of it financially. They can't afford to go out. Well, that isn't exactly true, because Rudy and he are always swapping bar stories on Sunday at Momma's house — it's Rita that can't go out. Now with twins she will have to go out and find a job before she finishes her degree. Hustle to work five days a week, hustle home again to mind the babies and hustle to bed, only to wake up and start over. Not much reward in that.

"Let's go look," Momma says. We do. There they are, two tiny babies, hardly more than ten pounds between them. Mother chortles away, waves and makes clucking sounds, and Bill says "ooh" and "ah" by turns. We present a complete picture, Momma hunched down chortling, Bill squatting with his hands in his pockets and me looking like a guard of some sort, a stoic fool watching and doing nothing. I decide to leave them there marvelling at the twins and go back to Rita's bedside. I just can't bring myself to cluck or "ah." Rita is lying there looking heavier than when she was carrying the twins. Her eyes are puffy from the effort of delivery. There is something else different about her; maybe it's the vacant look in her eyes.

"What's up?" I ask this as lightly as I can. I hope for an answer that won't plunge me into any sort of emotional journey into her life.

"Twins," she says with a smile. Her eyes fill with tears, though. She stares at the ceiling trying to hide them. The air is uncomfortable. It's the first moment of confidence between us. I can't believe I invited this but there isn't any sense not seeing it through.

"How are you going to manage twins and school?" I can't think of a gentle way to form the question. My voice softens though. The question comes out like a soft murmur.

"Ever the pragmatist. I'm almost through school." Then she sighs and frowns. She doesn't know how she's going to do it either. She looks straight at me. "We'll make it somehow. We always do. Besides, the twins are the end of the line." End of the line? What does this mean? More riddles. Bill and Momma burst through the door with Lacey, Rudy, Joseph and their spouses in tow. My question is lost in the excited hubbub of congratulations and joyousness. Bill can't hide his pride. He struts about like having twins was some extraordinary feat. They are identical, both girls. Everyone is chattering and smiling from ear to ear. Joseph shakes Bill by the shoulders. It's the most emotional I have ever seen him get. Rudy slaps Bill's back, which is what Rudy always does. Only Lacey congratulates Rita. Laughter and jokes roll out among the general commotion of joy. Rita lies there, a wispy smile on her face. A pretty Madonna, enjoying the attention. Behind the small smile rests a strange look.

I don't understand how they can say which baby has which parent's nose, mouth, cut of face etc. I haven't, as an aunt, been joyous about babies. The whole business of moving from "goo-goo, ga-ga" to "hi, hi" and "why, why" never did appeal to me. All I see right now are dirty diapers, open mouths and Rita locked into another six-year tour of duty before they are in school. I hear squalling at all hours of the night and no rest for Rita. I can almost imagine her settling into her master's thesis finally after a long day, and then the little ones wake up. I can see her hands curling her hair around one finger, the furrow of her brow, lost in concentration, and then her old familiar sigh of disappointment when they awake for another feeding.

Mom settles down first.

"Don't worry about a thing, dear. You'll have all the help you need." Don't you dare volunteer me up for another round of baby-sitting, Momma. I almost say it out loud. University is not like high school. I need all the free time I have if I am to get through. Rita shoots me a look. It must be written all over my face because Rita tells me that she'll be fine. She smiles sweetly at me. I don't like all her suffering courage much. Momma ignores her. She is on a roll. This is a cultural roll and so she throws herself into it full throttle. Help mode. Rita's need for a clear conscience and my hesitation don't count. The others leave to go have a look at the twins. Momma plans out loud how Rita is going to make it with the twins without quitting school. I stop listening.

Little John, Rita's last child, is six. It has been two years since I agreed to baby-sit him. Momma always took it for granted that when she said yes, I would do the job. I can hear our last fight over it. They are my nieces and nephews and I am part of this family, whether I like it or not. This is our way and so forth and so forth. I sat and listened to her scold me into compliance, then decided that when I went to university there would be no baby-sitting for anyone, that I would live on campus if that was my only choice. I did not have the nerve to say this to Momma. I had gone over to Rita's and told her privately. She never asked again.

My brothers' and sister's spouses return from the nursery. The women are cackling and teasing Rita, who doubles over in pain at every laugh. The key jingler comes into the room to tell us that there are only two visitors allowed at one time. Joseph and Rudy return just in time to promise her we will all settle down and be quiet.

"It's noon. I'll call Johnny to come and take Bill for a cigar and whatever else men do when they have babies. You boys hurry along with Bill and we'll go shopping and double up on a few things."

"Great idea." This comes from Monique, Joseph's wife. She is the family's resident cheerer-upper. She starts listing all the shops we should go to and all the nice things we can get the twins. Lacey joins her. Lacey's list is not as nice as Monique's but it is more useful and Momma clucks the boys out of the room. Rita, who is nearly asleep, hasn't the energy to say it's all right again, but she looks as though she wants to say it. No one would believe her anyway.

Bill lumbers out with the rest of the men to find Johnny. Rudy swaggers down the hall, his arm about Bill's shoulders. He is taller than Bill and broader and he looks as if he enjoys their difference in size. He's condescending to Bill, whose body has lost its youthful vigour. Joseph doesn't swagger like Rudy, but he isn't hunched like Bill. He is slim, prideful, maybe dignified in his bearing. All of them are smiling. I never noticed the similarity between my brothers before. Both of them have broad, disarming smiles. Johnny must have come right away because he has already joined them near the waiting room. Back-slapping and guffawing, they exit. The hallway echoes their joyous racket even as they disappear behind the elevator doors. I fail to see anything sexy about Ol' Johnny. He isn't bent over like some old men and he has an eagerness about him that's pleasant but that's all I see. I wonder if your sense of beauty of the opposite sex changes as you age. It must.

"By golly, twins. By golly, twins," from Johnny is the last thing I hear, and then they're gone.

Back in the room, Momma is staring at Rita, who is deep in thought. Some form of eerie communication is going on between them. Rita's face is wearing a stubborn look of refusal and Momma's gaze is challenging Rita's.

"What's up?"

Rita looks at me, then at the ceiling.

"She's old enough to know the truth. What's up?" I want to leave. Rita's face tells me the answer to that question is going to be terrible. No one says anything. They all wait for an answer from Rita. Momma's face takes on a no-nonsense-from-your-child look and Rita's forehead has tiny little beads of sweat forming on it. Her face softens, she sighs. She looks as if she is looking for what's up. Monique looks at Momma, then Lacey, then Rita. She does this a couple of times. I am really trying hard not to tell her to quit.

"I'm tired, Momma." Momma's eyebrows rise, as do Lacey's. This is not a full answer and both Momma and Lacey wait for the rest. I sit down in the only chair in the room. "Bill, he ... well, he's sweet ... most of the time, but ... oh Gawd. I hate myself already ... I didn't mean to get pregnant, I don't ... didn't want any more children. I am so tired." If it wasn't clear before, it is now. Rita means to leave Bill. She means to subtract his income from hers at a terrible time. She is tired of her marriage. The kind of tired that the crazies in *One Flew Over the Cuckoo's Nest* felt. I don't want to be here. I don't want to know the rest of the story. She is four months short of her master's degree. She returned to school after her third child. Now the why of it looks pretty clear. Go to school. Finish her master's, get a nice job. All the kids would be tucked into school when she finished. Nature punched a hole in Rita's life plan.

"I was young, Momma. I had no idea what ... Is it a crime to be dense?" She really doesn't want Momma to answer that one honestly. "Should I pay for the rest of my days?" That is what the marriage vows she took meant, till death ...

"Divorce?"

"Yes." They all look surprised. Monique wrings her small, thin hands and toys with her own ring but says nothing. Leave Bill? He dotes on her, is she crazy?

"Have you told Bill?" Now that is cold, Momma. I feel myself spiralling down into some form of sticky web. I don't like it. How do the youngest children of families survive knowing about separation before they've had a honeymoon? No one in this room is going to consider Bill in whatever they decide. I can't help feeling sorry for him. Rita looks at me. She doesn't want me here. She looks at Momma and Lacey goes blank.

"Go get coffee, Marianne." It comes out blunt. I leave.

"You'll be fine, dear." It's a loaded remark from Momma. She plans to help Rita get out of her marriage and so she can say it with conviction. The rest of us will have to fall in line. Rita is talking before I make it out the door. I hear sex and dissatisfaction. I imagine frustration too. Well, maybe I didn't imagine it, maybe I heard it. I can't be sure; I was too busy feeling like I didn't want to just fall in line with the rest of them conspiring against Bill and his chance of joy. I wish the news were on again. Somehow Momma and her fight with the TV has more appeal than the woman I hear in Rita's hospital room. Her voice sounds so cold, it's scary.

The ride down to the basement cafeteria in the elevator is a strange one. The elevator squeaks and clunks all the way down; it adds to the general melancholy I feel coming on. It seems slower than the ride up to Rita's room a few hours ago. I can feel its agedness and my own weighing on me. The cafeteria is gated up. There is a lone coffee machine outside the gate. Some man is there. Just what I need.

"Coffee?" he asks as I approach the machine. He's Indian but he has no accent. It throws me off a little. No, diapers, I think, but I nod yes, mechanically. He wouldn't understand. He cocks his head to one side and asks if the news is bad. "You bet. My sister just had twins and is about to get rid of her doting husband and my Momma and other sister are going to help her." I can't believe I just said all that. I try to smile. It comes out pinched and small. He laughs.

"I thought something dreadful happened at the hospital." I bite down hard on my teeth trying not to grind them. How can he take marriage and divorce so lightly? "You didn't lose anyone did you?" A brother-in-law is an obvious answer, but there is something else I lost. An elusive thing I can't get a grip on. I felt much better before I knew about the divorce. In fact, I felt better when it was only a sociology paper I had to toy with. Now everything looks old and tarnished in the face of my family's plot to rid themselves of an unwanted human being.

"Just my innocence," I answer. Why not tell this stranger the truth.

"Must have been quite a shock," he quips, then he stares intently at my eyes. I am not sure if I want to give him the rest of the cards in my deck. I measure him up. Over thirty, just barely, and in a maternity ward. His hair is carefully cut and styled. His clothes are casual in a middle-class sort of way. A burgundy sweater with a Southwest Indian design and black pleated slacks. He is well heeled and neat. He must be married. Too bad, he looks good. I could kick myself for that one.

"Me," he says, motioning a toast with his coffee cup, "I had a good day." He drawls it out slow and easy. "My kid sister just had a boy. She's naming him after me. How about that, eh?"

"My big sister has no name for either of her twins. My Momma is sixty and has a twinkle in her eye for some old geezer she thinks she wants to marry, but not before she helps my big sister dump her husband. Like as not, my mother and my sister are busy right now plotting just how to do that and still keep the kids in our family fold."

"That's a pretty full day all right." He hands me the coffee. I am a little pouty about how casually he is taking all this. "Where is her old man?"

"Oh, he is off with my Momma's boyfriend, who is helping him to tie a proud father drunk on. They are probably smoking big cigars too."

"You're Marianne, aren't you?"

"How do you know?"

"I go to school with your sister Rita. Your story sounds familiar. She tells it a lot different from the way you do, though."

"Besides, we look alike," it comes out in an almost whisper. He murmurs, "Yes, that too." His face reads out the rest of the story. This must be the study partner she is always raving about, the one Bill is jealous of ... the one she insists is just a study partner. Even under the hot glare of fluorescent lights his good looks are not dimmed. His conversation is interesting and he probably has a promising future. He looks like his life is essentially a sober one.

That had done it for Rita.

"Are you her lover?" I should kick my butt for asking that, but it's out there and I'm not about to back down.

"Yes." It's his turn to whisper. It sounds reverent. Definitely without guilt ... chaos ... the world is all about chaos. There is no order, certainly not a religious one. Morals are for dullards who have no passion with which to imagine complicating the world with needless pain, and virtue is for those who lack opportunity. Chaos. Mother rolls about in some little old man's sweet arms; sister Rita cheats on her husband. Bill drowns his suspicions in alcohol, hides his inadequacy in beer halls and loud laughter. Children pine for their fathers and endure the icy wind of step-fathers. Me, I volley between feeling sorry for Bill and denouncing Rita and her bigoted Catholicism that does not allow her to abort an unwanted child, but somehow enables her to be comfortable with adultery. I also wonder why I am so angry about something that really is no concern of mine.

"Your coffee is getting cold," he says.

"Oh yeah, I need another one for Momma."

He pours it. He doesn't know Bill. He has no memory of the simple-hearted man taking my sister and me for ice creams on hot days. It seems like a century ago now. In a way this stranger can't be blamed, but still, he invaded Bill's private dreams, stole the little joy this life affords us, and I don't feel like thanking him for his minor devotions to our caffeine addiction. I take the cups of coffee and turn to leave.

"Aren't you curious about my name?" He looks out at me from beneath tipi-shaped eyebrows, thick and black. I can see a ring of white around his black eyes. His attractive posture annoys me.

"No." Rude old battle-ax already. I smile wickedly. I don't even turn to face him when I say it. Chip off the old block. Block? Well, not quite. Momma stands solidly behind Rita and I feel a shade treacherous for not doing the same.

* * *

The world is crass. No matter how much chaos lives among her children, she just carries on as though all of it were natural, normal at last. Baby birds cheep-cheep joyously first thing in the morning and flowers go on blooming no matter how depressed humans feel. The sun shines bright and sharp through my window. I am offended by it. Yesterday, I was young. Today, the world opens up wounds, fresh and bloody, and still the earth rolls around the heavens, spilling sunshine just as pretty as you please, and I feel so old. She is a crass old mother.

My sociology paper still needs tending. It doesn't look so threatening today. I pick up all the notes, mull them over and begin. My date book on my desk reads, "Auntie Mary is coming today, yippee." I smirk. That was before the world fell on me. Auntie Mary, dear, I have a paper to finish and, come hell or high water, that is what I am going to do. Second-year sociology is full of theoretical grandstanding about the why of divorce, alienation of a social nature and so forth. About the only things these guys guess right is the problem. They have no idea about the why of things or the solution. They can't even face a single human emotion when they rattle on about divorce. It's as though it were some grocery item in their intellectual store which they purchase along with the piece of paper which gives them the right to peddle the items they bought. "Few citizens link divorce with increased alienation or the socialization process and its incumbent breakdown ... " That's OK, C.W., even fewer people link divorce with sadness or sexual dissatisfaction, but then, human sadness is not the subject of sociology. Nor is any other emotion, for that matter.

"Someone is here to see you." My mother peeks in the door and chirps the words through the slash she keeps narrowed by holding the door partly closed.

"Auntie Mary," I chirp back.

"Yes." Like it was a lucky guess.

"Tell her I will be out as soon as my paper is done." The door bangs shut. Strong hands, low tolerance for the antics of a devoted student. This time I don't change my mind and jump up. Life, dear mother, is full of disappointments. I have now integrated myself with the ranks of the rest of the adult world by becoming one of those disappointments.

I can hear her talking to Auntie Mary in the kitchen. Her voice is up a decibel or two. She wants me to hear.

"She is such a committed pupil." Mother does not see the need to change the word pupil to student when she describes my current occupation. It was pupil when I began school at six and it will be pupil until I actually become a sociology graduate. "Always busy at her work." I am not sure if that was to ease my rudeness or her embarrassment or Mary's pain of rejection, but I don't mull over it long enough to make up my mind or feel any remorse. I plow through theory after theory from a dozen different white, male scholars' perspectives about the why of divorce and quit when I have completed exactly ten double-spaced pages of typed words. I wrap it all up with a stupid statement about the unwillingness of sociologists to consider emotions as part of the study of human society, particularly around the issue of family and divorce. I remember nothing else about the paper.

Auntie Mary and Momma are still sitting in the kitchen with another round of tea and cookies in front of them. Auntie Mary's eyes light up when she sees me, then they take on an old familiar longing. Auntie Mary lost a daughter the same age as me. I bring an ambiguous mix of joy and sadness at the memory of her loss. At the same time that I have become a replacement for her daughter, I remind her that human life is irreplaceable. I thought I was used to it. Today, though, it bothers me. I feel put upon, pressured into being something I am not and never can be.

"Well, I'm off," Momma says and plucks her coat from the chair, turns the kettle off and slides her chair and dashes out of view in what looks like one magical motion. I ask her where she is going.

"To see your sister." She says it with a shade of apology because there is no invitation to come along in her voice. It is whispered over layers of ordinariness and a tad of shame about her carrying on visiting as though nothing were amiss. Bill still doesn't know, I surmise. "You and Mary will be fine without me." I am already tired of that line. "You'll be fine" has been uttered a million times before, always under unfine circumstances. She is out the door before I can comment on her answer or say something nasty about Rita, her stud partner — excuse me, study partner — or anything else about divorce, hardship, twins and children. I must look like I am thinking about all these things because as soon as Momma is gone Auntie says, "You look like you could use a stiff drink."

"You know I don't drink. Momma and I are dead set against it."

"I wasn't advocating it. I just said you look like someone who could use it." She slides out from behind her remark, smooth as butter. I am glad Auntie is still the same. Some people, like institutions, are sacred in their predictability. "You're taking this all pretty hard for someone who ought not to be even thinking about it, aren't you?"

"Taking what pretty hard?" Dumb remark. Insulting actually; Auntie Mary knows better than to fall for the dumb kid routine. I shouldn't even have tried it on her.

"Don't piss me about, Dearie. You know what I am talking about."

"I'm 'Sweetie Poo,' Rita is 'Dearie.' " Jeezuss, what is wrong with my mouth. My head volunteers itself a flinch in the direction of my shoulder. That remark should be punctuated by a slap, it was so rude. Nothing happens. Mary busies herself, pours tea and reaches for a piece of Momma's cake and sits silent. I disappear. Mary sits in the kitchen as though she is the only one there. I want to make up. The air feels solid around her.

"Sorry," I mumble, but she doesn't respond.

"Do you remember when Karl died?" It shatters its way through the wall Auntie Mary constructed, sharp and piercing.

"Dead ... Karl ... dead. Yeah." We don't normally bring up the dead.

"I told him. I said, 'Karl, don't buy another car. You know how you are, just get a little too much joy juice under your belt, you'll be out on the highway going over some cliff edge.' Sure enough. He buys a car, drinks too much and over the edge he goes." She lets this sink in. "She went with him. Seven times more a fool than Karl."

"I thought she didn't drink."

"Didn't save her, did it?"

"How come you only had two kids, Auntie?"

"You are a sweet, blind baby, aren't you. You wander about this world, the youngest of five kids, with both eyes closed and your ears shut tight, then you make judgements on all and sundry. Before you talk, you ought to open your eyes and take another look. What the hell do you think they're trying to teach you up on that hill?" A massive chunk of confusion lodges itself in the middle of my mind. What brought this on? Drunk driving, death and the numbers of children people choose to have doesn't get mixed in with sociology at all.

"They don't talk about humans in quite that way, Auntie."

"You do research up there, don't you?"

"Well, yeah," and I wonder just where I am supposed to look for the answer to this question.

"What does that mean ... research?"

This question is a lot tougher than the last one my mom threw out about what sociology is supposed to be. What am I supposed to say? They tell you to go to the library and look up a whole bunch of junk mail about a subject and write about it. That's research. Auntie can't possibly mean that. If she knows about me doing research, she knows what the word means. It is a trick question. I know it. No matter how I answer it, it won't be right; better just admit I don't know what she is talking about and hear her out. "What do you mean?"

She lights into me. "Re-search. Look again. Look again and again, before you draw any conclusions or make any judgements. That's what they mean. You sit here safe and sound and childless as can be. No decision you make is ever going to be quite this conscience or duty free. Karl's Rosie is dead. Karl is dead. All because my fool son had not the sense of dignity to refrain from drinking and driving. Hadn't the pride in his family to sober up and live. Is that what you want for Rita? 'Stay with your drunk. Maybe death will be your ecstasy, Rita.' Someone ought to kick your heartless butt."

Momma told Auntie Mary what I said after I got back to Rita's room. It wasn't my business. I knew it. But after seeing Sweet Honey at the coffee machine, I made the stupid mistake of championing unsuspecting Bill, who had been dragged off by my mother's boy-friend. I had even assumed that Ol' Johnny was part of the whole scheming scandal, and I hit the roof. Auntie Mary didn't know the half of it. I hadn't looked at Rita once. Never considered her life, her dreams or the disappointment Bill must be to her. Memories come flying back at me through the tunnel of my vision.

"I can't do my homework and baby-sit too, Momma." ... "OK." And I hear Momma say, "No, not on a weeknight." Hear Rita plead. She has a paper to do. Hear Momma say, "Rita, wait till they go to sleep." Hear Rita say, "Just once, just this once." ... "Rita, you listen to me. Next time you set about to give your sister another niece to feel guilty about not baby-sitting you better ask her for her per-mission to have the baby beforehand." Hear the dial tone ... and for the first time I imagine Rita's desperate tears. Not once did she ever show me anything but kindness and understanding. Momma is right. Rita knew and she learned to live with it. Bill is a drunk. I know it, but somehow I think Rita ought to learn to live with it, or like Rosie, die with it.

He was kind to me, I rationalize my defence of Bill. Human

beings ought to be kind to children, I argue. Besides, his kindness comes through a fog of blurry vision and dulled senses. Further, I don't have to live with him. They don't own a car either. Bill works as a roofer. He works steady. Rita washes clothes, cooks, cleans and cares for those children; soberly and seriously, like a driven woman, she sneaks studying in between all her crying. Sheer nerves keep her in gear. Their apartment comes into focus. I never really looked at it before. An old rickety table sits in the middle of the kitchen surrounded by four unmatched chairs. Unmatched dishes, most of them chipped stoneware, ratty old pots and pans float between unadorned walls and curtainless windows. The whole place is worn and tired.

"I think I need a stiff drink."

"Kick," Mary repeats her last thought.

"That too." I look up at the clock. Momma must have left before the news. It is just now going on to six. I feel like the good witch's bubble has just popped. I see Rita's face as I scathed her soul with hot words of shame. I knocked her up one side and down the other and never lost a wink of sleep over it. How did I get to be so creepy?

"Here." Mary hands me a hanky. I realize I am crying. "Shame is a worthy sentiment so long as you clutch it to work out change and don't use it to excuse yourself with guilt, child."

"Rita talks like you, riddles. Drives me crazy." I try to laugh. It comes out kind of constipated.

"When you fall down, girl, get up, don't wallow in it." I missed something in my life. I feel it. I am not much of a thinker. I mean, all those riddles Rita, Momma and Mary talk in go right by me. I whizzed through school, swallowed everything I read, secretly disagreed with most of it, but gave it back in neat little packages for fourteen years, and the only people to stump me were my own. *Something is going on here, Marianne.*

"What's Rita going to do now?"

"No idea. Better ask her yourself. I never speculate on a woman's

46

next move … Honey, didn't anyone ever tell you about love?" She reaches out and touches my hair, a winsome touch, light as rain.

"What do you mean?" I have the feeling she is talking about the kind of love that involves sex, but I don't feel like helping her. The door opens and a cacophony of voices pours in and closes off our conversation. Everyone trucks in behind Momma. Rudy, Lacey, Joseph, their spouses and all their kids come trooping through the door. The kids cackle excitedly and the brothers and sisters are whoopalalaing about the arrival of the twins. The spouses are speaking to each other in softened voices. The gang trots over to me as always and fawns over me. I am still "Baby," in spite of my despicable treatment of Rita. They all behave as though it had nothing to do with them.

This makes me feel unworthy. It is the first time I have thought about worthiness or the lack of it. The laughter doesn't let up till midnight. Half the kids are asleep in corners of couches, on the parents' laps, or the floor; the older ones are groggy and they don't look like they are listening too seriously to anything being said now. Only now does Momma announce Rita's divorce. An uncomfortable silence follows. Each one of them looks at me by turns, hems and haws slightly and comments about the regretability of it, and then they mumble something about how things have a way of working themselves out.

"How come we don't celebrate divorce with the same vigour as marriage?" I ask. "If it's better not to stay together, maybe we shouldn't be so glum about it." It is a beginning, is all I can concede to. I still can't dislike Bill, can't be happy about his upcoming loneliness, but I feel resignation coming on and I need to get on with it so I can look at life again with both eyes open and at least half my ears listening. I prepare to give Rita her due. She deserves something more than that old table and five raggedy little kids. I just can't bring myself to see that she deserves love too. That will have to wait until more calamities and bigger emotional traumas have crossed my path. It is enough for everyone here just to know that

Rita has made the decision. Rudy and Joseph open the six pack they always bring. Momma snorts as she always does and Auntie Mary joins them for one. Momma, Monique and Paula retreat to a corner of the kitchen while the main party, including Ol' Johnny, who has winked lustily at Momma's backside all night long, stays behind in the living room … Old fool … Momma set the tone for the family response to Rita's divorce before she left.

"Bill always did limp along with both feet planted firmly in mid-air." They all nod sagely. I am doing my best, but it all seems a little narcissistic. "Drank too much … stayed out long hours with the boys … long hours? … days is more like it … " I want to ask if the days and hours began before or after Rita went back to school, but I don't dare. I listen to the jostling and the jockeying for understanding and sympathizing with Rita, hoping my question might get answered without my ever having to utter it. "The first baby did it." … "Jeez, Bill didn't show up to collect Rita or the baby at the hospital when it was all over." … "Jerk." … "Hmn." … "Rita never got over that one." (Lacey and Rudy exchange this group of remarks while Joseph does the humming.) "Should have dumped him then." … "We always hope." … "Humans are the only animals dense enough to hope," Rudy ends it all.

The first baby. I take a closer look at all the faces in the room. The lines of them, the cut of the bones, the musculature are as familiar as rain, but the insides, the secret corners of their lives, their trials, their tribulations, are all fogged up under layers of pretence and secrecy. Baby. I really am such a baby. Rita's life has been one storm after another and I lived in a sheltered spot, not knowing the storms were raging on. Now they cut loose the foundations, hack at the walls covering my perception of their lives without offering me so much as a blanket. A chill sets in. My insides freeze. "I think it was the women," from Lacey, who gives Rudy an accusatory glance which he studiously ignores. The conversation folds in on itself. Joseph's face works overtime trying to dream up apologetic responses. Rudy doesn't like the direction Lacey is travelling in and Joseph can't think of a diversionary tactic. No one wants the family to split over this issue. Lacey gets close to discussing womanizing and woman treatment in general and somehow the rest of us know none of us wants to look at that. Quiet pensiveness holds Rudy still.

Soft murmurs leak from the kitchen to the living room. Do I sense the hush of silent tears through the murmur? "Yeah," Rudy begins again. "And he picked up some dandies all right. Imagine trading Rita off for the wharf rat down the road — six kids, fat and all." Rudy's comments clip a warning at Lacey. He threatens to get much cruder if she pursues her recrimination of Bill along feminist lines. She stands up to his arrogance, rolls her eyes and clips out something about plenty of other wowies coming from all directions, when Momma comes back into the room.

"I have enough for a down payment on a house," she announces to us all. The news falls soft as winter snow. It blankets the room with profound transformation, the way winter draws deep lines of difference between itself and every other season. Between life and death itself the snow of winter paints death in glorious cold. She could not have gotten a bigger rise out of us had she told us New York had just been nuked.

Buy a house? Ol' Johnny strokes her knee. She sits upright and regal. Challenge, her life is full of it. A sixty-year-old Indian woman with enough for a down payment on a house. Us? Buy a house? The whole notion is painful, absurd. Here we are, a bunch of ragtags trying to create a life from the ashes of a stolen land, stolen dreams, and our mother suggests we just bypass all that grief and buy back some of our stolen goods. No one moves. Rudy coughs slightly. It is like the grain of a giant cedar has been reversed before the carver's eyes. We all sit there with our mouths open while Momma dares us to deter her. She looks like she is calculating the number of reasons she has carefully crafted together into a single cloth, colourfully woven and sewn into a permanent design. Resolute, that is much too mild to describe the look on her face. Not a single cell in her whole body is about to be deterred. We can all go to hell; she is going to buy a house.

"Who is going to give a sixty-year-old Indian woman a mortgage?" Rudy cuts through our shock.

"No one, you idiot. The bank has already agreed to give it to Rita after she finds work." The split second of relief at not having to deal with the sociology of an Indian buying back stolen land is punctured by this piece of information. Rita? Like as not she and Rita have been scheming for years. Or maybe Momma has been scheming for years and decided Rita, of all her children, is her surest bet. No one in this family has ever gotten used to the holes this conversation seems to be filling up with right now. We are accustomed to rolling through family visits on coasters of sorry-assed and silly memories, worn out jokes and hee-hawing over the most trivial things. Tonight, Momma set a whole revolution in swing. Even Rudy is speechless.

The twins rescue us all. Lacey drags them up. Auntie Mary has not seen them, so Lacey fills her in about their little sobs, pinched by small lungs too tiny to amplify their urgent cries. This sets us all into the comfortable kind of motion we prefer.

✳ ✳ ✳

"Nappies." ... "Where do you keep your nappies?" ... "Over here." ... "Here, take this to the laundry." ... "Pass me the powder." ... "Oh, Jeez, this one ... ah'd." ... "C'mon Rudy, you started, you finish," and the laughter rolls out. The twins are home, so is Rita, and the house is kept under wraps. Momma turns the news on. Six o'clock, exactly one week later. Christmas is pushing at us through the television. The prospect of winter holidays seems oddly vacant in the wake of Momma's announcement about the house last week. "Not everyone will benefit from the food bank this year," the broadcaster says in that nauseous tone of indifference. "Surrey reports supplies are low." Momma's fist is up. It threatens whoever is in charge. "Don't you dare decide to deal my people out of the deck. Never fails, food is short, we're the first to have our rations cut." We are glad to get back to the normalcy of Momma's genocide plot routine. The story changes. The newscaster talks to a bunch of rough-looking Indians on skid row. She commends a single white man for "bravely facing rough customers with bannock and fish soup at Oppenheimer Park." The timing of the camera is perfect. Right on the cue of "rough," the camera focuses on the roughest looking Indian of all. It moves to some old white guy and the words of the broadcaster change immediately, "but some residents ... " and Momma flies into another flap. "Oh sure, camera is on our face and she says 'rough customers' but let a white face come into view and suddenly she discovers 'resident.' " The house conversation is buried beneath her nightly fight with the TV and the rest of us are busy overseeing the operation of readying the twins for feeding. I slip into the kitchen.

The conversation halts. Rita is serving Rudy's wife tea. Paula, I chide myself, her name is Paula. This past week has been rough. I can't stop picking on myself. I keep reconceiving of every old habit, all my words, the whole damned kit and caboodle of my thought patterns, and disagreeing with the lot. I need a rest.

The kitchen and the harmless gossip I thought women indulged in seems like a perfect refuge. I haven't even sat down and my mind is kindling guilt at never referring to Paula as Paula. Then I notice the silence, Paula's face, eyes red, staring down, and Rita and Monique pause, pregnant with secret knowledge of her tears' origins. I have been through this before, I now realize. Many, many times before. The room falls silent for a second on my entry; some key person looks at me with deep adoration and the conversation suddenly becomes trivial and focused on me. That is the architectural design of the house of protection they have all built around me. It is a house whose walls are built of secrets. I want to scream at them all.

"How did you do on your exams, Marianne?" Oh, shut up Rita.

Monique puts a cup of tea in front of me and Paula retreats to the bathroom, right on cue. I am tethered to the hot wire of my own rage, which is much too large to let go on my sisters. Not only have I been Baby for too long, but the blinkers I wore restricted my vision. Last week's stupid outburst at Rita is as much shaping the plot line of the current tension as is their habit of sheltering me from life's harder side. I really don't understand. I resent not understanding and I am not sure how much of my lack of understanding I am responsible for, but I am sure that it can't all be someone else's fault. I have a sneaky suspicion I could have opened my eyes sooner.

I hold fast to my rage. I tuck it somewhere in the hidden corners of my mind for later reference. I am getting good at saving things for later. I hope this is culturally Native and not European.

"I haven't got my marks back, but I don't have diarrhea." Everything moves slow. The last line reaches the middle of the room at the same time as Paula. She joins in the laughter that follows. The conversation turns to Christmas. The twins arrive and Rita begins a gorgeously melancholy rendition of "Silent Night."

I slip away halfway through the song. No one minds. Baby is not expected to keep up the flow of conversation, hold the fort or really do anything. I turn out the lights and close the door to my little room. This time next year I won't be here. Despite all, Momma and Rita will buy a house. My mother has never said she is going to do something and failed to do it. "Shepherds quake at the sight," and visions of my mother's more doubtful convictions pass by.

"I am going to tan that boy's hide," she had said about one of the village boys we used to live near long ago. "Do you know what he did?" We all knew. We had all helped. Stormy had locked the local white bully in the shed back of Olly's place with the pigs still in it. "That is *not* our way. Doesn't matter how that boy conducts himself. Nothing to do with us … " and she marched out the door, broom in hand, in search of Stormy. She blasted through the door of Stormy's house and in full view of his elder brothers and his mother, she tanned his hide with her broom. "Give it to him, Annie," Stormy's mother had cheered her on.

It all would not have been remarkable except that Stormy was seventeen. My mother's wrath was legendary. She was afraid of no one, certainly not Stormy. She landed the first blow and poor Stormy, caught by surprise, found himself backed up in retreat, his large arms fending off a continuous shower of blows as best they could, while my mother's mouth machine-gunned out a lecture on cultural genocide — "What is our world coming to when we behave precisely as they do?" — for a good ten minutes without pausing for breath or repeating herself once. I chugged out the door on the edges of her skirt as always and witnessed the wonderful chaos my mother could create over cultural integrity. I wonder about her decision to buy a house. I wonder if she knows what a major cultural turnaround the purchase signifies; then, before I can resolve the question, sleep carries me away.

＊　＊　＊

Babies just are. They have very small minds and no language. They wake, they sleep, they eat and they let go most of what they eat; then they sleep some more. In between they grow. What is remarkable about them is their effect on the adult world which surrounds them. No, not just the adult world but the world of children too. The twins are busy gobbling up whatever Rita can feed them and doing their best to become oversized, awkward and cumbersome, without showing any appreciable gifts or skills, but they continue to enthrall and entertain our family. Auntie Mary has been back and forth three times in the three months since they were born. The entire family has taken to visiting once a week. All day Saturday they marvel at the fact that they are still alive. At least I think that is what they are marvelling at, because so far their huge accomplishments amount to burping, holding their heads up for two or three seconds and smiling at the ridiculous antics of everyone around them. Babies don't say "goo-goo, ga-ga"; adults say it to them.

Our twins are special, so says Auntie Mary in lecture after lecture. Twin sisters mark our beginning in the land we now occupy. They also represent peace between the Nations of the West Coast. Another story rolls out, ancient and sweet like music. Auntie Mary's voice purrs, lilting and hushed, reverent, and the listeners hmnmhmn softy during her pauses and reflect deeply on the significance of twins. I am caught up in the reverie without bothering to contemplate the why of it. My acceptance of the significance of twins is absolute. The wonderment of our family being blessed by our entire lineage of infinite grandmothers, by their choosing to bestow twins upon us, brought so much peace to my troubled soul that I doubt I could have questioned the notion. The whirlwind of questioning I was caught in since hearing about Rita's coming divorce settled down only during those moments when the family gathered around to hear Auntie Mary tell another story about the specialness of twins.

Auntie is slipping into another story this one night when I am particularly determined to re-search my world. There are ten children in our tiny house — ten nieces and nephews engaged in various states of maturity. Two of the teenagers are listening; one is perched at Mary's feet, leaning on her old skinny knees, almost asleep; three of the older children are in the corner giggling; and the others are wandering about or watching TV, but all are reasonably quiet. The gigglers clasp their hands over their mouths, stick their faces in the pillows they lean on when overcome with the need to laugh out loud. The talkers whisper. The TV watchers sit close to the TV and keep the volume down and the wanderers carefully touch things so as not to rattle them or make loud noises. What does this mean sociologically speaking? I almost laugh, but at the same time it seems to me a serious question.

My imagination travels down the familiar halls of the school and I see noisy white youth running along hallways, shouting loudly, their feet hitting the floors of the hall as if they all weigh three hundred kilos. In the cafeteria, the few Native students gather in the quietest corner we can find and whisper to each other while the rest of the youth holler, throw things, including food, and play cards. *No fair. Some 17,000 students attend your school, Marianne; there are only ten kids here.* But even when there are only two or three of them at the bus stop they yell, curse and swear loudly.

Pictures of Momma dance in my head. "You take that schoolyard hack back where you got it and learn to talk, Rudy Carpenter, or I will thrash you." Momma's remembered voice is clear, ice-like crystal and each word crunches promise, but it isn't loud. Rudy is the oldest. All the rules come down to the rest of us through his attempts to violate them. The story is drawing to a close. My memory intrudes on the scene of silent musing and I miss most of the story. I realize that Momma doesn't even yell at the drivers that get her goat when we drive someplace; she lifts the volume more by projecting the sound across the distance — it isn't the same.

"Momma, I have never heard you yell." Surprise registers on everyone's face. Obviously I wasn't paying attention, but Momma answers, "Never will, either. Imagine behaving as though you were our earth mother herself, storming and screaming like the wind as though you had a right to. No. Not me. I am the mother of my lineage and that is it. I catch any one of you being that presumptuous and I'll tan you; don't care how big you are."

Auntie Mary is more poetic. "Wind is voice. Voice is wind — the instrument of earth sound. To elevate the voice to the song of earth storm is the worst sort of violence. Screaming winds cleanse earth, but humans cannot heal the spirit in the same way. Earth heals all of filth; only the earth can truly cleanse."

"What's the difference between tanning our hides and yelling?"

"Tanning your hide is preventative, a deterrent to further non-sense — consequences — but yelling is elevating your voice to the howling wind of your mother — dangerous, a breath sharp enough to tear holes in a child's little spirit. A tanning only hurts the body." No one was too comfortable with the closeness of the conversation but I didn't care. I doubted the wisdom of tanning, but didn't say anything because I agreed with the no-yelling principle. The poetry of Momma's and Auntie Mary's responses seemed to fit our good fortune; then Dorry slipped from Auntie Mary's knee with a loud clunk. She looked up, half dazed, half asleep and very confused. Laughter rolled out again from Momma's kitchen.

The babies, startled by the sudden change of tempo, cry. Commotion over the twins begins again, only this time I grab a nappy and a twin and set to work like the rest, indulging them with care. Momma turns the TV on and tells the Minister of External Affairs that he dare not plunge this country into war over Iraq, Iran, or any-place-else, because neither her sons, nor her grandsons, nor any other relative of hers in this country, distant or close, is going to traipse halfway around the world to kill other human beings, thank you very much. While pinning on Lila's nappy — I am sure it is Lila — I chuckle at the picture Momma must be making, her broom waving at this man who does not know she is alive and is the sorrier for that.

* * *

Winter left. It must have just up and died. Spring seemed to just appear one morning. It brought the usual rain and wind. Flowers blossom all over the place and school is nearly over. The twins are chubbing up and getting ready to crawl. Rita has had a hard five months. I guess we all have. Momma and me moved out of our bedrooms to accommodate Rita and her crew. We sleep in the living room and dining room, respectively, while Rita's older children usurp every square inch of available space. Study happens jointly at the kitchen table, usually in silence and well after eight and under pressure of time. On top of all this, Rita has to feed two babies while she pores over endless textbooks and masters her thesis. On top of that, we endure endless pleas from Bill for visitation rights. He never shows up and we face the disappointment of the older kids.

He is usually drunk when he calls; probably he forgets that he is supposed to visit. Women seem to get used to disappointment, but children seem to be forever heartbroken. Their smiles and their laughter grow less frequent. The lines of Rita's face deepen as she watches her children slip into depression. A depression she has caused. The novelty of the twins wears off for the older three and they want their daddy more often. They whimper and whine often.

Rita is dangerously quiet in the face of their depression. I don't remember ever noticing the internal drama of our family's life before now. It must have been there. I now know that Rudy and Paula fight over his womanizing, that Bill and Rita had not been getting along for some time and that Lacey is an equal-rights-for-women activist, which stresses her relationship with Rudy. We don't see much of her husband. I am curious about why, but don't ask. Probably something to do with her feminism. My eyes and ears are wide open now, but offer no solutions to all the cracking and popping surfaces. My brain is permanently disengaged. Meanwhile, Momma is caught up in the whirlwind of a grandmotherly romance with Ol' Johnny and doesn't seem to notice all the seam-stretching and stress on the family cloth, or does she not care anymore? Does she have to care?

It is on one of those days when I feel most powerless that Rita ups and bursts into tears. Amid a monologue of despair and recrimination she says she and Bill are going to try again. Why me? Why is she telling me this? The only social idiot in the family and she pours out her private torment and, with utter revulsion, prepares to return to the dead-end street of her marriage. It dawns on me. She hasn't seen her study partner for a month at least. It is not a good time to ask why. It would be crude to suggest that it was his absence that sparked Rita's concern for her kids, or that it was because of the kids that he stopped coming around.

"Rita. Would they see more of Bill if you got back together or would there be more of his drunkenness?" Rita plugs her ears. It isn't what she wants to hear. She stops scolding herself, though, and just sobs. I don't even know where the question came from; it isn't what I was thinking about. It just snuck up between the lines of my other, uglier thoughts and jumped out before I realized it was there. I don't feel the least bit sorry and I don't want to take it back. It hangs suspended in mid-air like the scent of old clothes you know aren't worth keeping but can't just throw away — words.

I reach over and put both hands on her shoulders, gently, so as not to disturb the flow of cleansing tears jerking from Rita. The question grows. It fills the room with the truth of its terrible answer. There will only be his drunken absence, his hangover-addled presence, and their longing will linger forever in Rita's aching conscience. Here or back at Bill's she will always be nagged with the horrible knowledge that she cannot provide her children with a father. Rita heaves some more and I realize that all her life she has comforted me, rocked me, but this is the first time I witness her pain and there is no amount of comfort I can give her to ease it. Sometimes shit happens.

Humanity is more apt to be bizarre than consistent. In the midst of Rita's terrible depression, in walks Momma's autumn — winter, really — romance. She giggles through the doorway, rattles her bags and entreats Ol' Johnny to stop patting her bum while her flattered laughter indicates she thoroughly enjoys his hand's attention. Rita scurries to the bathroom and no more is said about her return to Bill — ever.

Sometime between Rita's outburst and Momma's obvious girlish joy at Johnny's daring attentions, I stop calling them "old fools" and wondering what in the world old people do when they fall in love. Like all lovers, they peck at each other on the sofa, they pretend to watch TV. They sneak kisses at family gatherings when they think no one notices, and sometimes Momma does not come home — all night. The first time causes quite a stir. The entire family holds a major teleconference over the missing Momma, until Rudy — smart Rudy — figures it out. "She's getting her bones … " "Rudy," Lacey stops him. "How can you talk like that?" Rudy laughs heartily. Crude bugger.

She rolls home sometime after noon, two roses on her cheeks and giggles in her throat for days. I can't resist. "Momma, what is it like to be sixty and in love?" She looks at me and says, "Same as when you're young, dear. You walk down the street, hold hands and you think every grey-haired old lady is after your man." I laugh. "Well, some things are different. You don't have to seriously consider the possibility of children," she adds with a chuckle. Love closed Momma's sensitive eyes to Rita's dilemma, thank Gawd.

This time, Momma and Ol' Johnny roll in around eleven thirty. Johnny has been nipping politely sometime during the evening, because a soft scent of midnight in a brewery wafts in with them, and I know Momma would never break her code. She scuttles about the kitchen searching for an old quart jar. She has missed both news hours. I don't think much about it, except that Meech Lake fills up her threats at the TV and I have come to rely on her weird sense of logic to shape my own perceptions. The furor over Quebec's status and the failure to reach an accord are somehow related to us and I am not sure how. A comment or two from Momma would push my digging root into the subject. She is too busy romancing Johnny lately to help me along. Besides, I think I am a little conservative. I have come to enjoy an uninterrupted homelife, each day plodding into the next, and I miss the old broom and the rounds she fights with the TV. I have a feeling Johnny isn't going to go home. He putters about and makes tea while Momma fusses over her flowers — mostly daisies and mums. How appropriate.

"Mums for moms," he chortles, then pecks her cheek and strokes her hand as she bottles the flowers in a clear Kerr jar.

"We'll be needing a vase, won't we, sweet Mom?" My sense of it all changed somewhere along the line. I can't help chuckling to myself. The romance between them stands out in sharp contrast to the break-up between Rita and Bill and the doom that surrounds the marriages of Lacey and Rudy. They see me. They look at each other; both faces register tension. Something's up. They look as though they are discussing how they are going to rid themselves of my presence when my niece, slightly weepy, wanders into the kitchen.

"Auntie, I had a weird dream." Right on cue.

"That's OK, Babe, you can sleep with me tonight," and I wander out of the kitchen to the dining room which now serves as my bedroom. I squeeze up next to her in the single bed and murmur soft words of comfort. *This is getting to be a habit Marianne.* I look forward to Momma's house purchase, though so far, outside of Rita, no one completely believes it is going to happen.

Dorry's breathing jerks a little, then deepens, and sleep takes her far away to a gentler place full of different dreams. Her face softens, grows still and angelic. She murmurs a couple of sweet, almost childish sounds, then rolls over and curls up in a perfectly lovely little hook, face upturned to the moon and stars that twinkle outside our little window. One of the stars falls. I can't resist wishing on it. "Something good, Lord, just let something good happen for all of us." I look one more time at Dorry, her woman body pushing up and out on her childhood, her breath sliding in and out free and easy; then I too sleep.

The radio is on, loud. Gawd. The sun is barely up. The bloody birds are barely awake enough to chirp out a decent tune. What in the world is the radio doing on? I scramble off the edge of the bed. There is no way to have a decent sleep with a moving teenager on a single bed. I almost hit the deck, grab the dresser and heave myself upright, feeling foolish about my arms flailing to keep me from landing on my face. My mouth is engaged before my brain gets out of neutral. "What's going on? It's 6:00 a.m." I rattle and roll and mutter on my way to the kitchen.

"Hush up. We know what time it is." Johnny and Momma are huddled next to the radio; both pairs of hands guard steaming cups of coffee. Both their faces are bent in the direction of the radio. Why, I can't figure out. It was playing loud enough to wake me up. Are they both going deaf? "It's Meech Lake." The journalist hammers out reasonably ignorant questions, but fairly justifiable given Canada's general attitude towards Natives and Canada's vague perception of our connection to Meech. Despite a number of attempts by a dozen Native political organizations to be included in the constitutional talks over the last ten years, so far we are not considered a part of this momentous attempt to carve out a constitution uniquely Canadian. No one has been concerned until now. Me, I can't help wondering what magic has occurred to bring about an entire program devoted to Native leaders and how they "feel" about Meech, including a Native woman's sultry poem, sandwiched between the discourse of the two men.

"Asking too much? My good lady, you got the whole damn country, all of its resources, by dint of the bayonet and now you accuse us of wanting too much." My mother talks to no one, not even Johnny. "Is she an idiot?" She looks up at this one, maybe it is directed at God. The room has an ethereal quality to it. A soft, sunny May morning. A radio program about our feelings on Meech, and Momma looking up when she talks. Her questions don't have the usual tone of inquiry; they sound more like statements and they are all directed at some invisible figure who floats above her head. Her discourse with the TV takes on a ritual, ceremonial quality. I take her more seriously.

I wonder about old people, our old people. I imagine thousands of old Native men and women stationed dutifully at their radios all across the nation. All of them ask no one in particular if this journalist is an idiot; can't she figure out the simplest of historical realities? All believe their creator would not let these people get away with building a nation from the bloodshed of gentle folk. The lilt of the men's voices, their muted sense of surety, the very melody in them, match my mother's own reverent voice and Johnny's occasional assent at Momma's remarks. I feel large, awkward. I intrude on a private ceremony between our elders and the world. In the midst of it all, I realize something trivial. Mother never lets the journalist finish her questions. She seems to know the question before it falls out of the speaker's mouth, fully formed. I don't. Momma talks before the journalist finishes any remark and she answers for the two men, so I don't get a thing about what anyone is talking about. What affects me is the combination of sounds. I feel, sensing by the sounds, by the whole impact of the scene in the kitchen, that something new is afoot. The phone rings.

"Jeezuss, what is going on?" I fairly jump out of my chair and bang my knee on the table.

"That would be Lacey. She is the only other one with the sense to listen to the radio when we finally get a chance to discuss Meech." Her voice lacks the tonal sarcasm that usually accompanies words of this sort. She has a way of delivering hard words in soft tones. The soft tones are very persuasive.

"Pardon me," the sandpaper on my tongue is particularly thick this morning.

"Is Mom there?" Lacey drawls out slowly and quietly.

"Oh, hello Lacey. And a good 6:30 a.m. to you too. Is mother here? Well now, where else would she be a 6:30 a.m. on a Sunday?" Momma grabs the phone. Lacey is the last of the diehard older siblings who refuses to recognize me as anything but Baby. She talks past me and around me but never to me. I am tired of her bypassing me. I know everything she thinks and says because the entire family reports to me, but I never hear it from her first hand. When I am in the room she restricts her entire conversation to trivial pursuits and harmless nostalgia. In the hierarchy of her burgeoning feminist mind, my mother ranks first on the talk list, Rita is last and I have no place at all. "Oh, she didn't get a very good sleep, darling. Did you hear the program ... and ... Well, I could care less if it's a milestone to talk to us at all ... Not a bit grateful ..."

"I did not have a bad sleep," I say to Johnny, who smiles condescendingly. The steam is knocked out of my rage at Lacey by the realization that Lacey is telling Momma exactly what I thought she would: "At least they are finally talking to us." It isn't good enough for Momma, and a lively debate ensues. It ends with Momma assuring everyone in the world, including her Roman Catholic Lord, that these people all need a good hiding.

"Why is Paula likely to come over?" Momma's voice is rich with doubt and laced with a little fear. Lacey doesn't answer, just repeats herself, and Momma says OK. I can hear the whole conversation now because I have stopped telling Johnny what a ditz I think Lacey is and complaining about the way she treats me. Neither Lacey nor Momma has quite gotten used to telephone technology. Before we moved to town we had a rickety old CPR telephone — the wind-up kind. For the person at the other end to hear you, the speaker had to talk pretty loud. Both of them still talk loudly on the phone.

"Johnny, how old is Lacey?" I would have asked Momma but she went straight to the bathroom.

"She's the oldest," he answers. I know this. He only said that to stall for time so he could calculate just how old Lacey was by subtracting eighteen years from my mom's sixty. I want to chuckle at him and tell him I know what he is doing. I could have done this myself but I am lazy and thought maybe he knew the answer off the top of his head. Instead I wait passively for his answer and enjoy the scene. "Must be near forty-two. Lacey was born when your Mom was eighteen. I remember. It was the summer your Momma broke my heart." He laughs heartily, as if having your heart broken is such an incredibly wonderful memory. "Wasn't always this chatty. No. Quiet as a mouse. Richard came back from town with a railroad job — didn't have to go to war like the rest of

us. He scooped up your mom and I put'near died of a broken heart."
How do you spell "put'near," Johnny? I think but dare not say.

"This would be later, Johnny, after the war."

"Yep," like he failed to see the conflict of timing in his story.
"Yep. He'd been working on the tracks all through the war. Me, I
had to go overseas. We came back about the same time. Ended up
at old Miller's place, both of us with courting intentions. Richard
dressed up in fine clothes, spats and suits. Me, I just wore my old
overalls. Richard told railroad stories about arms shipments, troop
movements, train derailments, and I didn't say a word. Figure bloodshed wasn't the subject of polite conversation. What's there to tell
about war? I shouldn't a went. That's all there is to tell."

I don't get the story. My brain stretches, pulls and drags, but
nothing happens; I don't understand. I don't even understand
enough to ask a question that might clarify the point of the story.
I look askance at him and try to enjoy the conversation without
understanding the meaning of it. It is the first one we have had. I
blush. Ol' Johnny misinterprets my blush.

"Well now, all this business of romance is new to you, eh?" and
he winks. I nod, not because it's true but because I have no idea
how I should react to this.

"Pretty soon it'll be your turn. Just remember, Honey, shiny
things sometimes crack easy. I left the village after your mom married your papa. Never went back. Never married. Just drifted
through life, worked, ate, slept ... " The story loses its magic and I
realize Momma is still in the bathroom. I can hear the water running steadily. It has been running steadily since Johnny started
talking. Something happened. Johnny says something about "ran
into your mom a year ago by accident" and then quits, as if the rest
of the story is a foregone conclusion. I am glad his story is finished. I decide to phone Lacey and ask what she said to Momma,
when the doorbell rings. I put the phone down and turn just in
time to catch a glimpse of Momma rounding the corner and heading for the doorway.

"Come on in, Dearest." It's Paula. Both daughters-in-law share the same "Dearest" title, but I know this is Paula. Only a major domestic fight would drive a woman from bed on a Sunday morning at 7:00 a.m. Monique has never hinted at dissatisfaction with her double-income, no-kids life with Joseph; so this would be Paula.

They are all a mess; both kids have bruised faces and Paula is gushing blood. Momma shoots me a look. I run to the bathroom and get the first aid kit while Johnny fishes in the teapot for last night's tea bags and starts treating the two kids. Paula falls apart. I hand the kit to Momma. She begins to mend Paula's face. I go get Rita up — she'll know what to say to Paula. Rita takes a look at the bloody carnage and tells me to call Joseph and Lacey. Rita is angry. I notice how stiff and clinical my mother is, beyond reasonable rage. There is going to be major shit to pay here and I would not want to be Rudy just now. Paula's eye is cut up. A huge gash, must be an inch long, runs along her eyebrow, and both eyes are swelling up. She keeps trying to hold her face and Rita keeps slapping her hand mercilessly so Momma can stitch it up. Her face is going to scar. Jeezuss.

"Joseph," my voice answers his hello flat and toneless. "You better get over here. Rudy's finally done it."

"Asshole," he whispers and hangs up. I think he mumbled "be right there" to the air as his hand let the phone fall.

I hang up and dial Lacey's number. For some reason I plan a small speech. "Lacey, Momma and Rita wanted me to phone you. Paula has been hurt and they want you to come over here right away." It sounds stupid in my ear, hokey. Why am I making up a speech and rehearsing it? Lacey is my sister. The phone rings. Why the hell did he smash his wife and children's faces? I look in the direction of the kids, both have swelling eyes. Their faces, why their faces, keeps limping along inside my head like a broken record. The phone rings a half dozen or so times, long enough for the impact of events to hit me — huge, racking, ignorant sobs overtake me and the male voice at the other end drives my speech from my mind.

"Don't cry," the man's voice says. "Lacey is on her way," and she appears before Jacob finishes saying, "It will be all right, Sugar." Lacey marches through the door, assures me, "we'll fix it" between cursing the world, patriarchy, Rudy, racism and every other white male conspiracy against Native womanhood and swabbing blood from below the gash Momma is sewing up, while Rita gets another pot of very strong tea on the go and Ol' Johnny holds the two little ones and applies the bags to their eyes and sings, "All my trials Lord, soon be over." It takes me by surprise. He sounds Black when he sings the song. The sound of it, plaintive and haunting, makes me cry all the harder.

"Stop your racket," Momma barks at me between soft, consoling remarks to Paula. "You'll wake the dead," which really means the kids. Of course I do wake them up. I can't stop. They jump about me, crying and saying, "Don't worry Auntie, it'll be fine," just like their old gramma does in a major crisis. They honestly believe it will be fine, and I will never again believe in the fineness of the world. The room is a whirl of emotion and movement, horrific realization and painful sounds. I cannot heed my mother's instructions. I want to, but images of Rudy obstruct my ability to grab hold of myself for the kids', Paula's, or anyone else's sake. Rudy picks me up after school in his old beat up car. Rudy bandages endless cuts and bruises, tells jokes that allay fear, that drive pain away, gets me to howl at the moon with him, rides the same merry-go-round, laughs at the wickedness of the world, faces storms, storms of lightning and Daddy's disappearance from the world. Rudy, what happened to you? Where did you go? Rudy, handsome Rudy, ladykiller Rudy, and I retch.

There is elder cousin Walt, Uncle Walt, tossing Rudy bits and pieces of his life, while Joseph sits quietly in the corner. Rudy commands attention. Rudy sings songs to adoring relatives and Joseph, a wistful look on his face, stands in the shadow of his older brother, eyes full of hidden knowledge. It is Christmas. Dark winds howl at the night. Bitter cold creeps through the cracks of the old cabin. Momma announces her intent to move out of the village. Rudy wants to know why. "This old house was good enough for Gramma, why not you?" Momma hates the comparison, hates the implication that a breezy cabin is good enough for any human being. "I had to live with that for more than twenty years while your dad was alive. I am not putting up with it in you, boy." Rudy is up on his feet. Momma squares off and Joseph interferes. It is not much of a fight. Joseph, quiet and sure, is larger and heavier and, much to everyone's amazement, stronger. He decks Rudy.

We moved to the city by ourselves — well, without Rudy, anyway. Rudy stayed behind with Paula in Gramma and Grampa's old house until the number of children and Momma's nagging brought them all to the city. He worked from the first day he arrived. Roofing. Why didn't I think of it before? That must be the way Rita met Bill, through Rudy. Bill is one of Rudy's roofing mates. Good-looking Rudy and his beautiful wife, now scarred by her love of him.

Joseph and Monique arrive. Joseph will bring to Rudy the only kind of justice Rudy truly understands — a good hiding. But how did he get this way? The tears are still rolling out of my eyes liberally, but my body stops making noise. The scene is blurred, not just physically, but internally; the memory of Rudy lacks understanding. It gives me no insight. His rage was there before my memories began. My life lacks understanding. I managed to live twenty years without ever seeing anything clearly.

The end of my noise cues everyone. The commotion stops. Coffee is served. It is Paula's move. Joseph is on the phone; we all look at Paula and wait. He hangs up softly without speaking; must not be anyone home.

"I can't go back." It comes out desperate and unconvincing.

"Were you still thinking of buying that house, Momma?" Joseph asks.

"Grief, Joseph. The girl is half mangled, the kids are beat up, Rudy is gone, all hell has broken loose and you want to talk real estate." Lacey, bless her, blurts out precisely my own sentiments. Rita and Momma look a little confused, but not nearly as indignant as Lacey and myself. Ol' Johnny brings everyone back to reality on Joseph's behalf.

"Paula needs a home. We can't possibly all live in this here old house. We can't send her back to Rudy, can we?" We can't possibly all live ... does this mean Johnny is now a permanent member of our household ... reality blurs again. Joseph, with Johnny's help, takes the helm. He wants to know how much of a down payment we have. I don't really understand why at first, as everyone else slips into this co-operative mode. They answer Joseph's monosyllabic questions.

"How much money you got, Johnny?"

"A couple thousand and some."

"Exactly?" Johnny fishes for his savings book. I am getting a bad taste in my mouth.

"Two thousand, seven hundred thirty-three dollars and forty-four cents." Oh no. My savings. All the money any one of them has ever given me is about to be appropriated because one of my brothers turned out to be an animal. I just found a job. It doesn't pay much, but it has swollen my little bank book already. My book is full of family allowance cheques, cash birthday presents and Christmas gifts from Auntie Mary and every other relative who has done well on occasion. All of it is about to disappear.

"Momma?" Joseph looks at my mom.

"Fivethousandtwohundredtwelve and twothirtyfour"; she says the numbers like they are all one word.

"Rita?"

"I've only had three paycheques ... " Joseph waits for the answer without paying any attention to her apology. "Five hundred and seventy-two." She looks down and wrings her hands, then says,

"But I can afford a hefty mortgage payment." Momma's hand caresses Rita's. She looks straight at Joseph.

"Monique," he says.

"Eleven thousand, eight hundred and forty-two, Joseph." Her eyes open, drop, open, then drop again, a coded speech to Joseph. "Yes, Joseph, give it all to them. We'll always get by."

"Johnny, are your intentions towards my mother honourable enough to part with all that cash?" Momma gasps, and Joseph and Johnny smile at each other. Momma blushes, then laughs when Johnny says "of course."

Lacey is next. She is already digging around in her bank books — personal savings, joint savings, personal chequing, joint chequing — and carefully calculating the difference between the totals and the cheques she wrote. She subtracts her half of the money from the joint accounts after the bills are accounted for and adds this to the sum of her personal bank accounts.

"Twenty-eight, seven seventy, Joseph." It is already a lot of money. Maybe they won't need mine.

"Are you prepared to put your money down on something bigger than you originally anticipated, Momma?" Momma nods. They set to work and decide how big the house should be and throw around ideal locations. They don't mention me or my money. Joseph never actually asked for Lacey's money; she kind of offered it. I can't. I can't say anything unless Joseph asks. I contemplate lying about the amount, but they all know how much money I am worth. Last summer I bragged about how I was going to treat myself to a new car when I graduated. They must know I am more than halfway there. In any case, Joseph and his damned calculator can figure it out in a few moments.

Paula shakes her head. Good, Paula, tell them this is more than you deserve. Free me from my guilt, because I am not parting with a dime. Joseph looks at her, his eyes full of sympathy, but his face moulds itself into sterner stuff and he says she can go home if she wants but this is as good a time as any to buy the house Momma wants. "If you move in with Momma, then the house will have to be large — and the mortgage too. If you don't, it will be small and so will the mortgage. You will end up paying your share of a mortgage for a house we will all own, or you'll pay rent to some landlord for a house he will own. It is up to you, but Momma will get her house in any case." He closes the calculator up and slips it into his sports jacket pocket. Conspiracy. Joseph and Monique are part of Momma's scheme, probably were from the beginning. Where was I when they laid out their plans?

Paula nods "yes" and weeps again. Joseph tells me to pack my things; I am to stay with him for a while. Rude bugger. Why the hell do I have to pack up and clear out? He tells Paula to do the same. Oh, great. I get to play nursemaid to a miserable grass widow and her two kids, while the others hunt around for a dream house. The kids can stay here, he says. Paula will need the time alone to get through this. Right. The kids set up a howl. Joseph bends down and, in the sweetest murmur I have ever hard him utter, he asks them if their Uncle Joseph has ever let them down. He keeps asking until they both answer "No." Then he says they are to stay here with Gramma and their Momma will stay with him. He clips the words out slowly, full of no-ifs-and-or-buts and don't-argue-with-Uncle-Joe. He threatens them without altering the tone of his voice much. I can't help admiring his handling of the children's resistance. They bite it back, whimper and nod agreement. Was it Joseph or was it them? Was it the scent of co-operation in the face of crisis that hung in the air? Am I the only rotter here besides Rudy?

The phone rings again. I get up to answer. I gained weight sitting there. I am sure of it. It takes me three rings to cross the ten-foot kitchen. I leave them mumbling practical plans about who will sleep where and how long Paula will need to recover, while Paula weeps and submits to whatever plans are made. On the other end of the line a man is asking for me. Grief. I have forgotten about him already. Friday, I fell in love. It's only Sunday and he is calling me to arrange when we are to go somewhere and I can't remember where. I am so disconnected from Friday and work that I can't remember his name. Maybe he will hint. Maybe it's all right to ask, "Who is this?" Blurred and barely able to stand up, I mumble hello after he asks for me, then fall silent.

"Do you remember me?" So glad you put it that way, now I can truly indulge in humiliating myself. I lie.

"Oh, yeah. Hello." My voice lacks conviction. He laughs.

"Hello. It's Mark. From work. Are you ready for our stroll through the park?" So that's it. No, absolutely not. I am ready to piss on the Premier, shit on the President of the United States or nuke New York, but I am definitely not ready for anything so ordinary as a stroll in the park. Another lie? No, I can't face the deception I pulled on my family this morning; another lie is going to overload my capacity for guilt. Actually, I did not pull off any deception, I persuade myself. Well, my heart was in it, just their minds weren't. They didn't bring my money up because they did not think I was mature enough for something like co-operation with family ambitions in a time of family crisis. Maybe I better take the walk — nuking New York is clearly overkill, unreasonable.

"Hello," he says again.

"Hello," I say again. I think this is my third hello. I better fish for something a little more intelligent to say.

"I have had a rough day."

"Oh, well, I can understand that. It must be 8:00 o'clock in the morning already. Plenty of time to have had a lousy day." Right. "What's up, Marianne? Should I just hang up the phone with quiet dignity?" Above average intelligence, sensitive, but clearly he owns a healthy dose of self-respect.

"No ... Well, maybe ... You see ... Well, it is hard to explain." What am I supposed to say? My brother just half-killed his wife and kids and ran off. My family doesn't consider me an eligible adult capable of family co-operation. I don't think I am capable of mature co-operation either and right now I want to nuke New

York more than anything else in the world.

"OK, I understand." What he understands from that mumbo jumbo is beyond me. I don't understand what I meant to say, much less what I did say. The phone registers a dial tone just a couple of seconds later. I feel sick all over again. The entire kitchen is silent. All of them are wondering about my strange conversation. Just what I need to pick up my spirits. Now I have to tell my family that the call was from a man I would like to see, but it's all over, even though we never really got down to seeing each other because I could not think of a single intelligent thing to say to him, and I want to piss on the Premier or nuke New York. I would have to assure Paula that it has nothing to do with her; it is sort of like, well, I went semi-psychotic for a moment, forgot who he was, well, nuking New York appeals to me this morning for no particular reason, but you know how some guys are, no sense of humour, like you know, he couldn't get into it. Oh, Christ, I can't stand the sound of my own mind.

"I would like Auntie Mary to kick my butt just now." Joseph laughs. "OK, Honey. How much are you in for?" Not even close, Joseph, but I throw my car into the pot anyway without thinking much more about it. Momma stays on the theme of Mary. "She can put this all together for us." This remark comes in the middle of a call from Auntie Mary. Momma starts on her old track of genocide, cultural genocide, all the hate and venom of those other people turned in on ourselves.

"The very moment, the very day we stopped dying of disease, Mary, some mother's son among us killed his wife. I swear white men make me crazy. Now one of my own has joined the ranks of mercenaries out to do us in ... " I do hope Auntie comes soon. My lost love, Rudy's failed marriage, my disappearing future lifestyle and my eviction from this house — the home I grew up in — are making me lean in my mother's philosophical direction.

"Joseph."

"Yeah, Honey?"

"What kind of jail term would you get for pissing on the Premier?" The laughter from the crowd neither dampens my enthusiasm nor answers my question.

"Well, we need something." Momma says it kind of pouty. She interrupts her conversation with Auntie Mary to impress us with this piece of wisdom, then resumes talking to Mary. It surprises me. I asked the question they are all laughing at; why is Momma pouting about their laughter? In the middle of the last guffaw I see Joseph steal a secret look at Monique and wink. I feel like a complete stranger caught in a room full of people I don't know. They are all bent on integrating me into their family fold now that they realize I am one of them. A piece of me wants to resist, but the rest wants to know, understand, and be one of them.

"Besides the house, Joseph, what do we need?" I ask. The laughter grinds to a halt. Lacey sits up straight, sticks her aristocratic chin out and waits for the minute or so of silence that it will take Joseph to say he doesn't know before she plans to answer the question herself. I don't really want to hear from her. Her answers always sound a little too much like my arguments and counterarguments in sociology class: justice, peaceful struggle, resolute and relentless, pecking away at an impossibly large and invisible social order. I don't want to hear my own answers parroted, because they have never satisfied the deep yearning that plagues me more than ever right now. Joseph surprises us all.

"We need to dream. Then we need to roll up our sleeves and begin plugging away together and hack at our dreams — whatever they are — to make them come true. Unfortunately, Honey, that takes a lot more than some of us feel we have right now."

"Oh, for Pete's sake, Joseph. She wants something practical that we can actually do, a struggle we can win, not some idealist nincompoopetyjaw."

Joseph pays no attention. He looks at me from under heavy black arched brows, his sleepy-looking eyes veiled by stiff thick black lashes. He is gorgeous. I never saw it before, but he exudes extraordinary sensuousness and beauty, the sort that live deep inside a person. Monique smiles adoringly. I retreat to an imaginary world in which dreams are encouraged. Everyone talks at once. Some defend Joseph, others side with Lacey, and the kids interrupt to ask innocent questions. Dorry moves to stand next to Joseph and I let the hubbub go on while some piece of me I didn't know existed just floats about this unknown universe full of dreams.

✳ ✳ ✳

There are over a dozen people working in this office. Two other women are summer students like myself; the others, including Mark, our boss, are on regular payroll. No one refers to him as our boss. The term does not seem to fit into the order of things here. I know he is our boss and secretly tell myself to be careful. He is young and confident. His clothes fit neatly to his vigorous frame and his voice purrs steel as he instructs us in our work. He leans over our shoulders every now and then as we work. He smells of cologne. Funny I didn't notice the cologne during the first week of work, or during the interview.

Every now and then he looks at me quizzically, an earnest gaze directed at me above the official hubbub that goes on. His look stirs my imagination. My body comes alive. It gushes despite all my good sense. Jeezuss, my entire family is falling apart at the seams and my body decides lust is the best solution to all ills.

His office is right in front of the computer I punch at. I look up every now and then to watch him work, and dream his character into being. I watch his steady drive through the day. His hand runs through his hair as he barrels along, gets stumped, figures the problem out, then resumes his march across worlds of paper. His papers end up on my desk. Mountains of proposals, legal documents, research information and plans for the future of Native people in British Columbia. How does a body get to have their head so full of words, plans, approaches and solutions to the dilemmas of over fifty thousand people?

The documents are addressed to a host of officials and dignitaries. Some of them are letters addressed to Ministers, or Members of Parliament or the Legislature. They look like they are answers to letters already received. It stuns me that this young man with a fierce sense of concentration and passionate gaze can communicate with dignitaries with such modesty. He hands me my set of documents and letters with quiet dignity and asks me casually to print them out.

I am minding my printer. I feel his gaze and look up; he smiles boldly, then lowers his face. I can see him invite me, pull at the possibilities he has to offer. I want him to stop, to continue, to say out loud what is on his mind and to be quiet, all at the same time. A voice cuts through my tangent.

"Elijah." It's a voice full of triumph. Saul, the head of the Union of British Columbia Chiefs, strolls in after the sound of his voice. We all stop what we are doing. Elijah? Saul takes a look around, assumes some sort of bird posture, narrows his eyes, both wing tips on his hips, and speaks. The only other person I ever saw speak like this is Auntie Mary. There he is, short, dark, about forty-five and he talks as lovely as Auntie Mary and sounds just as wonderful. He pauses at the same moments she would. He leans back slowly, gracefully, then moves forward into his words. His body responds to his own sounds as though he is hearing the words for the first time. He waves his arms, sweeping gestures full of great deliberation, signifying gravity.

Almost immediately, I stop listening and watch him talk. I can't stop comparing him to my professors at school. The instructor's jerky movements always give me anxiety. The ums and ahs, the apologetic phrases thrown in because he has forgotten what the devil he was talking about and needs a conjunctive remark to stall for time, don't plague Saul's speech. I used to think Auntie Mary was the only person who could talk like this. Saul's oratory centres on some man named Elijah who said no to something or other.

I wish I had paid more attention to his words because everyone gets delirious over Elijah whoever and his "no." I fake it. I hee-haw around and repeat "isn't that something" like everyone else. I do so with some trepidation. I don't know these people and have no idea how their minds work. I do know my mother and she will likely have plenty to say about Elijah and his "no." Her particular sense of logic may not line up with these people's. I decide that I will not likely work here ever again and probably won't be seeing these people after the summer. If my mother doesn't like Elijah and what he said no to then I can acquiesce to her opinion at home, then switch to joy at work without much trouble. Likely I will never have to make a decision about it on my own, one way or another.

"Well, what do you say?" Mark leans on my desk, smiling from ear to ear. About what? Elijah? The speech? Maybe he asked me something personal ... no ... Elijah crowds everyone's communication today. I'm sure his question centres on some feeling I have about Elijah saying "no."

"Great." Somehow his face doesn't look like this is the sort of answer he expected. He smiles too hard. He stands up and swings into his jacket, then looks at me with anticipation. I suspect the question had nothing to do with Elijah.

"It's lunch time now," he says, like I was wondering about it. Is that what I said yes to? I hope so, because if it isn't it's going to be embarrassing when I stand up and he asks me what I am doing. I get up slowly. I can always fake going for coffee — he just keeps smiling.

"We can go to the little eatery just around the corner." Lucky guess, and I breathe relief. We aren't the only ones who are off to lunch. Apparently the whole office shuts down today.

Elijah said "no." I am glad we all traipse off together. In a crowd of talkative, festive Indians the story will unfold of its own. We are very fond of reliving dramas by repeating their details and hahaing them to death. I won't have to reveal my ignorance or my inattentiveness. There are enough eager participants to fill in all the blanks of my non-understanding. My lunch date is among the well-informed. He is not as poetic or as commanding as Saul but his knowledge is impressive on its own. He moves along the corridors of law, constitutionality and their significance to us, easily. I appreciate the clarity and fullness of his remarks. As I listen, I look for opinions that might clash with my mother's. It is hard to tell because his use of English differs so sharply from Momma's and I can't picture him with a broom. *For Pete's sake, Marianne, it's only a lunch date, not a marriage proposal.* I already stood him up once for a walk in the park; surely he invited me along as part of the general tide of office revellers. In the midst of the festive brouhaha around Elijah and our turn, rolling around the bend, at last he keeps up a steady stream of tiny devotions to me.

"What would you like?" My heart stops; there is more than one meaning in his voice. What would you like? You can have anything, anything you want, Marianne. I can give you … *Stop it, Marianne.*

"Denver."

"Denver it is … coffee … or something stronger?" There is just a hint of playful pout circling around his response to my answer. I blush inside.

"Coffee," comes up barely audible. *Get your hormones under control, Marianne.*

"How in the world could it be that they need unanimous consent?" Julie, my co-student worker asks.

"They tabled it wrong," and his eyes look at me, ask me if I am all right. I smile a thin "yes"; he smiles a layered "good." "The dumb buggers didn't follow their own rules for tabling a bill in the legislature." His leg touches mine gently, so gently I'm not sure it happened; then his look invites, whispers, well? I stare at my food. "Now they need unanimous consent to even consider the bill. All Elijah has to do is keep talking and saying no until midnight of

June third." Everyone laughs. We love it when white folks get tangled in their complex rules and regulations. His laugh speaks of silent invitations, studious inquiries into my heart. I feel naked, spirit naked, not physically naked. My spirit moves sensuous and free ... *Stop it.*

"That's a lot of talking; this is only the 11th," and my voice stops the laughter dead in its tracks. I want it to stop his looks and the reams of conversations underneath his words. I tread on dangerous territory. I don't know enough to carry on a conversation about Elijah. I should really keep quiet but he keeps looking, looking at me.

"Yes, it is." He says it like it's an answer to one of his questions he didn't ask out loud. "Cream ... sugar?" Sugar like it's my name. "But it's what we are good at." Good, Marianne, I'm good. His eyes tell me how good he can be, how good it will be ... . "He doesn't have to make sense, he just has to keep it up." It doesn't have to make sense, Marianne, Marianne, look at me, tell me ... "We are a tenacious people," I am tenacious, Marianne, "and given the stakes I am sure any one of us here could probably talk a blue streak." His voice is back to normal. They all laugh again.

"What do you mean he doesn't have to make sense, surely he has to argue the bill," Julie pipes up again. I know the answer to this one; no one can argue the bill until it has been duly tabled.

"Not according to their rules. They have to get the bill on the table before they can argue it. It has to be tabled properly and they didn't so now they need Elijah's consent. He gets to speak as long as he can keep up the flow of words. If he shuts up the speaker gets to call a vote." I am relieved he is not paragraphing propositions at me but sorry he isn't looking at me. "Gawd. He must have an endless run of stories to tell — they say he was quite the partier until a couple years back," and they all laugh.

"Didn't ever think our bizarre drinking habits would come in handy in the legislature," and they laugh.

"If he remembers them." They stop laughing. I just can't shut up; my hormone levels are too high; they are firing up my adrenaline which is wired directly to my mouth.

"Yes ... this is true. Salt?" I answer yes as flat as I can. "But he lived for twenty years before he partied, heard endless trappers' tales and went to residential school — that must be worth a story or two. He must have had a dream on one or two occasions." Do you dream, Marianne? and he is at it again. What are your dreams, Marianne? ... I can guide your dreams along trails you have never imagined. Do you want to dreamwalk with me, Marianne? Tell me your dreams. "Besides, he could keep on repeating the same story over and over, if he knows only one." Just one, Marianne, just tell me one dream — one impossibly sweet dream ... I am shaken.

"That would be embarrassing." I look at him, tell him this is embarrassing ... Saul studies us ... I can't bear the embarrassment. Please, please stop. His silence answers, please what, Marianne, please you? and my eyes flash *stop* — seriously stop. He shakes off my "stop" and focuses on the lunch and the celebration of Elijah. I have to cheer myself up; the change is too abrupt. I did not really want to close the door on him. "Excuse me, honourable gentlemen and ladies, few in number as I know you ladies are, I hope you like the first story because it's my only story and I think I will repeat it for the next several hundred hours," and we all get swept up in the tide. "Excuse me, you, over there, wake up, I am talkin' to you — don't sleep. If you listen you may get a better perspective on Humpty Dumpty. You may realize the extraordinary depth of the metaphor contained in this famous piece of literature. Of course, then again, you may not, but what the heck, let me say it again anyway." He isn't looking at me — I can't signal him. I brush his leg — gently, so gently. He turns. My eyes whisper, not here, I only meant not here — someplace else, sometime but not here, there are too many witnesses, my blood runs too warm. Mark is triumphant. Exultant in his victory over the inside of my heart. The luncheon, ladies and gentlemen, is a most delicious affair and it hurries the day to a close.

✳ ✳ ✳

Back at home, Momma and Johnny and whoever of the kids can stand it are watching all-news television.

"When did we get all-news cable, Momma?"

"Hush, Elijah's on." I sit next to Dorry and shuck my jacket and put my purse carefully onto the coffee table, then sneak into a chair and watch without making a sound. Elijah looks frail. His voice is so soft you have to feel around for the words, study his face for their meaning, but there he is, Elijah Harper, MLA from Red Sucker Creek, Manitoba, still talking. Even, steady sounds, statistics about the nature of our life in this society. Its treatment of us indicted. Historical accounts, contemporary accounts, minute after minute, hour after hour he goes on. Facts about his village, the residential school system — the death of our culture — and every now and then Momma is affirmed. "See," she blurts out so quickly compared to the slow steady cadence of Elijah that you don't miss a single word he says. Actually, he speaks so slowly that any Métis from my Momma's village could crowd a jig between his words, but the hum of his voice never ceases long enough for the Speaker to call for a vote, at least not today.

I don't know why, but I want to weep. I feel so consumed by the magic of it all, the absolute irony of it, the greatness and the simplicity of it, that I just want to roll all over the floor and wail. The plot. The physical murder of our whole people, is being documented by the man from Manitoba who sat silent in the House of Commons for two years. His frailness disappears in the folds of his steady gaze. He has waited for this moment. He sat in the back benches and waited. He knew his turn would come, and when it came, he could be glorious, is glorious; so much of this moment is his that whether or not he fails to filibuster won't matter. He is there and we all watch. Three generations of us glued to the words of a little man whose command of English is connected to some other language, some other rhythm, a rhythm my mother bemoans is lost. I loathe English, feel imprisoned in its dry and cold delivery of pain and truth. I never realized this until I saw Elijah speak. His English in translation is free of the dry, cold pain. Graphic and gentle, polite, free of the bullshit hierarchy, he drives on relentlessly, but not noisily. He carefully chooses each word so as to sound as unobnoxious as he possibly can, while he articulates, documents and advances the most obnoxious and despicable thing a Nation can do: attempt genocide on a people. I look at Momma and see heroism. I see her fight day in and day out all of her life. She struggles to maintain herself and her children, not just physically, but psychically, culturally, with very few tools. She wages a horrendous battle against terrible odds — odds we cannot possibly win against, but not for a moment does she ever give up the good fight. And there on television, for all the world to see, is the battle laid out, the struggle for personal and psychological survival of Momma and all our old women. There are their weapons: organized violence, conquest by sword and musket, organized child stealing through the school system and the Child Welfare Act, apprehension, terror, defamation of national character, racism, alcohol poisoning, imprisonment, hanging, language and cultural prohibition, total racial invalidation. And our weapons? We have but one: dogged insistence on truth. It is all so clear and so terribly beautiful. I sit and watch hour after hour with my family. I shed hot tears of shame, cooling tears of pride, sweet tears of recognition, tears of joyous truth until exhaustion overcomes me and I sleep.

✳ ✳ ✳

I am not much wiser about the raw facts of Elijah's actions but I understand their significance. I feel exonerated for a crime I never committed. I feel like my entire lineage since these people came has been on trial. We have steadily insisted on our innocence and now we have been granted a reprieve. Work begins to mean something to me. I can fall in love, with my nieces, my nephews, my mother, this man at work, our entire people. We all become worthy of love. I feel invincible, womanly, seductive and beautiful. At the same time, I want to weep because I know I have never felt this way before. Cultural genocide.

Visions of my Momma, adamantly insisting on old codes of conduct, and me, wishing she were not so archaic, dance inside. This is it. I lack the affection to believe in my mother. Elijah restores this affection. The nattering, the abuse, catalyze self-inflicted wounds and I, and children like me, grab daggers, aim them at our mothers' hearts and gash holes in their hopes, dreams and codes of conduct. Rudy, poor arrogant Rudy, becomes a casualty in a war we wage against ourselves. A war made of silence, despair and hopelessness. "To have dreams," Joseph said.

Not just any dreams, Joseph, I think as I sit at my desk at work. Not the kind of dreams they laid out for us — dreams of new cars and nightmares of the death of old things. They came into our bedrooms at night, invaded dream sleep, gave us dreams that ripped our souls out of our bodies and destroyed whatever bonds we had with our mothers. We had to love the enemy to hate ourselves. Rudy's swagger sounds the death knell between himself and our family. The swagger, the Macho man, the tough guy who talks just a little too loudly, is just a little too cheeky, too crude, too mean, is the harbinger of cultural genocide. The daughter who ignores her mother, fails to see inside her soul, re-dreams old visions into new escape, hands her brother the knife that cuts the cord and rips asunder the sacred bond of family.

Momma blames them, but I know we had to give up on ourselves and our families for the plot to work. We held the knife that cut us from our past. "Rudy, where are you now? I am bleeding, Rudy. I bleed ancient wounds. I need a bandage, a healing hand only you can give me. Rudy, come home." I wake from my reverie, prompted by someone's voice. It sounds so far away.

"Are you OK?" my co-worker Julie asks.

"Oh yeah, she's fine. She's just a-thinking," Carla from the back office answers and winks at my co-worker and nods in the boss's direction. They giggle. The screen of my computer shines green letters back at me. "Rudy, come home." Oh Gawd, shift control Y, delete line, and Rudy disappears. I manage a weak grin and go back to keying in the words that are supposed to be there. I will survive this. I will survive. I'll do what I am supposed to do and save all this craziness for later.

"It's lunch time," Julie repeats what she had said earlier.

"Oh," and I get up to leave. Mark is off in the corner. He and Saul are engaged in a serious discussion and a couple of other men have joined them. Lunch will go on without them. I wish I had brought a sandwich. Somehow, eating out every day feels wasteful, criminal really. Elsa needs shoes, Dorry needs art supplies, a whole list of family needs I had ignored until now jumps about in my mind. I never thought about the needs of my nieces and nephews before. My family looks different now. I look at my hands — moonstone and jade adorn them. I have several semi-precious stones, all set in gold, all gifts from my family. I wear them as though I deserve them. I realize now that my brothers and sisters and my aunt gave them to me because they thought they ought to. A family sense of duty I lacked guided them.

"There's an art supply store around here, isn't there?" I ask Julie on the way out the door.

"Yeah, just around the corner."

"I'll catch you in a bit. My niece has been dying for some paints — oil — forever. I think I'll pick some up."

"You'll skip lunch for some oil paints?" Carla asks with raised eyebrows.

"Not exactly; more like I will do my duty as her auntie. You know, parents give you what you need, but aunties get to spoil you." They laugh and wave me on like they understand.

*   *   *

Dorry put the paints to work right away. Until now the children were all a generic collection of wanderers, gigglers and investigators, without age, character or differences beyond that. Dorry, through her passion for art, becomes unique. She has always painted, watercolours full of fire and life, but from watercolour to oils is a giant step in the world of art. Almost anyone can turn a simple watercolour into a vibrant piece of art with oils, but Dorry has something more. There is depth in her composition.

Within days of obtaining the oil paints, she brings me a canvas. A solitary Native woman cradles a small child. The woman is a vague portrait of woman-shape, a little abstract and painted in bold blues, reds and yellows. She is surrounded by midnight blue dark. Streaks of yellow emanate from someplace past the canvas's beginning. Moments of hope in a melancholy scene. She finishes the painting and gives it to me. It inspires me to spend money on more canvas, and this moves Dorry to spend every waking moment of her free time painting, creating, re-creating our lives in dreams of colour and shape.

Canvas after canvas rolls out, full of hope, dreams and aspirations, all painted against a stark and brutal reality. Dorry knows something about the world we live in that has gone by me. At night we talk about her work. She understands the significance of every brush stroke of colour on her canvases. Where she got this knowledge of our lives and her vision of the future is beyond me.

On this one night I want to ask where her paintings come from, but think it best to wait and see if our conversations around her work will reveal her source of knowledge.

She has this one particular painting I am curious about. A solitary Black woman, sweet and innocent, is silhouetted over an indigenous woman, also young and innocent, in the foreground. Behind them the illusion of crowds and picket signs, with no writing

on them, makes the background. Both women are painted in red
and purple hues over and under the brown of their skin, but that is
not what I'm curious about. I want to know why the Black woman
was silhouetted over the indigenous woman. "What are the people
doing?"

"Protesting."

"What are they protesting?"

"Apartheid."

"Do you know what that is?"

"Oh yeah, Gramma argues with de Klerk all the time. She hates
apartheid. It's when they leave us out because we aren't like them
— white." I laugh. First, because she answers my unspoken question. Blacks in South Africa and us are the same for Dorry. Second,
because my Momma is not a wild card to Dorry. Gramma, my
Momma, expresses her sentiments. Momma's genocidal plot theory
doesn't confuse Dorry in the least. I wish I could trust my mom's
thinking this implicitly.

She rolls over and goes to sleep. In sleep her face retraces her
childhood. Her skin, smooth and soft, lies tight against cheekbones still hidden by baby flesh. Her body stretches its casing,
struggles to free new womanhood from the enclosure of innocence.
Half-child, half-woman. Fifteen going on twenty is what Momma
used to say about me when I was that age. Dorry looks more like
ten going on twenty.

She sleeps comfortable in her awareness of apartheid, the shame
of it is not hers. It is theirs. I wonder if she bought Momma's plot
theory too. It seems incredible to me that a dozen or so white men
sealed in some ivory tower actually planned our demise. A picture
of holocaust rolls into focus. No. It is not rational to think that
these people actually plotted our death. I start to laugh out loud,
then jerk with the effort of restraint. Dorry murmurs and rolls towards me. One arm flops over my stomach. My sister Lacey's child
is closer to me in years than my sister next to me. I have not thought
about this before. I should spend more time with Dorry, since the

experience of our lives is far more equal. Maybe I would feel a little less like a social idiot.

Sleep drifts in my direction. It warms my toes, travels through relaxed legs and swirls about my belly. I want to feel myself fall asleep. I want to capture the precise moment of becoming unconscious. Moonlight plays a lazy song inside my mind. Sunshine against gold drifts around it. Bronze skin against sunshine argues with the gold. Gentle confusion whirls in a crazy dance with moonbeams and I am gone without knowing just when I fell asleep.

I wake up disappointed. Dorry is up before me. She wants to know if I slept well. I lean on my elbow and dramatize my answer with a false seriousness in my voice. "Before or after you whacked me?"

She squeals a heap of "sorry's" and I have to tell her I was just kidding. She is here only for the weekend, as usual, along with the hordes of others. Momma insists her grandchildren stay with her on weekends. It turns our house into a mini-war zone or a busy bus station, depending on the humour of the children. Usually it isn't so bad, but it is always hectic. I want to sneak off on the whole works of them.

"Why don't you take me to an art supply shop and tell me about paints, Dorry?"

"Just us two?" Her face lights up.

"Yeah. All right." The tone of her voice changes when she talks about paints and art. I become the innocent and naive child and she the expert. I don't know why this feels as good as it does but I don't bother questioning it. I like it. Equality is not simple. It is knowing when you are not equal to the expertise of those you know are usually less experienced in most other things. It is creating the condition for the less experienced to feel powerful; no, not just feel, but be powerful. It is empowering others through their own expertise to teach and instruct, rather than always making sure you are the teacher.

Dorry comes alive in the art store. She talks about acrylics, oils, styluses, brushes of sable and a host of other tools I can't keep track of, and I know I won't remember much of what she says. She stops in front of this easel; she looks at it briefly, then carries on.

"Wait a sec? What was that?"

"An easel. It makes painting such a joy, easier." She keeps walking while she says it. I decide to buy Dorry the easel. After school is out for the summer, Dorry will spend weeks on end at our new home. Joseph is looking for one big enough to accommodate Momma, Johnny and me as well as Rita, Paula and all of their children. They want a basement on top of all that. A basement could be used to house a corner art studio. It isn't any easy task, but I am sure Joseph is up to it.

* * *

Lunacy is a much misunderstood phenomenon. For the whole first week of the Elijah "factor" I cannot get a grip on myself. On the outside I look fine, almost fine. At work, I manage to keep up a sane appearance, but at night, mesmerized by the actions of Elijah, I wander into spaces and time from an untravelled direction. One moment sociology comes alive for me. Then the white man's demon, his sense of intellect, his sense of the social, dance about all evil on the outer edges of my mind. The demons grab my heart. Visions of white men as a body grab the heart of the earth, squeeze and compress the fire of our mother. They grab their own daughters, suck them dry of life, cut their spirits loose from their bodies, and advance this madness as process, as thought. I wake up exhausted. I half understand why the world is so pissed off, and at the same time I feel completely crazy.

Lacey, whose feminism always scared the hell out of me, starts to make sense. The riddles Momma, Rita and Auntie Mary speak in used to annoy me; now I like the sound of them. I play with them, turn them over in my mind, form thoughts rooted in them.

The language of riddles is ever so much clearer, respectful, heart-felt and spirited than are the dissertations of John Stuart Mills and the good old boys. Even surreal stories by Johnny don't look as crazy as they did yesterday. The condescending men who have been my teachers move from the place where painful memory dwells to the disdainful side of my mind.

* * *

"Excuse me, but could we talk after class in my office?" my instructor says with great care.

"Yes." I know what it's about and already I am bored.

"This paper you wish to write requires an acute understanding of Mills's concept of utilitarianism — are you sure you are up to that?" Momma, it was never so simple as cultural genocide. You see, they not only invalidated all of our thoughts and our thought processes, but they also cancelled out our ability to get a handle on theirs. Two other white boys in my class are doing the same paper. I know their papers were accepted without question.

* * *

During the Elijah hours I realize I have been hauling ass across foreign terrain carrying two additional burdens on my back: racism and patriarchy. The instructors who tried to be liberal about women did not consider me a woman. I have been Native, generic and sexless, for twenty years. Elijah knows I am and always will be Marianne, a woman.

If I throw a hoop around the simple practice of racism or patriarchy and place it on anyone's table, it will be excused, "It could have been that you were young, it could have been that given your level of participation in class ... " The hoop will always come back to me. The excuses never comfort. It is not gratifying to hear bias excused as youthfulness either — bias paralyzes development, precludes intelligence. The drivel about my level of participation sounds too much like a general agreement with my lack of ability. That is how these burdens work; no matter what happens, it is the coloured girl's own fault. It works this way no matter who you talk to. That is precisely why, despite my love for Rita and her loyalty to me, I blamed her for her inability to stay married. We even blame each other.

Likewise my sympathy for Paula is moderated by blind love for Rudy. I stop feeling after deciding he is an animal. It is him I want to fix. Him I want to help. I cannot chase the demon who misshaped my sense of affection out of my head. Every day that Elijah talks about the process of nation building, the image of the demons who plague me sharpens. Every day he stands alone, guarding our heritage, validating our entire history as men and women, my betrayal of all that my mother and Auntie Mary hold precious hammers at my heart and turns my mind inside out.

If Elijah upset Canada, he upset me a great deal more. His message to us was profoundly simple: we are worth fighting for, we are worth caring for, we are worthy. No more mea culpa. We, as men, as women, as poor people, as Native people, as working people, are all worthy. No white trash, no savages, no broads, no squaws — just honest folk all wanting honest social affection. "When Native people struggle for their rights, they do so at some- one else's expense, because our rights, the denial of them, is inti- mately bound to the mistreatment of the aged, the handicapped, women and the abuse and neglect of our children and poor and working people. Our whole philosophy, our way of being, pre- cludes the mistreatment of anyone. Canada has not only erased us as a people, but it has cut its own people off from learning from us, and Canadians have much to learn from us." That is how I hear your words, Elijah Harper from Red Sucker Creek. Those words upset me. I have lived twenty years on this earth making faces at my mother's sense of justice and I live in terror of my sister's womanly consciousness and you stand there, Elijah, and affirm everything I know is dangerous to think, feel or believe.

My mind retreats to fantasy land, thoughts whirl at breakneck speed half the time. It would be OK if I were in school and no one expected me to pay attention. At school I am a generic Native without much capacity for thought, but here, in this office, it is assumed I have a mind and I am expected to be able to concentrate. It takes huge effort. I limp along. I am not doing too badly, when Saul decides to bring a colour TV to the office and play all-news cable all day. It drives me to distraction. My face is drawn like a magnet to the clean, smooth, unobtrusive lines of Elijah's face. My thoughts skip the data entries and wander around the hills of sociological theory and my own fantastic realizations. Momma shows up, harumphing at a store clerk, challenging some bureaucrat, or railing at some teacher. I wince with embarrassment. I know her challenge of these people has something to do with Elijah finding the strength to stand up each day, day after day, hour after hour, and talk the country to a standstill, but I can't change my heart. It is still ashamed of my mother, and her challenges to those people embarrass me still.

Lunacy: crazy, distracted intervals of inability to reason. My context, my back-up file of explanations, has been uprooted. The raison d'être of my emotions has melted into thin air. I am cast from my moorings into an unknown void. Thoughts spin about, surreal and abstract and multitudinous, but they have no stone to cling to, no brick on which to rebuild my house of learning. That is what crazy is all about.

"The dollar will drop if Elijah succeeds," the Prime Minister says. How could he imagine that any Native could be coerced by the devaluation of a loonie? Some of Elijah's own party members panic. The Liberal party leader freezes, paralyzed by the huge implications of Elijah's actions. Elijah's party leader expresses silent confidence in Elijah. She makes no comment to the press but she says nothing to Elijah.

"My dear fellow," my mother informs the Prime Minister after he made this remark. "We have no dollars, so it doesn't scare us a bit. We never wanted your damn dollars. Your money is filthy. We want our homeland. Even a fool such as yourself can figure that out." I roll all over the floor, laugh through my tears and cheer my mother on. She looks at me, shocked. No one in our family has ever found her funny before. I feel like Scrooge after his ghostly altercation with good will; I am hysterical, full of new knowledge for which there is no rational explanation. She gets over her shock within seconds and accepts I have had a change of heart. Oh Gawd, I hope life becomes this simple for me.

* * *

It is late in the day.

"Have you had lunch yet … Marianne?" Mark is cautious now. He circles around his affection for me, tests the water before he expresses it. His long pause gives me a moment to read the desire in his voice. His voice presses significance between the syllables of my name.

I fill my "not yet" with longing, and we are off again to another shaky start. At lunch we talk about the Manitoba chiefs, the behind-the-scenes support it is taking to keep Elijah on his feet. He tells me of the thousands of letters of support Elijah has received each day. Sadly, the death threats grow too. Mark is animated. Finally, he has a place as a man. I can't help asking why only men retreat to the backrooms to discuss strategy.

"What?" He looks confused, maybe even a little disappointed in me. "Why do only men retreat to the backrooms to discuss strategy? Oh please. You aren't a fanatical feminist are you?"

"Oh please, you aren't a fanatical patriarch are you?" I scrape the words out across layers of stone sharp and unrelenting. I want to finish with some sensible treatment on how fanatical patriarchs create fanatical feminists; they don't just drop from the skies all ugly and witchlike. The rocks in my mouth are too sharp. I know the words will come out cutting, so I just stare at him.

"I think we ought to go," he mumbles, and we leave. Outside the sun in shining. My mind casts grey shadows over its brilliance. Leaden grey, weighty grey, steel grey, hard and cold, spreads itself into a thin transparent sheet over sun's glory. I want to talk to Lacey. I know Lacey will be by tonight. It is Elijah's last night. He has already passed round three. If he can't keep it up today, we are lost. It is the fourth and final round.

In Mark's car on the way home, I think about Rudy. He could be so sweet, but he is also clear: he is a man. He is the head of the household. I think about that. The head of the household, as though his wife had no mind in her own home. It is his money, his time, his, his ... Resistance of the mildest sort from Paula to any of his dominions opens a chasm between himself and his wife. His wife. I watch Mark and see Rudy transform from a mild-mannered, benevolent patriarch to an incensed master when challenged. I wonder how close Mark is to this same pattern.

Halfway home I ask him to let me out; I want to walk. He stops and reaches across my chest and pauses before he opens the door. His face has softened and he studies mine for a moment, then whispers goodbye. In that moment my life hangs in mid-air, still and mutable. I want to say it's OK, but I know this would mean killing little pieces of me. I know the dagger he offers will be swung by me. I know that to hold woman inferior requires help from the victim, so I leave.

Outside, the sound of traffic comes at my ears through the tunnel of my confusion. Every now and then the murmur of cars sharpens, then recedes, drowned by the tornado of thoughts about Mark, manhood, Momma and womanhood and the nutty worlds we straddle. At work I bang out documents on an IBM computer all day. I return home to a mother who is toaster illiterate. At the same time, I am a serious social idiot and my mother is something of an analytical genius. We have never spoken in a language both of us agree upon and understand. The cultural genocide plot my mother insists keeps these people motivated is, on one level, absurd, yet between the lines of her insistence on their plotting lies a powerful sense of truth.

Footsteps come up behind me. Footsteps aimed at my back. I turn. James, big and blond. James, fellow classmate, honour student, running up behind me.

"Marianne," his voice bites off the technical formation of the sounds that make up my name without any heart. I can't believe he is calling me. In the two years I have attended school with him, he never so much as looked at me. Now he is hollering out my name and running like hell after my backside like we are long lost buds.

"Say, Marianne," puff, puff, he isn't used to running. His lips stretch across clean, even teeth into what he supposes is a wide open smile. I can't decide if he looks like one of those Jehovah's Witness missionaries or a salesman. Doesn't matter anyway.

"Let me catch my breath," he says, leans forward, bends his head full of wispy yellow locks and then sighs. I look. His shoulders are broad, his chest full of good-looking lung capacity and his waist trim; small, really. His face is tanned and unblemished. The lines of it indicate his life contains no major crises. He has probably never attended a funeral; likely all his aunts, uncles and grandparents are still in the land of the living. His parents are probably still married; likely don't care much for each other but have never had a fight in his presence. I cannot imagine him walloping some woman the way Rudy had. I look again and wonder why running a block has him so winded.

"So. What's behind all this Elijah stuff?"

"Genocide," and I laugh. He looks bewildered, turns a little red, grins like he doesn't get the joke but doesn't want to appear dense, so he chuckles pretentiously. I giggle. He shuffles a little, sticks his hands in his pockets, then remembers himself.

"Sorry. I mean hello, how are you? What have you been up to this summer?" This throws me off. He is lightning quick. He figures from my terse response that he has not properly engaged me in conversational foreplay. I want to marvel at the rapid contextualization process of his brain. I was making fun of his brass and he had not missed it. I tell him about my job instead. We are still standing on the corner. People have to go around us and between us to cross the street. We are inconveniencing the people who least deserve to be inconvenienced — the working masses heading home for dinner. "Maybe we should go somewhere for coffee?"

I look at him intently before I say yes. Maybe we shouldn't. Maybe his suggestion does not have the same weight in his community as it does in mine. When a single Native man runs up behind you on the street, shuffles his feet, sticks his hands in his pockets and invites you for coffee, he is making a pass. Yes, means you are willing. James, I reason, is a serious student. He wants to know about Elijah. Elijah is reshaping the direction of Canadian sociology. James is aware of this and wants to get in on the ground floor. I persuade myself his interest is purely intellectual and not personal. It is safe to answer yes.

We head for my favourite greasy spoon, just a half block from where we stand. When the buzz of work gets too much, I come to this place to be alone, just before I head home. It is the sort of café where all the tables are in booths. No one has bothered to remove the old jukeboxes that adorn the booths, though none of the customers has dropped a quarter in them for a long time. The jukeboxes have become part of the general ambiance of the place. No bright lights; the interior is dark wood and deep red leather covers the benches. On the counter near the cash register is today's paper, strewn about and well read. The customers are busy reading or seriously eating. The food is cheap and reasonably close to the everyday sorts of meals Canadians normally eat at home. The service is efficient, though no one here bothers to hustle for tips. All the customers drop ten percent of the cost of their meal on the counter as a matter of course, automatic and unthinking.

"Too bad there isn't a good cappuccino bar in the neighbour-hood," James says, as he settles into the booth. I can't think of why this is too bad. I laugh. Privilege has its amusing side. James smiles a bit incredulously. He has never experienced himself as a man with a sense of humour before. White male intellectuals are not funny. They are not supposed to be. Humour is cajoled out of them by well-meaning, gentle mothers. A gazillion "don't be sillys" discourage humorous behaviour. By this means, their sons are en-couraged to pursue academia with reverent diligence.

He wants to bring up Elijah. He wants to play with the socio-logical significance of him, the impact his actions will have on the future of sociology in Canada, but is no longer sure how to do that. Me, I can't play with Elijah. James senses my resistance, but can't identify its origins. How does it feel, James, to walk on for-eign terrain?

"Have you been following Meech?" Clumsy James — Meech has occupied all our class discussion for the past year now. Maybe he didn't hear me when I spoke. I see a gavel come down; I hear my mind say, I rest my case, you have just proven that Indians are capable of great invisibility in the context of Canadians and their sacred institutions. Until Elijah messed up the legislature, we didn't exist. I am sure Marley's ghost whispered in Scrooge's deaf ears for a long time before that fateful Christmas Eve. Scrooge listened only when threatened by his own journey. James now reckons I must have thoughts. Elijah's mind conjured a means to shut the show down and he proved once and for all that Indians "have minds." The genocidal plot is falling apart at the seams. There is no longer any terra firma for white men to stand on.

"Of course you have, we talked in class." He looks embarrassed. He fishes some more. You don't, as a golden boy, just walk up to some darky and treat her as equal if your whole life experience has been exactly the opposite. A whole series of contexts has to be accounted for and if you can't do that, communication is next to impossible. He is going to launch into a monologue of apologies for his behaviour, the behaviour of his whole nation, if I don't stop him.

"It is really quite simple, James. Elijah thinks we deserve to live. He believes we deserve to live despite the way we are, and because of the way we are. He bent his back to the plow and he is churning up old sod, dry from want of rain and hard from lack of attention. He sweats it out so that this country can imagine a garden. Imagine a garden which provides for us all."

He stares at me. I sip my coffee. His lips are slightly parted.

"I feel like an idiot." This isn't true. James has no idea what being an idiot feels like. What he feels is a strange sense that he is not superior, but it is too dangerous for him to bring this sense from his unconscious mind to the light of day. He calculates from the computerized dictionary of his mind that this must be what it feels like to be stupid.

"Pleased don't, James. I sat in class next to you for two years, long years. I commented in classical sociological language about the social condition Canada restricts us to. No one heard until Elijah messed the country up. Now you all want to say, sorry, I have been a jerk, I feel like an idiot, what can I do? Well, from where I sit, it doesn't feel or sound good, James." The gravel is now coming from my guts. I want to slap myself about the head and ears for being this honest. I spill my guts of stone for this white man, but I clammed up in the car with Mark. He toys with his spoon, while I play about trying to regain some dignity.

"I'm not a jerk." He says it softly, full of empathy for himself. "Ignorant, maybe even stupid, but that isn't a crime." He has no idea how my mother would cannibalize on that last remark. I am not persuaded, James, of the truth of your last remark. "I don't feel like it's fair to cast me into some permanent purgatory for ignorance." He pulls a major pout.

He is talking to someone whose people he ought to know have endured hundreds of years of criminalization because we are supposed to be inferior, and we have never been given an ounce of empathy. Purgatory is where I live, James ... your ancestors conjured into being its design and location, then consigned all of my ancestors to be permanent residents.

The distance between us grows. It takes on hopeless dimensions. Momma would never agree with him. She excuses thoughtless ignorance and stupidity in children and retarded people. The rest of us owe consequences for thoughtlessness. Momma makes people pay. He sits with his back to the window, which looks out onto the street. People pass by like shadows silhouetting his vibrant presence. The sun struggles to spill through the windowpane. Even as the sun burns his golden hair an indescribably sweet strawberry hue, I know he looks ridiculous. The sun elicits frailty from his being. The absence of control he lacked in the shaping of his life makes me want to alter the core of my being. I can't help filling up with empathy for this lost lad, who can't feel the same about the world, can't think beyond its surface and the tension of the moment. I imagine wind tossing his hair, teasing it. I imagine the sea roaring up green and frothy against the blond wisps of hair. I hold the blade of cultural genocide just inches from the thread of my spirit. I get ready to sever my roots and tie myself to his ready-made world. I have no idea how to put the knife down gracefully.

He must have caught my imagination running hot because his face changes. He looks at me for the first time. He calculates the cut of my face, the arithmetic of my body shape, the colour of my skin, and wonders. The silence of his gaze is velvet. I want to go home, retreat to the corners of my household I have not yet discovered. I want to reconsider Rudy, who could never be this soft, who could not afford to be this sensitive and vulnerable.

Rudy's sweet youth was whited out by boys who drove fast cars and played chicken with Indian pedestrians every Friday night.

He spent his vulnerable youth coming into being as a man dodging these cars and trying desperately in his moment of youthful transformation to hang onto his dignity. Pubescence is itself a horror show. It is accompanied by deep doubts about your sanity. Adrenaline rushes go in a million directions and nowhere all at once, creating their own madness. This death sport aimed at his whole race, coupled with his coming into manhood, crushed him.

I see this memory buried in the sea-blue of James's endearing look. The inability of our men to sit in stark libraries and contemplate life from lofty intellectual places becomes obvious. Rudy had his body, his tensile strength and his agile good looks. Raw proud flesh was all he had. "Ladykiller" is what they left him. And the ladies to be killed were limited in number and confined to our own race. The hoarding of intellect, its monopolization by white men, reduced Rudy to a body without language, love or thought. The garnering of power by white men, their clutch on our right to be, had burned white-hot in the entire musculature of Rudy's body. He was allowed only the procreator of his race to blame for the disembowelling of all his sensuous humanity.

"I'm sorry, James, but when you live next to people for several centuries and you talk to them day in and day out and they don't hear you, you get a little nasty." Dull, almost whiny, but it extricates me from the picture of blond against green seas.

"Are you feeling the same as me?" Idiot. I thought he had a mind. The lust between his legs has crept up to the empty spaces in his head and scattered his brains. He has no memories to smarten him up when he leaps into the abyss of thoughtlessness. No, we are not feeling the same.

"I don't think so." An incredible sadness grips me. Cynicism sets in. We are never going to feel the same.

"A penny for your thoughts." I know white people value money, but this strikes me as odd — a penny for your thoughts. I don't think he really wants to pay for what I actually think. It has no value to him, so I lie.

"I was just thinking about our twins. My sister has twins. They crawl now. It's Thursday and my sister has to work late; I should be rolling home to take my turn at rearing them. Thanks for coffee, James."

"Can I call you sometime, maybe for coffee — to talk about Elijah or something?" I don't ever want to see him anywhere but in the classroom. I can't say this. Truth is, I don't even want to see him in the classroom. It is all too sad. I want to be a sociologist, so I don't have much choice. I will be there next September in his class, studying his heroes, but I don't have to bring him into the intimate sanctuary of my family circle. The flattery of his desire excites me, betrays my deepest sentiments for a moment. I can't bring myself to say no. The excitement of flattery is one obstacle, but the pages between saying no and explaining why are even bigger obstacles. He would ask if it's because he is white and I might throw up. Let him phone. I'll tell him when I can't see his face. I mumble sure, give him my number and walk out the door. I meet the sidewalk of busy people and head home. Sun kisses my bare arms, browns them, and warms my inner soul. The faces of white Canada pale.

They patter by, women in high-heeled shoes and summer dresses, men in light serge suits, ties a-swinging; all hurry by. Patter, patter, shuffle, shuffle, click, click, some " 'scuse me's" as they waltz in and around the crowds. The street is a fashion show of the latest in colour, style and dress. The odd blue-jeaned Native slouches aimlessly by. Not a single white person is dressed exactly like another. Still, the sense of style is the same. Few wear jeans, running shoes and shirts. Jeans and shirts are a presentation of self that has come and gone. We wore them before and we still do. We live on the periphery of style. It doesn't seem to have meaning for us. Most of us don't work so we don't dress for it. No one bothers us about dress codes. No one ever really looks at us.

Mark's inability to include women in his strategy sessions comes back. It makes a crazy, painful kind of sense. Until Elijah stood up and whispered "no," Mark did not feel he existed as an individual man. His words held no significance. Society pressured his manhood, chided him for not being a man, then did everything it could to prohibit his flowering as a man. The world ordained that Indians should not work, that they should be drunk, shiftless and irresponsible, and they meant men when they said this. Now his words hold meaning. He has acquired a mind. He has become a man, a significant man. The heady rush of becoming swallowed his vision of my womanhood. It is too new, too delightful to share with anyone else but other men.

I watch myself walk down the street, gauge these people's reaction to me. I duck and dodge the bodies hurrying home. I wonder what would happen if I didn't do the side-stepping. I test it out and bump into the first white man in front of me. " 'Scuse me" he says, not looking at me. I do this over and over. The scenario is always the same. He sees me only after he bumps into me. I duck into a doorway and watch the street walkers. White men dodge and duck each other and their own women. Men of colour duck and dodge white men and women, and women of colour duck and dodge everyone. It is the hierarchy of things.

My mother looks different in this context. She refuses to duck and dodge. I thought it was so petty of her. Now I know it took something indefinable just now, but something I would like to know about, to carry on refusing to duck and dodge the whole world. Her crass resistance looks normal. Lacey looks sensible. But somehow we left our men somewhere a long way from the home fire. Maybe our resistance stayed alive because white women aren't expected to be responsible for anything but children. They are not considered intellectually astute either. In an odd sort of way, the world treats our women and white women the same. Maybe we are intact because we never left our traditional labour behind. Before they came, we worked, loved, reared children and kept the social relations of our families sane. We continue to do that.

Our men have been denied work, denied their role as providers, governors of our destiny. They were shoved under some rug after society performed a mass lobotomy on their brains. Stripped of their minds, they were left powerless, with only their maddened, violent bodies to beat out a terrible mourning song on the backs of their women. Ladykillers and cultural genocide.

I'm tired. It's D-Day for us. I imagine every Native in the country glued to their TV set. Elijah is going for the last round. My whole world is upside down. My family is busting up. I didn't even know they were having problems and now the problems festered into ugly sores that have become a terminal case of contagious fracturing I can't stop. I almost had a boyfriend and closed the door on him twice. Inside, I shut the door on the only white man who has ever expressed an interest in me. I buy my mother's genocidal plot theory, with major reservations about its validity. The social disorder in our community feels planned and executed with our help and there doesn't seem to be any cure. Elijah brought the truth home about the cause of the disease but has not hinted at any solutions. Right now it doesn't feel like there are any. I want to fall asleep for, say, twenty years and wake up when it's a different world.

I open the door carefully. My mother's voice assails the crack in my head space. Oh Gawd, what now?

"If you think for just one minute you can waltz back into our lives like nothing happened, you have another think coming." It isn't six yet, so she isn't talking to the Prime Minister or the Premier. I turn corner. She is on the phone. Dorry stands near the sink. Momma hangs up.

"The nerve." Yes. the nerve, Momma, my last nerve, the one you are stretching beyond its capacity. It feels weak, cracky, strained to the limit. She bangs pots and pans, rattles on about how "some people have no brains, think the whole world is as stupid as they are" and how she is sick to death of excusing stupidity in people who are not retarded. I am too tired to ask her what's up. Dorry whispers, "Rudy." Ah. Who else.

I lean against the corner of the hallway. I don't listen to any more of what she says. I try to collect all the broken pieces of my insides and put them back together. It isn't possible. I was never familiar with the pattern of my soul. I can't arrange the pieces in any coherent order. They float about wanting to be ordered. Each time I think I have it I find out several pieces don't fit and the whole fabric of me falls apart. Momma, please shut up. I slink away from the corner and almost make it to my room.

"That young man called," she says and then resumes her monologue.

"What young man?" I interrupt.

"Ooh ... You have more than one?" her eyebrow rises and her lip curls. Dorry winks and grins wickedly. Momma has forgotten about her nerves, idiots and how dares.

"No," and I dial Mark's number.

"Hello."

"Hi. It's Marianne." This comes out flat.

"Marianne." It is almost a question. Jeezuss, maybe it wasn't him who called. Then who? Now what? Wait ... no, it's my turn to speak.

"How are you?" Fake it. Maybe he'll give me a hint.

"Good. You?" He is as cautious as I am. Dammit.

"All right. What you up to?" It wasn't him. I want to slam down the phone. I can't. I should close the conversation but can't think of how to do this without embarrassing myself or admitting that some man called and I have no idea who it was. Now I feel like a complete fool because I have no reason to be making this call. Maybe I don't need one.

"I was just about to call you. Maybe I could come over and watch the showdown between Elijah and the good citizens of this country with you?" There is something suggestive about his voice that I ignore.

"Sure." The tiredness of an hour ago slips away. Jeezuss, what did I just do? This place is not ready for him. My Momma will not watch the showdown; she'll orchestrate it from the living room. She'll talk for Elijah, kick at the Prime Minister and the ten foolish Premiers, rail at the whole country and re-articulate the genocidal plot theory while Lacey rants about feminism and the stupidity of letting eleven men determine the fate of anything more substantial than an outhouse, and Rita and I hug the speaker of the television from a butt-up position and try to catch a little of what is being said. The kids will all be there. The gigglers, the wanderers and the investigators will shuffle over the hum of the gurgling twins.

Between all this, every member of my family will cast side glances in my young man's direction and assure themselves he really isn't much good for anything.

"When's a good time?" "Just before six." I give up. Besides being a social idiot, I am a masochist. I should have said my mother just died and I have to bury her in the back yard. Could we maybe do this another time? Instead my mouth went ahead and said come on over, witness the madness of my household. Go ahead, discourage yourself from ever considering me for anything but a candidate for a funny farm. Next month I will be twenty-one and really, spinsterhood is not all that bad.

"OK," and he hangs up. I didn't get a chance to tell him I don't live alone. I smile. The suggestion in his voice was a lusty one. He is in for a major surprise. Soft warm light dances about my toes. It plays about the musculature of my legs. It softens the tone of my frame. I feel aglow with sun-warmth. The music of the warmth gains volume. My stomach is churning with it. My head is light. My eyes close. I open them and stare at the phone.

"Yes, Sweetie Poo, it is still in your hands." Thanks Momma.

"He's coming over." It comes out flatter than I feel it. "How nice," Momma says this without conviction. Matter of fact, she sounds like she is convinced his presence is going to be a major disaster.

"Well, don't stand there, get busy."

"Doing what, Momma?"

"Oh, for Pete's sake. I am surrounded by stupidity. This place is a mess. Vacuum. You still know how to use a vacuum, don't you? Rita. Get out here; her beau is coming." Beau? She flies about the house, grabs whatever shirts, shoes, toys and papers lie about and runs to the closet and throws everything into it in some sort of psychotic heap. I make a mental note: don't let anyone open that door. Rita scurries about sweeping the decks that can't be vacuumed and Dorry throws herself at the dishes in the sink. Me, I slowly get to the vacuuming. I barely get started when Momma grabs the machine and tells me to go and fix my face. What's wrong with it? I go to the bathroom and look in the mirror. How do you fix a face?

The doorbell rings about when Rita and Momma flop on the couch. They have already grilled me with questions about his character, what he does for a living and what he is like. They assure me this will help them gauge how to conduct themselves. Not true. Momma and Rita's habits are unalterable. They will conduct themselves in the way they always do regardless of my briefing. They will embarrass me. I know this. Ol' Johnny is the most ridiculous of us all. He has spent the past hour or so jogging behind Momma, patting her butt, for which he took the occasional serious blow, after which he would giggle, then wink at me. The kids, except Dorry, are outside. They will stay out there for another couple of hours, unless someone calls them in. Dorry is in the corner watching the hubbub, inconspicuous and shy, but not naive. She is about to watch the drama of her auntie's first love unfold and looks like she knows it.

The doorbell rings again. "Maybe someone should answer it," Rita offers. I run. Before I open it, I cast a quick glance at Momma and Rita. Momma is on a chair, her hands folded neatly on her lap. She looks like she is seriously watching the TV show. Wrong show, Momma, you are watching *M.A.S.H.* It is not a serious movie. I contemplate telling her it's a comedy. My young man is still outside. I opt for opening the door. Wrong man. James, big and blond, is on my porch. A few meters away the right man is parking his car. I have to get rid of Mr. Wrong before Mr. Right gets to the door.

"James," good start. It is James, but he knows that. "James." When all systems fail, repeat yourself; it gives you a second to think of what to say next. Mark is closer to getting out of the car now.

"Hi. Thought I would drop by and watch Elijah's triumph with you." Just thought you would drop by. Just thought I was sitting here waiting for you to arrive like I had no one coming by. Just thought I would be alone on the most significant night of our entire people's modern history, waiting for Mr. Big and Blond to drop by.

"I don't think so, James. I have already arranged to watch Elijah's triumph with someone else. He is right behind you." I try not to glare.

"Huh?" He heard. I said it loud enough for the neighbours to hear. He takes a look at me before he leaves. Mark glances in James's direction, then stops, looks at me, back at James, and waits for me to signal him forward before coming any closer. I smile, Mark resumes walking towards the door. At the door he grins, says "hi" and waits for me to smile again. I step aside, smile; he comes in. He looks, grins; I smile; he removes his jacket. The ritual goes on like this for some time. Each move he makes is followed by a quizzical look and a small grin, my smile, then another move. Momma and Rita wait for the ceremony to end. He walks into the living room, looks back at me, a little surprised at the presence of my Momma and what looks like my sisters, but he smiles and awaits introductions anyway.

"Momma, this is Mark. We work together. Actually, he is my boss." Momma's eyebrow goes up — the right one — she puts out a hand. He takes it gingerly, grins, waits for her approval. Momma, how could you be so stingy? Her lips pull back into one of the poorest and tightest excuses for a smile I have ever seen. It is going to be a tough night. Mark takes in a little air and holds it. He knows it is going to be a tough night too.

"Mark. This is my sister, Rita." I can't believe it. Rita repeats my mother's performance right to the stingy tight smile.

"Ah, you are the sister who delivered twins," that takes the brace out of Rita. Her smile doubles.

"You know about twins?" she says.

"Of course he knows about twins. Marianne knows better than to bring a cultural idiot home." Thanks for the confidence, Mom. I am not sure of the truth of her last remark, though. I feel like a cultural cripple myself. The introductions are over when I finish telling him who Dorry is and Momma kicks into a conversation with Rita on a subject Mark could not possibly know anything about. Neither she nor Rita leave any room for anyone else to participate. Rita, without missing a step, crowds in my mother's direction and turns her back on us. He gets it and slips comfortably onto the couch next to me, opposite the corner Rita and Momma occupy. This is Momma's way of giving Mark the opportunity to have a quiet fight with me over the wrong man who just left. Mark obliges her.

"Who was that — the Fuller Brush man?" Who was that? I want to lie, but my sense of dignity stops me. I can't say, oh, he is just someone I imagined walking on the beach with, the sun kissing his blond locks a strawberry hue and the ocean rolling up green against his gold. I can't say he is someone who spent the afternoon gleeking at me in an old greasy spoon after I decided I did not want to ride with you. I have no idea what James's intentions are beyond Elijah and sociology. He came by without phoning, assumed I had nothing to do, no one to see, but what lay behind all this I am not sure. Shit. I gave him my phone number in the restaurant. It must have been James that phoned.

"Classmate. Wanted to watch Elijah and get a real Native's perspective on him." Pure speculation. It is not a bald-faced lie, just the next best thing. The answer implies that the man has no personal interest in me, something I am not sure of anyway. It leaves Mark's dignity intact and extricates me from what could be a sticky mess. At this point I don't have any sort of romance with either of these two gentlemen and I wonder why I am doing this to myself. Why bother to mislead the one about the other? He looks at me, full of passionate doubt. He holds the look. I have thirty seconds to alter my story. I don't. I look at him intently. He shrugs and hunkers down to watch TV.

It is an amazing newswatch. Momma doesn't argue with the journalist, the Prime Minister or anyone else. She sits for the entire hour in silence. I can't stop looking at her in disbelief. Even Rita steals the odd glance when she expects Momma to punctuate the program with her own remarks. After every glance, Rita looks at me wide-eyed, then at Momma, and we both exchange shrugs. This does not go past Mark. He looks at me, back at Rita, then watches the news again. He knows something is amiss but doesn't get it, and the news is too important to interrupt. He holds his curiosity. The drama will have to be unfolded at a future date.

The news isn't over for more than thirty seconds when the phone rings. "That will be Lacey. She is at Joseph and Monique's watching the news." Momma glances at me when she says it will be Lacey. It is her way of telling me to answer the phone.

"Hi Sugar, it's Lacey," comes over the phone. I answer her. I have the phone in my hand for only a split second and I can hear Momma asking Mark just what he does for a living.

Lacey … I want to talk to her. Just a second ago I knew what I wanted to talk about, but now with Momma's beeline at Mark, the subject is jarred loose from my memory and my thoughts are scrambled up in some kind of chaos in my head. The disorder is so thick I barely get out a hello.

"Are you coming … over?" Now Momma is asking what sort of future there is in Native politics — as a career choice, that is.

Oh Rita, can't you stop her? That is a dumb question, even for me. No one can stop Momma.

"Yeah. In fact, Paula, myself, Joey and Honey were thinking of coming over together." Lacey is the oldest. She takes the liberty of calling us by her own set of pet names. Momma is deepening her incisions into Mark's personal plans. Please, Lacey, hang up. I say a quick "OK, see you in a bit then." She hangs up. The dial tone sounds. I look at the phone for a second. The tone sounds so lonely all by itself coming through miles of wire. Dumb.

They all look at me. They know that was Lacey, they know she will come over, but Rita and Momma wait for me to report anyway.

"That was Lacey. She, Paula, Joseph and Monique are coming over."

"Oh, good. We'll have tea until they come." Momma's voice sounds like I better not argue. I file into the kitchen behind her and Rita. Mark stays in the living room. Momma looks at me, like following her into the kitchen is rude, so I go back and sit with Mark. I am not sure I want to. He is awfully quiet.

"Is it OK to smoke?" he asks.

"Oh yeah, Rudy used to do it all the time."

"Rudy?" he asks.

"My oldest brother … " I want to cry. Grief, not now. It feels like Rudy's absence tonight is the gawdamnest awful thing I have ever experienced. I want to curl up at his feet and be there at the last minute when Elijah wins the good fight. I must look sad because Mark touches my hair so gently I can hardly feel it. Then he lights up a smoke.

"Are you seeing someone else?" He asks it carefully. There is no edge in his voice. He tries to keep it free of moral judgement. He sounds like he is just some curious guy asking the news. His touch opened me up. I am vulnerable. I don't feel able to lie anymore. He already has one version of my story. This same question, approached from a slightly different angle, means he did not believe me.

"No." I answer too loud and too fast. It shouldn't matter this much to me.

SUNDOGS

"Was the man I saw at the door the man who called you earlier?" He presses awful hard for someone who sounds plain curious. I try to put all the pieces together, try to calculate how much he has figured out, so I can give him the straightest answer with the least truth. My mind is too slow. He draws in a long pull of smoke.

"Let me put it together for you, Marianne. Last month I asked you if you would like to do something on Sunday. You answered yes on Friday, then you cancel out on Sunday without any coherent reason. We see each other for lunch. You look a little more willing. We go out today and it doesn't seem to be going very well. Then you call me, sounding like you're returning my call, but I hadn't called you. I ask to come and visit. There is a man at your door. On his way out he looks at me as if I am the competition. I ask who he is. You say he is some nondescript student." Another pull on his smoke. He looks up into the air and then directs his attention to me again. "Marianne, I am no fool. Please, who is he — and tell me, am I competing with this white man?" His face is so close I can smell his cologne. I can feel the heat from his forehead. He is talking so low I have to read his lips. My heart is beating so fast I want to faint. Underneath all of this is a nagging suspicion of my own — what business is it of his?

"I don't know." He doesn't believe that. He bites his lip, sucks in air, lets go a sigh and then resumes smoking and looking at the ceiling. I want to enter into a pleading monologue and defend myself. This white guy called. I thought it was Mark. I gave him my number for innocent reasons. It all means nothing to me. It doesn't sound dignified even in my mind. I want to say I am lonely for Rudy. My Momma won't let him in our house and I miss him. I want to tell him about the storm of confusion that lives in my mind. It has been there for weeks, and the Elijah business is far more upsetting than it is inspiring to me. It sounds dull, so I sit silent. Soon I will have to say something. Lacey invades with her merry gang. The ruckus, I hope, will absolve me of trying to dream up an explanation for the wrong man showing up on my doorstep. It doesn't work. He has no interest in who just came in the door.

"He just showed up?" he pushes on.

"Yeah." Why is he asking all these questions?

"We have been working together for a while now." He tallies up the totality of our relationship. I do not want to hear this. Rudy is too large in my mind. I don't like having my life tallied up in this fashion. A scream is growing in the centre of my brain and spiralling out towards my mouth.

"Are you all right?" I must look awful for him to notice.

"No."

"Marianne." He doesn't say any more. Momma brings me tea. She frowns. She can see the conversation is not going well. I don't want her to ask questions. Please, can't we all just get focused and watch Elijah's last hour? I am desperate for an interruption. Any interruption will do. A thud sounds from behind the front door. Inhuman grunts and groans, interspersed with the odd human sound strung together in no particular order, come from behind the door. Joseph opens it.

Rudy is lying there, puking and cursing by turns. I will never again pray for a generic interruption. He looks at Joseph and tries to recognize who Joseph is. Rudy is blind drunk. His eyes are red. His clothes want soap and water and so does he. I stand directly behind Joseph, wishing I had stayed on the couch. I do not need to see this. Sobs escape from Rudy, huge wracking sobs that jerk my emotions around. Mark leads me back to the couch where I collapse, near to hysteria, in his arms.

My Momma is furious. She goes straight to her closet to fetch the broom. Oh no, it's the closet all the stuff is thrown in ... too late ... it all falls out ... she curses and marches back to the door. Dorry starts picking up the shirts and shoes and whatever else is spilled all over.

"Please, Momma, no Momma ... please." It comes out so quietly not even Mark is sure he heard it. He holds me tighter. Lacey is yammering about feminism, Paula is crying uncontrollably and Joseph is trying to get the women inside. It is not the sort of madness I thought would occur. Joseph wins. He convinces them to stop what they are doing. Rudy is still out there, likely choking on his vomit.

"Lacey, Rudy is precisely the sort of man you say he is, Paula, you have nothing to fear, and Momma, it is going to take more than a broom. You all watch TV and tend to Baby. I will deal with Rudy." Thank you, Joseph. Mark needs to know I am still a baby. I cry like a baby, am being cuddled like one and right now I feel like I need a great deal of taking care of, but did you have to say it?

Joseph and Rudy disappear. Momma is pinched. Rita is stiff. The kids are confused. Ol' Johnny takes this moment to tell a story.

"It was summer, party time. Not the kind of parties you young people have nowadays, but old time party. All the folks just enjoy the Saturday nights. Old grannies, little kids, young people, moms and dads all whoop it up doing a little Indian two-step or just sitting around talking, playing. You know." He doesn't wait for anyone to say whether they do or don't know. "Some guy takes it into his head to insult Big Lu. Big Lu is the biggest Stoh:lo woman there ever was, over six feet, must've been a couple hundred pounds. No sense of humour," he chuckles like having no sense of humour is something everyone should be proud of. We all watch him, unaware of the joke. "Next morning the man is layin' behind the row of houses, dead. Cops knock on the chief's door. Those days, the chief never got paid to chief around. Cops collect the body and ask the chief who dunnit. It's hot. Sweltering. Even the cactus is droopy. Chief says, 'The man had an off day.' Cops don't get it. See? … Nothing to cry over, little one." Cops don't get it? No wonder they don't get it. This moves beyond the bounds of riddle, Johnny. What on earth does he think I am crying about?

Mark is laughing hard. I can't believe he got anything out of that. I stop crying and stare at him.

"What's so funny?" Mark recovers himself and looks at me. I

am about over the edge, I must be. The leap into madness is so swift and smooth I don't even know when it happened. The entire household takes on zoological characteristics. Maybe this is a circus. Maybe ...

"The whole business has nothing to do with you, me or anyone else. What does it matter how the guy died or who killed him; he's dead. Big Lu is alive. There is nothing to cry about."

Everyone hmns, like they all got it. I cannot sink my teeth into a philosophy so complacent about death. Do they actually believe death is so commonplace, or did I miss something. There must be something more to the story that Mark isn't saying. Who are these people I call my own?

Mark says no more. He has left his arm where it was and I collapse into its crook while he engages the family in more conversation. He manages to get my mother on a roll that she really enjoys. Iraq, Iran and every-place-else gets turned over in Momma's unique way. I can hear Mark's appreciative laughter and feel his body shake. At a particularly rich remark his grip tightens. His tensed body feels good. I peek at his face between moments of introspection.

Flesh, honey-brown, pulled across a wide bone structure and accented by large, even teeth, sharpens his square mouth. His mouth is not quite pouty and moves in sensuous perfect rhythm to the musical strains of his accent. His words are carefully chosen for their soft, unobnoxious sounds. No guttural hard sounds interrupt the flow or cadence. Momma, Rita, Johnny and Lacey jump in and out of the conversation, augmenting the sound of his personal symphony. Ravel's "Bolero," its doggedly compelling drumbeat gently blended with lazy violins, floats about underneath his voice. I sink into the impossibility of unravelling my thoughts and gripping my own essence. Just when I am sure I will never recover sanity, he touches the hair on the back of my neck, twirls it in and around his fingers and re-roots me to the scene in my living room. I imagine his touch tracing the familiar lines of my body, travelling all on its own. Without hands, an independent feeling of pure loveliness, and it rescues me. But it isn't enough to drive me away from the abyss of my own despair.

It has been an hour and a half. In an hour the eleven o'clock news will be on. The final moment is coming upon us and Joseph is not back. I know Rudy will not be back, but Joseph is supposed to be here, sharing the joy of Elijah's victory. Momma's eyes dart towards the clock; her anxiety levels go up with each passing moment. Mark looks at me each time Momma looks at the clock. I shrug. I am much more concerned about the mess Rudy is in than Joseph missing the moment just now. Finally, Momma looks at the front door as though she wants to will Joseph through it. Mark helps her; I do too. Monique's hands pull at her skirt; her eyes stare at a spot on the old rug. She is beautiful, well heeled. Double income, no kids; isn't there an acronym for that?

"Monique, why don't you and Joseph have kids?" Everyone's throat lets go a gasp.

"When did you start sticking your nose in other people's bedrooms?" Lacey recovers first and lets me have it. I have broken everyone's effort to will Joseph home and cracked a hole in a major taboo at the same time. I amaze myself sometimes. Momma's head turns, snaps a full 180. Her eyes wear a distinct Joan Crawford sort of rage. Rita's jaw drops open and Monique now has a whole handful of her skirt in a clutch. Her face is blank. She looks like she is going to be sick. The air around me strengthens, thickens, and Ol' Johnny stares off into space. The kids are frozen to their seats; their heads move back and forth between their Gramma and me in unison and their faces look like they are seriously grappling with what is going on here.

Disappointment in my complete alienation from my family hangs thick in the air around me. The horror of the violation is that I didn't know the question was taboo until the moment of shocked response — Momma must know this.

No children, in the old days, spelled divorce. I know that, but did not for a moment consider it relevant when I asked the question. I was just curious. They seem to be so in love. Love and children are synonymous in my mind, maybe even inevitable in unions among us, so I wondered ... I wasn't suggesting they divorce over the question. What is the problem here? Is it because it isn't any of my business, or did the question suggest drastic solutions merely by its articulation? Surely someone else must have wondered about it at some point. Monique's face tells me that no children is not a matter of choice. I am truly sorry I asked, but it all seems too serious to just blather out a simple sorry.

Monique is special. From the day of her marriage, she busied herself with the work of integration into our family. She has no family of her own. She was adopted during the days when family records of Native kids were not diligently kept. They don't even know what kind of an Indian she is. Ours is the only family she has ever known outside of the white people she still calls Mom and Dad. I realize how painful this all must be — orphanhood is a terrible thing among people who hold onto lineage as seriously as we do. I think by bringing up the question I sharpened the pain of her absence of family. Not only has she no family, no blood relatives that she knows of, but she has no future lineage either.

Memories from a faraway place intrude. Our little log house is full of people. Tears are shed. Speeches are made. We are moving away from the village and everyone mourns our departure. They bemoan the disappearance as an uprooting of our entire lineage. The future clan our family represents is giving up the struggle to survive in an isolated and impoverished village forever. We give up our being. The union of the community, tenuous and weak already, is threatened by the subtraction of our lineage. The complexity of the community is simplified by our departure. The art, the music, the creative power, the knowledge we carry, are subtracted. The village will never be the same. Everyone feels it but they all understand it. Choice.

Choice is a sacred thing, old Charley says. Momma does not

have to live in a log cabin and struggle alone with five children. She does not have to haul water, live in the semi-light of kerosene lamps and send her sons out after wood and meat. She does not have to send her daughters out after berries, roots and medicines. No one has to fish anymore. It is law. The world landed on us all in laws. We are not children in the eyes of the law any longer. We are no longer émigrés. We are citizens. The citizens of this country don't have to struggle for survival the way we did in that little village far away. Momma is forty-three and single. Papa is dead.

Papa's death frees her. It drives her to seek a different world. A new life. She wants to begin again. She wants to take Canada on. She wants to be a citizen, a citizen who adds her own cultural stamp to the garden of flowers that blooms in the urban centres of the country. It hasn't quite worked the way she planned, but she has done everything she could to make the dream come true. So long as she has children and grandchildren, her dreams hold out possibilities. I have taken the possibility of children and grandchildren for granted. I have taken the existence of grannies and aunties whose names I know, despite the fact that most of them died before I was born, for granted. In some eerie way I know they all shaped my destiny, formed my being, before I was born. Monique cannot possibly feel this way. Without children, her own continuum is dead. Without family, she has no beginning. Between the layers of betrayal, calm wavers. Joseph wanders in. He feels the confused sentiments that hang in the air. He watches his hand as it carefully closes the door. He gathers the sentiments together and gauges their meaning for a moment, then he turns and walks to where Monique sits. She lets go of her skirt as Joseph kneels before her. Her face, looking carved and mispainted a ghostly white, is lined with a thin stream of tears. He takes both hands in his and whispers in a language I don't recognize. Mother, Johnny, Lacey and Rita slide from the room. Mark, myself and the kids follow.

Dorry walks beside Mark and me, upright and dignified, almost defiant. She wants the room to know she feels no shame for me. The kitchen fills up. The children retreat to its outer edges, except for Dorry. She stands in the centre surrounded by her adult world. She is getting ready to speak; everyone feels it and gives way for her. She strokes her chin and leans forward a little, like Auntie Mary does before her prose, graphic and significant, rolls from her tongue.

"I am going to paint a chasm, deep and dark, travelling along a tornado path to white-hot light. I am going to paint us young people clutching at the edges of the chasm, barely hanging on, and our elders will stand away from the chasm with their backs half-turned. Between our elders and ourselves, I am going to paint cities, red with war, and between it all, coming magically from the whole centre of the work, I am going to paint Marianne, one hand pushing up on the city and the other hand reaching out to the young and old." She turns and leaves the room.

Momma sighs. Her face looks vulnerable. I shrink from the vulnerability I have never seen before. Her eyes watch Mark's hand touch mine. Calm, the pain-inspired calm of enlightenment, fills her. I am not sure which words of Dorry's brought this on but the show of vulnerability and sensitivity assures me somehow of my place in this family, despite the show I inspired. She phones Auntie Mary because she has no words to respond anymore.

Elijah is not going to be celebrated here tonight. Mark whispers something about leaving. Probably for good. How could anyone entertain the notion of keeping company with such a perfect ditz?

Momma talks to Auntie Mary in another language that is strange to me. My family speaks languages I don't know. Rage, small and sharp, cuts through my sense of shame and shreds the fabric of my belonging to these people.

A moment ago I felt lineage, powerful in my veins; now terror peers through the gashes of rage's razor. Mark's decision to leave catalyzes a hacking ritual inside me. "Go ahead." It comes out blue and cold, plain and hard. Leave, you bastard, underlies it. Between his announcement and my angry words lie whole speeches, words, too many for a not-yet-romantic couple, one of whom is dying to watch Elijah and the other of whom is just dying to articulate.

He stares at me from beneath his thick, curly lashes. His eyes wrap me in their gaze; they call me. My blood betrays me. It pumps out desire into veins mixed with rage and terror. Desire blankets every other emotion. Ancient passion, the memory of creation awakens. My thighs tense, then quiver. My hands pulse involuntarily. That's it. I am going to take this body and trade it in on a new one. There is something major wrong with it. I feel babble coming on. Stupid babble about tired ... about genocide ... about rage ... desire ... tired ... desire ... terror ... desire, desire, desire ... My hand wakes up. Mark has my jacket in his. He moves in slow motion magic to hold me.

"Let's get out of here," husky and dark urgent words fire hot lava in my ear. They sear the skin on my neck and scream passionate promise to my aching self. I put my shoes and jacket on without taking my eyes from his. He watches. Eyes change, gain intensity, hope. I can hardly breathe. My knees loosen up. Blood leaves them. I lift my legs and move to the door and we leave. He closes the door gently and gathers me up and folds my body into his.

I don't remember much of the ride to his place. I don't remember whether or not we watched Elijah's triumph and don't care. I remember movement, touch, sweet breath, hot breath, music, unrelenting drumsong pounding out a kaleidoscope of sensuous passion to every cell in my body. I remember words. "I want you." Passionate pleas breathed husky and bronze against pale light. I remember blond against green burned by bronze fire. I remember desire, the restoration of my beauty beaten from consciousness by crude teenagers duped by illusions of racial superiority. I remember feeling, feeling womanhood gush between thighs holding manhood, a treasured glorious manhood, healed of the injury created by mountains of insult. Worthy love. Passions reborn in a world maddened by its own white megalomania. Dark desire, rich brown, then sleep — dream sleep. Of flowers. Of clean meadows, tall grasses, blue skies and peace. Peace burns the lies and pain dwindles to nothingness and disappears under fields of dandelions and rain falling gently into rivers that rush to Mother Sea to be reborn in the magic moments of desire. Yes Joseph, we must dream.

Morning comes too soon. He lies there awake, a cheeky grin on his face. I hardly recognize the room. I have to look at him twice to remember how I got here, then I smile and stretch, all peace and contentment.

"Was that good for you?" Wrong race, Mark. I roll over and look for my clothes. They are strewn about the room. Oh Gawd. How am I going to get up? How did I get into bed. Did I throw my clothes about like that? Look, there is my treacherous little bra lying there, both cups winking at me. Oh my Gawd. I pull the covers over my head.

He comes under the covers with me.

"We have to go to work," I say.

"Sounds like a pretty weak no to me," he giggles. I did not know men giggled. My body likes it. My mind is losing its resolve.

I must have drifted off. Mark is standing in front of me offering me clothes and saying something about coffee is on. We still have to go to work. I don't remember if we watched Elijah and I am now not satisfied with his refusal to answer my question about women and strategy sessions. It must be late in the morning; my head is operating in its sensible mode. Why ruin a perfect night? I dress, wolf back coffee, and we leave for work, babbling meaningless trivia about what paper needs to be bought, what faxes have to go out, and Mark finally says he taped Elijah so we can watch it later. How did he do that? Never mind, I will find out later.

I have no idea what is the matter with me, but the closer we get to the office the less I want to walk in the door with Mark. Everyone will know. That sounds really dense, likely half of Indian country was doing the same thing, especially if Elijah succeeded.

The dating ritual is all so new to me. He pulls up to the curb

SUNDOGS

and runs around to let me out. I bang the door open as he approaches and his knees take a good whack. "Sorry," and I close the door. He stands there wondering why I closed it, reaches for it just as I open it, and gets another whack for his efforts.

"Marianne, you are dangerous," and he laughs. I want to tell him I have misgivings about walking in together. My misgivings don't make sense to me, so I keep quiet. I don't feel like adding any more stupidity to the door routine. Too late anyway; he has my arm in his and he guides me right through the door in full view of everyone. I feel like I am being held up as some sort of prize Mark won overnight. Everyone looks, raises their eyebrows, then pretends to be hard at work. We are late, which makes our entrance too dramatic for my taste just now. I am going to get a ribbing. Mark continues his devotions to me for a few minutes before leaving me for his own office and I join the ladies at the machines.

"She is wearing roses on her cheeks," Julie quips to the girl at the front desk. They both look at Mark, who steals lusty looks at me, and the women giggle. I hate this about us. We all behave as though lust is so weird, remarkable, as though only the really odd young couples and the really foolish ever indulge in it, and as though teasing the new and unschooled is just what they need to smarten them up. I was nearly ten when I watched poor Rita and Bill subjected to this ritual. Mark helps them along. He gleeks at me, eyes full of obvious desire and triumph, with his lips pulled back in a knowing Madonna smile. He struts about full of male pride. Every time he looks this way he winks and parts his lips. His voice crows, cocksure of himself and full of it. I feel like smacking the grin from his lips. I feel like the pride of the Indian Nation. Emotions, paradoxical and contrary, argue in parallel lines inside me all day.

Time goes by slowly. The traitorous little beast of a clock is loyal to the teasing, the winking and the gleeking as well. Time might crawl but she has to pass. Mark strolls out of Saul's office, a hint of strut in his gait. Saul glances at me with both his eyebrows raised and grins approval.

Mark leans forward on my desk. Today the lean towards me is weighted with significance, power and public notoriety. I remember Rudy, cocksure Rudy, when he first came home with Paula. Paula, demure and innocent, wearing roses on her cheeks. I remember the moment the sureness went out of his step and he needed alcohol to put it back, but it put it back in a distorted form. His strut became a swagger, then reduced itself to a staggering caricature of his original pride and joy. After several years in the city, Paula became his source of shame.

I want to find the moment, imagine the incident when Rudy changed his mind about Paula. No. It wasn't his mind that changed. It was his heart. Pieces of his heart had been chipped away by the endless run of work and lay-offs that roofing gives rise to. Once or twice he had been fired for failing to show up. No one thought about how he felt about being terminated without dignity. It happens.

I look at Mark, my mind full of thoughts about Rudy and the process of his movement from pride and joy to shame, all wrapped around Paula like a second skin she had no choice but to wear. I look and wonder about Mark. What would it take to alter his affection? What ugly reality from the outside world would drive him to spray a different skin on my body?

"Are you awake?" I see my face reflected in his eyes. It lies. It doesn't look upset at all. I wonder why I feel good about its deception — easier than the truth, I guess.

"What?"

"I said, are you coming to our celebration?"

"Yeah." Elijah won. We won. It was a major win. Indescribable jubilance fills everyone. Between "pass the salt" and huge guffaws is wedged my tiny sliver of doubt. Rudy. Your face rests against a huge backdrop of white men, blond and soft, bodies slid into thin tailored suits, their necks adorned by lengths of silk. Men who carry briefcases, make plans, plot the course of history, discuss numbers, dollars, management, law and life seriously. Men who stroll with quiet dignity imprinted in the very sidewalks that path their lives. Rudy, bronze and dark. Dark. Light. Endarkenment. Enlightenment. This language has no discipline. It is used to brighten the world of white men and darken those who insist on their darkness.

"Canada will never be the same," and Saul lifts his coffee mug in a grand salute to the man who would change the face of Canada.

"Why not?" stops the joyous laughter. Saul is stunned, speechless. Mark looks at me, his face blank. They all wait for me to answer my own question. A small doubt about my loyalty is raised. Mark closes in on me. His touch assures me. It is a protective one but it doesn't feel like a permanent one now.

"Elijah may have stopped the process of constitutional betrayal, but Canada has yet to change. She is about to load a rickety old destroyer full of youth and send them to Iran or wherever, to kill men who look like all of you." My insides run hot. The response is instant. I have thrown water on everyone's fire.

"It isn't the same ... what has Iran, Iraq, got to do with us ... they'll never send the military on us." Carla says it without any deep conviction. The sound of my words runs sour in my mouth. The sour is about to become sorrow when Saul recovers himself.

"True. But we have changed. We are all intoxicated with joy. The joy of the good fight. The joy of victory. We have fallen in love with the prospect of dignity. We have reclaimed our affection for some very unloved and weary people. This would not be significant had it not been that this country and most, not all, but most of its citizens have put their heart, knowledge and actions to work, inciting a perverse self-hate among us." The lines of his face soften and blend with the murmur of his voice. Reverent truth presented from powerful convictions in tones so gentle I felt the words more than heard them.

"Then I'm not insane," I whisper. Mark's laughter fills the air, raven's raucous crow, spirited and magnificent. I have grave doubts about the attitude of our folks at this table towards the swelling Middle East crisis. I can feel behind the pride an ugly sort of narcissism I can't articulate. Mark's laugh lacks magic. My misgivings are pulling at the magic, stretching it, making it thin and weak.

"We have to talk," Mark whispers between the caws and laughter of the others.

"OK."

"See you all on Monday, bright and early," he says and winks at everyone. They crow nasal and lusty at us as we retreat. Monday. The day is only half over. I must have missed something. I still daydream a lot. I don't pay attention consistently but I am confident Mark will clue me in at some point without my having to ask. No one ever needs to know what is going on right away anyway, me least of all. Why did I say that? Me, least of all? Not least of all. Never least of all.

The street outside is not so busy. People glance at us the way they usually do but they don't impact on me in the same way. I look hard at the faces of the people who pass me by. Women, painted, their hair dyed and their shoes confined to spiked heels, click by. Fashion designers must be misogynists. The clothes women wear in the name of fashion restrict movement, entrap and enslave. Tight skirts, mid-calf length, hold their legs together. Spiked heels force their feet to mince their steps. It is all so annoying. Still, in the cut of their faces lies their individuality. Yesterday they were an anonymous mass, all crowded together in colourless lines in my mind. Today, the redhead passing me has a small nose; her eager look separates her from all the blonds, brunettes and other redheads. Each person takes on character different from the last. This blond has a generous smile; that one is taut with tension; each one jumps at me sharp, clear and different from the last.

"White people have become individuals."

"Yeah. It is the price we have to pay for becoming a people." This makes sense. We get into his car. I have not been home yet. I wonder if I phoned last night. Not likely; the trail of clothes looked a little too desperate to have been interrupted by a responsible phone call. Momma was talking to Auntie Mary when I left. That's right. I am in deep shit. I am also angry. They speak another language. My language, the one they hoarded and kept from me as though I were unworthy of my ancient self. Damn. We are on a side street behind a stop sign. Mark stops and side-glances at me, then smiles.

"Worried about your folks?" He turns out onto the highway and awaits my answer. It is such a large question, given my current context. I have created a whole new crisis of such severe dimensions that they were all driven to expose me to the language I didn't speak. Whole paragraphs crawl around. Paragraphs without order, structure or end. A simple yes would be too deceptive even for me. His hand squeezes my knee. I don't have to answer.

We pull up at his house; he laughs, then says, "You don't always pay attention do you?"

"Why?"

"You look like you are wondering what we are doing skipping work."

"The thought crossed my mind."

"Saul gave us the rest of the day off." He touches my cheek, "to celebrate Elijah ... Let's go inside and do him justice." Cornhusk, our voices have country cornhusk in them. Soft winds of sound breathed across taut cornhusk sing a melodious country song of passion. Plaintive elegance. The sun splashes gold across his honey-brown face. My breath jerks. He sits still as the afternoon. I smile. Eternity passes, he shuts off the engine and opens his door. I manage to wait for him to open mine this time.

Inside, he folds me up. He steps back to look at me. Looks forever. He plans ... My feet are planted a little closer to the ground today. I look about the contours of his house. Tastefully furnished, large and oak-filled. Simple house without plants or family photos all over the walls and stuck in every nook and cranny of every room. No kids' pictures or youthful paintings adorn the halls. A beige couch against oak end tables, a television and a VCR form a simple square in the middle of the large L of the living-dining room. Oak-trimmed cupboards accent the oak tables and chairs in the kitchen. Hallways stretch out far enough to accommodate four doors. This is a big house for one man. The sparseness of its furnishings make it feel lonely.

He is still looking at me. He removes his tie. He takes my bag, my jacket, then urges me toward the bedroom. I don't resist. Passion is a roller coaster ride to a place as near to heaven as the living ever want to be. Trouble is, when the ride is over, the concrete feels harder and your legs thicker and the only cure is another ride.

"How old are you?" The question punches out at me through the haze of dreamsleep fading.

"Twenty, why?" I hold my eyes closed, not wanting to know what time of day it is or what the damned sun is doing just now.

"Just curious."

"You?"

"Twenty-nine."

I open my eyes to look at the truth of his age and try to read his face. That is just one year short of Rita. It is a lot more years than I own. No raven tracks to indicate stressed-out nights, walking babies, breaking teeth, or struggling with books and brats year after year. There is experience written on his face, but it is the neat clean lines of experience free of hardship. I change my focus before his life's ease bumps up too sharply against Rita's hardship. The bedroom matches the rest of the tasteful simplicity and sparseness — austere living quarters without clutter. No kids' finger paintings or the youthful art of teenagers to comfort or annoy.

"Do you own the furniture or did it come with the house?"

"I own the house." His voice has a quiet, almost guilty edge to it. I am about to intrude on forbidden territory. Maybe, like us, he feels a bit traitorous about being a home buyer in the middle of white territory. I hold onto my next question; there is lots of time to etch the details of his life onto my consciousness. In my silence he takes control of our exchange.

"Do you like my house?" His voice is loaded. I am sure this is a trick question.

"Yes ... I mean, it's nice."

"I don't want you to go home."

"OK." Another night will not deepen the mess I am in.

"Good. I'll pick up your things tonight."

"Pick up my things?" I missed something. Did I stop paying attention at some point, or did I just miss his meaning?

"From your mom's house."

"And just move in ... here ... like that?" I panic. Move in, give up twenty years of my ordered life after one lunch and a couple of roller coaster rides. Is he mad? I hardly know him. I don't know me. In fact, I don't know a blessed thing about sweet bugger all. He probably wants kids. Kids ... Oh my Gawd, he, he wasn't wearing ... maybe it's too late ... I could be ... Stop staring at me, dammit. I look at the ceiling; it's got all this bumpy swirly white stuff on it. Looks like the dry waller didn't know what he was doing.

"It's too soon, too fast for me."

"OK ... How about just tonight then?" He plays with my hair. He can't possibly know the wire I am walking on is this tight. He cannot guess his remark would bring razors to my gut and that these razors would begin singing dangerous songs of resentment against the world, against the denial of language, against my womanhood. He can't possibly see my insides have been one storm after another for weeks on end. Storms without let-up, which do not halt and birth clear sunny moments. He can't possibly know I hate him at this moment, hate his assumption that I would move in without experiencing the wonderment of courtship. Ice froths thick over the words in my mind.

"You have no idea who I am."

"I know I want to be with you for the next twenty thousand or so days."

"Not good enough. I can't talk to you. You can't talk to me. You ask me to pack up and leave my family after twenty years as though they were nobodies. What makes you think I don't deserve to be courted?" The razors have escaped and slice the wire. I didn't know he was up there with me.

"That's mighty white of you."

"Shut up. Shut the fuck up ... You ... " I am up now and scrambling for my clothes, throwing them on in a hurried rage. My pants don't cooperate much. I jam my leg in, they tangle at the bottom. I lose my balance and have to jig a little dance to stay upright. This little manoeuvre destroys the impact of my rage. I have to concentrate to stay mad.

"Maybe you see dark meat and don't think of my right to be ..." Be what? Treated like a white girl, taken to dinner, adorned with flowers and endless phone calls — dated? I am almost dressed. Where are my damn shoes? He is up chasing me around the room. He passes me my shoes without thinking, then jumps into his shorts. I can't believe we're doing this. I am dancing into my clothes, trying hard to stay angry and he is chasing me around the room. The tantrum I am throwing is thinning out. I am half afraid I can't hang onto it.

"Wait, shsh, hold it ... OK, OK ... I'm out of line, I take it back." It's too late for him to backtrack; my rage has swollen again. I have puffed it up too big to wait, too big to be calm. I make it out the door before he grabs me.

This is not romantic. He managed to put his shorts on but the rest of him is buck naked. Buck naked? I wonder silently why I have used the word "buck."

"You haven't got any clothes on." The valve controlling the steam of my rage is easing up the pressure.

"Yes I do," and he grins at his shorts, bites his lip and gives me a pleading look. He doesn't look a bit embarrassed.

"You better go inside." I try to muster up some firm resolve.

"Not without you." He looks serious about this. I can't shame him. I feel compromise coming up behind and I follow him inside. My chest is heavy and my body moves slowly through the door.

"Mark'll go a-courtin', OK? ... " Then, "I didn't know you were so hung up on your family." Wrong words. Hung up. Jesus hung up, nailed to the cross over family. I'm tired. In my fatigue, I can't figure why this is such a negative. He is tender again. I am Lacey's nightmare. It is so hokey to be this weak-kneed and full of desire. It feels plain wimpy but I'm on my way again, riding a roller coaster built for two straight up and reaching for the stars.

"It's been a hard day. Don't get mad, OK? I want to talk. Maybe I want to listen, but what did you think I meant?" He says this as he finishes cinching the belt on his slacks.

"I thought you meant spend the night," the words come out all pouty.

"I want to tell you something about me. I feel like shit just now. How the hell am I going to say this without driving you away? I never courted any Native woman, and I have been with plenty — too many probably. Your feminists have a name for it — womanizer." I stiffen. He touches his hand to my lips. "Take it easy with me, Marianne ... it isn't a terminal disease."

"How many?" Now that was mighty white of me; even I could feel its whiteness.

"Next comes who, and I ain't buying, Marianne." The pale blue cold of his voice reminds me of my earlier words. I shrink back from my remark. His words hang in the air sharp and clear.

"I want to go home." His resistance to my departure is spent. We leave. Outside, the afternoon fades. The sun on the road west, tired as it looks resting at the edge of the earth, burns merciless heat. Mark is quiet for the whole ride. He looks tired too. In front of the house he parks the car and grips the wheel. I don't want to know what he is going to say but my feet have grown roots and planted themselves to his car and only he can extricate me.

"You're a wild card, Marianne. That ain't all of it. It's family, your sense of it, your family … Jeezuss, I am babbling." Join the club Mark, besides it's Momma who is the wild card. "Family for me is a drunk mother and father fighting their way through a dead marriage every weekend. It's neglect of every bizarre type you can possibly imagine and then some. My context is different from yours. I feel this awful doom about you right now. You're slipping away and the magic I thought I had with women doesn't seem to work with you."

I want to tell him his magic is conjured from the wrong potions but I don't want to slice the heart out of this relationship, so I don't. I sit there and fish for something we can both hang on to.

"Should I just walk away with quiet dignity?" I whisper. It eases his tension.

"No, but my getting to know you is going to be a lot more fun than vice versa. You don't have the same ghosts in your closet, maybe you don't have any."

"Then it should be more interesting for me." I notice a strange car parked in our driveway — a Honda Prelude, all shiny and new, squats there shouting money at me.

"Do you think they send detectives in Preludes after missing persons?" Mark laughs. "I'll hang in there until you stop laughing." As we move up the sidewalk towards the house, I wonder how long it will take before he no longer finds my bizarre behaviour amusing. I can't stop thinking about Shirley Valentine and Lacey. There must be some ingredient, some sort of glue that holds people together. I don't want the kind that bonds so fast that you are welded to marriage willy-nilly. I want the kind that holds you together without feeling like you have to fight your way to the end.

The car belongs to James. What is wrong with this man? He is seated on our couch with a cup of coffee in his hand. The air in the room feels stiff and the people all seated neatly on various bits of our furniture look even stiffer. It looks as if someone came in and arranged the seating for the greatest possible stiff effect. Momma's lips are pinched tighter than her usual mad look. The smell of coffee is in the air and James is sipping away. His stiffness looks normal. It's dead quiet except for the clunk James's cup makes against the end table as he puts it down to greet us. Good old Momma gave him the only chipped and stained mug we own. She sits next to him in a chair, her chin is out and her eyebrows are up. Her eyes form slits when I enter. This morning she would have been furious but now, with this white man inspired by me to plague her, seated in her living room, my entrance relieves her.

Mark hovers by the door, one hand on the knob and his head slightly bowed. He is ready to exit. I have not been honest with Mark about who this man is. I haven't been honest with myself either, and I remember imagining his gold hair against green ocean spray and feel shame curl its way up my neck. The knob under the hand makes a half turn, so do I. It's an impossible situation. I can't introduce this man to Mark without telling the truth. He does not look like an overzealous sociology student but I can't risk saying he is Mark's competition either. First, I could be wrong about that — but then I could shit bricks if I had a square ass too. What I really don't want to risk is offending Mark's dignity.

Just tell him to leave; Lacey would. I can't. I am too full of prepaid bullshit codes of conduct about rudeness and decorum to tell him to leave. Mark doesn't say a word; he just turns and leaves. I whisper goodbye to his receding back. No backward glance, just a brief look at the Prelude and he's gone. Life would be simpler if we could just say what we mean.

"Hello James," my voice is old, dead dog-tired and laced with shame.

"I was in the neighbourhood ... " his voice is full of "did I mess up?"

"And thought you would drop by," and throw a major wrench into my life. The hard edge in my voice relaxes my mother. She would have left the room had the man been one of ours intruding on my space like this. Her presence indicates her sentiments; she wants to see me shame this man. He looks a little guiltier. I can't shame him, Momma.

"I didn't know ... I should have called ... I did call, but ... I'm sorry." His words come out between layers of rock-hard silence. "I didn't think you'd mind ... I mean ... "

"James, what are you doing here?"

"Huh?"

"Pardon me," I correct him.

"Pardon me?" he asks, confused.

"What are you doing here?"

"I came to see you." Well, that is clear as mud and twice as noncommittal. I can hear my mother's audio presentation of how much like them I have become when I rattled her cage over sociology. I want to tell him I don't even want him to look at me. It's too brutal, and compromise, impotent and useless, comes up behind again. Elijah unwittingly rescues me from my own brutality by providing a harmless escape hatch. We discuss him for a while but the tension is still too thick, so he cuts the visit short himself. I feel like an old wife, an adulterous and not too clever one, who has been caught with the milkman.

"Sorry, Momma, the boy has obviously never heard of Alexander and his wonderful invention."

"Speaking of Alexander — " she cuts herself short. Her voice is rich with relief and gentle tenderness, with only a hint of sandpaper in its tones. I decide to tell the simple truth.

"Momma, when Mark wrapped his arms around me, Alexander and the whole damn world disappeared ... "

"Sounds like true lust to me," Lacey says from the hallway, and Rita and Momma squeal with delight. Risqué womanly banter chases whatever worry or anger my disappearance conjured out the door. Johnny blushes, utters "goodness" and leaves us to our naughty joy. Memories long dead for Momma come alive; she talks about her Richard, the storm of their romance and the roller coaster ride. We prance about the room mimicking Marilyn Monroe's walk and feel gorgeous. Momma gives us a walk and brings her youth into sharp relief for us; we roar, there is nothing quite like this moment.

"I'm going to call him." They giggle, watch, and lean into the phone. Four rings and an answering machine kicks in.

"Hi, this is Marianne — lonely Marianne," an "aah" from Momma. "I wonder if you could call when you get home and maybe take the edge off my loneliness?"

"Cheeky," Rita squeaks.

"It's 6:00 p.m." and I hang up. The reality of my silliness hits me and I wish I had not been so cheeky. That's when I notice Joseph is in the room. He looks grave. He watched the whole scenario with James and Mark from his silent corner in the living room.

"If Ol' Johnny wasn't up to competing with another Indian, what makes you so sure Mark is up to competing with a white man?"

"He isn't competing with anyone."

"I don't think that is how he sees it. Looks to me like that white boy was on a chase." More paragraphs. Joseph means more than he says. I don't feel up to asking him what he is talking about. I want to end the conversation before it takes me on any ugly roads. For thirty seconds of lustful play with my mother and older sisters I felt like a woman; now Joseph has pointed out my youth.

"I dream Joseph. I have to dream."

"Hnh." It's too loud, he doesn't buy the answer. Go to hell, Joseph. The phone doesn't ring. I wait for it to ring, I pray for it to ring, but it lies there as dead as Alexander. Somewhere towards dawn I drift into sleep. Love is a major pain in the butt; the ups are great but the downs threaten to cancel them out. I wake up dog tired and without any appetite. I must have swallowed a lead ball during the night and I complain about it to Momma.

"Must've slept with your mouth open," is all she says.

The house is alive. Kids wander about. Elsa is up with Paul and they discuss school, punctuating their discourse with huge groans and complaints. I don't envy the life we have sentenced them to; high school holds no fond memories for me. Lacey, Rita and Auntie Mary all file into the kitchen. Wait a minute. What is Lacey doing here?

"What brought you, Lace ... they nuke North Van?" Laughter, the healer of us all, rolls around the dismal mood and swallows it up.

"No, Jacob threw a tantrum and I left before he got out of hand."

"Don't talk about Jacob like that. He is a nice man — a little stiff but nice," Auntie Mary says. The laughter of the rest of us agrees with her comment about Jacob's stiffness.

"Seriously, he and the kids are out of town for a couple of days. I went out, didn't want to return to an empty house so I came here." Is that the glue that holds people nailed to rotten marriages — fear of being alone in an empty house?

"Dorry too?"

"Yeah, he took them to the Island."

"Them? Paul's here."

"Wade. They've gone to see their other Gramma."

Auntie Mary, who came to help solve the crisis I created the day before, is sensitive to the new one I plunged myself into last night. Two major crises cannot be dealt with at the same time. The crisis between Mark and me is the primary one, she decides, and so leaves the other for later. The tension I caused between Mark and me can only be solved by me and so she isn't sure what she is doing here. I don't have much faith in my problem-solving abilities. I am better at creating them. Life without romance is simpler; less exciting but definitely simpler.

* * *

At work, Mark ignores me. He behaves as though I am some office worker he doesn't want to know. He instructs me in the day's tasks in efficient and polite language. People stare at us. Now I know why in some places romance between work mates is frowned on. On Friday I decide to talk to him. I even get to the door of his office. He has rearranged it so that his desk now faces the outside window. His back is all I can see. It kicks the hell out of my resolve. I stand there for a few idiotic seconds, then leave for lunch. Lacey is at the door.

"Hi, Sugar." Lacey wants to give me some lessons in manhandling; I hope she means handling men — that doesn't sound much better. I can't resist taking a look at the office. Mark is staring at us from his window. It's such a forlorn scene, his face enclosed in bars and glass like that. He looks away when he sees me. Damn.

Lacey and I head for my greasy spoon. The conversation at lunch jerks along. Lacey rattles on about this and that without getting down to any lessons on manhandling and I am not paying much attention to her anyway. She notices and makes some remark about how bad I got it. It inspires her to wonder why this is my first romance.

"No one asked me out before."

"Come on, Sugar, you're a knockout. Don't tell me those Indian boys never noticed before."

"Lacey, there aren't any Indian boys at the schools I attend."

Our worlds parted years ago. Lacey grew up in the village, came here at twenty-one, dated a number of men before settling on her husband. She worked for years in this city and knows scads of our folks. It never occurred to her that her friends didn't have kids in every high school and college in this area. The thought of no Indian boys at school brings forward memories of the other boys. I had a few lewd offers; that was about it. They all thought I was ugly and only good for … I can't bring myself to even think of it, much less tell Lacey. I feel ugly just now. All that sociology and I haven't figured out a damned thing about why school went the way it did or why the boys were the way they were.

Tennessee Williams once said that truth is a desperate thing, and I need truth desperately. I would just like to be wandering along the beaches that circle the city right now. Maybe spend the whole day letting sea winds toss my hair and caress my body. I can't think of any believable excuse for not going back to work. Lacey looks like she understands and sits quietly. At the end of the meal we agree to meet after work.

Work is a horror story for me. I throw up whatever coffee I drink but I survive; what I can barely tolerate is Mark erasing me. I keep looking up at the clock every ten minutes or so, which only serves to slow its ticking time by some. Finally Lacey comes by to take me to her bar. She says she hangs out there when things get to her. She doesn't drink but she likes to sing. It's Karaoke night and she signs up for a few numbers. It feels good. We don't talk about much, just share a laugh or two and sing some songs.

She sings those country tunes no one my age cares for. Her voice is rich and twangy like those of the singers who originated the songs. The sadness of them chokes me a little. Lacey sings them as though she were really sad about the way things are going in the words. I can see why we love those sad old songs now.

The weeks drag by at the office with no change in Mark. In between, the Mohawks at Kanesatake occupy a bridge or some such thing. It seems incredible at first. The town wants the grave-yard to build a golf course. The Indians maintain the land is theirs; the town maintains they own it. I can't believe that the town could come to own our graveyards by legitimate means; more so, I can't believe anyone would want to play golf on someone else's grave-yard. The crisis escalates, the Mohawks arm themselves. The road-block they erect is ominous. A mountain of stone, cement, debris and other heavy things. The police attack and one of them is killed. The Mohawks maintain the man was killed by one of their own men. Government heads hold a major tête-à-tête and the army is called in to replace the Sûreté du Québec. Momma cries in front of the television each night, powerless to express the horror and deep sadness she feels. None of us can believe this is happening to us. I experience love for ourselves and sorrow I never felt before. I think of the hoop that is thrown out and how it always comes back pointing a dirty finger at us. The press fills its pages with broadcasts full of ridiculous comments about how this is not going to do our land claims struggle any good, etc. Not a word about the shame the Quebec government and the town of Oka should feel about golfing on other people's graves. Our land claims struggle has not been doing us any good anyway, limping along as it has been for a hundred years now. I think about the twenty-seven court cases we won. Don't know how to convey the land. Please, spare me. There is no longer a question in my mind about genocide. I still don't buy the plot part of Momma's formulation, but the genocide is clear.

I want someone to hold me, cherish me, to bring some hope to the despair, but I don't have anyone. I almost had Mark, but some white man showed up and he scattered to a different corner and now he refuses to look at me. Does it always have to go that way — just at the moment when togetherness is possible, the ghost of white men invades the small space between you and erects an invisible wall dividing you. We can't love each other and now they are out there bulldozing graves for a golf course.

Oka changes the nature of our work. There is a desperate tension in the air. We put everything on hold. Behind the crisis lies the threat of annihilation, and we all feel it. As the news reports and faxes tell us of the escalating amount of weaponry the army deploys against us, we all set to work with a will to try to stop the threat of death. No one in this office considers asking the Mohawks to lay down their weapons and dismantle the barricade. We all figure "no" is a good idea.

Faxes about Oka, reports on the state of the crisis, speeches by Saul, meetings, plans, press conferences and serious discussions about politics occupy most of our time. Sociology comes alive for me. All those theoretical tracts about the workings of government line up with our new sense of justice and the world that encroaches on Oka in a living, breathing form. They are no longer endless books of meaningless chicken tracks; they have a tremendous value in reporting the events of the summer and planning our next action. Sociology becomes a joggling table that structures the helter-skelter information that pours in every minute on fax machines.

Mark. I still miss the romance, its brief intense drama; each day I resolve to catch Mark alone and each day he manages to elude me. He learns to share power with the women in the office. We need everyone. All of us rise to the crisis like angels of a new faith, faith in ourselves. The process Elijah began is rolling out over the land, rooting itself in all of us — solidarity with each other. Sovereignty association as a possibility, as a solution, now looks sensible, possible. Tribal council after tribal council joins the fight. Individual after individual lines up with the Mohawks. Tear-filled calls from Elder after Elder inspire us to carry on supporting the struggle for a little graveyard thousands of kilometres away.

Between all this, Lacey, Jacob and I have taken to going out every Friday after work. We never get too serious; mostly we just laugh and joke about the craziness of the white man's world, his stiff asexuality and his pompous sense of smarts. In between the laughter and the songs Lacey and I feel a powerful merging of our sense of womanhood, race and class, in that order. As I suspected earlier, we do think pretty much alike. I wonder how that happened; our lives seem to be so different.

We are sharing a joke when Mark strolls in. Lacey and Jacob get up quietly and go dance. Here is my chance to resolve this one way or another.

"Hi." I try to sound calm and aloof, what for I don't know, dignity I suppose. It feels so false.

"I didn't know you hung out here." He looks slightly tired. His shoulders sag a little and fold inward. The effort to block an armed invasion at Oka is telling on him. We sit long after work should be over, collectively pulling at what intelligence and imagination we have, trying to dream up one more plan, one more activity that would convince this government and its people that our gravesites are sacred ground, not to be violated by golf balls. His back bent in this way looks as though it is waiting for a blow. When I left the office he, Saul and a woman and man from Penticton were talking vigorously. They must have just finished their meeting before he came here. I am not all that curious about what the meeting was about. I know it had something to do with Oka and strategy. He sits looking at me without any sign of self-consciousness on his face.

"Only on Fridays. Lacey likes to sing and I like hearing her." I don't know why I explained myself like that.

"How is James?" I can't deal with this now, after all the hopeful anticipation over you and me, privately making speeches to myself about how I would explain James away and none of the words making sense — I just cannot handle the question.

"I don't know." More paragraphs but this time they take on order and shape. Lacey never lets Jacob govern her. She is clear on that. I have spent every Friday watching the two of them, both opposites, bound by common passion. Lacey learned to keep a healthy distance between herself and other men, particularly white men. She flirts with her husband constantly and never so much as thinks about looking at anyone else. I know how the whole scenario between myself and James developed. I had left the door open a crack and he had seen it; the rest is history. I want to tell Mark things will be different but I will have to confess the business of the green light, the flattery I felt when this white man presented himself to me. The confession would only drive a permanent wedge between us and I don't think I can stand any more walls separating us.

It was Jacob who explained to me how white men made him feel — used to make him feel. "They put ice where fire should live; they fire you up when you want to be cool. They turn my insides and my outsides upside down." In pure metaphor and without moralizing, Jacob gave me a new perspective on the scene I created for Mark. I turned him upside down, from raven's cocksure self to defeat, in just a few seconds. I did not create the defeat, though I may have reminded Mark of it. I want to tell him that but can't.

"I haven't seen him since you saw him last." His eyebrows go up the way Momma's do when she doubts you. I ignore them. I can't answer the unasked question or the unsaid remark. The doubt is insidious. It overwhelms me, paralyzes me, but there is no way to deal with it because it is an unexpressed doubt — an implied one. In my mind, Jacob's words continue to roll about: "White men have everything except our bedrooms, and they want that too. What bugs me is that the plainest white people manage to grab hold of our most beautiful youth. Until I met Lacey they used to make me feel like they could have anyone they wanted." I remember imagining gold hair against green sea — adulterous thoughts. Mark stole my heart before I had a chance to become entangled in James's infatuation; otherwise the outcome might have been different. Mark sensed that in the room when I walked away from the door without noticing he wasn't beside me. James, big and blond, in my living room, and I erased Mark. The Oka crisis, the intense work and anxiety over a bunch of men and women I did not know, was uprooting an understanding of the mechanics of racism in my personal life. I can't possibly deliver this monologue to Mark because I am no longer sure of what he wants or what he is prepared to give me.

"I'm not the same, Mark." A deep sigh escapes. It feels old. It sounds defeated.

"I know." Defeat colours the cornhusk and violin tones in his voice. Defeat puts a little gravel in the melody of sound our men make when they speak, it grates on my flesh. *Talk, Marianne, say it, say you want him anyway, say you want to begin again* — but the words die. Mark isn't the same either. He still looks at me when he thinks

I am not paying attention, but his looks are much more serious, coloured with a whole range of emotions. His looks are richer but not so clear. The lust is not wild, abandoned. Thoughts govern his behaviour. Principles dictate his actions now. We sit silently for most of the evening and then he leaves. I watch his receding back, broad and square, covered in a trenchcoat, his head just slightly bowed.

✳   ✳   ✳

I am ready to burst; so much has happened in the last while, I have to say it to someone. Dorry opens the door by asking me what happened to the gorgeous hunk from work. I tell her I made him pretty mad. Tears roll out as I recount the story of Mark and James and the wreckage it has wrought on me. I want to fix it.

"So fix it." Just like that, fix it. I wish it were all that simple dear Dorry.

"I can't."

"I'd just phone him and tell him the truth. Gramma says … " and she launches into her own mini-lecture repeating Momma's dictum of honesty. No mess is too great that truth can't fix it; besides, if you leave it too long other dirt just keeps getting mixed up with the original mess, then cleaning requires ordering it out and tossing it all item by item — sounds painful. I still don't feel like listening to Momma so I block out the rest of Dorry's lecture and retreat to marvellous self-pity.

✳   ✳   ✳

The week rolls by, each moment stretches out longer than the last. I can't seem to hold up the weight of my body anymore. My shoulders want to fold up and sitting up straight is becoming a chore. I know I have to do something soon. This is ridiculous. I have to make a decision. One of us has to do something. Someone has to make a decision and turn this horror show on its head again.

Thank God it's Friday. Friday, and I have still done nothing to resolve my dilemma. By now I just want to know if the hope that plagues my doubts is futile. He has been looking at me every now and then all day. His shoulders don't sag and they aren't folded in on themselves. He looks surer of himself. Something is up. PRESS RELEASE ... PRESS RELEASE ... PRESS RELEASE ... PRESS RE-LEASE. Prime Minister Mulroney should step down ... All the words look strange on the screen, words I conjured from the notes I took in the meeting with Saul and some of the others and Mark. They come out so easy, it surprises me and for a moment I am glad I spent a lot of time at school. Saul's a funny guy. He dictates to no one. He suggests a press release, waits for objections, then asks what we think should go in it. We all pitch in our thoughts, then he asks me if I would like to write it. No one has ever said no to any of his requests but I wonder with a little amusement what would happen if someone did. Just then I look up and Mark is leaning on my desk, waiting patiently for me to look up.

"It's lunch time." I need more than an announcement, Mark. I look back at him, my face blank, and he lets go a small grin. "It's a big world out there full of strange mean people, you going to send me out all alone?"

"You have to tell me what your intentions are, Mr. Mark."

"This isn't the place for talk like that." His voice becomes light and airy, full of bedroom promise.

"I'm not that kind of girl."

"Why don't you give me a chance to talk you into it?" His smile is moving in and out, full of mischief.

"Only if you plan to keep company for more than three days at a time." I can't believe I let the words fall out so full of brass like that. Lacey drops endearments and devotions on Jacob all over the place and she doesn't care who is listening. My words sound pretty mild compared to how Lacey talks to Jacob.

"Are you sure that's what you want?"

"Yeah."

"OK." He is not so cocky as the first go round, but my question drove out the sense of defeat. His shoulders square up and his muscles retrieve their taut, capable character. It should not be this hard to love each other; the ghosts between us seem legion and all of them originate from the other world. Lunch is uneventful. We talk about things that feel safe — work, Oka and Elijah; between the lines lies the world of our alienation that is disappearing like smoke in the fire of our new sense of solidarity with others like us. We are coming alive after a long period of numb existence, paralyzed survival. Mark mentions the Iraq-Iran crisis that lingers bitter underneath the bright light of domestic crisis. The speed with which they dragged the army out is a dress rehearsal for real war. "They want war," he says.

"What do you mean?" I am curious what Oka has to do with the man wanting war.

"I think they have been heading for war in the Middle East for a long time. They dragged the army out at Kanesatake to see how wild the objections by Canadian people would be. Did you read the paper the other day? They sent a rickety old naval destroyer with a handful of soldiers. People who support us are complaining that the army should be in the Middle East — leaves a bad taste in my mouth." Who's the wild card now, Mark? For me the Middle East is a million miles away. I just want to end the Oka crisis without spilling Mohawk blood.

Bizarre, Rita is at home battling all sorts of insurmountable obstacles and I am creating them. I argue that even Momma thinks having loved and lost is better than not having loved at all, but this sounds hokey; besides my faith in Momma's philosophical direction is shaky. I think about Momma and realize Ol' Johnny's is not the only offer she has had. And Mark is no longer the only man who has indicated interest in me. All summer men came in and out of the office. On more than one occasion I received invitations to lunch or dinner — I turned them down. On Fridays, when Lacey, Jacob and I went out I did not sit out too many dances. I could have gone home with any one of the men I danced with, but declined. Momma had turned down a host of offers too.

I guess that is where my faith in my affection comes from. I chose Mark again after looking around at the world of men.

*   *   *

Momma asks me about my romance. I answer her with a lot of nonsense about his looks, his intelligence, everything but rock-hard information about where he is from, who his family is and why he is still single at twenty-nine. Momma takes it on. Sunday night and Auntie Mary arrives after a month-and-a-half absence. We all sit around the dinner table kind of quiet. The tension feels a little thick. Mary clicks her spoon against the side of her tea cup and they all look at me.

"He is married," is all she says. Everyone stares hard at their plate except Rita. I move from shock to confusion and plough right on to rage.

"Who the hell gave you the right to investigate Mark?" It slinks out full of threat at Auntie Mary.

"Where did you get the notion that you were holy, sacrosanct and disconnected from the rest of us?" There is no threat in Lacey's voice. It is an articulation of my life. No, not my life, just her perception of it. There is a price to be paid for being indulged consistently over the years. This is the consequence of belonging to family; it's a kind of curious contract of guardianship both the indulged and the indulgent all ascribe to. I had, without question, accepted their indulgence for twenty years. Naturally, this indulgence includes protection of the sort going on now. Protection from my own folly and the protection of the family from it as well.

Still, I resist; I don't have to like it. They all stare at me in horror, except Rita; she plays with her food. No one has ever talked like this to Auntie Mary since Rudy tried it some twenty-five years ago. The air is electric; currents of fear, shock and my rage all crisscross above us.

"So is Ron." Rita pierces the atmosphere of crisscrossed currents of shock and horror and a collective gasp goes up. Even I suck air. Rita's Ron is married. No wonder her romance with him is on again and off again. No wonder she wanders about like she is in a constant fog.

"Holy Mary," and Momma grabs her purple crystals from the shelf and murmurs fast; Joseph tosses his napkin at the table and curses; Lacey points out that half the women Rudy has womanized were married too; Monique spills her coffee on Dorry's lap and Auntie Mary says, "It ain't the same thing."

"Why not?" Rita has found some courage in the past few months. The words tumble out slowly. They sound genuinely curious, like she has been trying to figure this out for some time. Me, I just stand there purple with indignation while a little lizard of doubt crawls around the empty space fear has opened up in my gut. Momma's beads are not enough. My mother turns the TV on and rails at the Premier of Quebec loudly. "Don't you dare touch one hair on those boys' heads, damn you. You have done everything to us; robbed us, raped us, pillaged us, until we are no more. No more. No morals, no culture, just a bunch of raggedy Indians. Indians, not even people. A mistake. No identity." She drops to the sofa and sobs. We freeze where we are in astonished and disbelieving shock. We have never heard her yell before. She recovers instantly, gets up, collapses, then yells at the top of her lungs, "I'll fix you! I'll fix you!" and she throws one of the millions of stones the kids have collected at the television. A blue light flashes and the TV lets go a moan, then all is still, but for the terrified breathing of Momma's audience.

He is married. Despite my rebellion in the living room, I don't feel like continuing the affair. His marriage has reduced our relationship to an affair. I should have guessed. A huge house, a mortgage, reasonably new furniture. How could I have been so naive? I feel like a dirty thief in the night who invaded some Native woman's bedroom and stole the most precious thing in life, her heart's desire. I didn't know he was married but ignorance doesn't feel like a very good excuse. I didn't ask. I can see his house with their three bedrooms. Single men do not purchase large houses in anticipation of marriage someday; they inherit them or they buy them because they have a family. Native people have not been buying houses in the city for long enough for any of us to inherit one.

My mind is a fog. He seemed so sincere about his affection. Images of his face float over my self-recrimination. I believed his looks, his words; what had he said — "I want you" — not much commitment in that. "I want you" is not much of an offering. I had folded into his arms without being made an offering — genocide, cultural genocide, personal and ugly. No expectations. Where were my dreams of family continuum? I volley between wanting to hurt him and trying not to care. In between the hurt and trying not to care lie images of his wife, ghostly and sad. They shred my affection and conjure images of my own willingness to offer myself up in exchange for nothing.

Dorry holds me and whispers words I can't hear. The hum of her voice, the music of it, comforts me. Slowly, dark crawls up my legs to the fog of my mind and carries her voice away.

I get up earlier than everyone else and walk to work. I have to sort this out. I have to look at it, feel it through and decide. Truth is, my own commitment to self-satisfaction blocks my good sense, paralyzes my decision-making process. I decide nothing. I move robot-like in the direction of the office and resume work. I can't even look at him. I do my duty with dogged determination and great focus. It takes everything I have to walk through the door each morning and carry out the simplest tasks. He smiles shyly, probably wonders what is wrong. I don't know what my face looks like when it feels betrayed, but it feels tight. He assumes I have had a change of heart for reasons he fictions to himself, likely coloured by images of James, because he doesn't even ask me what's up.

No matter, I can't just up and tell him, "Well, I heard from a very reliable source that you are married, and you know, I can't like that, so, you know, let's just pretend all this never happened." I am scared to say anything because, truth be known, he could convince me to steal him in the night from the woman who now sits alone and hopes he'll come back. No matter how often I picture his sad and betrayed wife, his children, nothing works; the flame of desire continues to smoulder stubbornly and burst alive every time I feel his eyes on me. I wish I had not cancelled blond against green as a possible alternative.

I try to recapture the moment in the café with James, but his innocent and ignorant questions, his brazen invasion of my home, get in the way. The backdrop of his arrogance changes. The fabric of resistance and repression woven around Elijah and Oka has altered the texture of me. My mother has become a living, breathing person, full of good sense, and I am sorry I lowered the guillotine on cultural unity in my family. Dorry has become a painter of great worldly affection and Lacey is no longer a fanatical feminist in my mind. The whole world is upside down. We are no longer victims, but people who have made a decision, established a direction for ourselves after what seemed like a century of floundering. I no longer want to be apart from my family. I no longer want to wander in a direction different from them. In my mind, white men have become the rootless, the lost and the ridiculous. Maybe it isn't upside down, maybe it has righted itself.

I am no longer on the periphery of their world and cut off from mine; they are on the periphery of mine. I look at my world's interior, the agony of it, the colours of betrayal, much of it mine. I had no idea the quandary over whether to pursue a married man was so rich with love and sympathy for his unknown wife. I feel this love, as do Auntie Mary and Momma. It is different when a woman wanders out of her husband's door and seeks the company of another man. She will always return to her home, but when the husband wanders off he carries his sense of family with him. We don't feel the same about anything. What is the difference?

On some level I am cut off. My wild behaviour closed the door to Momma; she felt it. But I feel exactly the way she does. I am childless; Mark's wife must not be or they would not have bought themselves a house. He walked out on his entire family and then came after a childless woman, single; he offered only lust. It isn't the same. A wandering married woman still holds her family together. Rita dumped Ron when she first learned he was married, then she hooked up with him again. In between, she continued to mother her children, plan for their future and pursue the education she needed to have so that she could work and provide for them.

Where is Mark's wife when she is not at home; why doesn't she have the home? Where are his children? This phantom, this wife who has not evidenced herself in her home, fills me with horror. I betrayed Rita when I held Bill's heart up higher than hers. I can't betray this woman who has become a member of the family of Native women Lacey has inspired me to love. Momma, I am not culturally dead. Momma ...

* * *

A fax comes through. OKANAGAN PEACE RUN. Peace. It is what I need now. I need a reprieve from this war raging inside. I decide to join the runners. Lacey will laugh. I know how her mind works, she'll liken my running off to join the run to some guy running off to join the French Foreign Legion. Five o'clock and Lacey is a no-show. I linger about the office for another half hour. Mark is there too, shuffling papers like he has something to do. The phone rings, he answers it. His body changes, shrinks, tenses, achieves crisis posture and strides in my direction. I balk. I can't deal with any kind of a crisis right now.

"That was the hospital. Something has happened to Dorry, Jacob and Wade." Glass, my soul is made of glass. It fragments, shatters and crashes, then retreats to some indefinable place. Not Dorry, not Jacob and Wade the giggler. I hardly know Wade. My body freezes. Mark takes my arm and slides me to the car. He hangs onto me all the way to the hospital. Whatever walls were there before are down. I am vulnerable. I can't walk away from comfort.

In the car I call Dorry's name over and over. He talks, tries to comfort me, give me hope, but I can't stop the pictures of pain. Shattered glass makes cuts into the images of Dorry and her art. The car stops. I grab the handle, hesitate for a moment. Mark makes no motion to get out. I will have to make this journey on my own. The lights are up all over the huge foyer outside the hospital. Bold red lights shriek EMERGENCY at me. Shadows of white uniforms scurry past swinging doors. This building houses horrific secrets of pain, loss and tragic death. It is not a healing place. It is a place of shock and mourning.

Lacey is hysterical. I could never have imagined her in such a state. She clutches a gurney. The gurney holds someone on it whose face is covered. "Jacob ... Jacob ... " she keeps screaming. I want to vomit. "Not Dorry, please Jacob, not Dorry." A nurse and a doctor flutter over her; my mother clutches her; Rita holds Joseph, who bites his lip and rolls his magnificent face from side to side while water streams down his cheeks. Monique sobs uncontrollably on the other side of him. The room spins, the sound of grief tornadoes about in the spin.

Memory intrudes. Lacey returns home all grown up ... Lacey takes me shopping, puts new shoes on Sugar, picks out dresses and goes to parent night with Momma. She pours pride all over Sugar's every accomplishment, tones down the acid of Momma's discipline, excuses Rudy's bad behaviour, explains Joseph's aloof quiet and softens the blow of Rita's sudden aversion to six-year-old Sugar.

Lacey. I closed the door on her sometime during my adolescence. She waited for years for me to reopen it. Lacey's love has no account books, no payables and receivables; she never wastes it, but she never withholds it either. She has watched grief afflict others from her strange philosophical distance, full of faith that things always get better, and now the grief is hers. Death, genocide, has come to collect its flesh, our flesh, Lacey's flesh. Lacey, who has been a constant in a world of fairly insane variables is now on the edge, herself a variable. Rudy is there in a corner, on the periphery of our grief. He looks embarrassed at the grief, its thickness all out in the open, bared before white people as it is. Grief wracks the body and challenges the soul, it drives the unreligious to pray and mourn and question God's wrath; it punctures holes in the glorious trail of life. It sharpens your vision, deepens your perception. It removes the veil of insignificance that clouds youthful memory. But it only does this for the loved and the loving.

Rudy sits in his corner, lost in his own embarrassment. He looks as though he feels no grief. I picture his love for family leaking out in drips as his hands abuse his wife and children. As trauma follows trauma in his life he lets love for life go. He can no longer grieve.

Grief strengthens your resolve to live and love, if you let it go. Rudy has collected his grief and clogged the pathways to his affection with the weight of it. Lacey grieves, terribly, deeply; she is alive with her violent grief. Her song of grief is total, full of wonderment, inspired as it is by her huge will to live and love.

Blood races from my head; it pools itself into the veins near my heart, it travels through legs weary of standing. The room sways and consciousness fades. I wake up to the acrid abrasive scent of ammonia. Mark's face fills the field of my vision. I look about. I am on a gurney in a room, next to Lacey.

"Did they drug me?"

"No, you fainted all by yourself."

"Lacey?"

"They drugged her."

"Where is everyone?"

"Home. I followed you in, and opted to stay. They took Dorry away." How can he look so full of empathy for me?

"Dorry, she'll never have to live with feeling ugly."

"Don't talk like that," he whispers, his voice full of sorrow I can't believe he feels. What about his lost family, the family he killed by extricating himself from it?

"You're married," I say flatly.

"Is that it? Is that why you have been avoiding me?"

"I really want you to see me. See … I want you to look at me … Dorry painted … She drew lines of hope across our despair, the despair of ugliness erased not by burying the images but by painting thin rays of beauty and hope on our faces. She … her work. The colours, the sculpting of us, women like me, the sensuous movement of our bodies. No Marilyn Monroe images to lie, just us. Bronze on rust, gilded by sun, moved by rain, tears of earth spilled on canvas all shunted aside and yet still clinging to our own beauty. Why don't you look at us and see … ?"

High school, excitement, wonderment. I am thirteen. I stroll along lengths of corridor, hear whispers coming up behind my back. Laughter follows insults wherever I go. My shoulders fold, my steps harden, my voice is stuck in my throat. My pen freezes and I fall behind at school. Auntie Mary comes over and sees the mess I am in.

"No one promised you a rose garden," is all she says. At night I weep, pray to God to wake up white. I refuse to look in the mirror, can't accept the twinning of my face. I stop looking at boys and bury these new passions somewhere between the pages of books. I hurl my womanhood at libraries full of imaginative escape from my body. Dream myself onto the pages of Zola, Dickens, even Shakespeare. Othello becomes a woman, a desirable Black woman. I blacken Cleopatra, become her. She becomes me. I dream.

Joseph is in the room when I wake up the second time. He and Lacey are ready to go. Except for the paleness of her skin and the shaking in her legs she looks as she always does, capable and ready.

"Ah, Sugar," is all she says. Her own grief spent, she is ready to encourage Sugar. I want the earth to open up and swallow me. In Lacey's boundless affection there is a huge message I can't read. It looks as muddled as everything else looks but I can feel the message nonetheless. I want to buy a poster of Elijah in his triumphant moment in the Manitoba Legislature and throw stones at it. I want to scream at Lacey; how can she love so effortlessly, so deeply, and Rudy and I so little. Then I remember Dorry is dead and I am repulsed by the speed with which my mind turned Lacey's tragedy into a major self-pity session. Jacob and Wade were in the same car.

"Jacob ... "

Joseph says they are both in critical condition. We have to go home and be with Dorry in her last days here; she is dead. Her last days? — ah, the wake, that's right, we are all Catholics. It has really helped, hasn't it, Momma? Your beads, they didn't save a damned thing. What good is a clean soul ready for heaven when life is so dirty and short-term on earth for us? It isn't even self-manufactured dirt. We have to run about the outside world and collect the dirt, and then haul it home. The thought of going home and fiddle-faddling around with purple Catholic beads doesn't appeal to me but Lacey stands there hopeful so I get up and leave with them.

I thought Dorry would be at the parish church down the road. We have not been there for some time. I can't remember in my grief how long it has been — a year or two? Anyway last week is a million miles away; it renders a year or two ago impossible to imagine. Joseph pulls the car up at our house. I am too numb to ask him what the hell is going on and why he is at home.

The windows on the inside of the house have black curtains

on them. Strains of strange music come from inside. I hear bells, feet moving in time with the bells and drumbeats keeping time with the bells and I imagine I have finally gone and lost my mind. Joseph calls me back to the car. He has my mother's dead serious, do-as-I-say tone in his voice. She must have one helluva hellish helix of DNA. We all seem to have the same urgent quality to our voices when we want to impress someone that we are in earnest here.

"Dorry is having a traditional ceremony." I don't know what this means and I am damned tired of confusion, riddles and surrealistic stories I never get the point of.

"So what's your point?" Joseph ignores the stones these words were grated across before they left my mouth.

"Walk through the hallway to the kitchen and enter the living room from there. People inside will be singing, they will send Dorry along her starpath through her own song to join her grandmothers at the end of her journey." He shuffles on his feet and bites his lip. This is hard for him. He has to hold himself together long enough to explain the ceremony, and underneath he carries the knowledge that someone should have told me this before. Our family is not ready to bury our dead in their own way. Right here on the sidewalk in the middle of residential Vancouver on the eve of my favourite niece's death is the spot Joseph picks to tell me a little about ourselves. Good going, Joseph. What really repels me is Joseph's intimate knowledge of the whole ceremony. He has always known about it; my mind clickety-clicks along and I realize Lacey knows too, and she brought Dorry up to know. What was wrong with me knowing? Dorry's last painting takes on new meaning, the one with the small things, the big city and the young people in it. I was stuck in the middle, my arms outstretched, her hands touching mine. She painted herself with the old people. She alone faced me. He finishes. The words come filtered through the tornado of my own thoughts. I hope I can remember them. No matter, they can't take my indigenous education too seriously anyway. Besides, I have continuously astounded them over the years with my lack of indigenous decorum and they have always forgiven me. They will forgive me today, too, if I don't do it right.

"Will it be in your language, Joseph?" Both he and Lacey felt that one. We have not dealt with this small detail in my life. The "theirness" of the language they all speak occurs to them. It is incredibly hateful of me to pour my own grief on top of Dorry and erase her loss. I want to take it back but it is too late. Everything is too late; too late to teach me the language, too late to teach me the protocol for the ceremony that holds less significance to me than my fading Catholicism. I am a genuine heathen. I attended the Catholic church mindlessly for eighteen years, grew disillusioned, left it and now I stand before my family, a non-Catholic, non-Indian heathen. Both of them hold fast to their ceremonial sense of life, birth and death, and I stand alone among them without any faith in anything. I wonder how many other young heathens there are among us.

"Dorry is a dancer." Oh lovely. Just what I need, more riddles. Joseph is strained beyond his capacity now. There are too many volumes of instruction missing in my life. The gap is bigger than mere urban blight. An entire context is missing. My whole cultural origins are absent. Joseph has no idea how to refill the empty spirit of me. He looks twisted with pain, shame and guilt; no, not guilt. It's more like he feels the intense responsibility of it all.

If I say it's OK he will be relieved, but we both know it is not OK. I can't lie, not now, not anymore. I am about to enter the funeral place of my niece as a foreigner, one of them, a white person. They know Dorry tried to paint the gap between myself and all of them. What had I done as a little child that was so horrible that they drove me from the fold of family knowledge? All this aside, Dorry deserves to be buried the way she lived, full of her own song, travelling to greet grandmothers along her own path.

"Let's go bury Dorry," and I walk inside.

They aren't ready. The singing has begun, but the main preparations aren't complete. I do not have a place in this so I retreat to the kitchen table — they will signal me when it's time I reason. Momma joins me; her invincibility, her endless source of reserve strength, look gone. I want to get up and touch her but I can't. The mountain of my missing knowledge was built by her refusal to integrate me into the family and include me in its lineage. I am nailed to my chair the way Jesus always hangs nailed to his cross.

In the silence I watch Momma's face. I dream old memories of her into view and re-look at her face as it aged over the years. Her body returns to its svelte, dusky image of seventeen years ago. I am three. I sit on a rock dipping clothes in and out of an old tub of water. She wrings them out and pegs them onto a thin rope tied between two trees. Every now and then she peeks at me, winks, then smiles. I laugh. She is not dark like me; her hair is long, deep brown, not quite black. It is tied back in a single braid; wisps of naughty strands escape now and then and she blows them out of her way. Her hands never stop pegging the clothes even when she plays peek-a-boo with me.

Now, it's my first day of school — grade one; there was no kindergarten at our school. I am six. I have on a new dress full of frills and ribbons, red and blue plaids over burnt rust. "They'll match your gorgeous skin," Momma says and Lacey agrees. The kitchen is full of people, elder cousins I call Auntie and Uncle, Auntie Mary, her son Karl, and her daughter Jenny, Rudy and Joseph, Monique and Paula; even Rita fusses over me. In the corner sits Jacob, watchful and silent. Momma's hair is short, a few strands around her forehead are grey. Tiny little raven tracks around her eyes give her smile depth and character. The svelteness of her is beginning to disappear. It is our third year in the city.

Years fly by and I am twelve. The whole family is there celebrating. The conversation centres on how high school will be different for me. I have had a better beginning. No obstacle like language to overcome. Then it dawns on me; Dorry was too old to be in eighth grade. She lost two years struggling for bilingualism.

Was that what they meant by a better beginning? Do they know how terrible these better beginnings feel just now? What a decision our parents all had to face. Dorry's language was an obstacle to her at school, but so good for her in her life outside their world and inside ours. Not having my language was good for me at school, in their world, but it kept me alienated from my family. Dorry's paintings hang on the walls of my imagination. They are full of compassion, justice, insight into human love and our need of it. Did Lacey know it was better to impede her European education with this other language in order to ground her child in a world of thought a European education could never provide?

My mother's hair is short. She wears it curled and the grey sparkles lavishly in it. She is stout, not fat, but definitely not svelte either. People bestow gifts upon me to honour my long haul across the fields of elementary school. I look again at my mother's face. The raven tracks are deeper but not any more numerous. Two curved lines pair up along the contours of her cheeks inside and next to her nose. She is fifty-two and that seems like a lot of years to me.

The picture rolls relentlessly on and I am eighteen; it's grad night. Momma had to go down to the school and fuss and threaten every one of their ancestors in order to obtain the extra tickets to accommodate my whole family. I went with her. I ignored her words, pretended not to be connected to this lunatic who pours acid rage over all the respectable persons in authority. Momma gets her tickets and my entire family dominates the graduation ceremonies. It is the only time I was not a minority of one at high school.

The memory climbs up to this moment where I sit across from her re-looking at her face. My Momma's hair is all white and grey. The deep brown has been obliterated by the silver her years collected. She is stouter, but the power of her musculature, the ability to give me a good hiding, is gone. She looks weak. When did she become this frail? Sometime over the years her body changed.

Sprightliness died and she aged while I had not been paying attention. Her muscles sag under the black shawl and her hands look less threatening than I remember them. When did her hair turn completely silver? It has only been a few months since I noted how grey her hair was and how few dark hairs clung stubbornly to their original colour. I slow down the pictures of the last few months. It was only last week ... yesterday ... a few days ago ... it must have been after Dorry died that it happened, while I lay in the hospital.

"What day is it today, Momma?"

"It's Monday." I lost three days on the ward. Did I sleep them away? Lost three days? I lost years of Momma's life. I lost the process of her aging. I can't even imagine it.

"I'm sorry, Momma."

"Sorry?" she asks, a little thrown off.

"I wasn't there the day your last brown hair went grey."

"My hair was not brown, it was light black."

I bite back my laugh. I completely forgot. My Momma's sense of logic changes whole concepts in the one language we have in common. Unseemly as it is to laugh at a funeral, I can't help letting go a constricted chuckle before I swallow the laugh. She doesn't seem to mind.

"I'm sorry too. About the language ... not ... " she chokes up on her words. "I ... " and she stops again and struggles for the words. She looks around the room like maybe they are lost somewhere outside of her mind. I can't bear seeing her struggle for words like this. I stop her.

"It's OK, Momma, I have a hard enough time trying to understand your English. Another language would just confuse me." Momma closes her eyes. In the lines of her face I see an old woman of tremendous intellect persuading herself to find the words to make me understand that it was not for want of love for me that she held onto my language. I see her reach deep inside herself to some place where a tenacious belief in her capacity to think lives and pulls, pulls the words up and out.

"I didn't want you to speak this language. It is not my language. It is your father's language. Rita, Lacey, Joseph and Rudy's father's language — he never lived long enough to become your father. No one here except Mary speaks my language, so I didn't teach you mine either. I thought when you grew up you could choose — my language or theirs."

The distance between us closes a little. The difference remains, but it doesn't look ominous. She looks afraid; afraid I will choose the others' language, afraid I won't understand her words, afraid I will choose her language and afraid I won't choose either. It is her fear that shortens the distance a little more. My mother, the all powerful, becomes ordinary; weakness backdropped against her great strength brings her character closer to how I see mine. I understand, Momma, I understand. I realize I am desperate for this understanding, have always been desperate for it, and I am surprised how easily it came, how little effort it took to achieve this moment of understanding.

"I'm going on the Peace Run, Momma."

"Unhh," she says like she knew all along I would.

"I'll decide then."

"Yes. Yes ... yess." She says it as though my words contain some sort of profound perception of truth. Like this is the only way to resolve the riddle. What riddle? Confusion swells, small and insignificant, but still, she manages to confuse me. This time I have the notion that confusion is only temporary; eventually life unfolds the mysteries that confuse.

They are ready and we enter the living room together; Momma takes my arm and lets me guide her in. The ceremony fills the room with Dorry's presence. The song, Dorry's song, dominates the night. I retrace my love for Dorry and listen to her words as they float above the singing and dancing. I pay no attention to the language of her death watch. Instead, I drift along dreamways Dorry carved for me. She brought me to this arc. This arc finally bridged the chasm between myself and my Momma. She whispers songs of love to Momma in my ear and breathes a last "take care of Gramma" before she stops singing forever.

She paints the colours of death before she leaves. Colours death wise, for only the living suffer consequences. Do not weep; the dead have no hills to climb, no obstacles to hurdle, no roads to run. The dead are not confined to prisons of flesh and blood; if you must grieve, paint your grief the colour of your will to live. Dorry's colours are vivacious and bright. Death is the living colour of the affection for the future. It is the poetry of creation. Death is impossibly sweet music darkened only by the living, whose insides are painted the colours of dread. Only the living fear death, and the dead alone understand the colours of great peace.

Our grief has shrunk some by the time we put Dorry to rest in the ground. I really don't think she wants to be buried in a box six feet below the grasses where her decaying flesh is not useful to the earth, but there are some things you can't easily change. You can't leave your loved ones in a fridge while you ply the endless bureaucratic pathways to achieve the right to bury your dead the way you choose. I think Europeans must have begun burying their dead enclosed in boxes and lowered deep into the ground around the time of the plague, when death stalked them in their millions. Maybe they thought they could bury the disease that kept claiming them deep in the bowels of the earth.

I throw my handful of dirt and listen to its sandy, splashy thud as it covers a piece of the box. I hold my mother close to my side and Rita is on the other side of her. Joseph and Monique cling to each other and Lacey has hold of her Jacob and her son, Paul. Paul collapses at the gravesite before he is able to throw dirt on Dorry. Lacey squeezes Paul; her grip encourages him to throw his tiny stones.

The cousins all weep mercilessly. They cling desperately to one another. Dorry is the oldest; her untimely death robs them of planning their future. Their tears sound fearful more than sad. Rudy stands for a long time at the edge of Dorry's grave. I am not sure if he is trying to feel her loss or beat the feeling of loss back. I have no idea if either of these two things are even options. The sun plays about with his hair. Purpled auburn hues shine against the beginning of his own silvering. His shoulders sag thinly.

Paula does not acknowledge Rudy's presence and his children do so only furtively. Elsa and little Rudy cast fear-filled side glances in his direction whenever he is near them; if he addresses them they respond too quickly and Paula is even quicker at getting between her children and their father. It must have been hell for them for some time before he left, for his children to behave this oddly in his presence. Rudy stands alone and powerless at the gravesite of his niece, without the comfort of his wife and children. He dares not grieve, and thus cannot truly live. I imagine him translating powerlessness in the face of the outside world into overpowering his wife and children. It kills dreams in him. He exists, survives in a purgatory of his own creation; then I stop wondering what is happening inside him.

Back at the house we feast. Momma says it is time to laugh. We have to let Dorry go and heal ourselves, and she begins a whole series of nostalgic family remembrances — all of them hilarious and all of them without Rudy in them. Auntie Mary and Ol' Johnny kick into gear. Auntie with her poetic riddles and Johnny with his surreal stories that never seem to be connected to any reality I know about. I laugh though I still don't get it but I find it all wonderful and it feels so good to laugh.

It's late and the stories wind down and grow thin. We are all tired and storied out and laughed out but there is something in the air that keeps us rooted to the spot we occupy. Something significant needs to be said and no one is taking responsibility for it. Who ought to be saying it escapes me but I get the feeling there is a protocol about these things and someone is not living up to their duty. If just anyone were allowed to say it then Lacey would, so it must be some predetermined someone who isn't doing it. There are gaps that enlarge themselves of their own between each speaker.

Rudy takes the opportunity to break the wall of silence he is consigned to. "I'm going to Mount Currie." We all look at him. Our forbearance of his presence arises out of a deep sense of duty and not a desire for his company. For him to intrude on our heroic conduct of duty seems absurd. Mount Currie? Which part of it? Mount Currie, the community which hosts the roadblock on behalf of Kanesatake, or those who huddle around the few who drown the spirit of rebellion in excuses? The entire country — Indian country — and a good many white folks too — are busy struggling for peace. The reasons for our participation vary; some want peace at any price and others want sovereignty. What for, Rudy?

"The roadblock?" Lacey asks cautiously.

"Yeah." I wait for Rudy to stretch his legs out and apart, then tilt his head back in that old familiar swagger. He doesn't. He sits; his hands cup his bronze face and this quiet settles over him for the rest of the evening. The rest of us look at each other, raise our eyebrows and shrug. Right then, Momma announces my intent to join the Peace Run and all hell breaks loose. "They hate Indians back there ... You'll be alone on the road ... Rednecks with stones everywhere ... You might die ... What about school? ... " and Momma sits smiling and winking at me by turns. She has a secret I know she can't keep, so I watch the family drama unfold and don't bother to answer my sisters and brothers.

"Baby's all grown up now," Momma chuckles after the cacophony of objections simmers down a little. "And that makes all of you kind of middle-aged." I want to laugh. They all look disgruntled. I dare not; I owe them their dignity at least. In the bathroom, out of earshot, I let it go. They are back to normal when I return and Ol' Johnny is "hnmph, hnmphing" his way into another story. Fatigue creeps up on me in the final words of Johnny's story, right around the part where he says "see" and I don't see, so I turn in. This time, though, not seeing doesn't feel so frustrating.

I lie in the dark comforted by the murmurs of cornhusk over

violins in the living room. My body relaxes, drifts, but sleep eludes me. I am twenty-one today. Dorry's funeral ate up my twenty-first birthday. I don't know why this feels good, but it does.

In the days following the ceremony and after grieving for Dorry, I make ready to join the Peace Run. I arrange to meet them in Penticton on the day they will be leaving. Dorry's voice whispers to me — no words, just the sound of deep and lasting approval. I feel like I have finally figured something out. I have no idea what it is that I figured out but it feels good to feel this way.

Dorry and I spent many a night over the past few weeks labouring over my sorry love affair. She listened to me extol Mark's virtues and rage over his negatives. Now, here in the room we occasionally shared, thoughts of Mark return, but they don't come back the way they went in — unadorned and naive. I want to tell Dorry that, so I do. She feels dead but not gone; I don't understand that, but I am beginning to realize there are a lot of things you can accept without understanding.

My thoughts curl around the sociology of him, the social content that gets in the way of his wonderment. I come to grips with me, really; with my life, the sum of it. The essence of me hovers around the libraries of sociology. I resisted thinking until now. I look upon Elijah's bestirring of my thoughts as a royal butt pain, but I re-dream and rethink the business of sociology and me anyway.

I spent two years studying sociology and anthropology at university. Most of the time my studies consisted of gauging the personality of the professor, analyzing which sociological direction his mind bent in, and figuring from there what sort of paper I should present. I avoid all those sociology and anthropology courses which focus on people of colour and/or Natives, unless they are required courses. I remember one of my classmates, a Chinese woman who had entrapped herself in an Asian Studies course. We ate lunch together every Thursday. On this particular Thursday she looked sick.

"I am so tired of being singled out as the Chinese in-house expert." I apologize mentally to the woman I have not seen for a few months now. At the time she last spoke to me I was obsessed with looking at Asian faces. While she spoke, I marvelled how they could look so like us in a general way and so different in all of their specifics. Their comportment, their bodies, all reflect a commonality between themselves and us, and at the same time they are so different. Not exactly relevant to sociology.

She continues: "Each class makes me sicker than the last. My mind is treated like their personal property — I mean, they don't ask the English people in English Literature classes for their opinion ... This instructor finishes every paragraph of his lecture with 'correct me, Sue, if I'm wrong' and looks at me. How is a first-year student supposed to be responsible for correcting a Ph.D. in Asian Studies?" They all act like we have so little to our cultures and history that we ought to have learned it all by the time we are six or seven, Sue, but I don't say that. They also behave as though we don't have a culture complex enough to warrant consistent and steady study like theirs. They figure our history and culture are so simplistic that they can be acquired by the process of osmosis or some such.

"That's it. Tell him he ought to be more responsible for his class. He owns the words; he plugged away for at least seven years and he collects the paycheque. Tell him to teach."

She laughed nervously; then she said that she couldn't possibly do that. She couldn't possibly do that. I wonder about her now; in the silent shadow of impossible love, these words come back at me. I can't possibly seriously study and research and re-evaluate myself, us, and she can't possibly insist her professor take responsibility for his instruction of the class. I don't know enough about who I am to risk critical study and I couldn't risk taking courses designed by them and based on books their scholars wrote. She has a certain amount of faith in his instruction but can't possibly tell him to be responsible about his knowledge. It all looks huge. The hierarchy of their perspective is ominous; it blurs their vision and distorts even the simplest of concepts.

Everything they see becomes distorted and accepted by custom. The challenges my mother's generation posed did not have to be taken too seriously. Until my generation, no one had to listen to Native people. What changed all that? I do not understand the stories told by my Momma and Auntie Mary; the context for understanding them is missing. Maybe, in their musings over education, they tried hard to provide me with the raw data so that, as I ploughed through sociological theory, I could place their personal struggle in some sort of context from which they could grasp significance. Somehow, the theory of social change and the stories of our ancestors struggling to push back on the encroachment of these others did not line up together as neatly as Auntie Mary and Momma expected them to.

I understand the colonial process in theory — divorced from living people. Objectively it's all so simple. It is all about Samir Amin's unequal exchange economics; but how does this really impact on us? The steady thrust of colonial pillage, what does it do to a man's mind? The construction of images always coloured by hues of derogation, denigration of dark colours, the elevation of white and fair and light; how does this affect our perception of each other? When we walk down the street and recognize or refuse to recognize each other, how much of what we feel is enmeshed in the orchestrated symphony of colonial conquest? How much of what we forgive and don't forgive in each other is laced to the external images of our race?

My throat constricts. My heart slows down and my breathing labours. When we see blond women on billboards, do we invert our heart's response to the image of bronze and dark in the bedrooms of our nation? Is it in the kitchen that it all begins? Does the inversion of our hearts travel with us to work, school, home? Does it dog us, repel us one from the other, or is it something we rip out from within? Love becomes hate. The hate swells, we cut it out and love dies. Neglect looks all right after a while. Insensitivity becomes normal.

Or is it that we ignore the billboards and the concrete and the looks of repugnance on their faces? We develop an ignorant frame of mind. Ignore this person. Eyes that don't want to look. Don't see. This not looking, not seeing, negates responding and emotions die — love dies and neglect becomes normal.

What is the precise nature of encroachment? It can't be simplified to some plot of genocide, I know this, but the encroachment is so steady, so thorough, so complete that I can't separate out the pieces of it. I can't pull the encroachment out and disconnect it from conscious genocide. Land. Land. We are landless. The land dribbled through our hands in moments when disease and hunger rendered us impotent. Royal Commission laws. "There are so few Indians left in this village that this commission recommends appropriation of the land and the transfer of the remaining stragglers to another reserve." They became few in numbers because disease, induced artificially, killed them. The remaining sick straggled to another village. Culturally, the village could not turn away their relatives. The sick diseased the healthy, and another village was entrapped, endangered by their own culture. Wrong. Endangered by the crassness of the uncaring conquerors. "They are sick. They do not need land anymore. Some other village will take them in." And another village dies. A map comes into focus. 1906: 1,800 small tribes in British Columbia. It took only seventy-five years of settlement to destroy one thousand, eight hundred villages by this process. Statistics become faces, relatives, friends.

Every single one of these villages was constructed of families with relatives in other villages. Rivers of tears must have been shed. Death must have become so commonplace that we ceased to grieve. No, grief became so constant we ceased to want to live. We have never stopped grieving. Grief of mass proportions dulled our will to live. The young and the old always died first, until the grief we felt for lost ones became greater than our affection for life, new life.

To love a small child, mother and father, sisters, brothers must begin with the assumption that the child will survive and our responsibility is to ensure that their survival is painted in full colour, richly textured with hope and joy. Disease and encroachment killed our future. We were not merely impoverished but futureless. Prohibited from pursuing life as we knew it and excluded from the life they created, we came to understand that our lives had no value.

All of the other laws added to the general burden of devaluation. Loonies no longer are treasured things in today's economy. We laugh at them, create jokes around them and toss them into piggy banks and old quart jars like so much dross. The dollar has steadily devalued over the past fifteen years and we no longer are able to treasure it.

"I have never courted a Native woman and I have been with plenty." Paragraphs of sociological analysis lay within those lines. Truth is more than a desperate thing. It wants more affection than mere desperation. It wants life of universal proportions. Truth wants to know how it came to be and, at the moment of truth, the flashpoint wants transformation — new life. The shape of this new life is completely dependent on the parenting of it, the nurturing of it. That is much greater, Tennessee, than simple desperation. Desperation is merely the fire that sets the process in motion.

"I have never courted a Native woman." Neglect, a simple kind of neglect, invisible but tangible to the woman. Neglect in its most harmless form, normal neglect. Deep desire, the ancient need to mate, results in normal and invisible neglect for woman. Love in its brightest and happiest moment inspires only neglect. Love between us does not give rise to the patient sort of commitment building that will bring us through storms together.

These storms are not normal storms. They are shaped of shame and encroachment, storms made of the defilement of our race by the external world, storms constructed of steady invalidation of our wonderment, our sensuous, beautiful selves. These storms negate our perfect right to be, erase our right to blossom, to rage, to weep and to live. These storms are in addition to the storms that the concatenation of two separate individuals gives rise to independent of the external world.

Mark, if I ever were to refuse some request, deny any of your wishes, what thoughts would travel through your encroached body, your besieged mind? What colour would your storm take — the colour of my bloodletting? White-hot rage, rooted in the negation of my race's womanhood? Will I become the besieged, just as they have placed your own manhood in a state of siege, or will you simply trade me in on a new Native, equally unworthy of anything but small and normal neglect?

I do not want to grow old like my Mom. I don't want to spend forty years of my life nurturing children and fighting the encroachment of the other world on their hearts. I don't want to feel the horror day in and day out of watching my love of beautiful children uprooted and unable to do anything about it. I do not, in the autumn of my life, want to cling to reinventing spring, with all its procreative beauty, for sons who should naturally feel wonderment in the beauty of procreation. I especially do not want to reinvent ways of inspiring cherished feelings in my children at a time in my life when they ought to be finding ways to express their appreciation of me.

My mother is sixty. Her hair is completely white and grey; no black, light or dark, peeks through in the strands of varied greys that adorn her heard. She has no brothers or sisters outside of Auntie Mary left. Auntie is the oldest. I vaguely recall Auntie saying she was not in the village during the flu epidemic that took the lives of the others. It was the last of the great epidemics. Momma alone survived it — Auntie escaped it.

It was a story before today, "nothing to cry about" — you are alive. How does it feel to be nine years old and watch death steal your family in the night? One by one they die. It took weeks to claim them all. How did this invade my mom's nine-year-old dreams? I remember Momma; dim light frames her face; soft words trail about the room, lazy careful words, a reverent voice stretched thin and small. I know that voice now; it is full of impending breakdown. It is the voice of her wailing child spirit — the voice of terror.

"Momma and Papa died last." I was not even curious enough to ask how she survived. How did we come to have uncles made up of older cousins? In between the magic of human story lies a terrible truth; uncles made of cousins are a result of besieged death.

Momma tells us she is the only member of her family left now. I wonder about why she does not include Auntie Mary. I want to know. Both of Auntie Mary's two children are dead. Karl died not so long ago — he died childless, as did young Jenny. We did not go to his funeral; this is excusable, we had not the kind of money it would take to get there, but I did not feel Mary's loss. Her loss is complete — her lineage closed forever. Auntie Mary has nothing but her age and her fruitless womb. I don't want to be her, either.

No wonder those men at Kanesatake have armed themselves, armed themselves for our dead. Our dead constitute the lost potential for our race. They evidence our genocide. They represent the remnants of what might have been and never was — in their eternal sleep lies our grief, the grief that killed our will to live and love.

"I just thought I would drop by." The words line up next to Mark's and spell out the same meaning. No phone calls, no invitations to movies, dinner, dances ... just drop by; she'll be there waiting for small doses of neglect. I would have, just like I went home with Mark and jumped on his roller coaster after two lunch dates, one of them a public lunch to celebrate Elijah — to celebrate Elijah, not me or my womanhood. Yesterday, a long time ago, I would have been flattered, was flattered because truth is a desperate thing and young women dream of love. I dream of love so intently I will defraud the nature of it. I want love so desperately I will dilute my definition of it, erase the dream and repaint pictures of normal neglect on the outer edges of the canvas of love's colours. I will paint blind white light — the absence of colour — in the centre of truth.

Lacey ... fanatical feminism I called it, and in my mind and heart I slashed derisive lines through the truth of her woman heart. I didn't want to look in the mirror, imagine myself, re-create a seductive, worthy woman. I was willing to reduce my body to a vessel that pours out love until it is empty.

In the dark I imagine Lacey. She sprawls out over the kitchen table, leans into her own conversation, her voice husky and seductive, full of raven's laugher. She is forty-two. No deep lines furrow her brow; her skin is still smooth and dark and her body svelte. She looks well-loved.

She scares me. It isn't her feminism that scares me; it's the absence of my own. She expects love; she expects to be treated the way women deserve to be treated. Jacob responds. I don't have a clue how she managed it but she pried Jacob loose from the moorings white men tie our men to. Maybe she just never changed her heart about herself; maybe she never gave up.

"You finish high school, Sugar. It's all we ask of you. If you can't go further, we'll all understand." She said that and presented me with a gift of my successful completion of elementary school. She talked about how hard it was during the first years of her marriage to Jacob to complete high school and go on to college. Her children were small and the family burden great. It took her forever to meet the needs of family and school. I hadn't really thought about it. Lacey, you were already a well-loved woman when you entered that place. You were loved by a man who never looked at the world except through the vision you both shared. You never heard the boys and their whispers in hallways "cleutch ... squaw," while your blood ran hot with desire for personal beauty. You never had to read prize-winning poems about Cariboo squaws.

"So, are you going to the reserve to pick up a couple of oinks?" my one date in high school said to his friend. I sat in the car next to him paralyzed with shame. The other boy looked at me for a brief moment, then said, "Nah, I have to take Gerda to the movies." Chris asked if he meant the drive-in. They both laughed. "No, Gerda is not that kind of girl."

"Neither am I," and I left. Chris travelled alongside of me for a while, asking what the hell was wrong with me. It is hell wrong for oinks and squaws to own dignity. He told me to get back in the car. I didn't ... couldn't. Finally, he drove away. Under ordinary circumstances three miles is not a long walk, but my whole family knew I was out on a date. I was supposed to go to the drive-in with him; the stop at the A&W killed the movie. It was only nine o'clock, too soon for the movie to be over. If I showed up early they would want to know why and I would have to re-create the shame to tell them.

I wasted time. I killed it in bits and pieces. I don't know where it went, this time, or how it died, but the walk took me two hours — a movie-length walk home. I lost those hours. I lost years. I lost time in high school. I killed time, immersed in the wherefores of the literature, because the children of the authors were so despicably crippled by delusions of race that I dared not live. I retreated from my youth, buried it in books — preferred them to young men who had no appreciation for life or creation.

The alternative was to consent to sexual reduction: withdraw or be reduced. Erase yourself or consent to shame. That is the sociology of being Native and woman in Canada. It is the result of besiegement, encroachment, small neglect, impoverishment and mass death. I had my mind and spirit crippled by the choices they left open to me as though there were no others.

My mother's response, "love one another," was simple, but in the face of the colonial colossus it looks insane. Lacey, you believe in Momma's simple truth because you never had your blooming, tenuous womanhood violated in quite the same way. Lacey, you did not go to my high school. You worked at home alongside Momma. Lacey, you restricted your world to a coloured one; no white men were allowed in it. You re-created a village in the middle of Vancouver, a village full of Natives from all kinds of nations, all sorts of occupations, successful Natives, unsuccessful ones, good people, grumpy people, but all of them bronze, with cornhusk and violins in their voices.

Only feminists ever got through your door, and most of them were Black or Asian. You discussed white men and patriarchy all the time, laughed over their inadequacies, their impotence and their futile attempt to negate the majority of the world. You erased them while I was busy dancing to their crazy tunes. I competed with them and in my mind I still do. I had to find partners from among them to study and conduct group seminars with. I experienced the humiliation of being chosen last for group after group, or being picked only if someone else had no partner, because no one wanted to invest their trust in my intellectual potential.

Mark, you must have gone through the same thing. University is not as bad as high school; feminists and Asians dot the landscape of racist and patriarchal university students, but most are not free of racism. A few are aware of the common link between their particular besiegement and mine but we were still besieged. Women, whether we are white or not, are all besieged. Some of us know it. I wonder if Mark's university experience was dotted with feminists or people of colour, or if he experienced validation as a bronze-skinned man strolling to class with white female company who saw only a body. I don't want to know the answer to this one, so I succumb to sleep.

❋   ❋   ❋

The weight of grief is physical; weeping relieves some of its weight but it doesn't do it all. I translate this weight into a general gnashing at the world. I transform it into rude quips about the stupidity of the world, the utter irrelevance of the bulk of human interaction — nothing escapes my attack. What is not stupid is ugly.

Neon signs are gaudy; billboards are a stupid translation of our strongest sentiment — attraction between men and women — reduced to fanny-flashing by women organized by criminal men who foist designer jeans on the female population who hope to acquire the same fanny on the billboards in place of dreams of womanhood. Newspaper ads exploit the language of human aspiration: "revolutionary new soap ... save money ... get smart and buy," tacky slogans, all abrasive to the human soul divine.

Billboards make the ugliest use of literary devices in the history of humankind. The flashed fanny is a metaphor for woman's deep desire to love and be loved. Cleavage moves from a symbol of the natural procreative sentiment of woman to a gross distortion of lust. "So natural only her hairdresser knows for sure." Hair dye, repainting the illusion of youthful promise on the faltering selves of aging women who ought to know the promise is a lie, but who still dream. Silver — a jewel on a woman's hand, distinction on a man's head — is a source of shame for woman.

I satisfy my grief by telling myself Dorry will never have to see the world the way I see it now. I connect the fanny-flashing, the cleavage and the whiteness of debased womanly beauty to the ease with which men in power-broking positions in Quebec can play games on land housing our eternal grief.

The warriors of Kanesatake know the attack on their grandmothers' graves; the evidence of our genocide is an assault on their will to live. They take up arms, not to deprive anyone of life, but to show the world they are dead serious about living. We stand behind them, not because we want to hurt anyone but we are all dead serious about living. Every one of us is saying no to simplistic survival. We want to live. We want to experience the love and passion of social affection before we die. We feel this need to live so deeply we will risk life itself to feel blood pumping sisterhood and brotherhood to every moving cell in our bodies.

I want to feel that affection for my own. In the alienated distance between myself and my family wanders this great need to reconnect with my origins. The run for peace holds promise. It promises in every step across the country to fill me with affection for my own. It promises to give me the courage to take up the broken thread of my aborted past and march forward into life from a place where I am both familiar and accepted.

✻ ✻ ✻

I still have compassionate leave days left but I head for work anyway. I need to say something to Mark. I don't know what it is I want to say, but I feel this need to talk. I can't drag the words out for my mind to read, but I know they will come free of pretension when I see him. On the way, I let my grief for Dorry carve cynical pictures of urban Canada into my soul.

Mark is at the fax machine doing what I normally do when I arrive. His movements are graceful and decisive but his shoulders hint sorrow. His body looks smaller and less powerful from behind. He turns to look as soon as he hears the door close and I lean against the jamb.

"It's lunch time," a good Salish hint. It allows him to say he is busy if he doesn't want me and it leaves a sliver of dignity for the unwanted.

"I'll be with you in a moment," he answers.

Fatigue is an emotional thing. It inspires the spirit under siege. Unfortunately, when the weight of emotional fatigue is brought on by our own besiegement of one another, we despair. I add the weight of besiegement by his heart's desire to the weight of his besiegement by the colonial colossus he carries on his back. I wonder if our men ask themselves, "How can she do this to me; doesn't she know I carry the world, a world whose nightmare it is to vanquish me? I carry a world so base it would play games on my grandmothers' graves." I want to answer, "You can't relieve this burden by climbing on my back."

We go to my little greasy spoon. The walk is a silent one full of trepidation for Mark. He doesn't look at anything on the street. We weave through the pedestrians mechanically, each of us careful not to walk too close to the other. "You're married," I repeat over coffee, only this time I mean to see the conversation through. I try hard to sound calm and curious and free of judgement.

"Separated." He corrects me but it doesn't sound correct.

"But I see her ghost, sense her tears, feel the loss of her heart's desire. I see children missing their father. I can't mother any woman or child's pain."

He sighs and lights a cigarette. He looks at me as though he were trying to calculate how much truth I can handle. I want the whole truth, but I know about paragraphs, volumes of words, and I sympathize with his calculations. He fills his lungs with air, and truth, raw and unadorned, escapes filtered through the smoke from his lungs.

"We were young. We got married, had two kids, bought the house, the furniture, a new car. Something went sour. I beat her and she left. She and the kids don't want me to come back. They have someone else — some white guy." His whole body is stiff with the terrible truth of his story.

"But she is Indian," I say, and pain registers on his face. "You never courted her and I know why you beat her." The rhythm of my truth becomes dogged. "You don't see worthy women when you look at us. Every time some white man or woman looks ugly on your face you come home and wait for us to screw up and then you let us have that ugliness. It isn't for me, Mark," and I wait for his reaction. It doesn't come. He withdraws to someplace inside where no woman can reach, someplace where Native women have no meaning. I want to shake him from his silence, but I know I can't. I want to kill this feeling that I will always butt up against his silence but I don't know how. I can't go on talking to thin air and smoke, so I sit quietly. We both play with our coffee, then get up and leave simultaneously.

On the street I watch him view the world. His face runs a gamut of emotions while the world fills his vision. He reaches out with pain, revulsion, desire and frustration at every image on the street. Longing crisscrosses with the rest of his emotions and etches itself into the bronze of his skin. The human body is a strange and wondrous thing. Its spirit wants truth, but the body wants lies. Our bodies crave the lies of fashion and comfort. The debate that arises between spirit and body fragments our thoughts, distorts our character, and clean-spirited loving people become brutes during the twisted heat of argument. At the same time, fine clothes are not a criminal thing. Clothes, possessions, express who we are.

We stand outside the door of the café for some time. He looks like he wants to say something to heal the rift that keeps getting bigger. He searches for words, but they wander about in an order he can't get hold of. He sighs, looks again, bites his lips and shuffles his feet. His search leaves me with hope, and I don't mind his inability to find the words. I know how it feels for them to wander about in anarchic, inarticulate disorder. He sighs and puts out his cigarette, then grins.

"Don't forget to buy a good pair of running shoes."

"OK." It is the first time I have not felt sorry about looking at truth. Some strange new emotion I don't recognize is born inside. He puts his hands out. I don't reach for them; it isn't what I want; instead I lean into his body and fold myself there. He holds me; it feels different. His words come filtered through the black of my hair. "You are a worthy woman, Marianne; remember that when you want to give up." His voice is textured with the rhythm of sensuous promise — bedroom intimacy. I haven't heard this voice for a while. I miss it. I want to hear it for all eternity. We disengage and he says, "I'm going to miss your little philosophical cuts into my conscience," and giggles. We part. Truth is, I love him, not the way he is but the way he could be. I love what he hides and not the image he presents.

* * *

Preparations for my departure bring the whole family together, minus Wade, who is still in the hospital. Panic over the seriousness of his condition has subsided; he is doing fine now. Chaos reigns in my Momma's house as we bump into each other, checking and cross-checking lists of what I will need. We duplicate each other's efforts and shout out contrary instructions to one another. In a pile on the floor are my things. There are two sleeping bags, two back packs ... too many things ... two pairs of running shoes, one much too large ... what ... ?

"Hey!"

Paul looks at me as though he is about to be put on trial.

"He is going with you," Momma says. They have discussed this without me. They all look and dare me to say no. There are no warriors outside our men in this family; no women warriors. I want to resent this. Paul is being included in my trek as a kind of body-guard. My resentment drifts away when I look at their faces. No one wants me to go. They are all sure I will die out there. Paul is not going to protect me, they know this, but at least I will be with family when it happens. So much pain rests between the lines of hope on their faces.

"Whose idea is this?" I ask.

"Johnny. The old fool means to kill half my clan for the good fight." Momma mocks annoyance and Joseph's eyes smile. I know better. Joseph went to Ol' Johnny with his objections and Johnny persuaded Joseph to compromise. Stopping me was unthinkable to Ol' Johnny, and sending young Paul along was a way to assuage Joseph's objections, turn them into consent. I want to whack Joseph.

"Let's go, then." The soft shuffle of young Paul becomes a de-cisive stride. His body straightens and gains size. His movements acquire the grace and coordination of his ancestry. He is heading out on a journey of personal and family transformation and he knows it. He smiles and flirts constantly with the women before we leave.

Lacey drives us to the Okanagan starting point. The ride is a blur of sleep and boredom I can't bring into focus. This is the longest ride she and I have been on that I remember. All the way she gets Paul and I to join her in sliding our voices around country tunes. Paul's voice is a rich tenor as pretty as his mom's. Mine has no discipline — it rises and falls, then whispers and shouts — but none of us cares. We climb the hills of coastal mountain passes and level out on desert plateau. I have never been outside the imposing mountains and cedar of my home. Spindly sage and short pines dot the yellow-brown hills. Everything looks like it could use a drink. The sun shines hotter than I could ever imagine her. The air smells magic and powerful — sage, Lacey says.

Penticton lies in a bowl surrounded by hills almost bare of trees and edged by two lakes; the reserve lies in the hills west of the town. The road to the sweat lodge is windy and tree covered, greener than the rest of the valley. Green Mountain Road, the sign says, and we all laugh. The closer we get to our destination the more intense our emotions get. We arrive at the log cabin on Shingle Creek Road just in time for the sweat.

The woman conducting the sweat is smaller than anyone in my family — not quite petite. She is middle aged but houses youth in her body. Sensuous calm layered over a sprightly, youthful vigour gives her a look of wisdom. Her voice is soft and musical, accented by her other language. She explains the sweat and makes it all sound simple and ordinary. Lacey knows about sweats. She and Joseph mention them in quiet voices every now and then, but I haven't a clue what they are. I never asked them, was never curious enough. The woman talks in flat, even, easy tones about how it works. She has great faith in this "ceremony," as she calls it. I have huge doubts, driven by sociological blocks about the reasonability of indigenous "magic," but I save them. I want to run, bad. Bad enough to move through the ceremony without letting on I have doubts. Bad enough to listen and comply with whatever the sweat conductor says.

Lacey comes in with us. Thank God. Just before the process begins she cues me up in one of her old songs — chants. It comes in handy before the ceremony is over. Paul seems to have no trouble dashing off with the men — likely he knows this stuff too, and a twinge of resentment shocks me for a moment. I drive it away; it has no value to me now.

The runners are all at the ready. Drummers sing old songs from the back of a large pick-up, their man voices stretch themselves thin into violin-like womanly strains accompanied by a big drum. The first man in front, the old one, clutches the feather and runs it to a group of even older women at the edge of the community. The three of them jog across the bridge, grinning from ear to ear, and hand it to the sweat conductor's father. With style and flourish he spins about and trots the feather across the road. The ladies seem ancient and young at the same time, all a-giggle with the joy of bringing the feather into the village, and they fairly trot the rest of the way to the hall where we are going to eat and leave from.

I listen to the Elders address our conduct during the run. I hear the instructions from the old men. The feather is never to touch the ground or stop. I commit all the instructions to memory but I don't feel much — really, how the hell is a feather going to bring peace. I recognize the younger woman who is getting up to speak. She was at Saul's office not too long ago.

Her presentation is a lot easier to get my teeth into. She wishes us all luck. Everyone here is full of emotion. She bites her lip, sucks in her breath, elegantly brushes away a tear and tells us we represent the Okanagan Nation. Okanagan Nation? I never heard of that nation in any of my geography studies. No matter — I want to run. I will call myself anything they want me to.

We move onto the highway and head for the next Okanagan village. My insides shake. We all wear the same t-shirts and hats and black shorts the Okanagan Nation has made just for the run.

"Peace is survival" hats all bobbing up and down in single file, snaking their way at the edge of the highway and heading out on a seven thousand kilometre jog. I feel crazy, glorious wonderment and grave doubts, all mingled with great love.

Running is a solitary thing. It is a thing of the spirit and deeply personal. It requires great effort and an appreciation for the mundane; this I know from my high school track days, but this is not a race against other human beings; it is a race against time, against the army. I watch the thin line of men and boys jog ahead of me. Each is alone with their thoughts. The smallness of the human form against the greatness of our task hits me. I want to cry. I want to go home already. Here we are, a group of insignificant youth armed only with a feather and an eagle whistle, accompanied by two old men, an old woman and a pair of middle-aged drivers, heading down a highway to stop the army from killing people we have never seen. We will wrack our bodies, torment our muscles and haul ass across thousands of kilometres of spine-jarring road surface with nothing but our faith in our purpose, this little feather and an eagle whistle to save us.

I feel self-conscious embarrassment coming on. My entire educational framework tells me this is really far-fetched. My body carries me anyway; it trudges on with a will of its own. The hills of the Okanagan breathe all around me a different truth. My sociological structures have no relevance here. The men in the truck gather around the drum and sing songs of confidence to our young legs. It helps. The Elders greet us at the community's edge. People line the streets of our departure. I can't look at them. I can't look at Lacey. I know she wants to be one of the runners. I know she weeps for herself and her forty-two years — twenty too many to make this trek. I know she believes in this feather and I feel guilty that I don't.

I pull the face of the sweat conductor back into view. Her faith in our ability to make this run is infinite. Her trust in small things, our feather, the drum, is absolute. I hear her words after the sweat and over the meal — she is brilliant, clear, and her thoughts have sweeping world significance — yet, she believes. She is talking to some man about Law, constitutional law, explaining fine points about the British North America Act, the Meech Lake Accord and the struggle of the Okanagans for sovereignty on the political level — these words sound so disparate from her faith in the feather. My doubts shrink. My legs keep moving. I stop thinking about the distance.

I stop thinking altogether. When my brain rests, images are cut loose. Images of pavement coming at me, images of trees blurring by, images of sun, intense heat, sweat, a still and reticent sky, and the feather begins to take on a life of its own as it bobs up and down ahead of me. I see eagle, images of birth in hands with great faith. I feel power. I feel distance, backward and forward, coursing through pumping blood. I feel muscle, tense, relax, tense, relax, and distance is swallowed by the magnificence of my own creation.

I hear voices, familiar and unknown, whisper words of simple faith to my aching muscles. "It's a long way, but you'll make it." We have to make it. We have to complete this run. We have to breathe youth's sweet breath across eagle's feather, touch eagle spirit, and reclaim our bodies across this distance of our aching, breathing homeland. We have to see every inch of soil, the destruction of our mountains; we have to see earth, pulsing living earth under the heat of sweat and toil. Sweat and toil for peace. "It's a long way, but you'll make it."

We stop at other Native communities along the way. Each night bronzed faces feed us, bed us down in their little community centres, share laughter and build our courage with wonderful speeches rich in metaphorical images I barely understand. It surprises me that we stop only at Native communities.

"How come we don't stop in regular towns?" I ask the old man. He isn't sure what I mean. His loyalty to his people does not allow him to entertain any other notion but to travel from one Native community to the next. His answer is more an explanation of the significance of what we are doing from another angle.

"We are allies of the Six Nations. We are obligated to support their quest for sovereignty." Are all old Indian men like Johnny? I wonder.

I pick up my turn at the feather and begin again. Day in and day out, we take turns, men and women, pick up the feather and run her as far as we can. Some of the men are athletes. It shows. Two of them, an Okanagan boy from Penticton and a Hochunk La, raised in Minnesota, run much greater distances than the rest of us. Some of us run half miles. It doesn't matter, we are all treated like Jim Thorpe on a sacred mission. We all receive the same care and attention. I draw thin lines between the feather, the allegiance of Nations, the loyalty and the faith in our mission. Spider weaves its web inside my soul. In the centre stands my mother, her mother, her mother's mother — infinite lines of grandmothers who spiral out, gain numbers and accumulate strength in their numbers. The simplicity of their love, the greatness of it, spins a web of ancient power in places inside me I have never trod. The omnipotence of my grandmothers spins a thread tied to their centre, their original being, and adds my own being to its magical construction — family is a spider's web of continuum.

I listen to my feet drum steps to the rhythm of the songs in front of me. Each step peels away distance. Each step pounds peace, peace, great effort for peace. My muscles take up the song, run, run, run for peace, run, run, run for peace. Drive, drive, drive my muscles to peace. I see faces strain, relax, tense, strain, relax, tense, feel the rhythm of drum song under their feet, see them dig inside themselves, reach deep, and run some more. Klick after klick slips away from eagle's feather under the drumbeat of youthful steps.

I fall in love. No lust in this love to confuse and disorient — pure love, sweet and worthy. Every man and woman on the run takes on worthiness. We are worthy. We are sacred. Life is sacred. Eagle whispers from my feather across the hot breath of my effort, creation is sacred, and my body changes. It rearranges my pattern of thought, tears up page after page of nonsense, utilitarian and cluttered. Rips the hierarchy of arrogant men from my mind. Stone comes alive. Grass, each blade my relative, speaks to trees who weep for their lost ones, grieve their genocide. We are besieged, the winged, the four-legged, plants and us — we are all besieged.

The feather erases the state of siege from my mind. It has been so long that I can't remember not feeling besieged. No. It has been so long that the state of siege felt like freedom. Peace, freedom, freedom from grief, freedom, peace — peace the end of siege. End the siege of sovereign Mohawks who want to live. Want to experience the pure wonderment of creation.

This is the solitary gift the run gave me. Collectively, we have no end of trouble. These mothers and fathers love us desperately. But truth is more than a desperate thing. This love entraps us. This desperate need to care for us meets resistance. We don't understand our need of it. Do not want great love, desperate love. We want to run. We do not need order and organization. We need to run.

We neither understand the discipline of their affection nor feel the depth of it. We are young, forward; every adult looks backward for their colours and their definition; they establish power and curtail our need to run. We feel power, the absolute power and freedom of solitary running burnt on our souls. We resist authority. Their sense of organization and the discipline of desperate love cramp our legs. They do not see their own desperate need to protect us.

The runners tug at their new-found freedom; the organizers tug at the hoop of discipline and organization. Circles are made. We struggle to understand, communicate across webs of desperation and youthful confusion, but we keep tying ourselves in knots of misunderstanding. Still we run. Still the organizers hang in there and the people at home cling to the magnificent hope of thirty youth and three elders and a couple of middle-aged drivers who stretch their legs across huge distances to carry an eagle feather full of promise.

Lacey would have a field day if she were here. The attitude of some of the guys towards women is pretty rough. The first couple of days I spend my time watching the young men on the run. Everyone slips into this easy familiarity right away — I can't. They all remind me of Rudy and Joseph. Half the men swagger and talk tough, like Rudy, and the other half watch in thoughtful silence, like Joseph. Two of the boys seem different than all of the rest. They are chatty and friendly, without the swagger, and much more inclined to talk about the significance of the run. They remind me of the twins, oddly enough, and I miss home.

They talk a lot about sovereignty, and this confuses me. I came here to stop the army from killing Mohawks. I thought I was clear; I want to promote peace. These boys, both sons of Penticton, Okanagan spokespeople, have more complex reasons for being here. Their mother is a lot like Lacey, but much better dressed — I saw her at the Band Hall where we ate in Penticton, and once in Saul's office. She rises to any occasion, gives clear speeches about sovereignty and political struggle. She is a lot easier to listen to than Lacey. No riddles to work out later at night and try to figure out the meaning of, no stories, surreal and unrelated, to wrap myself around.

Her sons are about the same. They possess a plain narrative that doesn't confuse me. Each night one of them phones home and gets the lowdown on what the state of Indian country is — "Indian country" always makes me laugh. It reminds me of Lacey and Momma talking about B-grade western movies and teasing Rudy about rooting for the cowboys. It makes Lacey hysterical to recall Rudy whooppeeing John Wayne over Captain Jack, and my mind watches Rudy mumble, "Who wants to be a loser?" Who wants to be a loser? Stay loyal and you lose, fight and you lose. The choices are pretty narrow. The boys from the Okanagan present another choice. Between paragraphs about sovereignty, the sell-out politics of some of the chiefs, the loyalty of Saul, the wavering of George and the wonderment of Elijah, lies their love and joy for life.

It is all so new. I listen quietly to their conversations. They do not always agree, but their disagreement is couched in careful respect. Nothing is resented. Everything is a matter of finding the best plan. One minute they agree with us about the arbitrariness of the leadership of the run, next they caution us about the need for organization. I don't get it; they both seem to be content to plant their feet firmly in mid-air and look at every problem with a fresh start, free of emotional bias. They aren't the only ones like that, but I ride with them every day so I get to know them pretty well.

The prairie rolls out before us like the belly of the earth. Miles of flatlands holding fields of golden wheat interrupted only by the occasional field of oats and the odd rhythms of metal critters bobbing up and down, all lonely, in the middle of farms, is all there is. I am curious about the critters.

"What are those things, Pete?" We are in the back of the truck and it will be at least an hour before any of us gets a swing at the road.

"Oil rigs. Some are owned by independent oil companies like Alberta Natural Gas and Oil or Mohawk, but most are owned by the same multinational corporations that suck the oil out of the Middle East."

"I take it you're against the war in the Middle East."

"Everyone has a right to be. No one has the right to organize themselves to kill anybody." Monty says this with his eyes still shut. I wonder what he would do if someone marched up on him with a gun — how does he justify supporting the Mohawks?

"I thought you were asleep."

"He's just resting his eyes," and the rest of the guys laugh. Pete, the storehouse of economic knowledge, and Monty, the philosopher. I wonder if they know how much of what they think and say fits into the framework of sociological discourse. They both sound a little like Frantz Fanon and Samir Amin.

"And you're against apartheid?" I fish. I want to paint a clear picture of their whole approach to the question of sovereignty and this feels like a good place to begin.

"Well, I'm not, but they got the wrong race on the Bantustans," Monty drawls.

"Now, now, Monty, that's racist," Pete chides. His voice is not that serious about scolding him but he says it like he and his family don't feel quite the same about the question.

"I'm not racist, I like white people … think everybody should have one," and the gang cracks up. Pete's eyes are a-twinkle. He set his brother up. He knew if he chided him lightly about being racist Monty would respond in just this fashion. I realize these two boys have been pulling my leg since we began this run. The scenario always patterns itself the same way. Pete answers me in a way that rousts Monty into the fracas; Pete chides him and Monty gets to make the outrageous remarks both of them want to hear.

Somewhere between their word play lies an entire analysis. They aren't too showy about delivering it but they are real good about playing word games with the system and the loyalty of white folks to it. They laugh about every power source in the country, from parents to government. They play with institutions like they are meaningless. The only thing they never joke about is sovereignty.

"What are you going to do with white people — drive them into the sea?"

"We have never organized ourselves to rape people or land," Pete says matter-of-factly.

"Didn't you sweat up?" Monty asks. By now I am sorry I brought the question up, but I answer him.

"Yeah."

"We pray. We have no churches. No priests, just our own personal love for creation. All we have is a tradition of justice, peace and prayer." Hot rocks, open hearts and an eagle feather — I delete the prayer.

The prairie road is slapping my feet again. I look down the road again, pray for a bend, pray for a hill, pray for a break in the scenery. It dawns on me I prayed to this God for two decades and not once have I been answered. My mother's God, her Catholic God, her Pope. He is up there in his illustrious gold, red and white vestments of silk. "It is a sin to lust after one's wife." My mother shakes her broom at him, "And I suppose that will stop men from lusting after their neighbour's wife, you old fool." I gasp. "Momma, he is the Pope." She assures me she knows that, but she knows who put him there — men, and men are capable of great stupidity. I wonder why I am praying for a hill or bend anyway. The flatness of the prairie is shortening up the run.

I dream up the hills of home. I hike along their old familiar trails. Lacey leads the way; she natters about grandmothers and daughters travelling the same path, generation after generation. Deep green conifers guard our path. She talks to the trees, drops something at the base of them. I dream of Lacey. I imagine jogging between stanchions of omnipotent green instead of out here on this golden wasteland. Back in the truck I ask the boys where we are.

"I don't know, but Regina is just around the bend," and like a fool I look up and they laugh. There is no bend. My muscles ache, my heels hurt, the sun beats mercilessly on my head, the landscape bends my mind; it is so boring, and these boys make fun of me. I do not want to be a hero. I doubt my desire for peace. I miss my home. I miss green, deep green, and I miss hills, twisted windy roads, sunsets that go by unnoticed because the mountains dominate the view. I miss cool salt air breezes and I miss being Baby. I am tired of endless speeches in languages I have never heard, ceremonies that confuse my soul and the intense attention of organizers who constantly ask me how I am.

At home I am assumed to be all right until I give a clear signal that something is amiss. Here the cook, the old men, the old woman and every one of the drivers and the runners ask me if I am all right. When I have assured some forty people I am fine, they all take the opportunity to pull my gullible self into their sense of humour.

"Watch out for my frog, huh?" Lyle asks me seriously and I jump to miss the frog and the boys all laugh. They carry on forever on the theme of frogs and what I might have been thinking when I jumped. "Did you think he was raised up like farmers raise up cows?" Lyle asks and they laugh some more. It is depressing me.

"Did you see the little blade of grass pushing its way up through the pavement?" Pete asks as I climb into the truck after my turn at the run.

"He has millions of relatives all around you," Monty says. Forget it, boys, not this time. I just know that as soon as I comment they are all going to laugh at me again.

"You should try to get to know them." This comes from Lyle. I refuse to help them play another joke on me. If they don't tell me what they are up to I will learn to live with it. In the meantime, I am not going to respond.

"Every blade of grass out there is an individual, different from the rest. Tony is the one we passed who was poking up through the crack in the pavement," Pete continues. Now I am really mad.

"I don't want to play fool for your fiddle just now." Monty softens, assures me they aren't playing me for a fool. The scenery is not nearly as dull as I feel it is. For him the prairie rises and falls, not nearly so dramatic as the mountains of the West Coast but he can see a world of difference in the landscape. To the boy from Minnesota, mountains are dull, tall trees all look the same. It is only after you watch them, talk to them, get to know them, that things begin to look different. They urge me to try it. Next time I turn around I will look, but I know I am going to have to look awful hard to see individuality in grasses. I'll try anything — I need to feel better than I do.

I don't say this to them, even though they all look dead serious. I know just as soon as I agree they will all have a good laugh at my expense. I look back at them as blank as I can and one of them sings a soft old tune in words no one at home would ever recognize. After that I watch them run. Their faces look out over the vast prairie and emotions surface. Each of them looks like they hear a story of their own creation. They make up the drama of the world in front of them. They are buoyant and they look heroic when they run, their backs straight, steps light and rhythmic — they make it look so easy.

"Watch out for my frog, will ya?" Lyle says again as he passes me the feather. His face is gentle and full of affection. He looks as though he understands how desperate I feel. I smile uneasily and take the feather. The sun patches illusive water on the road ahead. It is a piece of magic. There is no water on the road. There is no moisture anywhere, not even in the air. The only water that exists in the world here comes from irrigation pipes on huge wheels. It is quiet, more quiet than even my imagination could conjure. Far away the pavement is smooth; under my feet it is rough, full of tiny round stones. There are two trenches on the highway where steady auto and truck traffic have worn the surface down. Hondas, Volkswagens, Fords, trucks of all shapes and sizes pass by. Some of the drivers honk and wave. I lift my feather in salute each time someone honks or waves.

I wonder if they know what they are supporting. Probably not. I am still not sure. I try to imagine the world of grasses. I try to see difference, give them character, but the logic of sociology blocks my view, gets in the way of my imagination. Spiritual balderdash, animism, idealist dialectics, all crowd the character of grass.

Things pop and crack more than usual today. It is our thirty-third day of the run. We have covered over five thousand kilometres in a relay-style race against time. The first part of the run was major detox city — our bad eating habits and whatever other poisons youth are wont to consume created no end of leg cramps and other discomforts. That's over with now. The clean-out launched by the sweat has been completed through the sweat and toil of the run. The Mohawk women who joined the run some time back bring reports from home. They phone their families each night. Rumours of attack abound. In tears they tell us of the feelings of desperation the Mohawk men and women behind the barbed wire feel. The desperation in their voices spurs us to try all the harder. Most of us are in great shape; however, the stress of needing to finish drives us to push too hard and the injuries begin again. Some of us report them, some don't; none of us takes our injuries too seriously. We just want to run.

In this one town in Ontario, hundreds of kilometres from the border, a crowd waits. It is an angry crowd, a small crowd, a crowd armed with stones. Stones hail from the arms of men whose eyes are filled with hate. Run ... carry out the run. We have to make it. Stones drop. Run ... carry the feather. We have to make it. Missiles of hate rain all around my frail body. Run ... carry peace. Peace ... run ... peace, sweat for peace. Rocks lock legs in cages of hate. Hate, acid hate, red-hot hate ... twisted hate ... run the hate from my legs. Run rage swollen in muscles, inspired by stones, run it far away. Shouts ... epithets ... "squaw" ... high school hallways ... "ugly wench" ... "go home." Run, run, run for peace. Feather, sweat, small things, rage rising, looms large, small things burn rage from my soul. Run, run, run for peace. Run for squaws, feathers, small things and great love.

It is over almost as quickly as it began. They are far away and somehow my legs managed to carry me. No, it wasn't just my legs, but small things huge in the universe of truth which battles lies. Small lies, petty lies and sick lies laid to rest by small things filled with vast truth. My feather engages my spirit and together they erase body hate. Those boys don't know me. Their stones cast in rage could not reach me. The names can't hurt. Truth is wind, wind whirling from sky, caressing earth, spiralling down into my body and spinning pathways along ancient trails. Truth is heart, dark and light. Truth is a prism that shines every colour imagined by the human body and then some. Truth is complex. It understands epithets rooted in pain divorced from subject. Truth, it moves through paralyzed cells, cancels fear, frees their movement and opens new vistas. Fear is a lie; courage is truth.

These boys are the bearers of hate; they are not the originators. Someone poured pain into their small bodies, translated pain into hate for bronze, for dark, and persuaded them stones would relieve them. Hate is old, decadent pain left to rot in the souls of men who have no language to translate grief into new life, into bright rainbows of living colour. Pained men without rainbows of truth, vision, hate. Stone ... the healer, stone ... the lover of small things, sailed by the feather, the bearer of truth. Peace, run ... sweat for truth. Labour for love.

In the back of the truck I make my face return to look at the images of twisted, pain-wracked bodies of boys whose stones aimed hate at my own wreckage. Rocks, innocent stones, dodge my body, protect my spirit and unleash new visions of old roads. Young white boys line hallways, whisper epithets at my humanity and lose their own in the process. Pain etches lines of hate in their faces and robs them of hope. In their pain they lash at me. They miss the source of pain — the origins lost to them forever. Hate is the end result of squeezing pain small, compressing it into dangerous locked cellular movement at the height of youth's vigour. Forced to traverse a path of rage, this pain transforms their bodies into acid vessels of hate filling and refilling the body with self-destruction. Hate wants expression. Express, push up and out. Hate must be expelled. These boys don't know how to expel hate, so they indulge it and retrieve it at the same time. In their frenzy they can only cling to their hate.

The universe is made of small things. The colours of the mundane people the world. Pain is momentary, small; light is huge, vast, varied, coloured. Life's significance is imprisoned by rage that hides the wonderment of small things. A feather, a flash of courage, and the universe that is my body opens up and stone, in its modesty, becomes my herald of glory. Stone envelops things perceived by open minds and big hearts. Stone knows great spirit is experienced through the love of the small and the mundane.

There is horror written on the face of the man I pass the feather to. Horror paints the bronze of the men in the back of the truck a khaki hue. They had to sit and watch in helpless horror from the back of the truck while stones hailed the smallness of me that clutched desperately to an even smaller feather. They wanted to reach out and touch me, embrace my fear, wash the ugly faces from the painted images of my mind. Paralyzed, they watched in silent horror.

Silence, horror's lover, lingers sensuous in the air that divides us. We swallow our food. We force it by the lump of silent horror in our throats. In silence we sit on guard against any further en-croachment. The runners withdraw from the wild horror of the run. We alone face the stones. We alone will face any further stones. The driver, his back to the runners, did not see the hate-twisted faces of the rock throwers. We, the runners, came through the gauntlet of raining stones. We divide ourselves from all else. We are the run.

In silent horror we dare anyone to send us home now. "Send them home ... Bring them back." These words ride the wind of fear and protective love at home. Small things make up the universe. Faith in the small things added one upon the other builds a universe of secure knowledge within us. The silence between us needs breaking. I have to say something to relieve the tension, the burden of betrayal that separates them from me.

"Well, that was a bit of an adrenaline rush," and they laugh. It softens the distance between us and adds to our solidarity, but it encloses the runners in a web that excludes the rest. The organiz-ers did not see what happened. The cook says "hello" and we mum-ble hollowly. We grunt exchanges with the organizers, who are concerned for our well-being.

"Clark has to go on to Ottawa because he is injured," echoes in the thin night air. They don't understand. We have to run now. The purity of our spirit, the sum of our loyalty to peace, depends on the millions of steps we all need to make.

We feel besieged by the organizers — encroached upon — and all hell breaks loose. The voice of desperate truth rages in our bodies. Truth is small, complex, more than desperate. Truth is made of the universal movement of all living things. It is stone's refusal to participate in hate's hail. It is hail falling impotent around a small feather. Truth houses the infinite, the finite, and the desperation of the loved and the unloved.

No injury can compare to our desperate need to cover the road with our private truth. I want Lacey. Lacey can see inside the spirit, small and wise. Lacey can see the truth, dark and light. I want to translate the gap between the sharp colours of hate and the long distance between the organizers and those who run. I want Lacey to tell everyone that the schism that has swollen large is false and grounded in the hate of others. It is rooted in the besiegement of our Nations.

The runners feel besieged by the organizers who say, "You don't understand. What happens if Clark is running on his injured leg and the stones ... " Don't understand? We understand; we are not running for the momentary peace of Kanesatake anymore. We run for greater peace — spirit peace. We don't understand the encroachment of the others, the bearers of hate, white and light. We don't understand how their encroachment becomes translated into a schism between ourselves and our organizers.

We walk away. I phone Lacey. Hysteria overcomes me. I babble about schisms, truth, hate, besiegement and grief. She tells me to come home. I refuse. No one is going to leave, not now. She says she will be out on the next plane. She sounds as though she has waited for this moment all summer long. I see her face on the road to Penticton, eyes grieving twenty years too many. I hear hope in her voice. She will have a place in this, our moment of glory.

I leave the phone and collapse to the ground next to a small laurel bush and expel my grief to the earth beneath me. Paul finds me and he folds me in his arms and rocks me. He sings soft strains of old words. Cornhusk across violins, dark and rich. My nephew is a man. I have marched along the road to death long enough to have a man-nephew. He murmurs, "Auntie Marianne ... " Mary ... Anne ... my Auntie's name is Mary and my mother's name is Anne. The night, stars lit, folds over me.

We wake by the bush. Dawn, chill and half lit, plunges us into the world of the living too soon. Sunrise, magenta against hot reds and layer upon layer of yellow-orange fire colours, greets us.

"Ah, Marianne, look at sister sun," and we smile. The day before grows small in the riot of sun calling us to life. Sun calls us to life. It's that simple. Small things built on vast planes. What was that story that Minnesota boy told us about sundogs? "Impossible images reflected under extraordinary circumstances." Sundogs. Twin suns; twins image my family, my mountain home backdropped by twin mountains with twin peaks, made of twin sisters. My mountains, an impossible image, mirror my family under extraordinary circumstances. My nephew and I twin, mirror lineage and battle stones hailed by hateful citizens under the extraordinary impossible shelter of a single feather. Sundogs, two suns, one a mirror, the other pure fire, magnificent fire.

Ontario is really different from the prairies. In some ways it looks like British Columbia in miniature. It is not flat, but its hills are small; the firs who adorn its landscape are smaller than ours and there is very little cedar and a lot more maple, birch and poplar. In fact, there are maples everywhere. I imagine all the scarlet and gold colours which must people the hills in autumn. The roads are windy and they rise up and down regularly. I am moving up the hill towards Terry Fox's last climb. I feel just a little nervous.

At the top, I can see the statue that marks his last step. It is huge, gorgeous in fact. Whoever did it must have felt the effort and the heroism of Terry. The air sits still around the statue. It looks so real I imagine it moves, hippety-hop. I shiver. The wind rustles as I pass him. I thought I could hear the in and out scraping sounds of his sick and determined lungs. The rustle of the wind picks up his song of labour — scratches its way across the trees in a coughing sounds, singing Terry's drive to this last hilltop.

Terry is a white boy and it surprises me to hear my imagination wander along the path of his last great fight in such vivid sounds and sentient touch. His hippety-hop steps seem to be right beside me. I keep turning to look. Hippety-hop, run against cancer, hippety-hop, beat the odds, hippety-hop, run for freedom, freedom from cells maddened by overzealous reproduction in crazy, life-consuming fashion. His arms lift up and down, small pistons power one and a half legs. Air goes in, hippety-hop, out, hippety-hop. A lone camper carrying his feather crawls in front of the murderous run. I imagine Terry small, minuscule in the universe of cancerous disease. My feather against the army, Terry's one and a half legs against cancer — hippety-hop. Small things battle impossible odds, huge worlds of disease and violence. I feel Terry's courageous spirit invading my own — no, not invading, joining me on this run.

I feel as though an odd and strange secret has just been told to me. I look behind me. Terry's metal image is small, but so alive to me. He knew something about life and huge affection, an affection he did not confuse with lust. He too must have felt the worthiness of millions attacked by cancer — this do-it-yourself industrial disease.

Momma's face tries to tell Terry they will abuse the money he will die calling into being. "Stop poisoning the air, the rivers and the oceans, stop stripping the food and firing it up with chemicals — that is the road to the end of cancer. Oh, poor Terry," and I weep. No one in the truck seems surprised at my tears. Paul takes me in his arms and rocks me. I manage to say something about Terry. I calm down and tell Paul the story of Terry, the breathing I heard, the coughing and the hippety-hop sound of footsteps trotting alongside of me. Paul talks about the Lions at home, our twin sisters. The spirit of Terry chose me to visit, he tells me. I am not sure I believe him, but my resistance no longer takes the form of sociological analysis. He says it with such simple conviction that my resistance wanes and grows small in the golden afternoon. The day is windless again and I feel myself drift around images of Terry, a boy with a deep belief in small things. I can't believe my mother's cynicism about white folks anymore, though her reasons for cynicism look more believable.

The day rolls by and conflict between the organizers and the runners increases steadily. I think the conflict is deeper than simple disagreement. I watch the protagonists, listen to the words of a few of the youth who drag up mutinous sentiments among the runners. I sneak around and listen to the words of the organizers. We come from two different worlds. Most of the runners are young, educated in European schools. The organizers are older, educated in residential schools or not at all. Being with each other, working together, plugging along daily in a sea of bronze is natural for older people. They have never had to plug away in a sea of white, ducking and dodging the burning spears of racism on a day-to-day basis. They have always lived and worked on the reserve, immersed in their community. Residential school may have been hard, but they were all Native in the schools, except for the teachers.

The youths' lives have been too different. It is intense for us to spend every living moment immersed in our own people. Our standards of judgement have always worn white faces. We have no standards here, just a sea of brown. It puts an edginess to our characters that is inexplicable.

"Paul," I say at dinner one evening, "we have never invited any white person to our house."

"What would we have them do?" and he laughs. I join him. The whole idea of white youth muttering over the marvel of twins, gurgling at them along with a dozen or so other people crowded into a small kitchen seems absurd. I imagine Johnny launching into one of his surrealist stories and saying "see" and some white kid saying, "no, I don't see," and when no one answers him he continues to badger Ol' Johnny until someone has to tell him not to nag. I think of Terry and realize white people don't fit in our homes, can't fit; the context which guides their behaviour is absent. They would end up alone, silent in some corner, feeling unsure about their whole personal human history — it would be painful for them. All the jokes would go over their heads. Some of the jokes would offend them. My mother's diatribes on the Premier would frighten them. Her lack of decorum, her different sense of courtesy, would rub them the wrong way. And likely after that, we would feel offended about their inability to look and see, then do, rather than nag us into silence about what we are talking about.

Some of the tension is cultural. It has nothing to do with racism. This realization is a deep source of comfort. It doesn't do much to resolve the tension, but it is comforting to know that our different sense of being is the root of some to it. I understand everyone's passionate commitment to sovereignty a little better now. In my lonely years in high school my withdrawal was my own personal defence — my struggle to hold onto my essential self, my difference. I re-search Auntie Mary and Lacey — look again. I re-look at the interaction between white youth, the loud, uncontrolled, shallow interaction and talk. I listen to the conversations of white girls in high school locker rooms and blush at the focus on sex, style and aesthetic looks.

I hear voices run by who is cute, cool, and who is a hunk. The boys are bodies to them, no substance, just bodies without character, history, or family. I think about the world of television, stereos, video games and spectator sports they come from and stop wondering about the shallowness of white youth. I see their elders crowded into old folks' homes or struggling to stay alive in cheap apartments on low incomes and wonder who their grandchildren are. I wonder why none of these kids' conversations ever focus on grannies or old stories. I wonder why I have never heard a single white child tell pioneer stories they heard from grannies on long winter nights. Where are the stories of the struggle of old white women to carve out a new life, divorced from their lineage in a land so far from their birth place? Sadly, I realize they must not have been told any such stories.

I chuckle to myself as I watch our family each year pack up our baskets and head for the last berry field on the periphery of the huge city that now sprawls out all over the old food-gathering places of our past. I remember this one white girl who had always been friendly. She hints about us "getting together" over the summer months when school is out. She would not have survived a summer with us, picking berries all day under intense sun heat. She would have felt lost in the steady banter of a family that always addresses its kin and expects everyone else to find their own path to integration into our family. It would all have been too much for her.

My mother moved to the city because life in our tiny village not far from Vancouver had been too hard. I realize now that she never intended to integrate herself or any of her progeny into the social fabric of white Canada. It was nothing personal, but their being, their essential character was not acceptable to her. Despite the fact that no white person has ever been welcomed into our home, they are never really absent either. They are constantly the subject of endless jokes; their ways are scrutinized, analyzed and contrasted with our own. I must have known somewhere in my unconscious self that inviting them into our midst would have cramped our conversations too. Our silence in their company does not define how we are, but it does say volumes about how much we are willing to share.

I remember the one sociology course I took in which Native Canadians were the object of study. "Natives are quiet people, they can communicate without talking or they can sit for hours, not speaking to visitors." Most of the class believed this. When I got over my shock I brought it up with Lacey and my mom, who answered, "We got nothing to say to them so we don't." I understand now what they meant. You just don't casually drop bombs over tea saying things like, "Well, it's nothing personal but we just don't like how you are ... I mean, you come from a cultural beginning we regard as essentially sick, inhuman ... you know, we don't believe you have a single redeeming quality in your whole way of life ... you suck." Lacey's words are a lot closer to my sense of meaning. Ol' Johnny had tried to help with a story:

"Old farmer Mckyntire used to come by. First farmer in our area. Worked them boys from dawn till dusk. Beat them if they shirked their duty — his horse too. Beat them all bad, broke the little one's arm, then complained about how useless the critter was. 'Critter,' his own blood, a critter. Harvest time draws nearer. Keeps saying he knows it's going to hail and drop his crop, he just knows it. Sure 'nough our good mother earth hears his prayers and she drops big stones on his tender crop — ruins it. Grampa warned him. 'Don't pray for hail Mckyntire.' No good. Them boys hunger. We offer food when they come by, Mckyntire says they're not hungry. See — they got no roots."

I see now, plain as day. No roots in truth, no roots in the earth and her ways and no roots in family. "They're not human." If they can't love each other how can we expect them to love us. If they can't see themselves in relation to the very soil they seek to urge life from, how are they going to see our affection for the earth? "They are not human" was not so much a denial of their humanity, but a recognition of the absence of humanity in their condition of life. The earth is powerful. Small things we are, small things we own, but the earth is large, her universe omnipotent. Bleed her, she balks; destroy her, she implodes and becomes not the sustainer of our lives but the harbinger of our death.

Lacey arrives late at night. She rolls up her sleeves and sets to work trying to bridge the gap between us and the organizers. She draws an arc across the schism and re-forms the spirited circle of our beginnings. She understands the runners and the organizers and loves us all. The rifts disappear under the magic of our own voice, our sense of humanity and our commitment to the run. She reconciles us to our horror, our emotional sense of betrayal, the natural response of the runners to surviving the stones. She convinces us that violence is inherent in the world created against our will, here in our homeland, but that it is not inherent in the people who live here; neither we nor they were born with violent spirits. We deal with it daily as small children, so it is no big deal to deal with it now — everyone here is an adult. Violence begins with the distortion of our ways, the distortion of the meaning of our ways. From that springboard come the stones. Those white boys are distorted boys, victims of their own violent perception of who they are and who we are.

"They're just ignorant," someone says.

"No, not just ignorant. No racist is racist for reasons of ignorance. The people who pass us by and honk and wave or greet us in the towns are just as ignorant as the stone throwers. No one in this country knows much about us, but some of them have translated the violence in their own lives into hatred for us. Some of these people had good beginnings and translate their ignorance into a desire to know. Our supporters want oneness with all humanity. Racists want to vent hate on someone other than themselves — but they begin with hate. These same racists batter their own women and children when we are not around to stone."

"Or they join the army to kill people they have never seen," I mumble. There are a pair of WW II war vets on the run but they don't seem to mind my remark. Lacey's magic wand brings a truce to the run. The miles go by thoughtfully and much more serenely after that.

Although Kanesatake and the besiegement at Oka is on the news every day, our little run doesn't get much attention. In British Columbia, roadblocks in support of the Mohawks fill the news. The roadblocks are costing the country money and so they are worthy of reporting. All across the country demonstrations fill us with hope. Most of the urban demonstrators are white. White people stand along the highway holding peace signs, Blacks and whites in Kingston are arrested for blocking the bridge during rush hour and daily petitions are signed and sent calling for a peaceful resolution to the crisis. Although white Canadians and Native people carry out their actions largely separated from one another, the sense of solidarity is powerful. We feel like this country will never be able to erase us again.

I run along the highway filled with a new sense of wholeness. Initiative, empowerment grace my steps and ease the tension of klick after klick of running. The situation at Oka deteriorates. We run night and day. A train of cars carrying old people and babies is stoned and an old man dies. We swallow the grief and struggle all the more desperately. The feather has to arrive on time.

Paise Platte looms in front of me; dark black night and fog create a weird sensation about the place. The truck is up ahead, five kilometres away. No one is on the road. It's 3 a.m. I hear sounds, footsteps coming up behind. No one is there. Nothing I learned in school or at home is useful here. The steps are beside me now.

"Hi," my voice shakes. Talk to him or her, whoever. "Nice night." Step, step, step. "Are you enjoying the run?" My voice is squeaky and thin. The night folds black around me, thick. The steps grow louder. A sensation of touch on my back. Put one foot in front of the other. I tell myself to keep going. I can't see the feather or my feet. I can't see the road, step, step, step. "Guide me, little eagle, breathe your sight into my soul." My body lightens, grows less weary and resumes. My footsteps become sure. The steps beside me take on a normalcy. Natural that someone from Paise Platte, long dead, should join me here. Probably some young voyageur from Montreal, a half French, half Native fur bearer who just wants to feel the trail under his feet, experience the splendid vigour of youth running across familiar territory. Oka is not far from Montreal. I decide the footsteps belong to some gorgeous young man who perished on his return from the Northwest Territories, maybe Rat Portage. He perished right here at Paise

Platte. Maybe he succumbed to the brutal winter. Maybe he had left Rat Portage too late to make the distance to Montreal. He fell in love with some Native woman on the road home. Maybe he tried to persuade her to travel with him. She could not leave her village, her family, her lineage, and he strayed past the safe zone. Snow death overtook him at Paise Platte.

He finds me here running his journey home. My youth, the bronze of my litheness in the black night recalls his lonely journey to the other world. He reinvents the longing for the young woman and his love, which became his executioner. His affection was total. It inspired him to risk his mortal life. Wonderment has its consequences.

Mark, his inability to see me, the wonderment of my body, his inability to aspire to anything more than desire, had something to do with the journey between Montreal and the Northwest Territories. I felt like this moment of death of the young man, my imagined story of him, was the last time brown-skinned manhood ever risked his life for love of me.

I weep. Weep for the last time any young man braved winter, risked not getting home for love of me. It must have felt this way for the Minnesota boy too. He ended his leg of the run sobbing and staggering towards me, the feather in his hand waving frantically at the air, like my mother's impotent broom lashing out at the Premier. I know I am never going to be quite this close to truth. I am never going to possess this sort of courage, but I also know that fear will never paralyze me again.

An old lahal song rings in my ear and gambling takes on new meaning. The paragraphs of communication that get stuck in my throat do so because I fear gambling my inner soul. On Paise Platte, in the footsteps and gentle touch of the young man long dead, I found my worthiness. It doesn't matter if I complete this run. I found the self I need to believe in. I witness the terrible journey we have to make to come home, home to the warm fires of our own ways, home to a place where great love peoples our private selves, where devotion lives, devotion so deep we will risk our perfect right to be. Deep black solitude is the birth place of my under-standing and the sweat, the blackness of it, takes on meaning. In deep black solitude my sweating body hothouses my renaissance.

I no longer feel cheated of my language. It is more than lan-guage. Words, language, communicate the internal self to the ex-ternal world. I had not known who this internal self was and so I could not present myself. Paise Platte, blackened by night and fog, forces me to retreat to another world of vision. Another kind of sight is born; that sight, that way of looking at myself, is who I am. Words cannot describe this process. It is felt knowledge, a private universe of sentient being, and it separates us from the external world and draws spiderwebs of silk between our personal universe and the people who nurture us.

The European world may be huge, full of loud machines and big houses, but it can't even nurture its own. It may influence the desperate need for nourishment of the spirit in negative directions, but it can only starve the soul. It can create rock throwers, golfers on graveyards, mercenary soldiers who will trot off to the Middle East to kill humans they have never seen, but it cannot nurture. It can create chainsaw-packing tree hackers, but its hierarchy, its obsession with profit, cannot afford to create compassion, the food of the human spirit. That's the sociology of being Canadian. Undernourished and mal-fed. Canadians are fed lies that blind them to their own truth, and the light of human worthiness is doused by notions of superiority that inflame their distorted character. This process creates an artificial and tenuous loyalty to hierarchy which is essentially murderous. The undernourishment cycle diminishes worthiness and translates itself into racism. It moves the population to a finite tangent of dehumanized proportions and misdirects their life journey. In the end, the philosophy, the very sociology of the madness they create, lead to the desperate need to reclaim their humanity. The rock throwers reclaim theirs by entrenching themselves deeper into their own life. Our supporters spiral out to the extraordinary opposite and fight the influence of profiteers. What a time you were born to, Marianne.

We are using up the muscle power of the runners. To run all night and day requires more than will. Even our athletes are beginning to show wear and tear. The drivers join Lacey and run. I watch them fight the added twenty years, valiantly. They wage a private struggle between their will and their aging bodies. Lacey amazes herself. She pits her forty-two-year-old musculature against endless miles of roadway, jarring pavement that rattles her body, and pushes herself to run like she has never run before. She feels pride, winks her self-appreciation at all of us. We swell with affection for her. In moments of quiet night, before sleep takes me away to a dream world rich with new affection, I weep with pride.

Forty-two looked so old until now. Youthful vigour returns to Lacey. Her tiny raven tracks become beauty marks of hard-won experience and not signs of losing it — beauty tracks of firm resolve and the strength of loyalty. We tease her and the other older women who run. One is much older than Lacey, but her jog down the highway does not seem odd now. The "running Mommas" are cheered every time it is their turn. It is so special when mothers long past their moment of vigour take on the work of youth and do it well. I know it is loyalty to us that keeps the older women running. Somehow their bodies, through their loyalty, translate spirit strength into physical strength.

As I watch Lacey and Tessa jump out of the truck and take up the little feather I think about my own mom. I do not want to grow old like her, I had said not so long ago — why not? I can't remember anymore. I watch these women and I feel like nothing could be more wonderful than growing old like them, like my mom, like all of our women. Laughter colours the world glorious in the worst moments of our lives. Humour lights up bleak days. This run is a bleak run, a terrible moment, yet we all feel so joyous about doing it.

This country feels no shame about the need for the run. The

good citizens who pass by and honk, who greet us in their hundreds and once in their thousands, feel no shame. It is shameful that forty young Native people and a handful of our elders should have to run a small feather across thousands of kilometres with prayerful visions of peace in their hearts so that death can be prevented. But the shame does not belong to any one of us. It is just there. It is there because we are so puny, the world and its view so large, but somehow the hopelessness of our fight has left and great love has replaced it. The universe is made of small things. No one feels shame because it has no meaning to us.

✳ ✳ ✳

In Ottawa the run is aborted. It is too dangerous, there is too much violence in Quebec. Natives are arrested without charges and held overnight. There is a multitude of reasons, but the pain of ending it before we reach our destination is horrific. We know about violence. We live with it every day. The reasons fall out of mouths empty of weight. I can't persuade anyone of our need to run. It is bigger than violence, bigger than incarceration, bigger than my body and its small life. We vow to return next year to complete the run. To me a year is a millennium. Each day this past year has been power-packed with turbulence and change. Each day seems like a journey across huge distances. A year is too long. We weep, say our last goodbyes and leave for home. Disappointment is deep, but I don't feel the same about it anymore. I accept the disappointment and my desire to complete the run and my feelings that a year is too far away in a different way. I joke with the men who have become like family to me for so many days.

On the way back I think about going back to university. I see James, gold hair and strawberry hues, seriously listening to me. On the ride back I begin to become aware of my body for the first time. I had put her through a lot of misery. My feet hurt, my ankles hurt and my hips feels like they have taken a steady beating. They have. We complain about the abortion of the run, relive our moments of glory, laugh about the aches and pains all the way home.

None of it seems to matter; we have sunk little webs of roots in the vast soil of our homeland. The run re-created each of us. We re-imagined ourselves in every step of the run, and acquired a vision of a different world. A world rich with peace. A world in which we are not invisible. A world in which we are not always running from behind, denied future. Denied access to the wonderment of being alive. We acquire a vision of the world in which the besiegement of ourselves, the encroachment upon our communities and the death and neglect of one another are no longer acceptable.

Despite the disappointment of not having our young bodies carry the feather into Oka, I feel good. I feel deep gratitude towards the Okanagan bands who financed the run and the organizers who ensured its success. They sponsored not merely a run for peace, but the rebirth of youthful purpose and future in forty very courageous young people, of whom I was one.

I stopped phoning home weeks ago. I could no longer bear to hear the "come home" pleadings of my mom. Her tears, her desperate fear, did not fit into the run. I had not called her to tell her about the stoning. We all agreed to keep quiet about it. After Lacey arrived, she had taken to calling Momma. They spoke in our ancient language — Lacey's father's language, my mom called it. I decide to learn my mom's language, not her indigenous language, but her philosophical language, her language of logic.

The soft guttural mutterings of Lacey seem too distant to the ways my ears work, and Momma's language with the rolling sounds of the Cree people in it are easier, but I still feel hurried. I want to know about her thinking more than I want to know the form in which she couches it. In private I try to mimic the sounds of Lacey and Momma. Momma's come but Lacey's stop dead in my throat. I know how it is to try and master a new language. You begin with baby talk and move on up the ladder. I am no longer a baby.

I can't wait to understand us. I have found the ability to put the pieces of myself together. Coherence is rooted in understanding the self in its own historical continuum, the logic that shapes the self is born of this. I left the run in Ottawa wishing Lacey would let me go on to Kanesatake. Some of the runners did, but she glared at me like I was totally mad so I never pushed it — I went home. It felt good to be going home.

The Minnesota boy's impossible image of sundogs still plagues me. How can there be two suns? None of the runners outside this boy has ever seen them. I wonder if his story is like the tales of Aylmilth or the Raven tales of Auntie Mary. Raven is a metaphor, I know this. Auntie Mary would rear up and growl in good wolf style if I said this to her, because for her the wandering journey into the imagination is real and more properly reflects human thought. The imagination is the governor of human behaviour and social interaction, much more than laws, courts or police. I know that too. Sundogs' equation with twins does not fulfill my perception of their magic.

I recall our second day in Ottawa. Pete and Monty's parents are there. The boys don't feel the same way around their parents as I do around my mom or even my brothers and sisters. They listen carefully to every word said, interject now and then, push deeper into the minds of their parents and guide the articulation of their parents' thoughts. I can't imagine myself being this bold. They are so sure of themselves that they audaciously rudder their parents' presentation of the significance of the summer of Oka. Joan and Stewart listen to them, let them guide their presentation, even the shaping of their thoughts. No, it's more than letting them, it's the faith, the acceptance of the existence of their sons' separate minds. Every aspect of the movement, the struggle for sovereignty, is presented from a basic viewpoint that fights against any hierarchy, even the age hierarchy directed at youth.

No one in this family sees heroes or genius outside the genius of the whole people. They slip into teasing themselves about being "piggy" in moments when they allow the hierarchy of the external world to creep into their sense of clarity with arrogant notions of personal genius. The knowledge of the family is a shared one. I get the impression that the whole family participates in the development of their collective thinking. Sundogs, impossible reflections mirrored under extraordinary circumstances. I imagine Momma as an indulged child; in her orphaned state she must have clung to the pair of wild cards in her memory and held on.

I already know that Monty and Pete come from the same twinning of separate Nations as myself. Their mom is a Métis and their dad Okanagan. She is the same age as Lacey and she wears her raven tracks of age with great dignity, but her thinking, her sense of logic, is like my mom's. The world of my mother is flat, no imposing mountains to paint metaphors of hierarchy on her mind. Just flat open spaces and small grass.

"I think it's wrong to stop the run," I said to Joan.

"The people have a right to be wrong," she answered quickly, and Stewart spoke to her maxim. He explained how racism affects all of us. "Miss Piggy lurks in the shadows of our lives. She blocks our sense of co-operation. The run is not going to accomplish what we dream of; the warriors of Oka can't do it and Elijah's small 'no' may have shaken us from a deep sleep, but we still have a distance to travel, not the least of which is to alter our perception of ourselves. People will always screw up — don't condemn us for being human. It's too easy."

"This is just the beginning," Joan says sagely. "Oka is just a beginning."

"Sometimes shit happens," Pete says from behind me. Then I watch them all. I see the nature of their interaction. Monty and Pete mirror the essential thinking of their mom and dad but they also added something of their own to it. They are freer than their parents. Their parents laid the foundation for the freedom of their thought, and the boys are much more comfortable than their parents with their freedom. No stress is painted in the boys' faces, but hints of it live on the faces of Joan and Stewart. The conversation rolls on and every now and then Lacey jumps into it. I get to witness the common rhythm that pulses with direction and power and weaves a web of certainty around us.

Each one of them forms a strand in the web of sovereignty. Each strand spins itself in its own direction, independent of the others, and yet is bound by a sense of co-operation and equality between them. Sundogs. Joan mirroring my mother and Lacey under impossible circumstances. Our whole life has been designed to kill all solidarity and co-operation between us. But here in the great meeting hall of the Assembly of First Nations, in a private moment, two women brought up miles apart under very different circumstances mirror the impossible. It is scary even in my memory.

Sovereignty — the impossible dream. Equality, solidarity with all creation — a pipe dream. Drum songs and pipe dreams. I wonder if some white people, in their terror of us, re-conjured our metaphors into negatives in order to neutralize them in our minds. Plot, it was a plot to belittle us, my mother's insistence comes back to me.

"We have an obligation to our history to do what we can — no more, no less," Joan says.

"We have a right to do what we can, free of other people's prohibitions," I whine.

"You don't have rights, you have obligations," Lacey answers.

"Sounds fascist to me."

Lacey looks like she is going to belt me. I know why she wants to whack me. There are too many pages of words to explain what she means. The sense of her meaning is so powerful and rooted so deeply in her being that she can't find the words to persuade me she is not a fascist. Besides, it isn't our way to defend our personal thinking. But then, it isn't our way to box people in a corner by calling them names either.

"The people as a whole have a right to be free. The individual has an obligation to cooperate. Everyone is obligated to speak their piece. I noticed you were quiet during the decision to halt the run," Joan says slowly and carefully, without a hint of hostility or accusation.

"I didn't know how to say it."

"Then you should have given us incoherent babble." Given them a gift of incoherent babble … I didn't think that was ever acceptable. I would have sounded dense. My pride got in the way. It was all so confusing.

Pride is good sometimes, but then sometimes it isn't. I feel like I am being ganged up on. I want to dig into the foxhole of my point of view, but I don't agree with myself either. My emotions want to run, but my mind, or is it my heart, sees things their way. I know Lacey is not a fascist. I said that to protect my faltering self. I don't want to be persuaded of this collective point of view. This new way of being puts me squarely in charge of myself, but at the same time it is a self that stands in the centre of a community of selves, all tough and resilient, with each one owning their own views.

"The essence of fascism is the individual taking precedence over the whole." Now a lot of sociologists will argue that point of view, Lacey. She has calmed down now and her voice returns to its tender approach to Baby — please, Lacey, don't condescend. I am not going to win this one. I laugh inside about the word "win" — I guess I have embraced the competitive spirit of the outside world, because winning sits front and centre in the language of my thought.

I lack clarity. Part of me is now rooted in these people but the roots are twisted up with the thinking of the outside world. I decide to give this new place I have found in my family a chance. I can always go back to the European world of sociology and academic discourse if I want. I untwist the snake of competition from the thread of me and let it go.

"No one wants to stop the run, not the organizers, not the runners, and certainly not the bands who put thousands of dollars and their best sons and daughters into the centre of it. But we have an obligation to the runners and their safety and the safety of the Mohawks. Your only obligation was to run. If one of you got hurt on the road outside Oka, not far from where they couldn't protect you, those warriors would feel responsible. It would enrage them, create unbelievable pain. They love you — do you know what that love is made of? So far, their actions have been defensive — nonviolent — but in the face of you or some other runner being violated on their behalf their defensiveness might change. We are responsible for the alliance between the whole of the Mohawk people and the whole Okanagan people," Stewart finished, his face full of affection for my small world of responsibility.

I get it now. Ending the run has nothing to do with the courage or ability of the runners to make it. It has nothing to do with our will, or our commitment, not even where our heart lies. It has to do with the Mohawk warriors' affection for us and their respect for the runners' courage and self-sacrifice. Truth is, if we got hurt, they would become incensed, so deep was their affection. They put themselves at the barricades in a spirit of self-sacrifice and great risk, but they did not want those who supported them to get hurt. Their love for others was greater than their love for themselves, and greater than their commitment to Mohawk sovereignty. No, not greater, but one and the same. My disappointment shrinks.

"Well, gee whiz, can't a girl whine and cry around a little?" And we all laugh — comic relief.

＊　＊　＊

My whole family and every Native any of us ever knew gathers at the house. It's a new house. While I was gone, Joseph had accomplished the impossible and bought a house. Likely he found the absence of my crisis intervention into the family peace freed his time to concentrate a little better on the task. My brothers clutch me like they are sure I have been raised from the dead. Dignified tears leak from Joseph's eyes but Rudy sobs uncontrollably. Everyone weeps. I break down too. I was so focused on completing the run I had not given myself permission to cry much. I cry for the long, lonely nights in a sleeping bag, the chill night air, the night I didn't have a bag to sleep in and the disturbing night run across Paise Platte. I cry for the fear I didn't let myself feel on the road under a hail of stones. I cry for the whole damned world of rot and decadence that could inspire young boys to wish me harm. I weep for every Native girl who has faced the same shame of hate. I cry because it feels so good to let it all hang out.

Momma's face smiles; tears track down deep lines, fill her crow's feet, but her body explodes with pride. Her womb birthed a frail little girl with extraordinary courage. From her came a girl who could carry a feather through hailstones of hate, body pain, prairie sun, thick fog, dense rain, chill night air, and fractured people, popping and cracking all the way. None of us considered quitting during the worst moments. Only injury drove us off the road. We quit for love of the warriors. We began the run for love and we ended on the same note. Now I know this is what my Momma is all about.

In my living room I can't believe that I up and quit my job, left the comfort of my family for a road run thousands of kilometres long for people I have never seen.

"You should'a been there, Momma; you should'a seen Lacey hauling her chubby butt over hill and dale."

"Lacey ran?" Rudy is astounded. She whacks him.

"Sick," she says.

"Well, it was a sorta kinda run," and I hunker down and imitate Lacey. She lunges at me, squealing with delight.

"Oh, yeah, and you looked like an Olympic star I suppose." She relates all the jokes the boys had whispered from the truck about the "razor" slashing cuts in the atmosphere, making their turn a little easier.

"I'm not that skinny."

"Did someone speak? I hear a voice, who said that?" and Momma grabs me and squeezes the hysteria out of me. She is going to say something I don't want her to. The teasing and the laughter are much easier to take. I know she needs to say it so I don't resist with any sort of will, I just get ready for the intense self-conscious feeling. The laughter subsides and everyone gets ready for Momma's words. The sea of bronze in front of me takes on an ethereal quality. We are not Momma and daughter but giants about to leap onto the pages of history. All of us here have faith in what is about to unfold.

"Marianne made this run. I didn't think she could. At times I didn't want her to be out there, battling all the odds. In private moments, I bawled myself out. I didn't do enough to re-create the world; now there goes my baby and my grandson taking up the good fight because I never finished it. When will it all end?" She stops for a long and tearful pause — the fatigue of our mothers' ancient deep surfaces when their last child has to face the struggle they tried so hard to wage without success. "I wanted to fix everything when you were born ... Each time my lineage birthed a new child I rolled up my sleeves and went out to fix the world." She has to stop again. Her lips are quavering violently. They try to force themselves into a smile. "Now I know that's a real crock." They laugh, but the sound of it is punches through our tears. I can't laugh. There is not a single joke between those lines, I am sure of it.

"Well, I must be home because you're all laughing and I don't get the joke ... " They laugh while I pause a moment to reflect on Momma's words. "I hear you, Momma, and the crock of youth is not listening to our relatives. We fill our crock with the sounds of everyone's lies without stopping to listen to our own truth." They all cheer. I do too. I could hear my Momma's language coming thorough my mouth and it felt damned good.

We all took turns saying something small and ordinary and

cheering like the speaker had unfolded the secrets of the universe. This is the first time my family ever patted themselves on the back for anything — cultural genocide. It can never work. Paula is laughing too. She and her kids sit next to Rudy. I watch his hand shake a little and reach for hers, barely touch it. She looks down and grabs his hand and holds it against her chest. Rudy's eyes fill up with tears of joy and ancient grief. I know how that feels, Rudy, I know how it feels. We are alive. We survived the holocaust, the most unspoken holocaust in history. We should have been patting ourselves on the back all along but we couldn't. The weight of grief unrelenting kept us all standing still. The good fight gave us the courage to move beyond grief and take up the business of living. Tonight, the room is a rainbow of joy and hope.

In the speeches that follow I learn that everyone else was busy while I was gone. No one sat on their laurels. My family geared up and went into action as a block. A great tank of lineage rolling out across Canada's golf greens.

The anecdotes are endless. Rudy was in Mount Currie on the day the police arrested the roadblockers. The RCMP went about their business with quiet efficiency. Everyone was put in helicopters. The press was sent away once the roadblockers were gone. Believing it was all over, they left. Fifty onlookers were on the hills above the tracks, mostly women and children. A lone Native man with a video camera stayed after the RCMP sent the press away. He hid behind a bush and kept his camera going and filmed the blood-letting that followed. On the news an officer denied that the police had used violence while the journalist questioned him on the phone ... "No, it was all peaceful, the roadblockers went peacefully ... " "Excuse me, I am looking at a video of what followed the arrest and it looks anything but peaceful," the journalist answers him. "What ... " she repeats herself and he hangs up the phone. "Well, there you have it," she says.

Then Rudy begins his own private testimonial. The room is quiet as could be. He watched men, gentle in their ways with women and children, become courageous and tenacious in their resistance. He heard brilliance from the mouths of babes, Elders, women and men. He learned the world was flat, that wherever hierarchy existed there was no love. Paula must be going through hell. She sits on the couch, a steady stream of tears rolling across her lovely face, battered and scarred by Rudy, while her kids cling to her in stoic silence. They aren't babies anymore. We have all been through hell. The crisis at Kanesatake and Elijah's "no" persuaded us to stop inflicting the hell of the outside world on the corridors of our own private universe. The warriors turned us all around and made us reconsider ourselves.

I leave the room to the crowing of Paul and his bragging about Pete and the Minnesota boy and recalling the hilarious events of the run. "Murphy's Law was written for us ... " Paul starts. The kitchen is a sanctuary. In the lines of it is drawn my mother's character. The character who laboured, loved and tried to protect her children for two generations. I can see it now. Photo upon photo stashed in every nook and cranny and covering huge amounts of wall space articulate our family history. I am lost in just looking at the faces, tracing the lineage similarities in the cuts of our jaws and the carving of our features. I look up and Momma is across from me.

"Who are these people?" and I point at an old woman dressed in a flowered cotton skirt and shirt with ribbons all over it; next to her is a man; a top hat adorns his head. He is wearing a bone choker and holding a pipe. He also wears a flowered cotton shirt with ribbons on it. She is holding a small drum. I don't remember ever seeing this picture before, but if I say that, I will get the why of the story and not the who of it.

"It's my Gramma and Grampa," she says softly so no one in the living room will hear. "It was taken in the days when we weren't allowed to smile." The venom of cultural genocide is gone from her voice. She knows it didn't work either. "Sarah and Dan, poorest people on the prairie." She looks at the picture like she is trying to find the beginning point of the story. "They had a lot of babies, and not too many survived — just like my Momma and Papa."

She must feel tough just now, none of her children have perished before their time — just Mary's two and a grandchild. Not bad, Momma, not bad. "Them boys at Kanesatake keep saying we don't want golfers playing games on our grandmothers' graves ... but I don't believe that ... They'd be playing golf on our babies' last playground." Playing golf on our lost lineage, my mind finishes the thought for her. It is as if it is too painful for us to say that yet.

"Bullshit!" Paul is yelling. We go to see what is going on. Lacey is repeating what she had said. The feather made it in. I can't believe they would do that to us. They swore the feather would be run in next year by the same youth who had to give up the run hardly more than a week ago. Lacey defends them. I can't believe Lacey agrees with such an obvious and cheap act of betrayal. It was our breath that blessed eagle's lone feather. It was our legs that pained their way across the country. They lied ...

"It doesn't matter. The feather made it." Momma says it quietly. I sway with the weight of this inglorious lie and listen to my mother side with the betrayers of youth. "Them boys need that feather ... they need the pipe and drum ... they need those small things to bring perspective to their fight. It shouldn't matter how we get the feather and the pipe and drum there. They need it — that matters." What is she talking about?

"It was our glory. They stole our moment of pride."

"Pride is not an object." There is an edge in her voice. "What makes you think your moment of glory is worth their lives?" Oh my Gawd, the business of cultural integrity can be so hard.

"You had your moment of glory. It came when you threw one foot in front of the other across thousands of kilometres of land after you had not slept and you had done without food. That was your moment of glory. It's who you are." Shut up, Joseph. Shut the fuck up. We wanted to run to Oka, to see the warriors, feel their joy when we arrived. "Will you risk their lives for your glory?" Paul sits down, tears rolling down his face. I do not want to hear this, feel its truth or understand its validity. More than I had wanted to run for peace, I had wanted to feel heroism, a power surge of electric recognition, stardom, and that possibility is dead. Our little feather, our pipe and drum are inside, snuck in by cover of night by a woman who sweated us up, then risked our natural rage in order to give the warriors the things they believed in. Our hot breath fired power into the wispy eagle feather, brought eagle in full flight to its lone self. Our voices sweetened the drum with the sacrifice of youth. The warriors knew that. They wanted our spirit without our bodies hurt. We ran the feather, the pipe and drum to the edge of Mohawk territory. They asked us to do that, to risk our lives that far, but no farther. They were responsible for our safety within the borders of their territory.

Now I wish we had accepted the invitation to go to Six Nations or Kanawake. Paul mutters the wish. Lacey asked him to wish for peace while he's at it. I turn to leave the room. Momma collars me. "We never leave a thing begun undone." I feel the staggering weight of my selfish needs pitted against the needs of the Mohawks; they don't compare. Forty runners' pride or sixty Mohawk lives — they don't compare.

"Why isn't life simple?" Momma laughs. It is not funny.

"I'm sorry, Baby, it's not funny," and she carries on laughing. I need the pipe and drum. I need my Momma's language. I tell her so. I need to know that all of creation's children are equal, from the snow flea to the whale; we are all just children of the earth. I have to know that small things make up the vastness of the universe, that love is built day by day, moment by moment, with great effort on behalf of the collective whole. I know it's her language. I want to know these things not just in my mind but in my heart. I want them to govern my emotions, my spirit and my conduct. Calm comes and I decide to phone Mark.

It is a long uphill climb, this love I want, only this time I tell him. I tell him I want to change not just the sociology of being

Native, but the sociology of being white. I want to roll up my sleeves alongside of him and labour. I want to climb mountains and watch sundogs caper on the prairie. I want to be free. I am sure he doesn't understand, thinks I have joined the surreal madness of Ol' Johnny, but he goes with it.

Mark doesn't bother to knock. He walks into the kitchen where I sit, still reeling over the truth of the feather. I know Lacey and Momma are right. We have obligations. We were obligated to bring the feather as far as we could and ensure that it made it inside without threat to Mohawk life. We did that. This truth still doesn't feel good, but I know it has something to do with the unfairness of our condition and not a thing to do with the intentions of the organizers or the courageous woman who risked popularity to carry out her duty. She risked our affection, not just popularity. I am trying to master truth with all its faces, its pain, its joy and its glory. I look and he is there in front of me. Over the phone it was easy to blather out all my emotions but now in the flesh I feel the old seizure of silence locking my voice up in her grip.

His legs cross and he leans into the corner with one elbow up against the wall and stares. He knows I am sad, beyond sad, and I can feel him wonder why. The inside of him goes to war; his insides fight for mine, fight depression, fight the terrible truth we seem to always have to rise above. His whole self floats across the room, breathes words into me, redeems my perception of my self, our world, the outside world, changes my agony to hope, frees the lock truth has gripped me in. "Dream Marianne, wild Marianne, uncompromising Marianne, dream new life, new visions, new vistas ... You ran, Marianne. You ran, conjured steps of hope for all of us. You pounded defeat into the stone of thousands of kilometres of road surface. You buried demoralization, killed cynicism, beat back the shame of being losers. Come to me, Marianne; we shall dream whole worlds into being."

The lust still lies there hidden between the lines of deep admiration. His solitary being explodes. He wears the heart of the man at Paise Platte. He holds the spirit of the run in his body. He offers endless loyalty to ourselves and our capacity to re-dream those selves inside him. You don't fall in love with a man. It is manhood — glorious humanity — you come to love. Love for humanity sharpens your love for the individual, and this love dulls the blade of Hollywood's romantic desperation until it dissipates and love for the human soul divine is re-created.

I see all the Rudys in our world — confused, entrapped and paralyzed — in Mark's face. I also see Pete and Monty's hopeful courage in his face, and his heartfelt appreciation of my thin, frail body, which houses a steel yarn of courage. In his eyes, I see awe, not for me, but for what we can all become. I see understanding play about the gentled lines of his face, dancing drum songs of desire and singing devotion to all indigenous womanhood.

Doubt. It is doubt which left us somewhere on the road. I inserted the cut that removed the doubt between myself and Mark, between ourselves and all our folks. I flattened the hierarchy in both our minds. Delivered us from the doubt that rooted us to the soil of arrogance. He can call me without hesitation, without wondering about his pride. He can call me without the tension of desperation wiring us to the other world. He calls me from that extraordinary place where the beauty of the world and all humanity lives. He calls without shame.

We float out the door wordlessly and wander into the night. I know the words we owe each other are volumes. Whole speeches must be said, spread across endless days. I want the endless days.

The stars are visible tonight. No clouds to cover their infinite dance. The night hums, pulses tunes, and the stars all wink in time with the hum of eternal dark. His hand slips into mine. I can feel his skin, the magic moment of his touch against mine; the blanket of warm, knowing touch blends with mine. Spirits twinned by faith in future. Hearts bound by affection for all creation. The touch of faith in the world has no colour. It is a spectrum painted in the colours of all the stupid, wonderful, blundering universe of human suffering and foolishness. Our constant search and re-search for a human path unending etches grey between the colours, but it doesn't matter. Tonight the holding fast to convictions that seem like impossible dreams mothers a new commitment and devotion to each other and our dreams.

"We may never win," and I can't help chuckling. He joins me. We both know it doesn't matter. I am aware he is leading the way, and that doesn't matter either. A grassy knoll swells in front of us. We climb over the knoll, across a pair of railroad tracks to a park hidden by the knoll and an old warehouse; to the right is the Alberta Wheat Pool. My Momma's daddy was one of the founders of the Pool. Before he died they gave him a plaque — a gold plaque. I remember Momma went to Edmonton to join her family when he got it. I asked her how it was when she came back. "Oh, you know my Momma. She had to repeat every bitter feeling she had fifty years ago. She complained about how he left her pregnant in the bush while old Fred traipsed across Alberta's North trying to organize a bunch of silly farmers."

"I'll bet she complained with huge pride layered between each complaint," Lacey had quipped.

"Well sure, she was married to a man who carried out his obligations to the people — even if he wasn't Native, he knew what he was about. She couldn't let him get away with becoming prideful though. It would be sinful." A farmer's co-op, a dream, a simple man trekking miles of frozen wilderness, and his wife taking up her duty in keeping him humble and honest about his dreams. Small steps on snowshoes. Miles of black night and Grampa, solitary in his quest for dreams, supported by a wife at home who suffered for the dream alone, solitary, keeping vigil over the family fire. Grampa had been young; unlike Terry Fox, he had been whole, but he took on the wilderness of Alberta's unpaved highways. He took on the crazy determination that separates most of Canada from the few. He let go of the kinds of things that keep us marking time, standing on the same spot day after day. He had faith. His wife had his faith. Momma must have felt that faith in exactly the way I am feeling it now.

I recite the story to Mark. He laughs and tells me Momma went to one of the demonstrations and without being invited she strode up and grabbed the mike. Everyone was whispering about "Who is she? What's she doin'?" All my brothers and sisters were trying to stop her. Without any ceremony she starts in on the rich: "I don't have much feelin' for the upper class. They're all a bunch of jerks held together by a lot of dough. That's who plays golf on graveyards ... " and Momma was on a roll. We both laughed at the image of Momma.

I can see the guy at the mike confused. I can hear the "Who is she's" mumbled between the MC and the technicians and my family. I watch my Momma pay them no mind. I can hear the crowd laugh and cheer by turns. It took sixty years for my Momma to command the attention her genius deserved, but it doesn't matter. Mark was proud of my Momma and her spunk. He tells me about the women he worked with over the summer, the good-hearted women who were an endless source of inspiration for everyone. Their tears freed him to look beyond the narrow definition of womanhood. Their courage inspired him.

"It isn't our way to abuse women. It shouldn't have to be such a costly lesson. When your mom got up there my sense of manhood all went out the window. She meant to speak, right there in the heart of white urban Canada — this little bush Momma. It was great."

"This is my Momma's country and she can do just exactly what she wants to in it," I say to Mark.

"You come from a long line of wild cards, Marianne."

✳ ✳ ✳ ✳ ✳

Part Two:

SOJOURNER'S TRUTH
and other stories

Bertha

The accumulation of four days of rain reflected against the street lamps and the eternal nighttime neon signs, bathing the pavement in a rainbow of crystal splashes. In places on the road it pooled itself into thin sheets of blue-black glass from which little rivulets slipped away, gutter bound. From eaves and awnings the rain fell in a steady flow; even the signposts and telephone poles chattered out the sounds of the rain before the drops split themselves on the concrete sidewalks. Everywhere the city resounded with the heavy rhythm of pelting rain. It cut through the distorted bulk of the staggering woman.

The woman did not notice the rain. Instead, the bulk that was Bertha summoned all her strength, repeatedly trying to correctly determine the distance between herself and the undulating terra beneath her feet to prevent falling. Too late. She fell again. She crawled the rest of the way to the row of shacks. Cannery row, where the very fortunate employees of the very harassed and worried businessmen reside, is not what one might call imaginatively designed. The row consists of one hundred shacks, identical in structure, sitting attached by common walls in a single row. The row begins on dry land and ends over the inlet. Each shack is one storey high and about eighteen by twenty feet in floor space.

They are not insulated. The company had more important sources of squander for its profits: new machines had to be bought, larger executive salaries had to be paid — all of which severely limited the company's ability to extend luxuries to the producers of its canned fish. The unadorned planks which make up the common walls at the back and front of each shack and at the end of each row are all that separate people from nature. A gable roof begins about seven feet from the floor and comes to a peak some eight feet later. Each roof by this time enjoyed the same number of unrepaired holes as its neighbour, enabling even the gentlest of drizzles to come in. The holes, not being part of the company's construction plan, are more a fringe benefit or a curse of natural unrepaired wear, depending on your humour.

None of the buildings are situated on the ground. All were built of only the sturdiest wood and were well creosoted at the base to fend off rot for at least two decades. Immersed in salt water and raw sewage as they have been this past half century, they are beginning to show a little wear. In fact, once during the usual Saturday night roughhousing which takes place on a pay night, X pitched his brother over the side. They had been arguing about whether the foreman was a pig or a dog. X maintained dogs did not stink and what is more, could be put to work, while his brother held he would not eat a dog, and food being a much higher use-value, the foreman was a dog. He then let go with a string of curses at X, which brought X to grievous violence. On the way to the salt chuck X's brother knocked out one of the pilings. It was never replaced. The hut remains precariously perched on three stilts and is none the worse for that. Unfortunately, the water that filled X's brother's lungs settled the argument forever. The accused foreman has since been known as a pig.

Not to discredit the company. In the days before modern machinery, when the company had to employ a larger number of workers to process less fish, it used cheaper paint — whitewash, to be honest. One day all the workers who had congregated in the town at the season's opening beheld a fine sight at the end of Main Street: exterior house paint of the most durable quality. These stains come in a variety of colours but the company, not wishing to spoil its workers with excessive finery, stuck with the colour which by then had achieved historical value.

The paint did not really impress anyone save the foreman. So delighted was he with the new paint that he mentioned it time and again, casually. The best response he got was one low grunt from one of the older, more polite workers. Most simply stared at their superior with a profoundly empty look. *Thankless ingrates*, he told himself, though he dared not utter any such thing aloud.

Although the opinion of the foreman about his workers had stood the test of time over the decade that had lapsed, the paint job had not been so lucky. The weather had been cruel to the virgin stain, ripping the white in ugly gashes from the row's simple walls. The rigorous climate of the Northwest Coast destroyed the paint in a most consistent way, exactly with the run of the wood grain. Where the grain grooved, the stain remained; where the grain ridged, the salt sea wind and icy rain tore the stain off.

At the front of the dwellings some of the doors are missing. Not a lot of them, mind you; certainly not the majority have gone astray. The plank boardwalk in front of cannery row completes the picture of the outside. Over the years, at uncannily even intervals, each sixth board has disappeared, some by very bizarre happenstances.

Inside, the huts are furnished with tasteless simplicity. A sturdy, four-legged cedar table of no design occupies the middle of the room. Four wooden, high-backed chairs built with unsteamed two-by-twos and a square piece of good-one-side plywood surround the table. The floors are shiplap planks. Squatted in the centre of the back wall is a pot-bellied cast-iron stove, though those workers who still cook use a Coleman. Shelving above the pot-bellied stove keeps the kitchenware and food supplies immodestly in view. Two bunks to the right and two to the left complete the furnishings. It was not the sort of place in which any of the workers felt inspired to add a touch of their personal self. No photos, no knickknacks. What the company did not provide, the workers did not have.

The residence, taken as a whole, was not so bad but for one occasional nuisance. At high tide each dwelling, except the few nearest shore, was partially submerged in water. It wasn't really such a great bother. After all, the workers spent most of their waking time at the cannery — upwards of ten hours a day; sometimes this included Sunday, but not always — and the bunks were sufficiently far from the floor such that sleeping etc., carried on unencumbered. A good pair of Kingcome slippers — hip waders — was all that was needed to prevent any discomfort the tide caused. The women who used to complain violently to the company that their cooking was made impossible by such intrusions have long since stopped. After the strike of '53 cooking was rendered redundant as the higher wage afforded the women restaurant fare at the local town's greasy spoon. Besides which, the sort of tides that crept into the residence occurred but twice or thrice a season. Indeed, the nuisance created was trifling.

Bertha is on the "sidewalk," crawling. The trek across Main Street to the boardwalk had taken everything out of Bertha.

"Fucking btstsh" dribbles from her numb lips.

She glances furtively from side to side. The indignity of her position does not escape her. Being older than most of her co-workers, she is much more vulnerable to the elements. Bertha donned all the sweaters she brought to cannery row and her coat to keep warm. She spent the whole night drinking in the rain on the hill behind the city and now all of her winter gear is waterlogged. The fifteen extra pounds make it impossible for her to move. She curses and prays no one sees her.

Her short pudgy fingers clutch at the side of residence number thirteen in an effort to rise above her circumstances. She is gaining the upper hand when a mocking giggle slaps her about the head and ears.

"Fucking btstsh."

Trapped. Emiserated. Resigned. What the hell? She is no different from anyone else. Her memory reproaches her with the treasure of a different childhood. A childhood filled with the richness of every season, when not a snowflake fell unnoticed. Her memory retreats to another time.

*　*　*

The early autumn sunlight danced across lush green hillsides. Diamond dewdrops glistened from each leaf. Crisp air and still warm sun excited the youth. Chatter and bantering laughter filled the air. Bertha in her glory punched out one-liners and smiled at the approval of the old ladies who chuckled behind their aging hands. Things were different then. Each girl was born in the comfort of knowing how she would grow, bear children and age with dignity to become a respected matriarch.

On the hills, basket on her back, Bertha was not called Bertha. She wanted to hear her name again, but something inside her fought against its articulation. In her new state of shame she could not whisper, even to herself, the name she had taken as woman. Old Melly staggered into view, eyes twinkling. Bertha didn't really want to see her now.

"Hey Bertie," a giggle hollered out her nickname, unmindful of the woman's age and her own youth. "I got some wine."

"Khyeh, hyeh, yeh" and the circle of memory that crept out at her from the fog dimmed, but refused to recede. You had another upbringing before all this, the memory chided her. The efforts of the village women to nurture her as keeper of her clan, mother of all youth, had gone to naught. Tears swole from behind her eyes. "Damn wine," she muttered to herself. In the autumn hills of her youth the dream of motherhood had already begun to fade. Motherhood, the re-creation of ancient stories that would instruct the young in the law of her people and encourage good citizenship from even the babies, had eluded her.

In the moment of her self-recrimination, Bertie contemplated going home. Home? Home was a young girl rushing through a meadow, a cedar basket swishing lightly against dew-laden leaves, her nimble fingers plucking ripe fat berries from their branches, the wind playfully teasing and tangling the loose waist-length black hair that glistened in the autumnal dawn while her mind enjoyed the prospect of becoming ... becoming ... and the words in English would not come. She remembered the girl, the endless stories told to her, the meanings behind each story, the careful coaching in the truth that lay behind each one, the reasons for their telling, but she could not, after fifty years of speaking English, define where it was all supposed to lead. Now all that remained was the happiness of her childhood memories against the stark emptiness of the years that stretched behind them.

Her education had been cut short when her great-grandfather took a christian name. She remembered a ripple of bewildered tension for which her language had no words to describe or understand what had gone through the village. The stories changed and so did the language. No one explained the intimacies of the new feeling in either language. Confusion, a splitting within her, grew alongside the murmur that beset the village. Uncertainty closed over the children. Now, even the stories she had kept tucked away in her memory escaped her. She stared hard down the narrow boardwalk trying to mark the moment when her memories had changed.

The priest had christened the most important man in the village. Slowly, christians appeared in their ranks. The priest left no stone unturned. Stories, empowering ceremonies, became pagan rituals, pagan rituals full of horrific shame. Even the way in which grooms were chosen changed. The old women lost their counsel seats at the fires of their men. Bighouses were left to die and tiny homes isolated from the great families were constructed. Little houses that separated each sister from the other, harbouring loneliness and isolation. Laughter died within the walls of these little homes. No one connected the stripping of woman-power and its transfer to the priest as the basis for the sudden uselessness all the people felt. Disempowered, the old ladies ceased to tell stories and lived out their lives without taking the children to the hills again.

For a short time, life was easier for everyone. No more shaking cedar, collecting goat hair or carefully raising dogs to spin the wool for their clothing. Trade — cash and the securing of furs by the village men — replaced the work of women. Bertha could not see that the feelings of anxiety among the youth were rooted in the futureless existence that this transfer of power created. A wild and painful need for a brief escape from their new life drove youth into the arms of whiskey traders.

An endless stream of accommodating traders paddled upriver to fleece the hapless converts. Those who lacked traplines began disappearing each spring to the canneries, where cash could be gotten. Young women followed on their heels. The police, too, gained from this new state of affairs. As the number of converts increased, so did the number of drinkers. Interdiction caught up with those unfortunates not skilled at dodging the police. Short stays as guests in the queen's hotel — jail — became the basis for a new run of stories, empty of old meaning. The rupture of the old and the rift created were swift and unrelenting. Things could be bought with money, and wages purchased the things of life much more swiftly and in greater quantities than did their pagan practices. Only great-grandmother, much ridiculed for her stubbornness, remained sober and pagan to her death. Her face lingered in the fog while Bertha wondered why the old woman had stopped talking to her. The process was complete before Bertha was out of her teens. Then she, too, joined the flow of youth to cannery row.

Bertha had come to cannery row full of plans. Blankets could be purchased with the cash she earned. How could she have known the blankets they sold were riddled with sickness? She paid the trader who delivered the blankets, as had some of the other youth.

She experienced the same wild abandon that life outside the watchful eye of grannies and mothers gave rise to. They learned to party away the days of closure, when there were not enough fish to work a whole shift. At season's end they all got into their boats and headed home. A lone canoe bobbed in the water just feet from the shore of their village; a solitary old man paddled out to greet them.

"Go back, death haunts the village, go back." Confused, they went back The story of the blankets did not catch up to them until years later. In their zeal to gift their loved ones they had become their killers. In their confusion and great guilt, wine consoled them.

✹ ✹ ✹

Bertha stared blankly at her swollen hands. With blurred vision she peered unsteadily towards hut number nine. It wasn't home. She had no home. Home was fifty years ago and gone. Home was her education forever cut short by christian well-meaning. Home was the impossibility of her ever becoming the intellectual she should have been; it was the silence of not knowing how it all came to pass. Slowly her face found the young girl leaning out of the doorway.

"Ssr."

She lumbered reluctantly to where the giggle sat, her mouth gaping in a wide grin, exposing prematurely rotten teeth. Bertha could hardly look at her. No one as young as this girl should have rotten teeth. It marred her flawlessly even features. The large, thickly-lashed black eyes only sharpened the vileness of bad teeth. What a cruel twist of fate that this girl, whose frame had not yet acquired the bulk that bearing children and rearing them on a steady diet of winter rice and summer wine creates, should be burdened with a toothless grin before her youth was over.

The consumption of wine was still rational in the girl's maiden state, though not for long. Already the regularity of her trips to the bootlegger was beginning to spoil her eyes with occasional shadows. Her delicately shaped face sometimes hinted of a telling puffiness. On days like that it was hard for the girl to pose as a carefree and reckless youth. Today was not such a day.

Bertha hesitated before sitting, staring hard at the jug on the table. Unable to leave, but not quite up to sitting down, she remained rooted to the spot. She struggled with how it came to be that this girl from her village was so foreign to her. The moment threatened the comfort of shallow oblivion the girl needed. A momentary softness came over her face as she beckoned Bertha to sit. "Relax, Bertha, have a drink." Bertha sighed and sat down. The girl shucked the tenderness and resumed her gala self.

By day's end the jug was wasted and so were the women. There had been conversations and moments of silence, sentimental tears had been shed, laughter, even rage and indignation at the liberties white-male-bottom-pinchers took with Native women had been expressed. In all, the drunk had been relatively ordinary, except for a feeling that kept sinking into the room. It seemed to the girl to come from the ceiling and hang over their heads. The feeling was not identifiable and its presence was inexplicable. Nothing in particular brought it on. Only the wine chased the feeling from the windowless room. For the giggle, these moments were sobering, but Bertha seemed unruffled by them. If she was bothered, she betrayed no sign. At such moments, the giggle snatched the jug and furiously poured the liquid into her throat. The wine instantly returned the young girl's world to its swaying, bleary, much more bearable state.

Bertha rarely left anything started unfinished, even as concerns a jug of wine. But the more she drank the more she realized she did not know this woman, this daughter who was not nurtured by her village grandmothers, but who had left as a small child and never returned to her home. She was so like all the youth who joined the march to cannery row of late. Foreign and mis-educated. Callous? Was that what made them so hard to understand?

The brutal realization that she, Bertha, once destined to have been this young woman's teacher, had nothing to give but stories — dim, only half-remembered and barely understood — brought her up short. Guilt drove her from her chair before the bottle was empty. The feeling again sank from the ceiling, shrouding the girl in terror. Foreboding feelings raced through her body, but her addled consciousness could not catch any one of them and hold it long enough for her mind to contemplate its meaning.

Bertha stopped at the door, turned and stumbled back to the shaking girl. She touched her so gently on the cheek that the girl would hardly have been sure it happened except the touch made her eye twitch and the muscles in her face burn. The realization that the gulf between them was too great, their difference entrenched by Bertha's own lack of knowledge, saddened Bertha. Bertha wanted to tell her about her own unspoiled youth, her hills, the berries, the old women, the stories and a host of things she could not find the words for in the English she had inherited. It was all so paralyzing and mean. Instead Bertha whispered her sorrow in the gentle words of their ancestors. They were foreign to the girl. The touch, the words, inspired only fear in her. The girl tried to relieve herself by screaming — no sound found its way out of her throat. She couldn't move. The queerly gentle and wistful look on Bertha's face imprinted itself permanently on the memory of the girl. Then Bertha left.

Bertha's departure broke the chains that locked the girl's body to the chair. Her throat broke its silence and a rush of sobs filled her ears. "Damn wine, damn Bertie. Damn," and she grabbed the jug. As the warm liquid jerked to her stomach the feeling floated passively to the ceiling and disappeared. Not convinced that Bertha's departure was final, she flopped the length of her body onto the bunk and prayed for the ill-lit, rat-filled cannery come morning to be upon her soon. Her body grew heavy and her mind dulled. Sleep was near. Before she passed out, her mind caught hold of the notion that she ought to have said goodbye to Bertha. Still, she slept.

* * *

Bertie's absence at the cannery went unnoticed by all but the foreman. The young girl had blocked the memory of the disturbing evening from her mind. They had been drunk. Probably Bertie's still drunk, ran her reasoning. The foreman, however, being a prudent and loyal company man, thought of nothing else but Bertie's absence. By day's end, he decided by the following reasoning to let her go: Now, one can withstand the not infrequent absences of the younger, swifter and defter of the Native workers. But Bertie is getting old, past her prime, so much so that even her half century of experience compensates little for the disruption of operational smoothness and lost time that her absence gives rise to. Smoothness is essential to any enterprise wishing to realize a profit, and time is money.

This decision was not easily arrived at. He was not totally insensitive to human suffering. He had been kept up all night weighing the blow to Bertie, and the reaction of the other workers that firing her might cause, against the company's interest in profits, before finally resolving to fire her. Firing her could produce no results other than her continuing to be a souse. As for the workers, they would be angry but he was sure they wouldn't do anything. In any case, he was the foreman and if he didn't put his foot down these Natives were sure to walk all over him. Her absence again this morning convinced him that he had made the right decision. Still, he could not bring himself to say anything until the end of the day, in case the others decided to walk off the job. No sense screwing up the whole day over one old woman.

In a very loud voice, the foreman informed Bertie's nephew that his auntie Bertie was fired and could he tell her to kindly collect her pay and remove herself by week's end to whence she came.

"Can't be done."

"I beg your pardon, and why not? I have every authority to fire every one of you here."

His voice rose and all became quiet but for the hum of machinery. The blood of the workers boiled with shame at the tone of this white man. No one raised their eyes from their fixed position on their work and no one moved.

"Can't be done is all," the nephew flatly replied without looking at the foreman. His hands resumed work, carefully removing the fins from the fish.

"I asked you why not, boy." Angry as he was, he couldn't fire Bertie's nephew. Had he been a shirker, he would have, but Bertie's nephew was one of the more reliable and able of his workers, so he could not fire him. All he could do was sneer "boy" at him and hope that this, the soberest and most regular worker, did not storm out in defiance of the foreman's humiliating remark.

"She's dead."

An agonized scream split the silence, and the knife that so deftly beheaded the fish slipped and deprived the lovely young girl of her left thumb and giggle forever.

Who's Political Here?

"Give me that, thanks," and I put the toilet paper back where it belongs, after catching it in mid-air before she managed to throw it into the toilet bowl.

"Excuse me." I grabbed the washrag and then both girls, removing them from the temptation of playing in the toilet by pushing them out of the bathroom, while my toothbrush vigorously scraped at my dentures. I strolled into the kitchen. My husband was standing there, looking kind of lost. He had that I'm-about-to-bawl-you-out look, so I started to ignore him before he even spoke.

"Do you think you could do laundry?" he said with the tone of voice that implies it has been at least a month since the last time I had done laundry and in between then and now I had been particularly unproductive. I put my teeth in, ran the water for coffee and mumbled some sort of bored affirmation.

"Could you pass me that hat?" He doesn't. He says something about not having any underwear, that it's in the laundry, and then I crawl over the table, grab the hat and, on jumping to the floor, snatch the matches from one girl's hand, then lean over to turn off the stove the other one has turned on. Thank Christ this kitchen is pathetically small. He leaves the room.

"Glgbltglgl-blk-th-blk," my youngest babbles, inflecting her nonsense in a way that suggests she knows what she is trying to say.

"Yeah, I know what you mean, I get that way sometimes too."

"Here, Mommy," the other little girl hands me her sister's shoes. She is three and really does know what's going on. We are all getting ready to go out. Mothers have an identifiably different sense of movement when they are getting ready to go out, and kids know it.

"Stiffen your leg, stiffen your leg ... stiffen, that's it, stiffen ..." Oh Christ, one of these days she is going to get it, after all. "*I* stiffen my leg when I put on my shoes." I hold her on my lap and Tania tries to help. She has reached the age of insistent and cheerful incompetence. I never discourage her assistance, so everything we do takes twice the time.

"Who are you talking to?" He is back in the room.

"Columpa."

"She can't talk."

"You asked me who I was talking to, not who was talking to me. What are you going to do today?" I grab the stroller, a giant second-hand English pram that no longer has the bonnet or basket, just the frame and seat, and haul it over the porch to the sidewalk. He has to follow me to answer. I think this humbling exercise of following me around and answering my questions annoys him, but he thinks it too petty to mention. Further, he is still a little pissed about the underwear shit — no pun intended. I come back in with him at my heels.

"I'm going to poster downtown." Terrific. He posters while I manoeuvre the logistics of shopping, nurturing and fulfilling my laundress duties. I take the shopping cart and the two girls and go out again.

"Where are you going? To do the laundry?" If I had the emotional intensity I would either laugh or cuff him, because this last remark is so obviously a disguised accusation of my general recalcitrance, but I have lost the heart to do either.

"Sure."

"How come the cart is empty?"

"I haven't finished shopping," to him, and "Take that out of your ear," to Columpa. "Only put your elbow in you ear." She tries, but fails, but keeps trying. At least her mind is off sticking the pencil in her ear and she doesn't cry when I put it in my purse.

"You said you were going to do laundry." He is whining now. There is nothing worse than hearing a grown man whine. Grown man. Since when have you known a man to really grow up, Lee. I agree that I am going to do the laundry, today, and put both girls in the stroller (back-to-back), and haul the shopping cart and kids down the lane. He is standing there on the porch looking dejected.

"Hey." I stop without turning around and try to bury the exasperation that wants expression. "You look like one of those sixteenth-century fish-mongers, pushing her cart with grim determination." He finds this amusing. One, I don't look like a European anything, and two, the word is fish-wif. Fish-wif means fish-drudge and is the father of wife, but I don't say that. I roll the buggy and pull the cart. I couldn't laugh but I did manage to turn around and give him a condescending smile. He is not an idiot and resents my lack of appreciation for his joke. Another obstacle to hurdle.

"Bldthbldbld."

"Cambie wants a cookie," Tania tells me.

"Does she?" Beats me how Tania can understand her babble. Of course, figuring out that the kid wants a cookie can't be too difficult because even if it weren't true, it would at least shut her up and she'd forget what she really did want. Last but not least, Tania's desire for a cookie would be satisfied. I get the cookie, grumbling a whole bunch of stuff about how I never had them as a child, they probably aren't good for you and so forth. They don't care much about all that.

On route to Safeway Columpa addresses every single citizen with a cute little "Hi," four or five times each. Every time she says it Tania insists I look at her and acknowledge her intellectual brilliance — until it about drives me to distraction.

"Hey."

"Sa-aay, Frankie. How are you?" When the only humans you have to talk to are under four and making demands or over thirty and barking out orders, and they all complain when they aren't fulfilled, you really appreciate some guy on the street saying "hey" to you, even if he is an obnoxious womanizer. He sidles over and asks what I am doing. I tell him I am on my way to Safeway to do a little shopping.

"Where are you going to put the groceries?"

"In the cart."

"How the hell are you going to wheel the cart and the kids home?" Men are not known for their resourcefulness. They are inhibited by their own self-consciousness. If it is going to look funny, they won't do it. I jump inside the cart's handle and hold the handle of the cart and stroller together, taking mincing little steps. Frankie laughs. I secretly curse him because my next-to-useless husband is downtown having fun postering while I have to shop and do the laundry and his jerky friend is laughing at me, but I don't let on I am mad.

He is gleeking at me now. I can hardly wait to turn forty. Then the men my age may be less obsessed with fucking. He offers help and I take it. I have to put up with gross physical nuances like having his arm accidentally brush my breasts, but I don't care. Under the coercive pressure of hauling fifty pounds of babies and another seventy-five of groceries a full five blocks, the stupid little rubs don't seem so bad. It's his great pretence at morality, his sneakiness and his belief that I belong to my husband that really get to me. If I were to suggest we jump in bed, he would ask me about my husband; he does not think of him while he is brushing my tits, though. *Ding-dong*.

I virtually run through the aisles, throwing things into the cart. The good behaviour mode of either of my children spans only forty-five minutes. I had wasted five precious minutes on the street talking to this fool and now they are getting restless. Screams, tears and tantrums are next.

Frankie is wheeling the cart and I am at the buggy's helm. We are moving fast. The girls love it. Columpa suddenly drops off to sleep in the middle of an incoherent bunch of babble that has a complaining tone to it. She starts swaying back and forth. Tania tries to hold her up. She is just barely managing to keep her sister in the buggy. I can't help laughing.

"You look beautiful when you laugh." Too much. It is the sort of remark you might hear in a John Wayne movie — you know, he has just paddled some poor woman's backside, she's hollering, falsely indignant, and he says, "You know you're cute when you're mad," and then they roll around — passionately — in the hay. I wouldn't care one way or another about a tumble in the hay with this guy. Sex, love and morals have never formed a triumvirate in my mind, and I'm still young enough to be gleeful over doing something I am not supposed to be doing. But the line was so bad. Still, I smile full in his face, encouraging him.

Tania is nodding out. At home, I put them both to bed, lock the door and confront his amorousness. He doesn't resist. It's all so naughty and hence lovely.

"What about Tom?"

"Christ." I had forgotten that I knew he was going to say that. "How long has he been on your mind? When did you start thinking about him, when you were ... "

He cuts me off. He just thought of it now.

"Well, in that case, we are all too late to do anything about it, so why don't we stop musing over hopeless things?"

The doorbell rings and I move to answer it. He grabs me and asks "what about him?" again. I wonder if some of the grey matter from his brain has sneaked out through his manhood. Jeezuss. The doorbell again. No time to convince this twit that people come in and out of my house all the time and it isn't anybody's business which of them I sleep with, most especially not Tom's. Frankie is not dealing with this at all well. He better not make some stupid suggestion about my leaving my husband or I will beat him to a pulp.

"Tom is in jail," and Don rolls in to take a seat.

"Great. You want dinner?"

Frankie comes downstairs and is calmly greeted by our mutual friend. Frankie's face is painted with thirty different shades of guilt. I try not to think about it. It didn't go by Don; the whole scene looks kind of funny.

"He is in jail," Don repeats himself with great patience, trying to articulate the significance of what he said.

"Yeah. I heard you. Do you want some dinner?" and I start banging the pots and pans. In 1974 I was still convinced that my whole reason for being was rooted in mothering my daughters, my husband and *his* friends. Don expected me to get all excited. What was new? He probably got drunk and landed himself in the drunk tank again.

"For postering." Well. Pardon my heresy, but that was worth at least one belly laugh. He must be the only person in Vancouver to have been charged with postering.

"It is fifty dollars to bail him out."

"Fifty dollars. Well, I just happen to have it in my ass-hip pocket. When does he go to court?"

"Tomorrow."

"He can stay there until then."

Don looks at me, a little pained. I want to say look, asshole, I do all the laundry, cook and clean after that man, type all his leaflets after midnight and mother his two children so that he can risk postering downtown. Who is in prison here? *My* sentence is "till death do us part"; he's going to be there overnight. I don't say it; he wouldn't understand.

In the corner, Frankie has gone catatonic with guilt. Don turns down dinner — he is miffed about my not taking the "jail in the line of duty" as seriously as I ought. In some perverse fashion he thinks that turning down a dinner invite is going to offend me. This guy believes that I cook, clean and mother because I really think it's the end-all and be-all in my life. He leaves, mumbling.

"I don't know if this is right." Frankie is still bemoaning our tumble in the living room, rendered all the more disgusting for him by the knowledge that Tom was in jail while he had been helping himself to his lovely wife.

"Honey, if you are talking about morals, it was all wrong." I hear the girls scurrying around upstairs. Frankie keeps mumbling about Tom, how we shouldn't have "done it," etc., while I bang pots and pans. Boy, men are miserable. They do everything they can to get between your legs and then whine about it later. I could have hit him.

"Mahmm!" My youngest is screaming and being hauled down the stairs by the oldest. She has hold of a toy that the other one is clinging to. Tania, in trying to get away from her, is dragging the little one down the stairs. They are both crying, someone else is knocking at the door, so I put the toy on top of the fridge without bothering to tell them they can't have anything that they fight over, pick them up, coo a little, then answer the bloody door.

"C'mon in." A couple more of Tom's friends come in and sit down. The conversation centres on his arrest. It's amusing. Arrested for postering. What next? I've heard that during the thirties they arrested people who made speeches without flying a Canadian flag, but this is forty years later. Maybe they'll start demanding that we get a permit to demonstrate.

"What do you say to the man? Uh, excuse me sir, but, uh, can I have permission to demonstrate against you? I mean, it's like a kid asking his mom for permission to curse the Jeezuss out of her." That remark brought laughter from me only. "Not funny?" I ask, serving coffee all around.

"Bad analogy," someone mumbles.

"OK." ... "Don't put your fingers in the butter," and I move it out of the reach of my youngest girl. "Put the hat back on his head," to the older one. "Cream, sugar?" ... "Practically speaking, fifty bucks is a bit of a wad. I don't have it."

They seem to understand, though their faces look a little

pinched. I resume cooking and someone suggests making a "run." I tell them that that is not a good plan. While Tom is home, I put up with that shit, but I wasn't about to while he wasn't here. The room gets a little stiff and quiet, the pair start to fidget, drink their coffee, mumble about things they have to do, then leave, along with Don.

Frankie is upset. "Why'd you tell them that?"

"Because I don't want them partying in my house." I grab a diaper, change the baby, wash my hands and tend to dinner.

"Don't you think it was kind of rude?"

"Yeah, that's why I told them no."

"I didn't mean *them*."

"*I* did. Pass me the cloth next to your elbow." He does. He just can't leave it alone. Somehow, he has it in his head that Tom would have let these two buy beer, drink and puke all over my house in full view of my toddlers, and while I agree he probably would have, he isn't here now and Frankie doesn't think it's OK for me to refuse them the dubious privilege of making fools of themselves in my house in Tom's absence.

"But ... Tom ... "

I remind him that he is not in a position to talk about what Tom allows or disallows, as it is a definite given that Tom has never permitted his friends to help themselves to his wife. That hits home. He asks what we are going to do.

"We? I am cooking supper and you are sitting there waiting for it to be cooked, passing me this and that as I might require. Pass me the salt." He does. Cambie grabs it before I manage to intercept his bad pass. I have to lean into the pass and try to get it from her before she pours salt on the floor. I don't make it. It is in my hand upside down.

"These guys need a good licking."

"Yeah, I know, but they are all grown up so it is kind of hard to convince them to bend over."

"I mean your daughters." Now he has really gone and done it.

"Look, sweetheart, you are really pretty and your body works the way it ought to, but father to my children you are not. Even if you were, I doubt very much that I would take your advice."

"Just look at them, they're wild." They are under the sofa playing in the box of shoes. The sofa is not really a sofa. It is two planks plunked atop four square bricks. They are too big to sit under it without raising the planks with their heads. It does look a little out of hand, but they aren't hurting anyone so I don't bother telling them not to have fun. Toys they lack and if I don't let them play with whatever is at hand, I will have to run after them enforcing ridiculous prohibition laws with violence. I have neither the time nor the energy, much less the inclination.

"I never did want to be a cop, so I don't see why I ought to run around policing them." He doesn't get it. Supper is ready and I take them to the bathroom to wash up. The baby keeps trying to grab the soap, the elder is obsessed with rubbing her hands together to create bubbles and foam. I manage to rinse them off and herd them to the table.

"What about us?" Oh, good Christ, here it comes again. Tania says, "What does 'what about us' mean, Mommy?" ... "Oh, never mind, he doesn't mean anything." ... "Then why did he say it?" ... "Well, what about us?" ... "Pass the butter. Nothing." ... "What do you mean, nothing?" ... "Yeah." ... "Mommy, I don't want da peez." ... "Eat them, they're good for you," and I plunk the food into the baby's mouth. "I really don't believe you, Frankie. I am married to your gawdamn friend for chrissakes." ... "Gawdamn for chrissakes," Tania repeats the choicer words. "Well, why did you do it?" ... "Look, I did not do it by myself, number one, and number two, we both thought it was a good idea at the time." ... "Don't put that in your hair." ... "Pass me a rag, she put it in her hair."

"This is a gawdamn zoo."

"You better leave, Frankie," I don't need anyone calling my girls animals to their faces. I put some more food in the baby's mouth. Tania is studying her piece of meat. I tell her it's probably best to study the taste and never mind how it looks. The phone rings and I jump to answer it. The doorbell goes off and the baby stands up on wobbly legs and half crawls out of the high chair. I holler at Frankie to help her. The person at the other end of the line says "What?" Frankie is too late and I curse him. This really offends the other person. I have to hang up on her 'round about the time when she is asking me what is going on.

I figure it out while I am comforting my little girl. Frankie is all indignant that I used him. If *I* had been upset about him taking me for granted, everything would have been normal. I was supposed to be upset and shocked about what we did and he could not handle that I felt no remorse, no guilt, nor any sorrow. How can one man be so many different kinds of a fool? I never did learn to act ashamed, so now he was going to make me pay by picking my life apart, including attacking my parenting skills and the conduct of my children. I wanted to tell Frankie that the lady on the phone was Tom's girlfriend ... that he doesn't think I know about her ... Tom thinks me a fool who believes the relationship is strictly political, but I can smell her all over him when he gets home after "serving the people" with her — whatever that means. I don't say anything because he would insist that that's different.

Frankie doesn't leave. The doorbell rings again and he goes to answer it. More of Tom's friends come in. They all discuss the "politics" of Tom's arrest.

"He was probably arrested because the subject matter of the poster was South Africa," someone says.

I resume doing dishes and mothering my daughters and only half listen to the chatter. Some of it is pure theatre. It seems absurd to me to attach a whole world analysis to a simple postering charge. It never occurs to anyone that maybe cops and business people don't like their "property" smutted up with lefty posters. They act like it was part of a global capitalist conspiracy to arrest their leader, Tom. An attack on freedom of speech, at least.

"We don't have freedom of speech in this country," and I

mumble out a little lesson in Canadian legalism. "Parliament is accountable to the Crown, not the people; human rights, free speech, etc. are not part of our judiciary."

No one pays any attention. Patti has come over and joined the guys in the "rap." I can't figure out why she is so acceptable to them. When she talks they respond. I find her exaggerated, rhetorical claptrap annoying — they eat it up. I get the feeling from all of them that college kids puff up their minds in order to feel like they have some sort of meaning or universal order to their lives.

Patti has been having an affair with Tom. I don't mind that so much, but I think it kind of cheeky of her to come by my house and expect me to wait on her hand and foot while she is helping herself to my husband, ostensibly behind my back. She is no ordinary woman. Most of the women who come to visit me, my friends, help with the dishes, the kids, stuff like that, while they're here. Not this one. She acts like me and the kids are dead except when she wants coffee. She has some sort of secret inside of her that inspires men to respect her brain and not intrude on her person by reducing her to a servant. I envy her position.

She holds her coffee cup up and says "thank you" to me. It's weird, but before I slept with Frankie I used to think of all this as normal. Now, I just look at her dumbly. Annoyed, she gets up and tries to pour herself a cup. The kids get in the way (perfect timing, girls), and she puts the cup down. She suggests making a "run." Again I say "no" and they all get this funny look on their faces like they're constipated. Patti asks why not.

"Because I said so." I go to the door and open it. The room empties of all the visitors except Frankie. He is not happy with the kind of person I'm becoming but he can't leave me alone. I go to put the girls to bed. Frankie sits downstairs in silence while I read them a story or two and make a couple up. At 9:00 p.m. I am lying on the sofa and Frankie mumbles that he doesn't understand me. I don't understand me either, I tell him. It seems kind of lame that I should think all of this adultery stuff a pile of cow dung, but it is what I think. I'm jealous of Patti, not sexually, but because my husband and his friends accord her her mind. I can't explain that to Frankie. I can't tell him that she has something that I obviously lack — something that tells all of the men around her that she is to be taken very seriously — and that I would like to have some of that. I sure as hell can't tell Frankie that he means nothing to me beyond that one sexual encounter, which I don't care to repeat. What a mix-up. It's all too complicated and inexplicable for me.

"Go home, Frankie. Tom is in jail." I roll over and face the wall. Everything is fuzzy after that. Rolling, changing emotions float around inside me as I lie looking at the old hand-besmudged wall and wonder what is happening to me, why I don't care about Tom's incarceration the way the others do, don't feel its earth-shattering importance, and why all of a sudden I resent them not thinking I am clever. Somehow what I am feeling seems more important to me than Tom's incarceration, and I think they should see it that way too. The changing emotions roar around inside, taking up speed and intensity until fear starts to ride over it all like the surf in a stormy sea. Panic almost overtakes me when my old granny's face grins through the wall.

I had not seen or thought about her since the last tear I shed just after she died a dozen years ago in our old backwoods bush home. I hang onto the picture of her face against the white wall I am still staring at. It calmed me some to see her. She was telling me that confusion is just like any storm — it rages, but at the end is the beautiful clear light of day. Stop it, and you lock your confusion up and stay that way. Let it roll, let it rage, and she fades.

I did. I had no idea that a storm of thoughts could be so exciting. Like a hurricane, crazy and destructive, some of it; sometimes like a flood and at other times a tornado, but always the thoughts and feelings were exhilarating. I don't remember much of what I thought about — not much of it settled down for me to hang onto, but the last thing I remember is seeing my girls and thinking, yes, they are wild. Wild, untamed, not conquerable, and I was going to go on making sure they stayed that way. A wicked little grin came over me while I was tossed about in the sea of my own storm, my wild little girls at my side and blessed sleep beckoning me home.

Worm

Written in collaboration with Sid Bobb

All of my stories are written to entertain and teach my children. "Worm" is special to me because it is a synthesis of a story given to me by someone else and worked up in my own imagination. It is the story of the momentous struggle my three-year-old son had coming to grips with life and death and with the loneliness that separation from his sisters gave rise to. It took him two weeks to tell me the story. Because he knew I was a writer he kept saying, "Write this down, this is my story." The language is partly mine, partly his; likewise we share the story in its telling.

A fat, glossy, peach-coloured worm with a blue vein encircling his middle rises from the ground, pushing aside small bits of earth that cling momentarily to his sticky body, unmindful of the eyes studying him. Insistently, doggedly, he wriggles his front; middle and rear follow suit. Another inch of turf is covered.

"Worming ... worming ... worming along." Siddie's words come punched between cheeks squeezed by delicately clenched fists pressed hard against his face. Lips flupping out mumbled sounds at worm, who's just inching along.

"Doin' his bizness," flups through his contorted little face.

"Worming his way out of dirt bizness. Trouble must be dirty," he surmises, "dirty bizness, cuz Mom always sez, 'you mustn't try and worm your way out of trouble.' Wormin' is when you move up and down and sideways but your body someways goes straight." It was for the crouched little boy a revelation, though he did not see or feel its significance. Worm showed him by doing his business.

"He is so shiny and pretty pink, nice and wigglesome. I wonder how cum big people don't likum?" Fat, pink worm stops and the tip of him worms forward to wiggle in the thin shaft of sunlight that has squeezed itself through the myriad of salmonberry leaves to the black earth below. Sunshine, so little of it gets squeezed to this corner of the yard.

The yard. The little fellow's mind, like a moving camera, travels back to the time when the yard was a tangled mass of roots and spikes he kept tripping over. Then uncle Roge, 'n' uncle Dave, 'n' Wally, 'n' Brenda 'n' Lisa 'n' Cum-pa came. Everyone was rushing around, digging and pulling roots and carrying them to where the fire was going to be, only Dennis didn't know it wasn't a fire yet, cuz he kept saying, "Take roots down to the fire." Siddie chuckles to himself at the image of his step-dad.

"That Dennis, he just kept hollering, 'take it down to the fire' and everyone took the roots to the fire." Siddie knew it wasn't a fire. It was a stick mountain, but he didn't want to hurt Dennis's feelings, so he pretended it was a fire just like everyone else. He looked up. Stick mountain is still there, a lonely sentinel watching out for the return of all the people. A great wrenching clutches his small chest, twists itself into unspeakable pain.

"Tania ... Cum-pa," he whispers mournfully to fat worm, and silent tears wash both little fists that press themselves tight at the touch of his tears. The realization that divorce has separated him from his beloved sisters falls on him with terrible force.

"The back of my hands is wet and shiny like you, fat worm ... are you lonely too, fat worm?"

An alert, red-breasted robin from her perch in the apple tree overhead has decided the crouched figure below poses no threat to her midday meal. In one graceful motion she sweeps down and snatches the worm out from under the boy's gaze.

A tiny piece of earth drops on his face, mixing with the tears that course down his cheeks to splat on his grimy hands. A scream swells from inside, gains volume, but is stopped in his throat by the picture of gold and green overhead, at the centre of which a cheeping pair of gaunt babies cry out their incessant need for food. "Worm death is pain, baby birds are joy and somewhere in between wiggles loneliness." A little cloud scuttles across the sky, blocking out the brightness of nature's colours, and the tears clean his cheek of earth's trace.

A large pair of hands scoop him up. He buries his face on the chest of the big guy. The soft murmurs of the man erase the remnants of the lonely scream the boy could not cry out.

Maggie

Mama worked. In the early morning hours she rose, set crab traps with our little skiff, and after breakfast she pounded them up and sometime in the afternoon she took the crabs somewhere to be sold. She came home near to our bedtime. Maggie told me she remembered the very day Mama went to work for cash money. Maggie knew why too. Mama's marriage was a mess. Sometime after our dad left, she acquired a lover who didn't care much for her dependents. Maggie told me he was just a plain brute. I remember doubting her, thinking maybe it was us. All four of us were there, unwanted by our own dad, when he came. I could never see the point of wanting more from this stranger than what our own dad was prepared to give, but Maggie wouldn't hear it: "He is sick."

It was 1956. The year we got a television. Mama tried to finish work by six to watch the news. Maggie popped the corn and made tea and got the rest of us settled in to watch the show. The new black-and-white console stood out in stark contrast to the bare walls of our hold house with its overly simplistic furnishings. An old couch and chair, an oil heater which never seemed to have any oil in it, and a brand new television. All of us lined up on the couch quietly staring at the news, none of us figuring these things really happened.

When Mama was late, Maggie mocked the newscaster, filling

up the broadcast with words of her own. "Anti-colonial Black move-ments in Africa threaten" came from the newsman, followed by Maggie's "to 'kick ass' with white folks today." We laughed nerv-ously. No one in our community dared used the word "white" when talking about the others. No one told us it was forbidden, but we had never heard white people referred to as anything except "them people," and always they were mentioned in hushed tones. Maggie's cheek and brass scared us. She knew something was amiss and somehow figured "kicking ass" could fix it.

After the news, Mama closed her eyes and asked Maggie to read. Mama had four books: a Bible, an unabridged dictionary and two novels, *Germinal* and *Les Misérables*. Maggie threw her heart and soul into her voice when she read, dramatizing her own passionate dream of poor people "kicking ass" with "them people." Mama never suspected a thing.

In the early morning light I would sometimes wake up and catch Maggie writing in her diary, painting with words whatever pictures of the world she wanted. Travelling to places she had not been, and imagining herself doing things she would never be al-lowed to do.

Sat., Dec. 10, 1956

"Joey, Joey, Joey," an exasperated mother picked up bits and pieces of an electric train, shut off the power source and muttered softly the name of her errant son.

Joey was long gone. His little league cap plunked jauntily atop his fiery red hair, a glove in one hand, a bat over his shoulder and a softball in his ass-hip pocket. He had sauntered off to the cow field for a game with the boys.

On the little league team Joey was the back-catcher, but on the cow field he was agreeable to whatever position his mates wanted him to play. Today, he was first at bat. Tony was the pitcher and he threw Joey a dandy — WHAP! A line drive heading straight for sleepy Dave.

"Shee-it ... Chrisst ... Jeezuss," and a half-dozen bewildered boys circled Sleepy Dave, who lay peacefully motionless on the field about where the short stop ought to have been standing.

"Will ya look at the lump on his head?"

"Yeah." ... "What a beauty," and other such mumbling carried on while Gary ran for his dad. The story ends here, because adults are not allowed in the diary.

She finished reading me her story. I asked her how come mothers were allowed in the story.

"Mothers are girls, silly, they never have to grow up." Maggie shaped me. Maybe it was what happened a little while later which made her words stick so well in my mind. What she said was true. Even the ladies from our own community called themselves girls — little girls, growing girls, old girls, but all girls nonetheless. It took twenty-four years, amid much brouhaha and some pies in the faces of a few politicians whose names I disremember, for me to say *women* and not girls, but it happened. It was kind of hard for me. I was among the first young females to gain adult status, and it took me a long time to figure out what being an adult entailed. Maggie must have known:

Tues., Dec. 13, 1956

"Ann, put that down. Annie, for gawdsake." A firm wrist jerked the hammer from Annie's hand and the mouth who owned the hand spat out some nonsense about "gurlz, 'n' hammerz, 'n' shugger 'n' spice" and other such claptrap Ann tried not to think about.

"Why don't you play with your Barbie doll or something, for chrissakes."

"Cuz Barbie don't drive truck and I don't like pointy tits."

The woman cursing Ann gasped, turned white and red by turns, and finally sent Ann to her room: "Until your father comes home." In her room Ann lay back and laughed about the look on Mary's face when she had found her pounding nails into the garage floor. Even more precious was her mother's look when Ann disclosed her awareness of truck driving and tits.

I was curled up into a fetal position before Maggie finished reading, terrorized by the strangeness and the boldness of her story. No one in our village mentioned tits out loud. It was like we all pretended women didn't have such things. Maggie told me tits were used to feed babies, but I had never seen the young women feed them in such a way. I disbelieved her.

* * *

It was near Christmas and we were busy. For catholic women Christmas means a lot of work. Mama left the crab nets to cut apples and deer heart and grind it all up with suet to make minced meat. She got us all busy candying fruit for umpteen cakes, cooking pumpkins we had grown for pies and tarts, and baking, baking, baking. For three weeks now the house would be warm and Mama would be home. Mama kept up a constant chatter while we worked, spinning hilarious tales and making us all laugh. Except Maggie; she was outside chopping wood and splitting kindling or drawing oil, and she never heard Mama's stories.

Dec. 15, 1956
He was here again. Loud and mean ...

On the morning of the last day of school before the Christmas holidays Maggie was particularly quiet. She stared out the kitchen window at the beach below for what seemed like forever. The water was choppy. Choppy water meant cold. She didn't move; she just stood there watching the water thrash about. I moved up behind her, a shadow wanting bodily recognition. I watched the water and tried hard to feel what she was thinking, to see what she was seeing.

Each wave brought gallons of water forward to the shore, only to be hauled back by some invisible force to someplace no one ever saw. With all its steady movement, the ocean water never seemed to get anywhere. Odd how the movement of the waves didn't seem to have anything to do with the tide sneaking off a couple of times a day like it does.

"You see that, Stace?" The sound of her voice startled me. I didn't know she had seen me standing behind her. "There's a huge vacuum somewhere in the bowels of the ocean, sucking back the water and cutting it loose again. Regardless of the direction of the tide, the waves always seem to travel towards the shore. They are, tide and waves, as separate as a pair of divorcés with common children." Her voice took on a low, husky quality: "Mother sea is magic." She looked down at my face with the same condescending look old people use when they know they have pulled the wool over your eyes. She stroked my hair gently, put her arm around me and we both turned to watch the water for a while more. Little white-caps popped up here and there — ocean now — liquid cold. They looked like living creatures, swimming out there on the breast of the sea. Maggie groaned, wondering out loud if everyone was as pained as she was about the cold, softly whispering that they didn't seem to be.

"Do you want to eat?" The sound of Mama's voice startled her just a little. Maggie once told me that when she was staring out the window like that she'd kind of go a bit deaf. Mama's voice seemed to come through a tiny hole at the end of a long tube and it was almost painful to break loose from watching the water to listen to Mama.

Asking any of us if we wanted to eat was kind of rhetorical. Eating was not too regular at home, so we were always anxious to get on with it. Especially this time of year. Good Catholics like we were, we sacrificed immediate eating for Christmas celebrating. Maggie was always hungry. She was the thinnest of us all. Never in all her eleven years had she ever turned down food. But it was

like Mama to ask. Her sense of courtesy forbade her ordering us to
do anything except stop fighting.

Without answering, Maggie moved slowly towards the table.
I don't think she realized she still had a hold of me. I matched my
footsteps with hers and we moved to the table kind of stuck together.

She sat in silence for a long time between eating. I remember
how she watched us with intense fascination, chuckling out loud
at the smaller of us. The younger, fat, chubby hands grabbed at
their food. They clutched their bread overzealously, mish-mash-
ing it with their fingers, as though afraid someone might snatch
food from their tender grip. The older, more competent hands
held their spoons gracefully, their owners consuming the meal with
steady determination.

Maggie was always looking to see who wanted an extra bite.
After our plates were empty, if one of us looked around she would
spoon a little from her dish into our grateful mouths.

Most days Mama would disappear amid a flurry of instructions to Maggie and a furious pace of eating, dressing and hurrying out the door to check the traps. Maggie was left to mother us.
Chins were wiped, hair brushed and clothes fussed over. She read-
ied our lunches and hollered at Grampa in his cabin down below,
where the littlest ones stayed till Maggie and I came home from
school.

On this morning, time was running out. Maggie wolfed what
food was left, reached for her jacket and we headed out the door.
Her face wore a funny look of agitation. Christmas. Mama was
still here. No traps to set. Maggie didn't have to take the little ones
down the hill; still, she hesitated a little at the door. Mama mumbled something about "looks like snow" as we set off down the
street to the bus stop. Maggie's body jerked, but she never turned
around to see what Mama was saying.

Noon, Dec. 16, 1956

It is so cold, so cold. Not one set of hands seemed to mind getting ready to go out in the cold. I'm alone, so alone. The personal bride of cold. My insides rant and rave at the freezing rain, scream for relief from this dread of cold. This dread no one seems to share.

I have been "kept in" again. These fools have no idea their punishment is such a welcome relief. Alone in the classroom, I am spared having to face the cold and those little brutes they call my fellow pupils, with their hideous minds, who think mocking the earth-tones of my skin a great source of joy. How did they get this way?

This morning it was windy and raining a light frozen rain. It hit my face in sharp pinpricks. I hunched pathetically inside my jacket, but it didn't do a thing to keep the cold out or the warm in. I scrunched my fists into my jacket sleeves, but that too was a bit foolish. The cold crept inside, past my arms and clear to my chest. My body rattled, my walk laboured, my teeth clattered senselessly inside my head. Stacy trundled alongside of me, oblivious to the cold.

※　※　※

Maggie had told me not long before how she hated her teachers. She held them accountable for some of her emiserating and useless struggle against the cold. They were responsible for Maggie having acquired the asinine practice of lugging home a number of unused text books, exercise books and other such stuff as hopeful teachers insisted she would need to do her homework. She wrapped the useless books in a plastic bag and tucked them under one armpit. Invariably, they slipped and fell — like mutinous little beasts they jumped out of the bag and into some puddle. The leap to the dirty water always made Maggie laugh. She refused to do her homework. The struggle escalated. She told her teachers she was not going to do it — five hours of "this boring shit" was enough for one day. Her slender hands paid dearly for such honesty.

They had been keeping her in at noon and recess, and once a week the principal sought to force her hands to apply themselves more diligently to her homework by administering a few blows. She could have done without the blows, but didn't mind being kept in. She missed no one on the playground, viewed all white people as some sort of blight sent over by some wicked demon to plague us. There was not a single white person in the world whose company she would ever appreciate.

She hissed when she spoke of them. I cautioned her to try and "get along." She refused. When I told her the old people admonished us to appreciate all human beings, she retorted that none of the old people ever had to sit next to them hour after waking hour, watching the way they looked at us. They never had to face their ignorance, their mindlessness, their loudness. No. White people were a plague of locusts sent to torment us. When she wasn't ranting about them she as laughing at their stupidity.

She and I were sitting together on the bus one day, about a mile down the road, when she laughed out loud.

"Do you know, Stace, we're still going to be studying reading and writing when we are seventeen?"

"No-o." I was horrified.

"Yeah." Persuasively she argued between giggles: "I asked yesterday. I said, 'Mrs. Jamieson, I've been studying reading for six years now, when do you suppose I will have learned it?' She sez, 'What do you mean?' so I said, 'Well, when do you stop studying reading?' Then she sez, 'You don't. In high school it's called English. You study English all through high school and if you go on to university, you study it there too.' Well, Stace, right away this numbskull says the wrong thing. I said, 'Oh, and university English is for the slackers who never paid attention in high school?'

" 'Certainly NOT!' she sez in an offended kind of voice. Well, Jeezuss, Stace, what in the world do you figure takes these people so long to learn to read the very language they claim to speak?" She laughed. It wasn't the kind of laugh you let go when you are really enjoying yourself. It was the sort of cynical laugh you let out when you find something really stupid, but hopelessly unchangeable.

It was all too much for me. I laughed. Comic relief, I think. It didn't much matter — neither of us was going to go to university.

✻ ✻ ✻

The day got colder. Later in the afternoon, the sky spilled an apronload of her largest snowflakes on the ground. Not believing sky was really going to do that, Maggie had let herself get another after-school detention. I saw her leaving the classroom, her teacher shrieking "Get down to the principal's office this minute," and heard Maggie yell back at her "Go to hell, hag." I tried to make myself small and invisible in the hallway as I sneaked up behind the open office door.

The principal was probably a good man, but he was always on the side of the teachers — never considered the students' point of view. Bad for discipline, he must have thought. He came out of his office to where Maggie was sitting on the blue bench.

"Well, whaddaya say?"

"I hate cold." I knew it was the wrong answer. I wept from behind the door. *Don't do this Maggie*, I begged silently. *Don't be cheeky. Maybe if you said "sorry," he would let you come home.* I saw her face in my mind, her full mouth pursed in stubborn resistance. I shook in anticipation of her missing the bus. Mama never understood. She would be angry again. I could hear what she had yelled many times: "Just once, Maggie Joe, just once, you would think you could cooperate, do your damn school work and make it home on time to get your little brothers. Grampa's old …" I could see Maggie praying for Mama to be on her side, just once. *Maggie, please hush and say you're sorry.*

"What?" the principal asked, not understanding her answer.

"I beg your pardon," she corrected him, and the world grew large for me. I shrank behind the door, leaned against the wall and sighed. *Maggie, Maggie, Maggie.* She meant no harm. In Maggie's mind no hierarchy existed. Proper English and polite presentation were demanded of her, and so she demanded the same sense of courtesy from the principal.

"You know, young lady, your impudence will not see you through life."

"I don't see why not. Your rudeness hasn't hurt you." It was the last straw. I gave up hoping and left to catch the bus alone before I missed it too. I wanted to weep for her on the bus ride home, but pride bit my lips shut. I thought about Maggie having to walk home, three and a half miles by road, and wondered what went on in her mind to drive her to such madness. A little piece of me argued with my heart. *Maggie, you have got no sense. You shouldn't have done that. Why can't you do your work and just go with these people?* But my mind could not argue away the picture of Maggie, fearful of the cold, struggling to get home in the half-light of winter, dodging cars and dogs because some power-hungry creep kept her in.

I couldn't stop seeing Mama, incensed with Maggie's rebellious ways, and Grampa, crippled with arthritis, scuttling after the little children, unable to keep up. Mama, tense, wound up tighter than a drum, hauling traps, pounding crabs, day in and day out, and never making enough to feed her young. Maggie threatened our survival. She never got old enough to see that, but Mama knew. Intuitively I understood it too, in much the same way that I "knew" things Maggie thought and did.

An hour of sitting on the blue bench thinking about going home in the dark must have knocked the fight out of Maggie. When the principal let her go she mumbled a flat "thanks" without a hint of gratitude in her voice, and turned reluctantly towards the door. She paused a moment before leaving — I guess to consider asking him if she could use the phone. She must have decided the cold of the snow was warmer than the chill of having to beg, because she didn't say a thing. She left.

When I got home I offered to look after the little ones, hoping it would soften Mama's rage at Maggie's recalcitrance. They bubbled about, asking for Maggie. I told them she was still at school, for which I was battered with a whole series of "why's."

"Teacher kept her in."

"Why?"

"I don't know."

"How come?"

"I don't know." They badgered me until I told them she got a detention. They wanted to know what that was, what it looked like. Exasperated, I barked out "never mind," which made them cry for Maggie. I turned the TV on so they could watch cartoons while I stared out the window trying to picture Maggie's way home.

Dark would have settled in by the time she left the school, bringing a mean cold. I imagined her pencil-thin legs, unprotected, her little canvas running shoes soaking up the wet cold snow as she hurled her body against the wind. I pictured her hurting, hurting like a licking never could. Even the middle of her mind must have hurt. Three and a half miles by road or a mile straight through the bush. I knew that, dark and windy as it was, she would choose the bush, tearfully battling the cold one more time.

Sometime after four

My legs feel so thick. I don't know where I am. The wind is biting my chest. I can't drag myself forward anymore. The wind's bites have become more vicious. I tried, Mama, I clawed at bushes and branches, trying to pull my thick legs along, until my hands, too, grew still with the cold. The howl of the wind is a musical call, calling me to join it. I can barely write anymore.

She sat down on a fallen log in front of a baby cedar. The sapling danced for her, and the howl of the wind became a musical call to her to join them. She bid her diary adieu. They found her, half-lying on the log, still holding the plastic bag, just a hundred yards short of the road — almost home.

> *Dear Diary:*
> *Have you ever felt so cold*
> *you were warm — sleepy tired?*
> *Happy to give up the ignorant*
> *fight against the cold?*
>
> *Please, I haven't deserted you*
> *It's just that I am so lost*
> *and cedar calls me, dancing,*
> *swaying seductively ...*

✳ ✳ ✳

> *Dear Maggie:*
> *I typed out the contents of your diary and am keeping the copy. You noted on the very first page that should anything happen to you, the diary could be my friend. I really don't believe your diary wants to stay in this world without you, so I am returning her to rest with you for all eternity.*
> *Mama*

> *Dear Diary:*
> *When you see Maggie, tell her I love her and miss her beyond words.*
> *Stace*

Mama and me sneaked into the church at dawn and slipped the diary (minus the first page) into the coffin holding Maggie. In the stillness of the white dawn, before the tears came, I thought I heard Maggie say, Please Stace, little sister, tell them, tell them, I just couldn't fight the cold anymore.

Mama sat in despondent silence for days after your departure, Maggie. Her body was at your funeral but her heart didn't believe you were really gone. Christmas came and went without celebration. On New Year's Day, Mama's eyes filled with water and she mumbled, "Maggie got lost, that's all there was to it. She wanted to come home, but she got lost." She rolled a cigarette and asked me to read *Germinal*, "the part where the young girl becomes a woman just at the moment of her passing." The face of Maggie danced upon the page, her last look one of panic as she wandered in a tighter and tighter circle, struggling to find the road. My voice rolled out the drama of Zola's young woman, who, like Maggie, had never been a child. It filled up with the steely yarn of Maggie's courage as Zola's woman-child fought for her life from the bottom of a mineshaft.

Eunice

I was just a little dry when Nora called and invited me to this meeting. I decided the gathering at Eunice's home would wet my writer's whistle. I agreed to go. There is no place for women writers, Native or otherwise, to gather together and engage in the sort of word play that would give them the endless run of story lines or unusual turns of phrases which could ignite their imaginations and help them along with their next book. For most male writers, the Austin or some other bar suffices, but as yet no one has devised the sort of coffee house with a kitchen table atmosphere to suit women writers' intellectual needs. Complicating all this is the numbers of us who have children. I am something of a fanatic on that score. With four children, I have always felt writing was a cross I chose to carry between wiping noses and throwing quick meals together, rather than a profession. A series of meetings between women had a magical appeal, even if its aim was only to organize a reading on a community radio show.

Nora had taken great pains to identify each woman and characterize them, including some of the more intimate details of their lives. Her descriptions were intended to help me understand the participants in a way that would guide how I treated them. I was familiar with all the writers but Eunice — she was agoraphobic, seriously so. She had not been out of her house for some eleven years. I didn't react over the phone, but this bit of news did spark some anxiety in me. White women, particularly writers, have changed over the past decade. In the mid-seventies, white women were still extremely defensive and ignorant about Natives. Vague recollections of really idiotic conversations nagged at me: "Why do Indian women drink so much ... why can't they look after their children ... if they are so poor, why do they continue to have large families? ..." My need to be with other writers took precedence over my misgivings about meeting with a white woman who had not been around during the years in which those questions had been rendered inadmissible in our company. *Please, Eunice, don't be ignorant*, I pleaded while filling my coffee thermos and getting ready to head out the door.

I must have been late because everyone was relaxing in Eunice's living room and sipping herb tea when I got there. The conversation was rolling around a familiar ache in my heart — the gnawing need for a women's and third world writers' hang-out. Some place kitcheny and sober enough for us to gather around and talk about works-in-progress. The inevitable discussion about the politics of being women writers followed. SKY, a Chinese woman struggling along with her first novel, wondered out loud, "Why do we have to drag ourselves through the agony of digging deeper and deeper inside ourselves for words to paint our lives when a conversation or two with other writers would do the same trick with much less strain and greater results?" Because women are still islands, but I don't say that.

Eunice responds, "There is some advantage to the process of self-examination. It gives us a handle on private truth — something you don't find much of in male writing." Eunice's ability to write without ever leaving her home begins to make sense. The pain of being bonded to her kitchen, the imprisonment of domesticity and the joy of it could fill volumes. In my silence, I don't feel so different from Eunice. My second book was out there, folks were buying me, sticking me on their shelves. Unlike the first time I had published, this go round I had agreed to trot around on the usual speaker's circuit in order to help book sales. We were both somewhat comfortable in our feminine invisibility, only Eunice stayed there, while I merely desired to. Each reading, each performance upset me, sometimes to the point of sickness. I cut these thoughts short of envy for Eunice's disability.

I am lost in a kind of reverent retreat, drifting irresponsibly in and out of the conversation without helping it to focus on the project at hand, but still wearing a look of attention on my face. I am waiting for the women to climb out on the sort of tangents poets get to, which could lead to my next piece. I am feeling mercenary enough to let the chatter roll in any direction it chooses. The subject isn't useful, something about yuppie food and health, so I look around and repeat the key lines of the living room. The shades of colour reflect the inner colours of Eunice's soul — warm earth tones with the odd streak of bluish grey hues, all gently arranged. It strikes me as odd that the colours of autumn are comforting, not stark and painful as one might expect. Eunice's hair is warm reddish brown with streaks of grey in it. The grey matches mine in a pleasant, not fearful way.

"Were you ever encouraged to write?" SKY's emphatic *"no"* jumps out at us. It about sums up the experience in the room. Women are rarely encouraged to write. We drift into the clothes our various types of discouragement wore. I had divorced my first husband over it.

"Drastic," someone remarks.

"Not really," I say. "My mom always wanted me to write. She would do anything to promote my writing as a child. It was almost sacred to her. While everyone was working for our common survival, she let me read or scribble. It shaped me. Made me obsessive about it. I couldn't grasp why this man failed to see my writing as more important than the damn dishes."

SKY wasn't so lucky. Her parents were concerned about her career and seeing to it that she lived a comfortable, affluent life — and writing doesn't give you that. Amazingly, she is squeezing a rewrite of her novel in between nursing shift-work at a hospital and single-parenting her son. Me, I would rather be poor.

All but Jamila have vivid recollections of our first pieces, what happened to our early efforts, and the furious battles that burying our noses in books and dictionaries and then typing till all hours of the night gave rise to. Jamila, ever the intellectual, does not remember not writing and hence cannot remember her first piece. Her father encouraged her. Inconceivable. She has been writing since she learned to read. It was commonplace for her. Life's memories are made of the eventful, not the commonplace, I note mentally, and fall back into silence.

A lull in the conversation sets in and the producer of the radio show tries to bring some order to the gathering, summing up what we have accomplished and outlining what still needs to be done. Politely, she hides how little we have gotten done behind words that make it seem like more. She has an agenda and refers to it. We appreciate this. An entire twenty-four-hour women's program has been planned for the celebration of International Women's Day. She managed to get us an hour before the midnight time slot. The reading was to fit the theme "the politics of international feminism," and the group here reflected that. We all nodded. Times were discussed and some thought about who was going to introduce who was dealt with. Before she got any further down her list of items on the agenda, I broke discipline.

"What's across the street, Eunice, a school?" I am actually thinking about how dull the view must be for her; an empty gravel yard dotted with sterile box-shaped buildings isn't the stuff of great poetry. What a dense assumption that turns out to be.

"Oh that, that's my sociology project," she laughs back my surprise. "Every day I sit here at noon and study the students. No kidding. I have come to some interesting conclusions about teenagers. They do the same thing every day — very conservative. They stand in the same spot — very territorial. They belong to groups and always rejoin the same one — very cliquish. In fact ..."

I leave Eunice pulling the other women into her web of storytelling and pursue my own interests. Eunice has a very typical Canadian white woman's voice with a very untypical "so glad you're here" sincerity to it. I am aware that my indigenousness never leaves the minds of white folks. I am a Native writer, never just a writer, but Eunice doesn't seem to see me that way. The paleness of her rounded face indicates a life without sun, and I am thrown back to a time when I couldn't handle the world outside. I wonder what would have happened if I had stopped trying to go outside, if like Eunice I had given in to my trepidation. I recount the number of times I "came to" in some phone booth, hysteria consuming me, trying to remember my gawdamned phone number so someone could come and get me, my poor kids and my second husband taking turns talking me down enough to encourage me to leave the booth to check the street names so they could find me. And then, the kids having to stay on the phone talking to their crazy mom while their step-dad came to get me.

I flush at the memory, then force myself to focus on Eunice again. She talks the way she looks, even, round tones that float about the room without quite filling it up. I get the idea her husband plays a big role in the management of her household. I want to chuckle at the thought of this faceless man hauling kids to doctors, dentists, school field trips and parent-teacher meetings, but I don't. A piece of me wants to say how hard it must be for him. I bawl myself out. I really loathe the sympathy I can sometimes come up with when men are stuck with doing the work women consider normal living. If *he* were the disabled person I know I wouldn't feel the same way towards her. I'd be saying something dull like "she must be strong."

Just then Eunice comes up with, "My Gawd, did you know there are 700 pagans in British Columbia?" Out of the blue, just like that. I'm anxious to see how she intends to make sense of it.

"I was sitting at home the other night and I turned on the news channel — only an agoraphobe would do such a thing — and

266

guess who is talking direct from Holland? Our very own Premier. He's saying there are only 700 pagans in British Columbia. Where are they?" Love it. We speculate about how this idiot managed to count that high and imagine him running about the province spying on the religious activities of various people, scouting out pagans and committing them to memory, and my mind returns to that other place. I can't stop cheating everyone. Nora jars me loose before I get too deep.

"Lee, did a publisher ever turn you down for reasons you felt were culturally or racially biased?" She up and stepped right into it, like I'd set her up.

"Yes."

"What was the excuse?"

"It was a story about a Native woman who had worked in a cannery and drank herself to death. They said, 'Take the drinking out and we'll buy it.' I took my story back. It is kind of hard to take the drinking out of a story about a woman who dies of alcoholism." Everyone laughs. Wicked. I was now pulling her in and playing the moment for all it was worth. Nasty.

"Who the hell was that idiot?" from Nora.

"You," I answer with feigned modesty.

"Aagh," and she falls over. "*Makera* readership was liberal. I mean the whole world could blow itself away and they wouldn't care, so long as no one talked about it. My Gawd, what a payback. You know, the first lesbian story I ever wrote got exactly the same response. 'Take out the drinking.'"

The quiet gets a little sticky, but not unbearable. We aren't really sure what all this means.

"Maybe they can't look at it because the invisibility they are responsible for creating is the cause of our death and they don't want to know that. Anyway, in some ways we have come a long way. We could never have laughed about such things as this fifteen years ago," I offer. We agree on that. Eunice, meantime, is in some kind of shock.

"You're Native Indian, aren't you?"

Oh Christ, here it comes, as I answer "yes" and numb up for the next line.

"How stupid of me, now I see it. I guess you get enough of that? I mean, I knew you weren't white but ... Oh, I better shut up before I get both feet in my mouth."

The stiffness in the room is palpable. It dawns on me as odd that Nora, who told me what everyone else was all about, including their racial and national heritage, had not mentioned mine to Eunice. At the same time, I am watching Eunice really intently. She looks as though she doesn't really give a tinker's damn about my race. She was surprised she hadn't seen it, was all. Only Jamila is not paying attention to the tension.

"How come women don't write about political meetings?" she asks as though the question were not new. She was lying back more like some Honolulu poolside tourist than a serious writer. Eunice mentions weakly that she doesn't go to meetings, but that she's getting ready to. The latter remark came out punctuated by a false sense of enthusiasm, while the former sounded a little guilty. Nora had prepped us about Eunice in the hope that none of us would blurt out any painful remarks like this. No one says it, but we all feel like Jam has spoken out of turn. Eunice talks about her impending "coming out" ceremony — a meeting of disabled people — and we just listen. Meetings, I tell myself, serve political ends, but they are not that political. Agendas, concealed and open, tend to obscure the politics of our lives. Besides, the rhetoric that gets thrown around in meetings is really rather boring. I recall my efforts to get here, running about readying my four kids for my departure, giving last-minute instructions about their care to my husband and finally robbing my change bank of loonies so that I can buy gas on the way — that's political. The hint of inadequacy in Eunice's voice about the question, too, was political.

The agenda begins winding down. The producer has given up trying to get us organized. She mentions topics for next week's discussion, including planning the logistics of Eunice's participation. Bad timing. Eunice, still raw from the political meetings question, looks uncomfortable, like her being on the show is going to be a lot of trouble. I suppose producers have a different mind set, but I can't help thinking the question was framed a great deal more importantly than was necessary. What sort of logistics do you need to plan to answer the phone? Eunice, on the other hand, presumes that anything involving an agoraphobe is bound to be troublesome, and she patiently awaits the plan. I'm embarrassed for her. I think about missing her in the studio and leave them all there while I look out on the schoolyard and imagine the stones, millions upon millions of them, each with its own grey originality. I relive Eunice's poetic, locked-in existence. I imagine her words carefully chiselled from her aspirations to chart her own course. A plain grey stone that sought her own preciousness, wanted to be alone, rather than conform to all the rest. I used to think my attendance at meetings was all that essential to my writing, but I doubt that now. At one time, I even wanted to write about the meetings. " 'This meeting is now called to order,' the chairperson pounded her gavel and the crowd slid into their seats, obediently. The loud murmurs of conversations hushed and everyone waited in anticipation for the proposed agenda to be read." As I stare hard at the schoolyard stones and imagine the cliques of teenagers gathered in the same spot and think about the cliques that gather at meetings, I am struck by the emptiness of the question.

The faces of the other women blur while Eunice's becomes clear. I want to tell her that she hasn't missed anything by not attending meetings. Her life was shaped by her desire for feminism outside the isolation of agoraphobia. At home alone, she could only remember the world as it was, and reconstruct it in the way she wished it to be. It had driven her to solitary exile and she had managed to turn the exile to account. Now she wanted out. It was a cherished goal for her. She wanted to be with other feminists. The power of her isolation, complicit as she was in its creation, escaped her. Few people possess the courage to sit in solitude with their private selves, unravel all the junk they collect by living, and then march out into the world unencumbered, with a different sense of what they might create out there. It was a goal, but I didn't believe that not attending meetings was what she really missed about not being out there.

Outside she sees teenagers and sociology and I see stones, sameness, individuality and power. The stones stretch and rearrange themselves into mountains. Hillsides, covered with huckleberries. I imagine Eunice and me trudging along the mountains of my birth, picking berries. I see the sun capture the gold and red of her hair and hear us conjure up our next poem, but I don't say a word. A brief goodbye and the meeting is over.

Yin Chin

for Sharon Lee, whose real name is SKY, and for Jim Wong-Chu

she is tough,
she is verbose,
she has lived a thousand lives

she is sweet,
she is not,
she is blossoming
and dying every moment

a flower
unsweetened by rain
untarnished by simpering
uncuckolded by men
not coquettish enough
for say the gals
who make a career of shopping
at the Pacific Centre Mall

PACIFIC CENTRE, my Gawd
do North Americans never tire
of claiming the centre
of the universe, the Pacific and
everywhere else …

I am weary
of North Americans
so I listen to SKY

As I stand in the crowded college dining hall, coffee in hand, my face is drawn to a noisy group of Chinese youth; I mentally cancel them out. No place to sit — no place meaning there aren't any Indians in the room. It is a reflexive action on my part to assume that any company that isn't Indian company is generally unacceptable, but here it was: the absence of Indians, not chairs, determined the absence of a space for me. Soft of heart, guilt-ridden liberals might argue defensively that such sweeping judgement is not different from any of the generalizations made about us. So be it; after all, it is not their humanity I am calling into question. It is mine. Along with that thought dances another. I have lived in this city in the same neighbourhood as Chinese people for twenty-two years now and don't know a single Chinese person.

It scares me just a little. It wasn't always that way. The memory of a skinny little waif drops into the frame of moving pictures rolling across my mind. Unabashed, she stands next to the door of Mad Sam's market across from the Powell Street grounds, surveying "Chinamen" with accusatory eyes. Once a month on a Saturday the process repeats itself: the little girl of noble heart studies the old men. Not once in all her childhood years did she ever see an old man steal a little kid. She gave up, not because she became convinced that the accusation was unfounded, but because she got too big to worry about it.

"Cun-a-muck-ah-you-da-puppy-shaw, that's Chinese for how are you," and the old Pa'pa-y-ah would laugh. "Don't wander around town or the old Chinamen will get you, steal you … Chinkee, Chinkee Chinaman went downtown, turned around the corner and his pants fell down," and other such truck is buried somewhere in the useless information file tucked in the basement of my mind, but the shape of my social life is frighteningly influenced by those absurd sounds. The movie is just starting to lag and the literary theme of the pictures is coming into focus when a small breath of air, a gentle touch of a small woman's hand invites me to sit. How embarrassing. I'd been gaping and gawking at a table-load of Hans long enough for my coffee to cool.

It doesn't take long. Invariably, when people of colour get together they discuss white people. They are the butt of our jokes, the fountain of our bitterness and pain and the infinite wellspring of every dilemma life ever presented to us. The humour eases the pain, but always whites figure front and centre in our joint communication. If I had a dollar for every word ever said about them, instead of to them, I'd be the richest welfare bum in the country. No wonder they suffer from inflated egoism.

I sit at the table full of Chinese people and towards the end of the hour I want to tell them about Mad Sam's, Powell Street and old men. Wisely, I think now, I didn't. Our sense of humour was different then. In the face of a crass white world we had erased so much of ourselves, and sketched so many cartoon characters of white people overtop of the emptiness inside, that it would have been too much for us to face the fact that we really did feel just like them. I sat at that table more than a dozen times but not once did it occur to any of us that we were friends. Eventually, the march of a relentless clock, my hasty departure from college the following semester and my failure to return for fifteen years took their toll — now even their names escape me.

Last Saturday — seems like a hundred years later — was different. This time the table-load of people was Asian and Native. We laughed at ourselves and spoke very seriously about our writing. "We really believe we are writers," someone said, and the room shook with the hysteria of it all. We ran on and on about our growth and development, and not once did the white man enter the room. It just seemed too incredible that a dozen Hans and Natives could sit and discuss all things under heaven, including racism, and not talk about white people. It had only taken a half-dozen revolutions in the Third World, seventeen riots in America, one hundred demonstrations against racism in Canada and thirty-seven dead Native youth in my life to become. I could have told them about the waif, but it didn't seem relevant. We had crossed a millennium of bridges over rivers swollen with the floodwaters of dark humanity's tenacious struggle to extricate ourselves from oppression, and we knew it. We had been born during the first sword wound that the Third World inflicted on imperialism. We were children of that wound, invincible, conscious and movin' on up. We could laugh because we were no longer a joke. But somewhere along the line we forgot to tell the others, the thousands of our folks who still tell their kids about old Chinamen.

* * *

It's Tuesday and I'm circling the block at Gore and Powell trying to find a parking space, windows open, driving like I belong here. A sharp, "Don't come near me, why you bother me?" jars me loose. An old Chinese woman swings a ratty old umbrella at a Native man who is pushing her, cursing her and otherwise giving her a hard time. I lean towards the passenger side and shout at him from the safety of my car: "Leave her alone, asshole."

"Shuddup, you fucking rag-head." I jump out of the car without bothering to park it. No one honks; they just stare at me. The man sees my face and my Cowichan, bows deeply and says sarcastically that he didn't know I was a squaw. Well, I am no pacifist, I admit: I belt him, give him what for, and the coward leaves. I help the old woman across the street, then return to park my car. She stays there, where I left her, still shaking, so I stop and try to quell her fear.

She isn't afraid. She is ashamed of her own people — men who passed her by, walking around her or crossing the street to avoid trying to rescue her from the taunts of one of my people. The world rages around inside me while she copiously describes every Chinese man who saw her and kept walking. I listen to her in silence and think of me and old Sam again.

Mad Sam was a pioneer of discount foods. Slightly overripe

bananas (great for peanut-butter-and-banana bannock sandwiches), bruised apples and day-old bread were always available at half the price of Safeway's and we shopped there regularly for years. I am not sure if he sold meat. In any case, we never bought meat; we were fish-eaters then. I doubt very much that he knew we called him "Mad Sam," but I know now that "mad" was intended for the low prices and the crowds in his little store, not for him. In the fifties, there were still store-owners who concerned themselves with their customers, established relationships with them, exchanged gossip and shared a few laughs. Sam was good to us.

If you press your nose up against the window to the left of the door you can still see me standing there, ghost-like, skinny brown body with huge eyes riveted on the street and the Powell Street grounds. Sometimes my eyes take a slow shift from left to right, then right to left. I'm watchin' ol' Chinamen, makin' sure they don't grab little kids. Once a month for several years I assume my post and keep my private vigil. No one on the street seems to know what I'm doing or why, but it doesn't matter. The object of my vigil is not appreciation but catchin' the old Chinamen in the act.

My nose is pressed up against the windowpane; the cold circles the end of my flattened nose; it feels good. Outside, the windowpane is freckled with crystal water drops; inside, it is smooth and dry, but for a little wisp of fog from my breath. Round o's of water splotch onto the clear glass. Not perfectly round, but just the right amount of roundness that allows you to call them o's. Each o is kind of wobbly and different, like on the page at school when you first print o's for teacher.

I can see the rain-distorted street scene at the park through the round o's of water. There are no flowers or grass in this park, no elaborate floral themes or landscape designs, just a dozen or so benches around a wasteland of gravel, sand and comfrey root (weeds), and a softball backstop at one end. (What a bloody long time ago that was, Mama.)

Blat. A raindrop hits the window, scrunching up the park bench

I am looking at. The round *o* of rain makes the park bench wiggle towards my corner of the store. I giggle.

"Mad Sam's ... Mad Sam's ... Mad Sam's?" What begins as a senseless repetition of a household phrase ends as a question. I know that Mad Sam is a Chinaman — Chinee, the old people call them — but then, the old people can't speak goot Inklish. But what in the world makes him mad? I breathe at the window. It fogs up. The only kind of mad I know is when everyone runs aroun' hollering and kicking up dust.

I rock back and forth while my finger traces out a large circle which my hand had cleared. Two old men on the bench across the street break my thoughts of Sam's madness. One of them rises. He is wearing one of those grey tweed wool hats that people think of as English and associate with sports cars. He has a cane, a light beige cane. He half bends at the waist before he leaves the bench, turns, and with his arms stretched out from his shoulders, flails them back and forth a few times, accentuating his words to the other old man seated there.

It would have looked funny if Pa'pa-y-ah had done it, or Ol' Mike, but I am acutely aware that this is a Chinaman. Ol' Chinamen are not funny. They are serious, and the words of the world echo violently in my ears: "Don't wander off or the ol' Chinamen will get you and eat you." I wonder about the fact that Mama has never warned me about them.

A woman with a black car coat and a white pillbox hat disturbs the scene. Screech, the door of her old Buick opens. Squeak, slam, it bangs shut. There she be, blond as all get out, slightly hippy, heaving her bare leg, partially constrained by her skirt, onto the bumper of her car and cranking at whatever has to be cranked to make the damn thing go. There is something humorously inelegant about a white lady with spiked heels, tight skirt and a pillbox hat cranking up a '39 Buick. (Thanks, Mama, for having me soon enough to have seen it.) All of this wonderfulness comes squiggling to me through a little puddle of clear rain on the window.

The Buick finally takes off and from the tail end of its departure I can see the little old man still shuffling his way across the street. Funny, all the cars stop for him. Odd, the little Chinee boy talks to him, unafraid.

Shuffle, shuffle, plunk of his cane, shuffle, shuffle, plunk; on he trudges. The breath from the corner near my window comes out in shorter and louder gasps. It punctuates the window with an on-again, off-again choo-choo rhythm of clarity. Breath and fog, shuffle, shuffle, plunk, breath and fog. BOOM! And the old man's face is right on mine. My scream is indelicate. Mad Sam and Mama come running.

"Whatsa matter?" ... "Wah iss it?" from Mama and Sam respectively.

Half hesitating, I point out the window. "The Chinaman was looking at me." I can see that that is not the right answer. Mama's eyes yell *for Pete's sake* and her cheeks shine red with shame — not embarrassment, shame. Sam's face is clearly, definably hurt. Not the kind of hurt that shows when adults burn themselves or something, but the kind of hurt you can sometimes see in the eyes of people who have been cheated. The total picture spells something I cannot define.

Grandmothers, you said if I was ever caught doing nothing you would take me away for all eternity. The silence is thick, cloying and paralyzing. It stops my brain and stills my emotions. It deafens my ears to the rain. I cannot look out to see if the old man is still there. No grannies come to spare me.

My eyes fall unseeing on a parsnip just exactly in front of my face. They rest there until everyone stops looking at my treacherous little body and resumes talking about whatever they were talking about before I brought the world to a momentary halt with my astounding stupidity. What surprises me now, years later, is that they did eventually carry on as though nothing were wrong.

The floor sways beneath me, while I try hard to make it swallow me. A hand holding a pear in front of my face jars my eyes loose from the parsnip.

"Here," the small, pained smile on Sam's face stills the floor, but the memory remains a moving moment in my life.

✳ ✳ ✳

The old woman is holding my hands, saying she feels better now. All that time I wasn't thinking about what she said, or speaking. I just nodded my head back and forth and relived my memory of Mad Sam's.

"How unkind of the world to school us in ignorance" is all I say, and I make my way back to the car.

Dear Daddy

I am going to be fourteen next month. I am almost grown up now, so I thought you might like to know what kind of a child I am before I am not one anymore. I know you don't know very much about me because I could never tell you — you weren't there to tell. Oh, I understand you tried to be there, Daddy, but it just couldn't happen. I know it wasn't your fault. Still, I thought you might want this letter to help you see the kind of girl I have been without you.

I am not very tall, about five feet, my hair is long and Mommy says I am pretty — but that's how love-eyes see. I am honey-brown, amber coloured. I never see girls like me on billboards, but I don't mind, most of them aren't modest.

Do you remember when I was three? No? Well me and you got lost. We were out with your friends. The big people, you, Mary and her man, were drinking. You got drunk, you argued with the taxi driver and he threw us out and then you punched him. Sister and I and Mary were scared. We all took off and then you and I played that game. Damn game. We were walking in front of Mary and Sister — at least we thought we were in front — and you said "Let's hide." They disappeared. We couldn't find them. It got cold and dark and you kept asking me where our street was. I knew the name but couldn't read the signs. We both started to cry. It was the first time I made you cry.

Mommy was trying to have another baby and wasn't happy with Sister and me — maybe that was why she wanted a new one. We were both bad. She yelled, "Go to bed" a lot and then she would talk through her teeth. "You are going to go to bed, gawdammit," and she would spank us with the wooden spoon. We were scared when she was so mad. All that hate in her eyes. We would beg her not to hit us, especially me, because Sister would always get in bed before she came with the spoon but I would get hit.

"Bend over," she would yell. I would dance up and down and around begging, "Please, please, no, Mommy, no-o, no-o, no-o."

"If you don't bend over I am going to hit you anywhere I can." Then I would run all over the room, over the bed and around the chair, trying to get away from her. She hit me all over. All the while I would beg, "Mommy, I'll be good, Mommy, I love you, Mommy, please, no, no, no." I didn't mean to be bad. I just couldn't get into bed, so busy was I with trying to get away from the damn spoon. Finally, I would fall on the bed screaming, she hitting me all over until she got tired. You don't remember, Daddy, because you weren't there. I think Mommy thought you weren't there because of her. Was it us, Daddy? Was it because you didn't like us to be bad?

Sister told Mommy she hated her. I know why. Mommy cried and cried. That was the end of the winter she hit us. She still yelled at us, but when she started yelling she would suddenly stop and go to her room, like she thought she was bad. Sometimes she yelled at you. Once she threw milk on you. Yelling like she was full of hate. I know you don't remember, but I can see her now, yelling at your lifeless form on the couch, your old newspaper covering up your face and your feet.

Then she had her baby and he took up most of her time. She started to leave us alone more. He was so tiny and kind of help-less-looking. He couldn't laugh or play or anything. Mommy laughed more. Just once, though, I saw her lying down looking up at the ceiling like she was dead. She couldn't hear me when I asked her as nice as I could about supper for Sister and me, so I learned to cook.

We both were going to school then and I wasn't so lonely. Before the baby I had to go to kindergarten for a while. The kids called me names and I got into fights and Mommy said I didn't have to go anymore. She had such a faraway sadness in her eyes, and then she hugged both Sister and me for a long time. She didn't make a sound, but I could feel the wet against my hair from her tears. After, she made tea and told us little funny stories about four bratty little kids and we all laughed.

Sister quit kindergarten too. The teacher made her sit in a corner every day for three weeks because she didn't have carrots and celery, just peanut butter — Sister liked peanut butter. It got on the carpet and Sister got into trouble. Mommy went to the school and the teacher started to yell at her. Mommy squared off, hands on her hips, and bellowed right back. You remember, Mommy has a big voice for such a little person. The teacher started to talk nice, but Sister still refused to go to school and Mommy took her home. Even after the teacher said sorry, Sister never went back. I was lonely again.

Mommy yelled at other people, once at a guy driving a car that almost ran us over. He got out of the car, but she wasn't scared. I think she could have beat him up, but he got back in the car. Another time someone pushed her and the baby; she hollered and pushed right back. She handed me the baby first, of course. I wonder if these men are ashamed to be so afraid of such a small woman.

It was around then that I learned about "can't afford this and that." We were on welfare, you see, Daddy, and Mommy was sneaking and going to school. Welfare wasn't supposed to find out or Mommy would get into deep trouble. We were kind of proud of her, going to school, looking after us and trying to fix everything so she could get a good job and me and Sister and Baby would never have to have "fast days" again. Did I forget about "fast days"?

Every end of the month we would run out of things like food and Mommy talked about the old days when our people — she always says "our people" — used to fast and clean out their system. We didn't mind.

The welfare found out about school and Mommy got cut off. She looked thinner and sadder. She just said she would have to find a job sooner than she wanted to, and she did.

The people next door moved away. We were the last kids on the block and we had no one to play with after school except each other. It was hard, now that Mommy was working. I had to get Sister ready for school and she wouldn't listen too well to me. I'd have to say over and over, "Come on now, eat your cereal, c'mon now, put your boots on," and like that until finally she'd be ready. She still sang then, Daddy, like a little bird. I forgave her for not getting ready because she sang to me the whole time I was cooking mush and putting her socks and shoes on. Mommy kept warning her, "You are old enough to remember this. When you are seventeen, little lady, you will be embarrassed at not dressing yourself when you were seven years old."

Work must have been good for Mom because, although she always seemed to be hurrying, she laughed and treated us better. She stopped being so sad and she never looked out the window for you anymore. I asked her if she was ever going to bring home a boyfriend. "What for?" she said. "I got all the friends here I need. I sure don't need another round of misery." I didn't understand her. I thought she meant she didn't miss you, Daddy, and I was scared. How could she not miss you? Sometimes I had bad dreams. I would dream the welfare took us away and no one missed us, not even Mommy. Daddy, where were you?

We put holes in our ceiling with our umbrellas and then we were scared of the mice falling through the holes. We had it coming, I guess — we were naughty to put those holes in the ceiling. Anyway, Mommy said, "It's your own damn fault, now go to bed." Not loud, she said it kind of cool. It took me such a long time to

stop crying and finally fall asleep. I knew better than to make noise
— just tears trailing down my cheeks and Sister's soft deep breathing, the dark and my crazy imagination working overtime, whispering evil about you and the mice.

Morning always came, though. I don't remember when I first
noticed that. One morning Mommy was singing in the kitchen. I
realized it was the first time I had heard her sing in a long time.

"Do I look any browner?" she asked.

"No-o," I answered soft and slow, wondering what the heck
she was up to.

"I am an Indian now." She said it as though it were something
you could become, and I began to think she was really losing it.
She went through a whole bunch of explaining about Bill C-31. I
hear that line a lot since she got her "status back." Bill C-31. You
know when you are ten, Bill C-31 sounds like the name of some
kind old man who runs about fixing things for Native women. What
did it all mean? Well, it meant Mommy could go to school and we
never had "fast days" again. Finishing her degree was a lot of pain
for her. She wasn't young and learning didn't come so easy as it
used to, she said. She wept through math, physics and chemistry,
and didn't do too bad in English. When she was almost a teacher
she told us that as soon as she got her degree we would move out
of the city. Then you wouldn't know where we were, Daddy. Didn't
you want to know, Daddy, or was it all too painful being married
to my mom?

Baby knew by then that you weren't coming back. He still
looked out the window every now and again and asked if you are
at "wirk" and when were you coming home, but not even he believed his question anymore. We all thought if we were good you
would just walk right in the door again. I think about that now —
the long periods of time between your coming home, Mommy
telling us you were out working, and eventually we would learn
that you were just gone, "pulling a disappearing act." You snick-
ered when you said that. It wasn't funny, Daddy.

I started to grow up the other day, Daddy. I realized that even when you were home you weren't really there. You were a body on the couch. I know now that you and Mommy had not slept together since the baby, but you took three years, three painful years of going and coming — us not knowing when or if you were going to return — to actually leave. Every old Ford Baby saw, he would run after it hollering "Daddy, Daddy, come home," and he would cry. Mommy would bite her lip and we would all go home and hug each other. She played "Pretty Brown" hundreds of times for us the first couple of years after you went. And Sister, she stopped singing. It was the one thing you really loved, we all loved. I didn't dare ask her about it. She didn't need to feel bad about not doing it on top of losing the joyful reason she did it for in the first place. Daddy, she sang because it was the one sure-fire way of making you smile. Daddy, I never saw you really laugh, and I would like to see you bend your head back the way Mommy sometimes does and really let out a gut-busting laugh.

Time muddled along for us over the years and I am sitting here at the window of our own home (Mommy bought it not so long ago) watching the ground break up and spring struggle to push back winter. There is a lonely little crocus looking up at me from her purple and yellow blossom, winking, as I write this letter. Time closed in on me like a fine, fine rain. The world got small and I don't remember when it happened. I peeked at the world through a thin veil full of small holes. The veil lifted and I realized flowers bloom in spring, die before fall; trees shed leaves every autumn to sleep during winter and somehow all this has to do with the greatness of the world. I can touch the greatness, feel it, and as I write this letter the unhappy feelings that were so large when I started have grown small.

I realized just now that despite all the lonely nights of tears and missing you, in the day we laughed, we ran, we jumped, we did schoolwork, and it was only in those few moments just before sleep that we thought of you and missed you. We carried on living. All this time I had written sad feelings onto my dreams just before I slept, when really, Daddy, I grew up without you. I don't suppose you ever had to deal with missing us. I know now why you were always on the couch buried under a newspaper at nine o'clock at night. Mommy still won't talk about it, but I know, and it's OK. You see, Daddy, you are the one to be pitied. I don't think you can laugh at your own folly, overcome weakness or see a little crocus on the lawn and imagine it winking at you.

Love always,
Your daughter

Polka Partners,
Uptown Indians and White Folks

When I was a petulant youth, it never ceased to amaze me how we could turn the largest cities into small towns. Wherever we went we seemed to take the country with us. Downtown — the skids for white folks — was for us just another village, not really part of Vancouver. We never saw the myriads of Saturday shoppers battling for bargains, and the traffic went by largely unnoticed except that we had to watch out not to get hit when crossing against the light. Drunk or sober, we amble along the three square blocks that make up the area as though it were a village stuck in the middle of nowhere.

I was part of the crowd sliding along the street towards the park. A hint of wind laced the air. Six leaves curled around crazily just above the sidewalk. Ol' Mose was leaning against the mailbox chuckling at the same leaves. It was fall. Ol' Mose had that wistful look on his face — he was thinking about home, missing it. The colour of earth death, the scent of harvest amidst the riot of fire colours, like a glorious party just before it's all over — earth's last supper is hard to deal with in the middle of the tired old grey buildings of the downtown periphery. I can see the mountains of my home through the cracks between the buildings that aren't butted one up against the other. It seems a little hokey to take a bus across the bridge and haul ass through nature's bounty, so I don't do it anymore.

"Say," Mose almost straightened up in a subtle show of courtesy meant for me. I laughed before he said anything funny.

"You still holding up that ol' mailbox? I thought I left you here yesterday leaning on the same box." Mose laughed and told me he was just keeping it company till Tony came out of the store.

"What's he doing at the tailor's? Don't believe I ever saw one of us going in there before."

"His sister is getting married. He's buying a new shirt."

"Well, hell, must be his favourite sister. Turning the old one inside out was good enough for the last one who got foolish like that." Tony comes out of the store grinning from ear to ear, proudly displaying a brand new bag.

"First time I ever bought something no one ever wore before." We examine his new clothes without taking anything out of the bag and head in the direction of the café. Every urban reserve has its café. In Vancouver it was the 4-Star, but it could have been the Silver Grill in Kamloops or any small, Chinese-Canadian café in any other city that was clean, plain, a little worn-looking and with food about the same. Jimmy the waiter likes us and the manager doesn't like anybody.

We don't go there to eat much more than a plate of fries, a cup of tea or some wonton soup. We talk, laugh and behave like we were visiting our neighbours rather than dining out. When the bill comes we all dig in and put our collective cash on the table hoping it adds up. Once we were a few cents short. The manager was about to give it to us and Jimmy slipped in the nickel. We gave it back to him about six months down the road. Jimmy tried to make a joke about "interest" but we didn't get it, which made him laugh all the harder and like us even more.

"Oh shit." In the park across from the café some guy was bent over another guy, cleaning out his wallet. Tony and I broke into a run.

"Hay-ay." The roller tried to bolt but I ran him down and thoughtlessly scolded the purveyor of the passed-out man's purse before I relieved him of his catch. Tony standing behind me must have geared up my mouth. I peeked inside the wallet — there was a whack of cash in there. I looked at the victim: a pricey leather jacket, wool slacks, gloves, Italian shoes and long black hair. He was an uptown Native, slumming, I guessed. Without feeling anything about what I was thinking, I wondered where all these uptown Natives are coming from, and pulled out a couple of twenties and handed it to the thief. He thanked me and took off.

Tony looked askance at me and asked if we should wake him up, like he thought it would be a good idea to just leave him. Mose grunted something about how he looked like your regular tourist. I gave them one of my *c'mon you guys, he's one of us* looks and moved to the bench he almost sat on. A few slaps and a pinch on the sensitive part of the neck brought him around. He grunted like a bear coming out of hibernation and sat up on one elbow, nearly falling off with the effort. I didn't recognize the booze he was drinking; must be some kind of fancy liquor I didn't know about. I leaned into his face to identify his tribe.

"My, Granny, what big teeth you have," he said, squinting up at me between glances to the left and right. His hand reached for his hip.

"It ain't there," and he sighed without swearing. I handed him his wallet.

"You didn't steal my wallet just to shame me, so someone else must have taken it and you retrieved it — correct?" Every syllable fell out of his mouth clear and accentless.

"Where are you from?"

"Isn't it customary in Vancouver to begin with hello and how are you, maybe what's your name, before collecting vital statistics?" The arrogance I recognized, but I couldn't put together the words to answer his question. Vancouver had become a collector of Natives from all over. Where you were from determined how

we treated you in some way I couldn't explain, so I ignored what
he said.

"You're bigger than most but you don't look prairie, so you
must be from Ontario."

"That too. Where am I?"

"Pigeon Park. Where are your glasses?"

"Huh?" and the blast of unfresh booze made me step back.

"Your glasses."

"Now that is twice in a row you have identified a fact of my
life without ever having seen me before. You are a clever little girl,
did you know that?" He was upright and looking at me different,
studiously, I think. A small crowd gathered behind me.

"Wrong two out of three. I am clever, but I am not little or a
girl. This must be the first time you been here." Titters from the
crowd.

"Bingo." His mouth formed a perfect smile, white teeth even
and well cared for. He is beginning to look like a polka partner
from the other side of the tracks that form my colour bar. As I walk
away, Tony is wearing a smug grin and Mose is chuckling. Polka
Boy knows he's been told off. He's European enough to imagine he
was getting somewhere, but Indian enough to know he's blown it.
He doesn't look all that confused.

Mose jumps into small talk like there hadn't been any interruption in our conversation. "So Frankie bought a new car." We
laugh. Frankie has owned and junked a perpetual run of cars but
none of them could ever have passed for new. We get all caught up
in laughing about the aging symptoms of all the cars he ever bought.
Polka Boy recedes into the train of Frankie's cars and their missing
parts that grew in Frankie's yard like a graveyard. I am already
slipping away from the laughter and dreaming of Frankie and home
and thinking he stays on our little reserve just so he can keep the
train of wrecks coming, or else he'd have joined us on this side
long ago.

Frankie is inside the café surrounded by the regulars and bragging about his Salish Cadillac. "Not a damn thing wrong with it, talked him into lettin' it go for twenty-five bucks."

"Did the chauffeur come with it?" and everyone cracks up. The conversation rolls around the parameters of our village and the odd or funny stories about the people in it. I stop listening and think about polkas and Prince George and the only Indian conference I ever went to. Everyone there had been uptown, dressed in the Sunday best of white folks. It surprised me at the time. The music was the same, but the people were like the man in the square. They pinched out their words, pronouncing every single letter and whistling out their s's as though they were all terrified about saying fis' instead of fish. The polka music brought out the risqué side of me and despite my better judgement, I had opted for a mattress thrash with some guy.

It was like tying on a good one. The morning after sharpened the loneliness. I guess loneliness is the mother of all promiscuity, because here I was thinking of doing it again — only now the body had the face of the man in the park. It shook me a little. I reached into my pocket, calculated my share of the food costs and wondered if I had a free quarter. The banter at the table took on a slippery quality. I couldn't focus on the faces. My hand toyed with the quarter and of its own accord put it to rest in the folds of my pocket.

✳ ✳ ✳

Time crawled by all winter. I spent most of it staring at my mountains just across the water, watching snow woman dress them up in white and wishing I was lost there. Every now and then I'd venture out to the old café, but Polka Boy seemed to spend a lot of time there. His dress code and language never changed, but he did learn to turn the volume of his arrogance down enough to grow on everyone. He was at the 4-Star talking up this "centre" he wanted to create. He captivated the imaginations of the regulars. I am not sure whether it was him that scared me or his centre. No one here dreamed dreams like that. Life here is raw, wine is drunk not because it is genteel, but because it blurs, dulls the need for dreams, knocks your sense of future back into the neighbourhoods of the people it's meant for — white folks.

I stared out of my window at the street below as though somehow my eyes would screw out from the sidewalks the words to describe my feelings. Why the hell did anyone want a centre, an office? We had the café. It was a hangout for those of us not quite cognizant of the largesse of the city, but aware we were not truly alone. Bridge Indians. Not village, not urban. An office is urban. Somehow Jimmy the waiter, the cranky manager and their café kept us just a little village. It was a place where we could locate our own in any city. Like an urban trail to the local downtown village. This guy wanted to sever the trail.

I scribbled little notes to myself: *"the Silver Grill in Kamloops, the 4-Star in Vancouver, Ken's Café somewhere else ... An office is not a hang-out."* Scribbling didn't help and I took to the wine bottle. In those days I didn't have much respect for my private words. The blur of the wine and the rhythm of country music and Patsy Cline crying in my living room didn't do much either. After a while the blur became stark, the pictures stayed real. What got blurry was my capacity to think about it, to see my way out, and that got unbearable too, so I left it behind. I was feeling like I needed to see my way out, even if it was only a dream, when I stumbled into the café.

I had been holed up for a while. I joined Frankie's table. Aside from his penchant for buying old cars he also served up his own kind of journalism. He ran down the news ... Rufus had sobered up in great anticipation of the centre and making the village more respectable ... Polka Boy was soon to rent an office and some Métis woman was going to be the secretary. I tried not to encourage such talk. You don't need hope to cloud your life either. I stayed long enough for Tony to tease me about how I looked as though my best friend had died, and everyone chided me for being a stuck-up hermit.

Outside spring had sneaked up on my world. Spiky slivers of earth-milk squeezed from her voluptuous breasts streaked across my face. I imagined the crocus flowers of home forcing their way through these sidewalks and trees, buds upturned, lining the dingy street. A frightful clatter of bumping, grunting and laughter from a group of villagers and my almost-polka-partner right there in the thick of it all broke my reverie. They were actually moving into a little storefront on the drag. I followed the racket inside. Everyone who had a sense of stability for our sorry little half-village was there, save Tony and Frankie. It was Polka Boy's community cen-tre/street patrol come to life.

I could barely stay on my feet. The room pulsed with move-ment and the people receded. My imagination ran on about the reality of it, arguing with the impossibility of it surviving. I saw the street, its frail dark citizenry rushing pell-mell towards this dream and imploding at the end of the dream's arrest. For arrest it would. No one would allow the total transformation of this end of town into a real community. Its attraction, its magic, lay in re-maining a peripheral half-village that could accommodate senti-nels — not people, but sentinels, alone on a bridge, guarding noth-ing.

My smile hardened itself onto the line of my face while my insides cried in silence. My words, empty of content, fell in bro-ken shards to the floor before they reached the faces they were aimed at. Nonsense greetings, mumbles of "how are you," dropped unanswered. They were busy. Every lousy piece of furniture — the old black telephone, file cabinets, coffee makers and cups — was carefully hauled in as though it was the finest possession these poor folks had ever seen.

I pretended to be caught in the wonder of it all. "Here, put the desk over there, no, here, plug the phone in, couches over there," and soon I was in the centre of it, as though it had been my idea all along. It was a star-quality performance for an Indian who would never see Hollywood. I kept it up all through the move. At home later, Tony and Frankie's faces haunted me. It occurred to me that they had been sitting at the back of the café alone for the first time. Tony didn't buy the dream and Frankie had no interest in dreaming for the folks down here. He had never left our reserve.

I stopped dropping by Tony's place for the regular tea and laughter while I wrestled with joining the gang at the centre or stubbornly clinging to the old café. It took a couple of months, but I did join the ranks of staff and volunteers who manned the office and conducted the street patrol. The office: it never struck anyone as hilarious at the time, at least no one laughed out loud, but the office was about as unofficial as it could be. One dingy little storefront on the drag, with its unwashed windows, worn linoleum and walls that sorely wanted finishing. The desk we had was not quite old enough to be antique but worn enough to be a joke, and the file cabinet needed a wrestler's touch to use. It had all been furnished by people who had bought their furniture second hand and had made a good deal of rugged use of it before handing it to us. But it was ours and we had never had a storefront that we could enter, have coffee and get treated like real customers.

We had a real secretary who hauled our butts across the fields of office life in the other world. She was appalled by our office and the nature of our work, but by and by she got used to it. Her first day would have been a major disaster had we noticed anything amiss, but naive as we were we didn't pay attention to her wool suit and high-heeled shoes or the cloying scent of her perfume. She coached us in filing, telephone reception and office politeness, though she could never get us to stop asking people if they were related to so-and-so from such-and-such if the name sounded familiar.

She came in one day full of her office etiquette and told us the mayor was coming. A hubbub of questions sprang up — "Who is the mayor anyway? What does he do? Why is he coming here? When?" — without regard to answers. She shut us all up, then told us what to say to sound smart without giving anything away. She ended the lesson with "and don't ask him about his relatives."

Old Rufus was best at it. He had had a lot of experience as a kid with tourists in his West Coast island home. He and the other kids had learned to small talk while they fleeced them of whatever quarters they could get. The mayor loved him. Edmonds came in shortly after the mayor's arrival. The press was there and the place was a general zoo. I was squeezed up in the corner. I knew enough about who the mayor was to stay in my corner. He was head of police and that was enough for me to have nothing to say. Edmonds puffed up his chest, asked the mayor if he liked Edmonds' clean suit. The mayor said a constipated-sounding "why, yes," and Edmonds was on a roll.

"How is your grandmother?"

"She's dead."

"Too bad, mine too ... mmm, mm ... and where are you from?"

"I am from Kitsilano," and Edmonds corrected him, "I mean, where are your grandmothers from, what part of Europe?" ... and the secretary grabbed the mayor and pointed to the statistical breakdown of newly employed youth, etc.

Ol' Edmonds didn't catch on to the coaching, and the secretary had a few laughs about that later. "How is your grandmother?" and she would bust up. Defensively, Rufus pointed out that it must have cost Ol' Edmonds five bucks to clean his suit. It was the first time I ever saw an Indian laugh at how we are and Rufus felt it too. I couldn't put my finger on it then, but it occurs to me now that Edmonds was something like our unelected chief. He was the one we all went to to settle disputes or claim the dead. She shouldn't have laughed.

Polka Boy was our boss and he spent more time at a place called head office than he did down at the storefront. Everything was going so fast. I got to be friends with the secretary, who took me uptown every now and then, showed me other places she had worked. Great anonymous buildings, filled with women who sat behind desks in assembly-line style, banging out pieces of paper with weird words on them like "accounts receivable," "correspondence," "budget reports" and such. A couple of times we went in. She chatted with the women about everything from the new technology to new hairdos. When they laughed they seemed to hold the laughter in the way a kid squeezes air out of a balloon so as to make just a little squeaking sound. It all felt so bizarre.

Then I was beginning to feel weepy, like there was something being born inside and growing of its own will — a strange kind of yearning. The tears began to possess a beginning, an end and a reason for their growth. Although I didn't really want to know, it came anyway, flash-flood style. As the mystery of office work fell away from these women, the common bond of survival was replacing my former hostility. The sea of white faces began to take on names with characters.

It was around this time that the doctor came. She wanted to start this clinic and was asking us to help. Us? Help a doctor? I plugged my laughter with "What do you want us to do?"

"First, I am a lesbian feminist."

"Is that a special kind of doctor?" The secretary and Polka Boy both laughed. I wished I had gone to school past seventh grade.

"She's gay," the secretary translated.

Thick silence followed. We didn't quite know what to do with the information. Some hung their heads like they'd rather not know. I wasn't sure what this had to do with the question ... did she want us to help her find a woman? ... change her mind? I knew better than to ask. I looked at the boss, the guy who gathered us here in the first place. He was studying me intently. He slowly re-positioned himself before speaking. I had the feeling that he had set this up. She didn't need us to help, she needed him, and he wouldn't move without all of us and somehow he thought I was the key to getting everyone else's co-operation.

He went into a monologue about the number of accidents, the deaths of our people on their way to the hospital or in the emergency room, and patiently painted a picture of racist negligence for us. A clinic with a friendly doctor would assure proper, immediate care. *Where the hell is all this going?* I didn't say that, I just looked away like the rest. I guess he decided to gamble on our assent because at the end he just said, "We can't promise you won't get abuse from some of the street people, if that is what you are asking. We can guarantee the staff here won't bother you. We don't care who sleeps with who."

Oh Gawd, this is going to be a mess. We all knew one of the guys was gay. We also knew he had to hide this fact from some of our lovely clientele. We further knew that he had never publicly admitted it to any of us. It was an open secret. We all side-glanced him. He stared catatonically off into space.

The meeting was over, chairs were put away and I got ready to go out the door. A hand tapped my shoulder and the boss called me aside. In the little walled-in space behind the storefront he asked me what I thought.

"That you're about the densest Indian I ever met."

"Why?"

It was too hard to tell him that white people cannot deal with the beauty in some of us and the crass ugliness in others. They can't know why we are silent about serious truth and so noisy about nonsense. Difference among us, and our silence, frightens them. They run around the world collecting us like artifacts. If they manage to find some Native who has escaped all the crap and behaves like their ancestors, they expect the rest of us to be the same. The reality that some of us are rotters is too much for them.

"Don't ask me, I don't know who your mother was." Pretty low. He sat bolt upright in his chair and then waved me out the door. We were never close. Until then, he treated me in the same distant and friendly way he treated everyone else. At times he had been disgustingly condescending, even arrogant. After that remark he got real cold. At night I looked out my window, screwing my eyes into the sidewalk, and cudgelled myself for saying anything about his mother.

I could hear the rich laughter of Tony and his family next door. Probably Frankie was there cutting up the rug and laying out the laughs. I missed them.

I knocked. They didn't answer. I wondered why my feet just didn't walk in as usual. Shit. I must have stood for a couple of minutes arguing with myself. For the first time in my life it didn't feel right to just walk in on Tony. I made up mind to go home and then the door swung.

"Jeez, Sis. You scared me. I thought you must be a cop or something." I backed up and he came out with me. We were both leaning on the porch and Tony started rolling a smoke. I handed him a tailor-made. His eyebrows went up.

"And do you have a savings account too?"

"With or without money in it?"

He laughed. "Well, now, you tell me."

"With."

He turned to face the dark, pulling hard on his cigarette. My hand holding the extra tailor-made dropped uselessly to my side. That, too, was different. Nothing was usual anymore.

Tony's voice purred on, gentle and slow. He told me they were dredging and filling False Creek again, making it smaller. Pretty soon we wouldn't be able to tell we had ever been here. I knew he was talking about me, us, changing our ways until we were just like them. I didn't say a word and he never got any closer to really telling me off than that. I left as soon as the story was over. Back in my room it dawned on me: he hadn't invited me inside. And the weeping began again.

The doctor worked out. We fell in love with her. She was soft spoken, thoughtful, and enjoyed a good laugh when things looked their worst — just like us. She could hear every word you said and understand where they were coming from. She put up with no end of junk from some of her customers — patients she called them — and never laid their stuff on us. I got so caught up in the wonder of it all that autumn came and went without me thinking about the beauty of the colours of impending earth death or yearning for my mountains. Already, a slushy abysmal snow was trying to cover the sidewalks with some dignity. My mind was wandering around the endless days and nights of laughter that brightened the office down here. I had not thought of Tony or Frankie for a long time and the weeping got lost somewhere in the joy of our work.

I scraped all the tops of the mailboxes on the way to work, trying to get enough snow to toss in the boss's direction. He seemed like he wanted to break the ice between us and laugh again. This would do it. The door squeaked when I opened it. *Doggone, now he'll see me.* I slipped my hand with the snowball behind my back and peeked inside, softly giggling. There he was, holding the weeping doctor, a faraway, angry look on his face. My insides started to shake. I tried not to think about anything. The snow was melting and my hand started to freeze. I tossed what hadn't melted outside while I urged the door shut as though reverent silence would fix things. I took a quick glance out first, so as not to hit anyone with my snowball. It had started to rain and I just closed my eyes. "Here it comes, here comes the night" was squeezing itself out on the radio.

"The clinic didn't get its funding and we are moving uptown." The words came out measured and flat.

"Why?"

"The city said they could not justify funding a racially segregated clinic."

"I meant the moving," bit words through clenched teeth. How could he possibly think I cared more about the clinic, her white do-gooding conscience work. The office, that was ours. He squeezed her, she mumbled that it was all right. I didn't look at her. He started in about how the Indians uptown were getting themselves into hot water fighting each other in the bars and the city ...

"I don't give a shit about a horde of uptown Indians with too much money and not enough sense not to kill each other. This ..." I never finished. I bolted, slammed the door so hard the glass broke. I reeled on home, thinking about winter, polka partners and this dirty town. Visions of assembly-line women office workers still going about their jobs and white women doctors setting up shingles in other parts of town crowded between the sight of him moving despite his better judgement. My knees felt knobby, my legs too long, my hair lashed coarse at my face and the tawny brown of my skin became a stain, a stigma, like the street. Hope. Expectations. Great expectations I had never had. An office. A simple gawdamned office where we could breathe community into our souls was all we hoped for, and it had been too much. I staggered down the street trying to hold onto little trivial bits of life that might help stabilize the rage. Old sidewalks are the only things in the world that age without getting dingy and dirty looking. The older they get, the whiter they look. Appropriate. And I am mad all over again. My feet play an old childhood game, "don't step on the crack or break your mother's back." Funny, I never thought about the significance of the ditty before. "Break your mother's back," and the first day the doctor came rolled into focus ... "Don't ask me 'who is your mother?' "

All the games I ever played came back. Rough games, games which hurt the participants, filled my memory. "Let's hide on Ruby," and little Ruby standing there in the middle of the sidewalk, silently weeping. Old Grandma warning us, "Whatever you throw out will come back to haunt you." She never said it with any particular tone of voice — just kind of let it go, matter-of-fact. The old mailbox is turned over again. I set it right and lean on it and think about deserting Ruby like Polka Boy is deserting us.

Grandma, I wanted to say, you don't know the half of it. How was I suppose to know that the things I threw out would come back on the whole kit and caboodle of us? The liquor store to the left is calling me. I answer. Overproof rum, that'll shut the nagging little woman whispering conscience material into my ear. Some old geezer wants a quarter. I am pissed enough to tell him to shut the fuck up. I look, open my mouth and then change my mind and move towards home.

Tony must have been watching me from his window on the old worn balcony of our project apartment house. I wasn't inside but a minute and a knock brought him through the door. He sits across from me just about where the slash of the curtain cuts a little sunlight onto his face. The rest of the room is semi-light. The trail of sunlight against his northern features makes him seem prettier than us from down here. No fat cheeks, just neatly chiselled high cheekbones, flesh stretching over them tight. His jaw is square and the hollow of his cheeks darker, sharpening his perfectly straight nose. He knows I am looking at him. He lets me despite his embarrassment, maybe sadness. I've known him nearly all my life and this is the first time I've ever thought about how he looks.

"Can see the liquor store from here ... looked like you were considering going in."

"Well, I never."

"Saw that too. But it don't stop me from wondering why. It's been a while for you, hasn't it?"

"I guess I don't feel so young anymore."

A healthy "mnhmnh," and silence. In the still quiet I remembered Tony and Mose outside the tailor's before all this. I didn't go to the wedding, didn't even ask how it was. I was really scraping around inside my head trying to think about all the changes that had happened inside of me, trying to place snippets of new knowledge I'd gained and old habits I'd broken and make some sense of them. They whirled too fast. Memory after memory chasing each other in no particular order. It made me dizzy. The weeping is filling my gut, then Tony's voice tears up all the images.

"Saw Frankie today. Crazy guy. He ain't supposed to be driving. You know Frankie — talk a salesman into buying his own dictionary." My face wants to grin. "Cop stops him. He forgot to signal. Right away, Frankie jumps out of the car, lifts up his hood and pulls the plug out of the cap and tells me 'try her now.' " I'm smiling, nearly chuckling.

"Dumb cop says, 'what seems to be the problem?' and Frankie says, 'I do not know, officer, it just won't start.' He says it kind of condescendingly, but the cop, he don't notice. 'Let's have a look,' the cop says. Pretty soon, Frankie's in the car trying to start her while this cop is out there trying to fix what Frankie broke." The thought of Frankie and a serious young cop fussing over a half-dead Chevy in the middle of downtown traffic cracks me up. "Cop finally figures it out, all kinda proud, Frankie is no end to thanks, even puts the hood down. They say their howdy-dos and off we go."

"Cops can be extraordinarily stupid."

"Now, now," Tony says, "you know they hire only the smartest morons. Now, you going to tell me what the problem is? I didn't come here to entertain you for nothing, you know." He is serious. It dawns on me that Tony hasn't been serious since he was a kid. Was it seventh grade? Yeah, in seventh grade Tony walked out the doors of that school and never went back. Why the hell did he leave? His question is still hanging on his face. I don't think I can answer him. Every time I try to think about that place too many thoughts get all crowded up together and none of them ever sits still long enough for me to figure anything.

"You really liked the place, didn't you?" I nod. "Yeah, that boss of yours, pretty smart guy. Just breezed into town from Harvard or Yale or whatever university he come from, set it up and now he's breezing out again." He waits for this to sink in. "Come on outside, want to show you something." On the balcony he lights a smoke and leans into his own conversation. "See down there, Stace, just over there by the water. One time, Ol' Marta tells me, the shore come forward on the inlet — maybe a quarter mile or more. These people filled it up and put a sugar refinery on it. Yeah. Sugar is sweet, but you eat too much, you want more and pretty soon you're like Joey, forty and crippled with arthritis. You know what I mean, Stace. One day water, next day sugar, next day pain."

"Shuddup." I lean against the wall. He tosses his cigarette over the balcony, tips his imaginary hat and strolls off. My bleary mind begins working away, trying to get a hold of the significance of the story. It repeats it as though to memorize it so I can run it by me one more time on some other occasion, when all my parts are working. The sun is sinking under a pall of dirty blue-grey haze. What was it? One day sweet, next day water. No. Shit. I lost it. The phone rings. Shit.

"Are you all right?" It's Polka Boy. I consider slapping the phone on the table and then hanging up. The image makes me smile. Childish.

"Yeah. Shouldn't I be?" Someone should have kicked my butt a long time ago for letting the acid leak into my mouth and burn holes in my speech like that.

"You didn't look so good this morning." He is purring. That voice I recognize. Bastard, I think. I can see him leaning back in his chair, teeth flashing and voice curling up out of his lips, confident and self-assured. He doesn't remember that I have seen him have seductive conversations with almost every other woman he talked to over that old black phone. He just can't help it; his sympathy begins and ends as a sultry invite. My tongue freezes. I stop helping him with the conversation.

"Look, I would like to talk to you about this. I did what I could. Maybe not enough, but I ran out of words. The boys at head office ..." Uncomfortable for him, these pauses — he can't handle dead air space. He fills it up with more bullshit. Then, "Can we meet and talk? There are some things you could help with." I see clearly for just a moment. That look he gave me when the doctor came. I could feel his look through the phone. Get the lead street girl on your side and the rest will follow. I could help him bring the downtown folks uptown.

"I can't haul furniture." My voice is as dead as I can make it. He doesn't notice. Maybe he can't hear. I laugh to myself. The bugger just can't stand losing. One last kick at the street. Pluck the rose left behind by tragedy. I want to play him. Hurt him, the way he hurt us. *Don't be a fool, guys like him got little tin badges and water pumps for hearts. They aren't made of flesh and blood.*

I can hear the tail end of his last line, "I didn't mean that." It sounds like a salesman who thinks he has his foot in the door. A wispy goodbye I was sure he didn't hear and I gently put down the receiver. Without bothering to turn out the lights I slept. Slept the sleep of the dead. Dreamless. Lifeless sleep. I didn't ever want to wake.

Sunshine plays softly with the colours of my dusty lamps. The radio is playing old tunes. It must be noon. "You are my sunshine" cranks out, tinny and ridiculous. I have heard that tune till I could just puke. Whoever she was, she did not live here, did not harbour futile dreams of dingy offices, and she never had to wrap up in a blanket in the dark without any hydro. She didn't know how it feels to crack cornball jokes about no hydro as though it was the best damned bit of fun you had had in a long time.

Hydro. Today's the last day.

I walk downtown. The office is just a deserted hole now. A dead office looks smaller, more confining than one alive with busy people. Memories of the people float about, wafting to the corners of my mind. I look away and stare hard in the direction of the hydro office. The sound of the street, the roar of cars grows louder. The murmur of hundreds of voices drowns the voices of my memory. I'm walking, not staggering. I can't resist peeking in at the 4-Star. Jimmy is still there. He is drumming the counter. Bored. One lone old white man sits in front of him eating his soup. Jimmy doesn't bother looking at him at all. "Nobody I know," and I laugh at the remark he always whispered to me whenever a white man entered. I decide to stop by on my way back.

I pass through uptown Granville on the way to the hydro office. There they all are, a new crew, fixing up the building, and in the middle of the crowd is my smiling Polka Boy. He sees me, lets his lips form a smile just like nothing happened. One day water, next day sugar, next day pain. Must have been the Pepsodent smile that reminded me, and I smile too. My eyes face his, but the whole of me is not looking at him anymore. The light changes and I turn, one last wave, and cross. Everything after that is mechanical and unmemorable. I pay the hydro bill, experience rudeness from some prissy white girl and tell her that I understand. She works in an office. She looks as confused as Polka Boy when I leave.

Charlie

Charlie was a quiet boy. This was not unusual. His silence was interpreted by the priests and Catholic lay teachers as stoic reserve — a quality inherited from his pagan ancestors. It was regarded in the same way the religious viewed the children's tearless response to punishment: a quaint combination of primitive courage and lack of emotion. All the children were like this and so Charlie could not be otherwise.

Had the intuitive sense of the priesthood been sharper they might have noticed the bitter look lurking in the shadows of the children's bland faces. The priests were not deliberately insensitive. All of their schooling had taught them that even the most heathen savage was born in the image of their own sweet Lord. Thus they held to the firm conviction that the sons and daughters of the people they were convinced were God's lowliest children were eternally good. Blinded by their own teachings they could not possibly be called upon to detect ill on the warm broad faces of their little charges.

Charlie did not do much schoolwork. He daydreamed. Much standing in the corner, repeated thrashings and the like had convinced him that staring out the window at the trees beyond the schoolyard was not the way to escape the sterile monotony of school. While the window afforded him the luxury of sighting a deer or watching the machinations of a bluejay trying to win the heart of his ladybird fair, the thrashings he knew could be counted on for committing the crime of daydreaming were not worth the reward. So, like the other children, he would stare hard at his work, the same practised look of bewilderment used by his peers on his face, while his thoughts danced around the forest close to home — far away from the arithmetic sums he was sure had nothing to do with him.

He learned to listen for the questions put to him by the brother over the happy daydream. He was not expected to know the answer; repeating the question sufficed. Knowing the question meant that, like the others, he was slow to learn but very attentive. No punishment was meted out for thickheadedness.

"What is three multiplied by five, Charlie?" The brother's brisk, clipped English accent echoed hollowly in the silence.

Charlie's eyes fixed on the empty page. His thoughts followed the manoeuvres of a snowshoe hare scampering ahead of him and his half-wild dog. The first snow had fallen. It was that time of year. The question reached out to him over the shrieks of joy and the excited yelping of his dog, but it did not completely pluck him from the scene of his snow-capped, wooded homeland.

"Three … times … five?" muttered Charlie, the sounds coming out as though his voice were filled with air. A tense look from the brother. A quizzically dull look on Charlie's face. All the children stared harder at their pages — blank from want of work.

He was still staring at the teacher but his mind was already following the hare. Did the brother's shoulders heave a sigh of disappointment?

"Thomas," the boredom of the teacher's voice thinly disguised.

"Fifteen," said clearly and with volume. Poor Thomas, he always listened.

The bell rang. The class dutifully waited for dismissal. The brother sighed. The sound of scholarly confidence carefully practised by all pedagogues left his voice at each bell. Exasperation permeated his dismissal command. It was the only emotion he allowed himself to express.

As he stood by the doorway watching the bowed heads slink by, his thoughts wandered about somewhat. *Such is my lot, to teach a flock of numbskulls ... Ah, had I only finished and gotten a degree. Then I could teach in a real school with eager students.* Each day his thoughts read thus and every time he laid out plans to return to university, but he never carried them out. At home every night a waiting bottle of Seagram's drowned out his self-pity and steadied him for the morrow.

✳ ✳ ✳

Charlie was bothered at mealtimes. The food was plain and mo-notonously familiar: beef stew on Monday, chicken stew on Tues-day — the days with their matching meal plan never varied. Un-varying menus did not bother Charlie though. Nor was it the plain taste of domestic meat as opposed to the sharp taste of wild meat that bothered him. He was bothered by something unidentifiable, tangible but invisible. He couldn't figure it out and that, too, both-ered him.

From the line-up, he carried his plate to the section of the eating hall reserved for sixth grade boys. He looked up to watch the teenaged boys exchanging flirtatious glances with the young girls in a line opposite them. In the segregated classes of the school, boys and girls weren't permitted to mingle with, talk to or touch one another. They sat in the same eating hall, but ate on separate sides. Charlie bored quickly of watching the frustrated efforts of youth struggling to reach each other through the invisible walls of rigid moral discipline erected by the priesthood.

His eyes began wandering about the eating room of his own home. The pot of stew was on the stove. It always had something warm and satisfying to taste in it. He scarcely acknowledged its existence before he came to residential school. Now he saw it each day at mealtime.

At home no one served you or stopped you from ladling out some of the pot's precious contents. Here at school, they lined you up to eat. Each boy at each age level got exactly the same portion. A second plate was out of the question. He felt ashamed to eat.

A stiff-backed white man appeared in the room and the low murmuring of voices stopped.

"EAT EVER-Y-THING ON YOUR PLATE!" he bellowed, clicking out the last *t* on the word "plate." His entrance never varied. He said the same thing every day, careful to enunciate each word perfectly and loudly, in the manner he was sure best befitted the station of principal of a school. He marched up and down the aisles between tables in a precise pattern that was designed to impress on the boys that he was, indeed, the principal of the school. Finished with the last aisle, he marched stiff-legged out the door.

The boys were more than impressed. They were terrified. They likened the stiff-legged walk to the walk of an angry wolf. They had come to believe that whites were not quite human, so often did they walk in this wolf-like way. They knew the man who had just pranced about the eating hall to be the principal, not by the superiority of his intellect as compared to the other instructors, but by virtue of his having the stiffest walk and hence the fiercest temperament of the pack.

Night came and Charlie prepared for the best part of his incarceration. Between prayers and lights out, the children were left alone for fifteen minutes. Quickly into pyjamas and to the window.

The moon and the stars spread a thin blue light over the whitening ground below. Crystal flake after crystal flake draped the earth in a frock of glittering snow. As always, a tightness arose in his small boy-chest. He swallowed hard.

"LIGHTS OUT!"

Darkness swallowed the room and his little body leapt for the bunk with a willingness that always amazed him. He did not sleep right away.

"Hay, Chimmy, you got your clothes on?"

"Yeh."

"Ah-got the rope."

"Keh."

Runaway talk! Charlie hurriedly grabbed some clothes from the cupboard beneath the top of the nighttable he shared with another boy.

"Ah'm comin' too," he hissed, struggling to snap up his jeans and shirt.

"Hurry, we're not waitin'."

He rushed breathless to the closet and grabbed a jacket. The older boys had already tied the rope to the metal latticing that closed the window. Each boy squeezed through the square created by one missing strip of metal lattice and, hanging onto the rope, swung out from the window, then dropped to the ground below.

Safe in the bosom of the forest, after a tense but joyous run across the yard, the boys let go the cramped spirit that the priesthood so painstakingly tried to destroy in them. They whooped, they hollered, bayed at the moon and romped about chucking snow in loose, small balls at each other.

Jimmy cautioned them that that was enough. The faster they moved the greater the head start. They had to get through the forest to the railroad tracks by night cover.

The trek was uneventful. The older boys had run away before and knew exactly where they were going and how to get there. Stars and a full moon reflected against white snow provided them with enough light to pick their way along. As time wore by, the excited walk became dull plodding. They reached the tracks of the railroad sometime near daylight. All were serious now. They cast furtive glances up and down the track. The shelter of darkness was gone. The risk of discovery became real in the bright light of day. Surely the priest had sent the police in search of them by now.

The boys trod light-footed and quickly along the track-line, fear spurring them on. A thin wisp of smoke curling upward from the creaking pines on their right brought the boys to a halt.

"It's mah uncle's house," Jimmy purred with contentment. The empty forest carries sound a long way in winter, so the boys spoke in whispers. It never occurred to the other boys to ask Jimmy what his uncle's reaction to their visit would be. They assumed it would be the same as their own folks' response.

A short trek through the woods brought them to the cabin's door. Uncle and Aunt were already there to greet them. They were now used to the frequent runaway boys who always stopped for a day or two and then, not knowing how to get home, trudged the nine and some miles back to school. The holiday, Uncle mused to Aunt, would do them no harm. Besides which, they enjoyed the company of happy children.

A good meal ... a day's play ... nightfall ... heavenly sleep in this cabin full of the same sweet smells of his own cabin brought sentimental dreams to Charlie.

Charlie's dreams followed the familiar lines of his home. In the centre stood his mama, quietly stirring the stew. Above her head, hanging from the rafters, were strips of dried meat. Hundreds of them, dangling in mute testimony to his father's skill as hunter and provider. A little ways from the stove hung Mama's cooking tools. Shelving and boxes made of wood housed such foodstuffs as flour, sugar, oatmeal, salt and the like. All here was hewn from the forest's bounty by Charlie's aging grandfather.

Crawling and toddling about were his younger brother and sister, unaware of Charlie's world or his dream of them. Completing the picture was his dad. He stood in the corner, one leg perched on a log stump used as a kindling split. He had a smoke in his hand.

No one but his wife knew how his thoughts ran. How he wondered with a gnawing tightness why it was he had to send his little ones, one after the other, far away to school.

Daily, he heard of young ones who had been to school and not returned. More often, he would come across the boys who recently finished school, hanging about the centre of the village, unwilling and poorly equipped to take care of themselves. Without hunting and trapping skills, the boys wasted away, living from hand-to-mouth, a burden on their aging parents. One by one they drifted away, driven by the shame of their uselessness.

It was not that they could not learn to hunt or trap. But it takes years of boyhood to grow accustomed to the ways of the forest, to overcome the lonely and neurotic fear it can sometimes create in a man. A boy who suddenly becomes a man does not want to learn what he is already supposed to know well. No man wants to admit his personal fear of his home.

The pull of years of priestly schooling towards the modern cities of a Canada that hardly touched their wilderness village grew stronger. For a while, family and city pulled with equal strength, gripping the youth in a listless state of paralysis. For some, the city won out and they drifted away. Charlie's father worried about the fate of his young ones.

His private agony was his own lack of resistance. He sent his son to school. It was the law. A law that he neither understood nor agreed to, but he sent him. His willingness to reduce his son to a useless waster stunned him. He confided none of his self-disgust to his wife. It made him surly but he said nothing.

In his dream, Charlie did not know his father's thoughts. He saw his father standing, leg-on-log, as he usually stood while he awaited breakfast, and he awoke contented.

Jimmy's uncle had given up wondering about the things that plagued Charlie's father. His children had grown up and left, never to return. He did not even know if there were grandchildren.

He lived his life without reflection now. Jimmy was the eldest son of his youngest brother. It was enough for his life's labours that this boy called him grandfather out of respect for the man's age.

"I'm going to check the short lines," he said, biting into his bannock and not looking at the boys.

"Can we help?" The older boys looked at their plates, studiously masking their anxiety.

"Sure." Staring at them carefully, he added, "but the small one must stay." The old man was unwilling to risk taking the coatless boy with him.

Charlie followed them to the edge of the woods. He knew that no amount of pleading would change the old man's mind and crying would only bring him shame. He watched them leave and determined to go home, where his own grandfather would take him to check his short lines.

The old aunt tried to get him to stay. She promised him a fine time. It was a wasted effort. He wanted the comfort and dignity of his own cabin, not a fine time.

Charlie knew the way home. It had not taken him long to travel the distance from the tracks near his home to the school. He had marked the trail in the way that so many of his ancestors might have: a rocky crag here, a distorted, lone pine there. He gave no thought to the fact that the eight-hour trip had been made by rail and not on foot.

The creaking pines, straining under the heavy snowfall of the night before, brought Charlie the peace of mind that school had denied him. A snowbird feeding through the snow curled Charlie's mouth into a delighted smile. A rabbit scampered across the tracks and disappeared into the forest. He had half a mind to chase it.

"Naw, better just go home." His voice seemed to come from deep within him, spreading itself out in a wide half-circle and meeting the broad expanse of hill and wood, only to be swallowed by nature's huge majesty somewhere beyond his eyes. The thinness of his voice against the forest made him feel small.

The day wore by tediously slow. Charlie began to worry. He had not seen his first landmark.

"Am I going the right way?" What a terrible trick of fate to trek mile after mile only to arrive back at school. The terror of it made him want to cry.

Around the bend, he recognized a bare stone cliff. Assured, he ran a little. He coughed and slowed down again. He tired a little. He felt sleepy. He touched his bare hands. Numb.

"Frostbite," he whispered.

In his rush to leave the dormitory he had grabbed his fall jacket. The cold now pierced his chest. Breathing was difficult. His legs cried out for rest. Charlie fought the growing desire to sleep.

The biscuits Aunt had given him were gone. Hunger beset him. He trudged on, squinting at the sprays of sunlight that cast a reddish hue on the snow-clad pines in final farewell to daylight.

Darkness folded itself over the land with a cruel swiftness. It fell upon the landscape, swallowing Charlie and the thread of track connecting civilization to nature's vastness, shutting away with maddening speed the last wisps of light from Charlie's eyes.

Stars, one by one, woke from their dreamy sleep and filled the heavens. Charlie stumbled. He rose reluctantly. His legs wobbled forward a few more steps, then gave in to his defeated consciousness, which surrendered to the sparkling whiteness that surrounded him. He rolled over and lay face up, scanning the starlit sky.

Logic forsook him. His heart beat slower. A smile nestled on his full purple lips. He opened his eyes. His body betrayed him. He felt warm again. Smiling he welcomed the Orion queen — not a star constellation but the great Wendigo — dressed in midnight blue, her dress alive with the glitter of a thousand stars. Arms outstretched, he greeted the lady who came to lift his spirit and close his eyes forever to sleep the gentle sleep of white death.

Lee on Spiritual Experience

California must be a magic place. Not only will it be the first state in the U.S. of A. in which the minorities combine to outnumber the white folks, but its colours dot our northern landscape. Pinks, pastel blues and rose-hued beiges colour new homes and apartments, diluting the powerful deep green of our mountains almost as though we needed some of the soft colours of California's desert to tone down the depth of our green.

Colours aren't the only things that have made their way across the forty-ninth parallel. In the mid-sixties the great flower child movement, or hippie movement, spilled onto the landscape of our hitherto apathetic social conscience. In the eighties new wave ideology began rushing north and we all became gripped by a deep need for spiritual enlightenment — real spirituality, the kind that motivates humans to behave more humanly. California catchwords colour our conversations: environmentally safe; politically correct; therapy; harmony and spirituality. (Now some nationalist is going to take exception to Americanizing what is seen as best about Canadians, but I heard all of these terms in San Francisco before I ever heard a Canadian utter them. Honest.)

The new wave movement for spiritual renaissance brings my folks back to the front of the bus, so to speak. Native North Americans are very spiritual — everyone knows that. Just before I go to read a new set of poems for Background Theatre, I watch David

Suzuki on television; he is popularizing us again. "If we don't listen to Native people, who understand, have always understood the need to live in harmony with nature, who possess a spiritual bond with nature ..." As he speaks, I wonder about myself. Almost every important Native person I know has had some sort of powerful spiritual experience, except me. *Never mind*, I tell myself, *not having had a powerful spiritual experience has not dulled your vision, or your imagination.* I turn off the TV and sort through my work.

Let me say that I love a Six Nations Mohawk, married him and still continue to experience intense passion and wonderment after ten-plus years of living with him. Although our marriage has slipped into the comfort zone — you know, we get up every day, shit, shower and shave and go off to our different jobs (writing now being my job, since publishers have started to market my words) — I can still be aroused to passion at thoughts of him. As the picture of Suzuki fades, I think of Dennis and decide to read my bent box poem about this lust/love. I further decide to pattern my reading after Pauline Johnson, Ka-Nata's first published Native poet and actress-comedienne extraordinaire.

The reading is in the whale room at Stanley Park. The park was Pauline's last place of comfort during the lonely days of her dying. It is all so fitting.

I always experience a deep sense of unreality, a feeling of unphysicality, before I read. Today, the absence of bodily consciousness is stronger than usual. There are three other women reading ahead of me. I know this, but my body doesn't seem to, and so it impatiently trots in the direction of the podium before my turn. The audience chuckles, the master of ceremonies corrects me and I return to my seat. My face is smiling sheepishly, but I am not quite in touch with myself so I don't feel my lips forming their embarrassed grin.

I watch the whales while the others read, and then drift off into my own world. "Properly rude," Chrystos would say. The whales are swimming about somewhat neurotically, as all people do when caged on a reservation too small for them to enjoy living. They are swimming in circles with Hyak, the man, on top and the two women underneath, in stairwell formation. Beautiful people of the sea. Poetry in motion, and I am lost in the sleekness of their skin, the elegance of their motion, and saddened by their imprisonment.

My turn. "I'm really glad to be here tonight. Of course, every time I step out of that two thousand pound killing machine some man named a car, I am glad to be anywhere." The audience, mostly women my age, chuckles knowingly, and Hyak stands up in all his tumescent glory and chatters at me, seductively. "Yo, Hyak," I address him and carry on with my routine. "I turned thirty-nine last week, which was very important to me. It marks the last year of my youth, which is a good thing because I am the mother of four teenagers and I ought to grow up before them. This is the year I have been waiting for, the year in which nature does her duty by me and makes an adult of me.

"Maybe it has already worked, because I learned something about teenagers this year. Teenagehood is a crippling disease. I can tell because none of my children can walk anymore. Bus fares and car fares are eating up what little extra I have earned in royalties from my work. I raised every one of my children to be long-distance runners, but as each reached teenagehood they ceased to be able to walk to the corner store. And it doesn't stop there.

"Teenagehood is also mind-crippling. Remember when they were five years old and they knew where everything was? You would come into the kitchen amid the orchestra of sound made by lids, pots and pans that the little ones were banging to create the kind of music only five-year-olds can appreciate. Never mind, I told myself then, when they are older they will know where the pots and pans go. What a dream. Every time I go to cook, it's a major search to locate the tools of my trade. These children, one of whom has lived here for nineteen years and all of them for at least thirteen years, again and again put the pots and pans in a place different from where I've instructed them to.

"The other day my son who had just turned thirteen came into the kitchen with his fifteen-year-old brother — the one who decided last summer that 5'4" was an unseemly height for a man and set about adding seven or eight inches to his body. (I don't know whether it was seven or eight because my neck doesn't naturally strain sharply enough to properly assess his new height.) This mini-eruption has cost the fifteen-year-old in agility. He makes it into the chair all right, but his hand flies out and knocks over his glass of milk. "Poor judgement," he mumbles, not moving. I ask the thirteen-year-old to get a dishrag: I already know the older one doesn't speak this kind of English anymore …

" 'Eh?' very Canadian and very typically teenage.

" 'A dishrag,' in that tone of voice only mothers use.

" 'Where?'

" 'Oh, try the stairwell.' Disappointingly, he does. I give up. He is afflicted: my last little genius has caught the disease of teenagehood and now I must wait another six years for him to recover. I join my other son in apathetically staring at the milk plik-plik-pliking to the floor. I am in a marvellous state of self-rescue-catatonia therapy. My husband returns at the same time as my younger son; the one confused at not having found the dishrag in the stairwell and the other bewildered by my catatonic milk-spill watching.

"My husband, bless his heart, has become accustomed to this behaviour in the past few years and associates it (incorrectly) with my poetic disposition.

"Seriously, I love my children, but I look forward to the end of their adolescence."

Hyak is still jabbering at me, standing perfectly vertical, his huge manhood waving at me. *Hyak likes my poetry* I say innocently to myself and wonder what that thing waving at me is. *I must ask Dennis*, I note mentally. I read my love poem and Hyak looks as though the poem was written specifically for him.

Halfway through the poem, it dawns on me that these people

are as captivated by my physical presence as they are by my words and voice. I feel, for the first time, absolutely lovely. I know I had no control over the face I possess, the contours of my cheekbones, the shape of my mouth and large eyes, but I can't stop feeling glad that these people think me lovely. I can't stop taking credit for it.

I rush off the platform to my husband's side and Hyak resumes his swim immediately after my reading. Dennis touches my hand and says as he always does, "You did fine." I am not sure if it is his touch, his words or both, but this exchange always brings me back to the physical world.

"What was that thing waving in front of Hyak? It seemed to come from the middle of his body," I whisper.

"What do you think it was?" he says with the appropriate leer in his voice. A leer I had never heard him utter before. "He is a mammal, you know."

"No-o." Disbelief, shock and embarrassment all riddle my denial, but my insides confirm that *that* is exactly what it was. I think about spiritual experience, California colours, new wave and Native people. *And doesn't all that say something about your character, old girl?*

Too Much to Explain

She sat on the upper level of the lounge, her chair up against the wall. She didn't want anyone behind her tonight. The table she leaned on was small and dark. There weren't many people in the room; it was, after all, a Tuesday night in October. He was late. It twisted her insides that he didn't have the decency to be on time. Just once, just once, you would think the bastard would be on time, she thought with more venom than was called for. She tapped her cigarette rapidly at the ashtray and scolded herself for smoking so much. She closed her eyes hard to shut out the hum that plagued her ears. The sound of the tapping did little to cancel the hum and closing her eyes did less. She knew both gestures were futile, even absurd, but she made them anyway.

He entered the room with grace and dignity, took a quick look around the room from the doorway before he recognized her tucked up in a corner. *He's probably sizing up the women*, and the humming grew sharp. She resisted putting her hands over her ears. He nodded in her direction, smiled and strode over to the table.

From the door he had noted that she was thinner than when they first began seeing each other. Still, even thin she was lovelier than the other women he knew. He grinned at his own foolishness. It was not that she was so much lovelier but that he loved her; he liked the way his heart clouded his vision. She had been tense and inattentive lately. He wondered if this outing would suffer the same fate as the last two at Joe Kapp's. He tried to stop thinking about the harangues that had marred the last two occasions. Her smile quelled his momentary cynicism. He was embarrassed by his private recollection and his own suggestion that there might be a pattern developing here.

He stroked her hand lightly and pecked her cheek, then swung easily into the chair. She was nearly finished her margarita. His automatic display of affection did nothing for her. She feared that this exhibition was conducted more for everyone else's benefit — the way the lead wolf in a pack might covetously snuggle his females before younger hopefuls. She resented what might have been a perverse show of male possession. Her hand fidgeted slightly under his caress. A piece of her wanted to scream at him, but she knew that would not be rational. Rational people do not scream. The waiter came up just behind him and asked what they would like to order.

"Two margaritas," and he winked at her. She interpreted the wink and his sickening overconfidence as arrogance, mentally adding this to the list of his crimes. *Gawd, what am I doing? Don't blow this,* and she felt colour come involuntarily to her cheeks. The floor floated towards her as the humiliation she felt filled her face. She argued with herself. *He's taking me for granted ... Gawd, what a stupid catch-all phrase that explains nothing and everything that goes wrong between people. The waiter probably thinks I'm one of those ridiculous women lapel-roses that can't speak for myself.* She ignored the fact that she was still toying with a margarita she had ordered earlier.

The waiter rested his eyes on her momentarily, awaiting confirmation. She felt his gaze but ceded nothing. Seeing that she was not going to look up, he shrugged and left.

When she looked at the floor her lover was not sure whether she was bored or angry. Then he flushed. He had answered for her again. The realization brought a knot of anxiety to his gut. He sighed annoyance and looked off into space, waiting for the barrel-load of condemnation that would assault his character, but it didn't come. He relaxed slightly, not bothering to reflect on his own internal need to eat up life's mundane and trivial decisions with his own decisiveness.

The pianist in the corner was plunking out a sad tune, "Moody River"; the sound was all the more melancholy in the absence of song and band. Just an old Black man, pecking at an even older piano. Pictures of her childhood home, the river and her solitary vigil next to it swam through her head. Her face wore a wistful smile when it turned to look at the piano player. Then her expression changed as she craned her neck to see.

"Dammit, the pole is blocking my view."

"Would you like to move?" he asked, trying to accommodate her. The question jarred her. A veil of darkness filmed her eyes.

"Why?"

Oh Christ, instant replay. When will I learn? Every time she invites me out like this, she gives me a hard time, but he didn't say that.

"Well, so you can see the piano player." He lit a cigarette. He rarely smoked and this little display of anxiety annoyed her.

"What do I want to look at some old man for?" She was rigid now, her words came out clipped into neat little pieces and were fed to him through tight lips. He sighed heavily, and even that she interpreted as male condescension in the face of a typical female airhead. The ringing hum in her ears gained volume as a steady stream of accusations whirled about insanely in her mind. Small bits of reason argued with the multitude of doubts until she finally regained her control.

He stared at the margarita in front of him and let his frustration drift around the dimly lit bar while his fingers played with the salty ice ring on the glass. Fatigue crept up on him like a faithless companion. He had been through this before with other women. He was beginning to think that this affair was going nowhere. Age and passion kept him rooted to his chair. He felt weighed down by an anchor of his own making.

"How did your day go?" She carefully laminated the remark

with layers of creamy sweetness. Surprised relief overtook him. *He knows I'm pissed, why doesn't he say something ... stop that ... Gawd,* and she recognized the voice that dominated her thoughts. She fought to still the voice, to stop the incessant humming. *Think of the river.* It swelled to a torrent and gave way to a memory she had thought dead. The flooding banks and the ranting of her mother returned to haunt her and she wanted to faint.

"Another day of make-work. If the new plans aren't ready soon, I think I'll lose my mind." Her glazed look did not escape him, despite her fawning attempt to disguise it. He ignored it. *What the hell am I supposed to do?* he asked himself. The question was in fact an old justification for doing nothing.

"Don't mock me." It slipped out too fast. *Oh Gawd, there it is, it's out, he'll guess.* Her fingers grabbed the napkin and tried to wring the thought out of her mind by twisting the paper into a white snake of anxiety. Far from surmising any hint of her mental turmoil, he was confused by her response. Neither confusion nor any of his other emotions had ever prompted him to self-examination or indecision before, and he didn't bother thinking about it now. The waiter rescued her with another useless interruption.

It looked like they would be harassed all night by the waiter's bored attentiveness. Her lover considered leaving but didn't want to ask. *No sense inviting trouble,* he told himself, and let the notion pass.

"I wasn't mocking you," he said with exaggerated warmth. The pianist had stopped to change songs, so his words echoed loudly across the emptiness, despite his effort to utter them softly. He reached for her hand. She feared that noncompliance with his overture would call attention to her near admission, but his hands inspired a feeling of revulsion that she could not let go of and so she dropped her hands to her lap. She concentrated on them guiltily.

"OK, what is it this time: my disgusting sexism, my appalling arrogance, or are you just generally dissatisfied with the meaninglessness of our relationship?" He laced the question with threat. His voice lied about the concern for his character that his question implied. The noise in her ears rose an octave. The pitch of it deafened her. It blocked out the reality of the bar. The roar of the river on top of the ringing in her ears distorted everything.

The table became a watery, seductive maw, the glass a slender woman staggering and begging to be let go. The weaving woman-glass swayed frantically in the clutches of her own liquid indecision, its every movement an accusatory cry to her for decisiveness. She threw the glass at the table. The margarita bled the content of her memory across the table and it leaked onto the floor. She jumped up babbling about stress, weakly trying to submerge her behaviour in neurotic nonsense. He signalled the waiter, relieved that he had not seen her throw the glass, and was sorry that his remark had been so harsh.

She stood aside while the waiter finished mopping up the drink with his rag. Her body hung limp against the wall. She knew she couldn't keep this façade up much longer. She wanted the floor to swallow her. She prayed that the river of her maddened mind would drown her. Anger abated, he looked at her more seriously now than he could remember doing. Her thinness took on dimensions of anorexic vulnerability. Her strangeness seemed less excusable.

"Is school getting to you?" he asked. She clasped her hands together with too much vigour. That voice, that "Nancy nursey" voice, drove her to the edge. She struggled to collect herself. She fought to rest her nameless agitation on something plausible.

"Don't patronize me. Who do you think you are? You just sit there like you are the only person in the world who can handle life. You don't think I can deal with anything, do you?" The words jerked out too fast between clenched teeth. Her eyes narrowed to slits. She would have said more but the stupid waiter was back again like a phantom, cajoling them to have another drink.

"A double daisy for me," she hissed.

"Huh?" The rude bugger didn't have the sense to say "pardon me." She didn't answer. She turned to face the wall and tugged at her cheek with tensed fingers.

"Two double margaritas," her lover said politely. The waiter sensed the tension and left quickly. She wanted to start in on him again, but scenes of the river broke her concentration. Instead of the usual hazy images of the past, the pictures took on a dangerously lucid clarity. *Maybe if I just let it happen ... maybe if I just lose myself in the lousy nightmare of it all instead of trying to stomp it out with rattling nonsense ...*

He was near the breaking point. *I'm just a gawdamn nail-pounder, not a fucking therapist. What the fuck do I know about her feminist anxieties,* and he closed his eyes. This was more than he could deal with. *Fuck yourself* was what he wanted to say, but he continued sitting there for reasons he could not adequately explain to himself.

The blood drained from her fingers and her hands shook from the loss. Weakly, she stood up and numbly walked to the bathroom. He paid the bill. When she returned they left.

The sound of the traffic failed to reach her and he had to hold her trembling body against him at the curb to prevent her from stepping out among the cars. He let her lead him into the blackness when the traffic cleared. The world was getting farther away from her. She needed to hear the water, it floated around in her head like a torrent of frustrated feminine rage, liquid unpredictability. They walked wordlessly forward and the hill rolled up behind their scurrying legs.

False Creek lurched into view at the bottom, a poorly lit facsimile of cultivated wild wood and trail. Over the hill of manicured lawn and untended brush the creek stretched out purpleblack against a neon skyline. No other lovers were out. The night was cool and the city's citizenry were already asleep in anticipation of the morrow's work.

They climbed down the man-made stone embankment. At the bottom, she sat with knees up, her shins folded in her thin, shivering arms. She hugged herself, waiting for the ringing to subside so the pictures she had long suppressed could return. She forced herself, in the comfort of the night's quiet affection, to watch it all.

He wrapped her in his jacket and waited helplessly. He had no idea what was going to happen but his sense of chivalry and his knowledge of the city would not allow him to desert her. He resigned himself to a night of cold anticipation.

From the riverbank she saw her mother struggling with her husband, screaming at him to give her her papers ... silly little bits of brown bags and napkins that she had scribbled on. He had caught her scribbling poems again. Her six-year-old body watched him through her woman's mind, and the clarity of the moving picture in her mind surprised her. At the end of her memory's eye, her mother disappeared over the roar of the river and her drunken father staggered uselessly after her, calling her name as though she were deserting him and not perishing under the hands of his drunken rage.

"They said I was crazy, a bona fide nutcase." Her chuckle came out a murmur. It was the kind of chuckle women let out when they suddenly discover that the mysteries surrounding unplugging a toilet are pathetically simple and wonderment is unwarranted. Her lover lived quite outside her range of subtle emotional variance and so thought the chuckle evidence of the truth of the findings of whoever "they" were, rather than recognizing it as the "I'll be" chortle of realization. He didn't want to hear it. *Christ, what am I supposed to do with this?* He didn't move or answer her aloud. There must be more, and he waited for it. He stared at the lights reflected against the water and thought about how they, too, made a crazy dance pattern against its smooth surface. He rested his face against her neck, trying to search his mind for some hope.

"I spent most of my childhood yo-yoing between lonely foster homes and a mental ward ... Shit." She began to rock back and forth. Her memories rolled into the smooth lap of False Creek as the wall of fear and veil of confusion lifted. She couldn't leave the brutal trap her father had set for her. The little girl, traumatized by the scene, had jumped inside the same trap, running a marathon of imprisoning relationships because she had not wanted to remember.

Now the trap sunk.

"The little girl just had no words." He couldn't accept that she was crazy, but this last remark wanted some point of reference to make it rational. If he accepted her insanity he would have to declare insane the hysteria of his mother, the violence of his sister and her breakdown and his own maddened binges of the past. He would have to condemn them all because he just wasn't cut out for looking inside at the why of himself or anyone else. He resigned himself to a crazy destiny, half wishing that he had been born snugged up against the distant mountains of his ancestors a half millennium earlier.

"You don't have a monopoly on craziness," he said dully. She laughed at his flat sense of self, at the hopelessly two-dimensional perception that he clung to, and she wondered if the man who defined neurosis wasn't just a little like her lover. Without feeling the least bit guilty about the unfairness of leaving him like this, she handed him his jacket and left without saying goodbye.

He followed her up the hill and she left him there in a tangle of confused babbling while she climbed into a cab and drove out of his life. It was all too much to explain. How does one begin to unravel the accumulation of thousands of years of entrapment to a man bent on repairing the rents she occasionally made in the machinery of the trap.

"I just don't feel desperate anymore," was all she could come up with. As the cab sped away she could hear him holler in self-defence, "You really are crazy."

Sojourner's Truth

From inside my box, an ugly thought occurs to me. I know what hell is — actually, I knew it all along, but in my haste to barrel along and live, I had not thought about it until just now. Hell just might be seeing all the ugly shit people put each other through from the clean and honest perspective of the spirit that no longer knows how to lie and twist the truth.

Can you imagine, there you are watching some maniac jerk his wife or kids around, pulling arms out of their rightful places in sockets and you walk on minding your own business, only this time you don't feel like just shuffling along and ignoring it. Your spirit cries out for humanity, but all you get to do is weep and remember that you didn't care when your soul was housed in living meat. You could have struck a blow at violence against women and children, but the little whisper from your living soul was drowned by the reality of all that flesh.

In its final resting pose your soul knows that all the maxims that guided your hypocrisy are just so much balderdash. "Spare the rod and spoil the child." "Don't let her get away with it." Who ever heard of such a ridiculous proposition! "Don't drop the apples, they bruise easily" is more like it. Pictures of all the lickings I laid on Emma and the kids file through my mind. In my newly dead state I try to rationalize one more time: if you don't subject the kid to a certain amount of brain rot, the kid is apt to object to even a minimum of authoritarian discipline. Hell is seeing the lie in all your excuses.

My thoughts come to an abrupt halt. I know that I am in the box and must get out. How convenient: the very moment you realize that you must get out, there you are outside, watching everyone from the most advantageous viewpoint. They are all gathered around the box. Those that talk are whispering as though they might interrupt the soul of me; others are in tears. The kids are playing. Why everyone gathers around the boxes housing the bodies of the dead is beyond me, though. The truth of me has long left the box.

The truth of me is a little unnerved by the realization that there are not as many living bodies gathered around my box as I expected. I face it, though. What the hell did I expect? I didn't do anything to inspire anyone to show up and grieve my departure, permanent though it is. (At least there aren't any Chinamen.)

Oh God, there are a hundred thousand Chinamen living in this city and I cannot count even one of them as a human being who will miss me. I weep. No tears, just the kind of pain of the inner self that goes with the action; the sort of hot, wracking emptiness, but without the tears to cool it off. There aren't any Indians or Blacks. *Oh God, there aren't even many white people here.* I lived for seventy years moving around in a sea of almost a million people and only fifty show up to bury my body and bid my spirit adieu.

"It's a crying shame, he wasn't that old." Thanks, Mike, but it really isn't a shame. Death is natural, but then we are inclined to add shame to all that is natural. The naked body and spirit are deep sources of shame to the mortal beings crawling about the earth. Life does look a little different from the vantage point of death.

A ripple of pleasure overtakes me as Emma speaks. "You know he didn't take care of himself." It is the worst she could come up with and still wear a mask of polite mourning. Hate jumps out at me and for a moment the essence of me is seared by it. A storm of hidden knowledge, secret pain, leaps at my soul, accusing, huge in its condemnation of my treatment of her as wife. I can see where it all comes from: the mind-bending brutality, the intimidation, the violence, the erasure of her soul — the screaming soul she denied. *Oh God, the living body of me scarred and twisted the very soul of Emma.*

In a corner, my brother and sister are secretly plotting for the spoils of my bodily being. Jerks. My spirit rolls back to my own plotting for the spoils of my parents before they were properly laid to rest. The twisting begins again, the terrible, unbearable heat of deceit in life burns my soul in death.

Oh God, I cry, *Don't do this to yourselves.* No one hears me. It is a little confusing being dead. You feel more alive than ever, except no one knows you are there. No soul present actually misses me, most particularly not Emma. She is relieved.

Shit. And mountains of it appear from nowhere. Shit-loads tumbling down from above me. A wall of crap. *I don't believe this.* The spirit of me is swept up in this sheet of rank-smelling human feces. *What's going on here?* We hit the water together, the shit and the truth of me. The water is filthy without the help of the crap. Rushing along, spreading itself out and running for the vast, bankless river of salt, the crud holds my truth in a vice-grip of gut-wrenching stink. *What the hell is this all about?* The water ejects me at the exit of the river, just next to an old man sitting on a park bench reading a newspaper.

I remember it now. Three million metric tonnes of untreated sewage dumped into the Fraser River, protested, of course, by a few crazies — college rejects, calling themselves eco-something-or-others. *Oh God. I wish I had been one of them.*

Hey, you oughta be reading that with a little more soul, old man. The polluting happened before I died so my words are wasted, but the truth is, it still goes on.

On the wings of a snow-white dove, my truth sails across the vast expanse of weeping earth and choking fauna and my soul mutters helplessly to the wreckage below: *Jesus, I didn't know.*

"Oh yes, but you didn't seek." From out of the blue, he appears on the tip of the dove's other wing, looking just as normal as can be. He can't be normal, though — he must be just as dead as me. The dove dips and drops us both in a mountainous wasteland — earth brutalized by a flurry of murderous chainsaws that massacred her treasured children. Not satisfied, man consigned the weak, the unusable seedlings and brush to a widow's pyre.

Didn't seek? I repeat dumbly.

"Yes, you know, seek and ye shall find," and he fades away.

WAIT.

No presence, just a soft chuckle and a clean voice: "You silly fellow, you cannot command another man's soul here."

Oh Lord.

"That's another thing, that whole business of lords has no roots in heavenly reality." At first I think he is kidding. But after I listen to it, I realize the whole notion of lords in heaven is ridiculous. It could not have been contrived by ethereal souls.

From inside the stone walls of Parliament, the House of Lords drivels nonsense while their lying souls convince their mouths that the bullshit they are peddling is true. I can't believe that I ever had faith in these fools. It's embarrassing. "Apartheid is not a question for us to address," some wigged lord with South African investments is saying. *I'll bet not. After all, you're the white guys.* I would laugh, but the truth stops me, and there in the kitchen of my own neighbourhood is Mike, being disgusted by all the uppity Blacks "who had a lotta nerve shooting us," and the body of me is agreeing. The blood of Soweto runs thick in the kitchen. The screaming pain of children being shot fills me. It muffles the stupid words uttered by pompous arrogance, and soils forever my truth.

A child, heartsick and ashamed, appears in the schoolyard with my grandson, who leads the others in cruel taunts against the solitary child.

Oh don't. Jesus don't.

"I never did. I always maintained that all children are a great offering to life." There he is again and the truth of his African heritage is written on his soul.

Actually, I was talking to my grandson.

"His name is not Jesus," and he disappears.

Is this all there is? Endless pictures of the whole suffering world? The wind carries my longings to the mouth of a poet whose words are secretly laughed at. *Oh God*, and a vast sense of nothingness sweeps over me. The nothingness is unmoving, cloying it its inertia. It suspends my soul in a terrifying void. It ends as it began, suddenly and of its own will. Nothingness is scary, but still it offers temporary relief from the tearless weeping. Since I came to this Godforsaken place, I have felt happy but once.

In the meadow where the void jerks to a halt, children are playing, chasing elusive butterflies. Peace rests within me. Laughter delights their little bodies, captures the heart of the grasses, and the trees chatter, echoing the sensuous happiness of childhood. The sun whispers gently and its light plays about on the skin of the earth's young. Grass, trees and little children are bursting with peace and joy. It is the first moment of rest for my soul.

"Growth is joyous. The knife that inhibits growth is the sword of death," the grasses breathe in blessed refrain.

The children disappear and a plane carrying defoliants flies overhead, spraying the meadow below in preparation for clearcutting the forest at the edge of the meadow. The horror of the whir from the airplane's engine slaps the peace from my soul.

Jesus, when does it all end?

"Be clear. When does what all end?" (*Jesus, I am getting tired of this guy. Every rhetorical or philosophical remark prefaced by his name calls him forth.*)

"You won't be so tired when your novitiate is over. I don't have to answer forever, you know." I did not know that there are no private thoughts in heaven. Jesus smiles.

Well, the butchery?

"Ah," and he leaves. The earth sighs to the sun, "It ends when the body of people stops hiding from the truth of the spirit." It seems too simple.

"It is simple. Why are you, of all people, doubting that?" she asks. And suddenly I need the comfort of Emma's long-suffering presence ...

* * *

"Hallo-oo, how are you?" and the lilt in Mike's voice veils his discomfort at seeing Emma again. He doesn't want to know how Emma is. His deception is an ugly sight. Deception has got to be hell's inner face. A deluge of scenes of deception bombards my truth: verbal garbage, physical garbage and most criminal of all, food garbage — all deceptively rationalized as respectable by the bodies of humanity that race across my view. The souls of people take the shape of their deception, and the eyes of my essence ache with the unbearableness of the sight.

Jesus. What is going on?

"Well, this is heaven and here you are, dead, looking at life through the honest eyes of your soul."

Well, if this is heaven, what is hell?

"You already know the answer to that one. Perhaps you want to know more about how it all works. You see, heaven is simply the sky. At the point of mortal departure, your spirit gets to walk the wing tips of the wind, witnessing the reality of your life. The soul is not blind, however. In death the truth is not dressed in the deceptive clothes of mortal flesh. The soul is incapable of rationalization."

You mean I have to watch, over and over, everything I have just seen?

"That is about it, but for a minor exception."

What do you get to see — the same thing?

And he laughs. The sound comes from deep within the earth, rich and resonant. It spreads out thick and joyous. The winds catch the laughter and layer the seas and grasses with it. Embarrassed, I try digging around inside for guilt to hide my shame. Only shame blossoms, relentless in its flowering. I yearn for the agony of guilt to absolve me. I fall over in a foolish, prostrate position of remorse, but guilt does not come.

Oh Jesus, can't I even enjoy the comfort of guilt?

"Oh no. Heaven is not like that. Here, there is but pleasure and pain. You see, if pain were experienced with the absolving comfort of guilt, it would be impure. Guilt is an intellectual contrivance that reduces the pain the spirit needs to experience if it is to alter the actions of the body. In that sense, guilt is the ultimate deception — hell. The spirit resides in heaven; it knows not hell."

Holy mother of Jesus. I can't go through this for all eternity.

"Yes you can. People do it all the time." She says it without sympathy — it's just a matter of fact; an eternal reality.

"Hello, mom," Jesus purrs.

"Jesus, how nice for our paths to cross."

Christ, this is insane. I balk at the bizarre meeting between mother and son, two thousand years dead. In my mortal life the idea of Mary as Jesus's mother ended with his birth.

"You called?" Jesus interrupts my thoughts.

I meant God, really.

His voice swells with magnificent urgency: "Man, in his opportunist desire to ease life and deceive himself that the torment of others is no concern of his, distorts the natural world of the spirit. Man creates a vision of heaven and hell for himself that he might justify his selfishness and appease his conscience while outraging human and natural life. God, good, all began as the 'great offering' of one's life to the world. But now, it is a catch-all word for every kind of desperate anguish living mortals wish to hide from. The offering is disempowered, destroyed, and its meaning lost to humanity by the distortion of godliness. God has become the mantle for the greatest human atrocity — war."

Horseshit, I snap, and it begins again, the crap, the children, the hunger of humanity.

Oh Jesus. I want to go back to my box and rest.

"You can't. It has been buried. Heaven is the sky and you cannot return to the earth. How long did you think eternity was?" Jesus leaves and the terror of having to walk the winds witnessing my life's trials without the comfort of his company follows his departure. The memory of my mortal life, cold nights warmed by Emma's yielding flesh, fills me with desire. *Emma, help me.* Below my shameless begging stands Emma, staring hard at the window of her quiet living room. She neither hears nor sees a thing. She is busy making a decision.

"He seems like a nice fellow. Not like the last," she whispers silently to herself, not even according me my name or the title of husband. "Ah, courtship; if only love could grow from the sweet seed of courtship to the lovely flower marriage was intended to be." The inside of her new love lays itself bare to me. While the man's body anxiously occupies my chair and waits for her reply, his damaged soul shouts his truth at mine. I try to warn her but know she hears not a word. Alone at fifty-six, afraid, desperate for affection, Emma says "yes."

In the beginning he is sweet, as though he has not fully awakened to the realization that the courtship is over. For a while there is laughter in Emma's little house. But, as men are wont to do from time to time, he screws up at work. The boss gives him what for and he comes home, full to the brim with another man's anger and his own humiliation.

Like a replay of my own mortality, the beer follows, then drunken, impotent raging about the boss and wild, unreasonable demands on Emma. She is slow to move on his drunken commands. (Sabotage, I had surmised as a living person, and quite correctly. What woman jumps happily to a drunken husband's command?)

Then the fists fly. The thud of human meat battered by the hammer that a man's hand can be. The tears, the screams, the agony of his perverse triumph over the lively body that he alone has reduced to limp life. And my wasted soul stretches itself over her body in a futile effort to protect my Emma from this other man's fists.

Inside the body of Emma a black emotion rises and spirals to the centre of her being. The soul of me catches in the madness of her emotion, captivated by her bleakly intense struggle to convert her outrage to despair. A crazy cacophony of raw passion carries me to that magical place where all feelings begin. A single crystal teardrop, alone in a fit of rage, rests peacefully. In shocked disbelief my truth stares at the perfect droplet.

Jesus ...

"But it is beautiful, isn't it?" His voice brings momentary relief from the desperation that lingers in the clarity of the tear.

Is this all there is left, just one tear, one tear to account for her entire life?

"Imagine, if you will, that she can hear the mutterings of her innermost self and rise up. Imagine the great flood that this little tear could become in the tide of her resistance. Bear witness, my friend."

Jesus fades and compassion rises in the soul of me. My soul envelops the tear. I plead for its life, praying for it to swell and to multiply. Softly murmuring, I cajole the tear to grow. *Not twice, Emma. I am dead. Surely you must know that I should never have lived thus, comfortable with your suffering. Emma, hear the words whispered to thee by thy self, thy perfect self. Abide by thy perfect right to be.*

I stretch my truth throughout her body, grow small around the tear, my soul rhythmically undulating with my fervent desire for her salvation. My love reaches its purest moment. Spent, my passion drapes itself in a perfect circle around the lonely tear. I feel her body rise. I hear the resounding "no" from every cell of her flesh. In my death watch, there is a great rejoicing. The knife in her hand drives through the sleeping man's heart. The blood mesmerizes her and then the wall of tears drives me outside her self.

But more my spirit knows. Police and courts are next. Emma sits in wordless teary repose, my own madness her defence. "Not twice." The very words of my soul she repeats to her counsellor.

From my sky perch I am compelled to watch. Jesus comes first among the throng that gathers. Curious, I ask why his presence.

"This is the very thing to which I am called, the judging of the meek and courageous by the lords of violence."

Nine Black boys gather next to us, giggling and shuffling and watching by turns.

Who are they?

"The Scottsborough boys. You must remember them."

How could I forget. The boys hung for a rape they were much too innocent to commit. The madness of racism runs sour and ac-rid in my soul. I, coward that I was, sanctioned the dirty deed. Sympathy, simpering and jelly-soft, obscures my outrage.

It must have been terrible for them to come here.

"Not at all. They have enjoyed themselves immensely since being freed from the prison of racial violence. Why, they have participated in every glorious riot, in every movement of Black resistance from Birmingham in 1948 to Soweto, just a short time ago. They have had their vengeance."

Is there then only freedom in death?

"Quite the contrary. When the slave is no longer a slave, what you have left is an ex-master. If the master insists on protecting his position with weapons, the slaves will have to covet the gun."

The congregation includes the strangest people.

Who is the funny-looking little fellow who speaks a strange language?

"Why, that's Vladimir Ilich Ulyanov; you probably know him as Lenin."

But he is an atheist.

"Heaven is the one place that does not discriminate."

The congregation swells its ranks with the champions of the meek and the poor; those who so loved the world that they sacri-ficed their selves that justice to earth and people might prevail. Marx, Fred Hampton, Jackson, Krupskya, Gwarth-Es-La and his standard bearer ...

These people are all rebels.

"Yes, they are all in their own way like myself."

I am no rebel.

"Ah, but you unlocked the door to Emma's rebellion."

The court case drags on in its usual ceremony of arrogant rigidity and stupid exactitude of language without sentiment. My life with her is dragged forward, couched carefully in legal mumbo-jumbo. Her character is attested to by women who assure the world that Emma was a kind and devoted wife to a brutal first husband. Even our children testify that they and their mother had been abused. Emma rises to her own defence. She refuses to deny that her hand held the knife that stabbed her second husband, but she confesses no guilt.

"I am a christian woman. This is supposed to be a christian country. Jesus himself forbade the abuse of the meek, but he did not deny our sacred right to resist abuse. 'Where ye shall have no justice, ye shall have no peace.' The man that would batter his wife is less than a serpent. I was born three months ago; until that day, I wandered the world a slave … "

"Oh, ain't she a woman? … Ain't she a woman?" and the tall reedy body of an old Black woman waltzes and sways to the music of her own words.

Who are you?

"Why, I'm Sojourner Truth. An' Emma an' me was born on the same day. I was delivered from slavery at fifty-six years ol' and so was she."

"I should have killed that first brute," Emma says, "but he died on me. And this lawyer sitting here doesn't know what he is about. Didn't know what I was doing? No one who feels the plunge of a blade through a human heart can ever testify that they did not know what they were doing. I knew I stabbed him. I knew it would send him to his maker. But I am guilty of no crime. I did not kill a man; I stabbed a snake."

The judge looks aghast. She feels her own emotion rising, contemplates quitting herself of the case, but a voice whispers from within that the jury, not she, will be pronouncing the verdict on Emma. She remains riveted to her throne. She counsels the jury that she must resolve some legal questions before they can retire to decide Emma's fate, and she buys time for her own troubled soul.

In the week that follows, the congregation remains vigilant. There is a hubbub of discussion about the possibilities that lie ahead for woman and earth should Emma win. Joy hangs in the air, visible as Thoreau's lily. Even the old woman next me, grim-faced most of the time, chuckles now and then.

What is your name?

"Emily."

Carr, the artist?

"Hmph."

I am honoured, I pule.

"I would rather you be pleased."

The week draws to a close and the judge counsels the jury. "The defendant takes precedence over her own counsel. Indeed, according to Benjamin Franklin, Thomas Jefferson and the 'defender of the constitution,' Daniel Webster, the founding fathers of this United States of America intended the values of this country to reflect those of the New Testament. The jury is to decide the fate of Emma in accordance with the book of Revelations and the word of Jesus. There is no doubt that Emma slew her second husband, but the law governing America and finally Emma, is the law of Christ."

The jury retires, armed with twelve New Testaments. And the heavenly congregation replies in blessed song:

Praise her soul, she saw the light.
The truth of this sojourner,
has been seen at last.
Praise her soul, she saw the light.

World War I

I wonder about memory sometimes. As a child I, along with a host of other children, listened to story after story without ever considering we would one day want, no, need to repeat these stories. I have repeated a number of such stories to my own children on long winter evenings during winter sleep, but until now I never wanted to write any of them down. Some I will never tell, but this one is curiously apropos of our times, and it gnaws at me as though it wants to find its way to dead wood leaves. I never thought much about the accuracy of my memory. Fiction does not require it, but this one isn't fiction; it happened, even if it didn't. Right now I don't even trust my memory to tell you who the bearer of the tale was. I was busy stewing over this when it struck me that the gift I possess lies in coming to grips with the essence of a story and combining this essence with my own specific imagination.

In my memory, no two people ever told the same story in exactly the same way. The bearer of the tale embellished the thread of the story with their own fabric. It would be sad should this written version come to represent the last word in the story; hence, I caution you to read it and re-imagine it, tell it to yourself with your mind wide open and full of your own embellishments.

There is a rush upon us, a tidal wave of soul searching of the past. All manner of youth are returning to the firesides of the elders in our community to gather yesterday's stories and commit them to memory. I don't feel this urge as deeply as I ought to. I return to no one to refresh my memory, perhaps because I am old enough to believe that, young as I am, I understand what I heard, and perhaps because I believe that the thread of it, not the precision of its retelling, is what is important.

For those with a penchant for verbatim accuracy, the story will offend. I don't apologize. For those who learned from the story when you first heard it and let it guide your lives, the story will enthrall and inspire, and this I am keen on.

✳   ✳   ✳

Characters:
HIM, un-named animal, probably extinct
SHE, definitely extinct

Two eagles, an ailing old man and his long-time mate, enjoy his last movements. No tears from her, just resignation. She watches him draw his last breath, noisy and full of objection to the termination of his life. His passing occurs amid a storm that rages across the bits of land left by rising water. Great bodies pool into lakes fed by a confusion of streams which melt with salt water of the seas. A tempest of liquid — swirling, bubbling and prohibiting the flourishing of new populations — had gone unnoticed by the old woman until her mate's life was over.

In the joy of their union, she had not thought about the shrinking of the landscape. With his death, her eyes opened to the creatures huddled together between the mass of moving lakes, streams and sea, birthing and perishing on the narrowing ridges before maturity reached them. She knew something momentous was about to happen.

The bird people were reduced to flying incessantly, sneaking up on the entrapped four-leggeds while they slept, in order to garner a few seeds and insects. Confined to ridges, the animals grew sour, mean, bickering among themselves, unable to develop the character of their race in a balanced way. When hunger came upon them, and it did more and more often, they snarled, nipped, and occasionally ate one another. Their sleep was incomplete as the sleep of the hungry is apt to be.

Suspicion, hunger's lover, distorted them, grew to paranoia; bickering became feuding and genocide threatened the people. Rain was anticipated with dread. It filled the lakes, overran the streams and halved the little existing ridgelands, decimating entire populations. Whole species came and went during the rains. Plant life perished and starvation, not the simple hunger that natters at the body between mealtimes but starvation of the sort which emaciates and destroys the body, swallowed one species after another. Eagle, her mate gone, took it upon herself to examine the world.

✳ ✳ ✳

From a ridge, he watched the water swell. His ridge was shrinking, the water was swallowing the bit of earth under his feet. Great huge raindrops pelted his coat. Shivering, he peered over the landscape with panicked eyes bulging inside their fleshless sockets. He staggered towards the water, scanned the next ridge: maybe it would produce a drowned rat, a mole. Despite his fear, he leapt into the raging inferno.

Each pathetic stroke brought new panic to Him as the water, maddened by the rain, rose and fell, pulling at the living skeleton, thrashing at it as it struggled to reach the next ridge. A mouse, eyes blank with lifelessness, was tossed to Him in midstream. He swallowed it. Whole. Barely chewed its scrawny body. He gagged, the blood rushed to his head, dimmed his eyes, his stomach worked overtime trying to digest the thing. Water snuck inside his nose and stopped the need to gag while it threatened his lungs with asphyxiation.

Memories tormented Him, memories of his young eaten by himself, and of his mate, murdered in his bitter determination to survive. These memories stilled his legs. *What is the point, you have no mate, your survival is limited to this, your last swim.* The thought of the end of his species calmed Him. *No more scrounging, no more swimming for new shores, the end of eating newborn in vain attempts to survive.* His relief at coming to the end relaxed Him and his body gave up its desperate strokes, acquiescing to a melancholy dreamlike floating on the crest of the torrent of water.

From deep within the bowels of the earth a volcano erupted, driving the water straight up and fanning it out. The sea raged, churned, and bits of earth were cast to a special place. *Dream, old boy, dream of earth lush and green, of landscapes rich and relenting, dream through the whirl of sea and flying earth.* Stone, inert, cool stone driven from the sea, fell layer upon layer onto the ridge in front of Him. Earth bits covered land and island mountain was created. Animals in their multitudes peopled this new place while he floated on the sea.

He was aware he was dreaming. He knew he dreamed this dream in one last attempt at eternity. Sleep, deep, dreamless and long, came upon Him and he all but succumbed to the ravages of the rain and sea. Eagle, in her wanderings, came upon Him. She thought of SHE. SHE, lonely, her life empty of the company of her own. Eagle whistled and Raven joined her. The thought of gifting SHE with one of her own appealed to Raven. (Raven is not always a trickster; sometimes she's downright kind.) She swooped down and plucked Him from the turbulent waters and tossed Him to the shores of their island mountain home. Eagle tracked SHE down and whispered of the presence of Him.

SHE's cool tongue caressed his cheek and cleaned his aching body. It woke Him up. SHE looked at Him from well-fed eyes. Jealous, he snarled. SHE arched, threw Him already-chewed food and left. *He'll be back, come fall, with something different on his mind,* and with that SHE scurried up the hillside and disappeared into the trees.

He sniffed the food. He had had experience of eating too quickly in a starving state. He pecked at the mash, swallowed patiently, let it settle, then pecked a little more. Hours passed before he finished. He could feel the old strength coming back. It filled Him with the confidence of the capable and well-fed. His mind did not function well yet, so he forgot where the mash had come from. By morning, he rose strong and agile.

Sound. The wondrous sound of life touched his ears. Birdsong, muskrat, rabbit, even the dull hum of moles burrowing beneath the land made Him dizzy with happy anticipation. No memories of a treasured life, rich with children, intruded upon his glee at the paradise of living meat he had been cast into.

He could not be blamed for not knowing this mountain was special, a place apart from the rest of the world, rich with plant life that was endlessly available. *The bird in front of me will do,* and he stalked it, though it wasn't really necessary in this place. No animals had any idea other animals would eat them. Bird pecked at the seeds about her, leaving the leaves for Him, and nodded in innocent greeting. He looked a little strange to bird, prancing about like that, but bird carried on eating nonchalantly.

Crunch, her neck broke, blood spilled, a scream from her throat issued forth and it was all over. Several of her family rushed to the scene. He went wild. Eyes bulging with the memory of hunger, he exacted bloody carnage on them all. Screams of perishing birds filled the air. Others came, batting wing against flesh, pecking at Him until, exhausted, he fell to the ground. Bones of bird lay scattered in great numbers. The living relatives of those who owned the bones stared in silence.

After a time, they spoke. "He looks like SHE, but there is something different about Him." ... "Where did he come from?" ... "The water must have brought Him ... hmnmn," and a profound respect and a wee bit of terror of the seas was born among them. Anger, new and uncontrolled, consumed the youth. "We should kill Him," they whispered to one another. "Why?" queried the old birds, "perhaps he is ill." "Vengeance," came the reply. Youth harangued at length, full of the sort of outrage peculiar to the young, righteous and lacking in foresight. The elder birds, fearful of the consequences of killing another person, counselled the young: "We'll go see SHE first. He is, after all, one of hers." The young birds, angry as they were, lacked the courage to move without the sanction of their elders. (It was a different time.) Reluctantly, they agreed.

As with some gentle-hearted women who love too much, SHE excused Him. "He was not from here, he didn't understand our ways, he had been starved, something no one on this island mountain could possibly understand. Let us give Him a chance to grow accustomed to our ways and see." Time passed and he continued to eat small animals, despite the gentle admonitions of SHE. The birds grew passive about his habits, as he had come to prefer the four-legged people to their own race. He had never repeated the carnage on them since his first day on the island, and the bird world began to forget that once they had all considered themselves one people. The land abounded with small animal life and he seemed always well satisfied without threatening the survival of any single species. An old inertia settled in around the eating habits of Him, even among the animals.

SHE, try as she might, could not convince Him to eat the plant mash everyone else ate. That it was better food seemed irrelevant to Him. As sometimes happens among people, certain curious individuals attracted by someone else's bizarre behaviour are influenced to emulate that behaviour. So it was that rat was the first to note that meat filled the body with a pleasant kind of fullness which was good for dreaming. A lazy relaxation resulted from the consumption of flesh and seemed better than the fulfilling, quick energy of the mash.

Despite his eating habits, SHE loved Him and was soon pregnant. Her knowledge of birth, creation, was scanty. The change in her body was marvellous. The children came in great numbers, soft and sweet, full of innocent trust and complete dependence upon her. SHE thought, as some women are wont to think, that children would bring love to the tortured soul of her mate. SHE awaited his transformation.

It didn't come. His soul had perished in the sea of forgotten dreams. One morning SHE awoke with one less child. Rage, Shock,

Grief, all made her crazy for a moment; then practical necessity cooled her emotions and SHE packed up her remaining children and retreated to a secret lair in which to nurture them. His blood and his cynicism filled the souls of some of them, while others tended to be like her. Hunting tiny prey came naturally to those like Him, and they set about capturing and consuming mice against her wishes. SHE, loving mother that she was, remained forever disappointed at their misbehaviour, but could not bring herself to disdain her young. SHE nourished them in the way they chose.

Her eldest son had a penchant for birds, and like his father, felt territorial mastery deep in his loins. He forbade birds in his kingdom, eating them should they transgress onto his territory. The old rage came back to the birds, whose land base and freedom shrank under the dominion of this prodigal.

In the night, second son dreamed of his sister, tender and warm, and he sought her. At first she resisted, but eventually her time came and she succumbed to the perpetuation of her species. The cynicism of their father was assured in their union. Like a prairie fire, the heady, dream-like satisfaction which followed the consumption of meat spread. Muskrat ate fish, fox ate rabbit, rat ate mouse and deep sadness settled in SHE. Her union with Him had brought pain to the land and it grew too large for SHE to bear. As SHE lay in her cavern, nursing a new batch of children to independence, SHE let go one last whimper and died.

* * *

Old eagle watched this and wondered at the meaning of all this change. She watched somewhat dispassionately, thinking SHE had always been too soft-hearted, but SHE's mate was swinging the world too much in the other direction. Eagle felt SHE loved too much, too earnestly, and in the end, was consumed by it. A cold shiver travelled up old eagle's spine as she realized that perfection had died as a human quality with the passing of SHE.

The bird people learned to fly away whenever the citizens of the four-legged race approached them. A youthful eagle, sharp-eyed and brilliant (in a military sort of way), noted that the bird people outnumbered the four-legged people. He counselled the others to war. "The largest among us can deplete the smallest and most numerous of them. Hawk, take mole, mouse and the children of muskrat. I shall have raccoon, rabbit and the children of cougar and fox; gull take fish; you small birds can take worm, insect and spider. Together, we can rule the land. Terror will drive the animal race back into the sea."

Now this was curious. Eagle wondered at such folly. Since when has command of the plant world ever been a goal for either race of people? Still, eagle said nothing. And it came to pass that the four-legged and the winged people went to war. (Now modern men of the two-legged variety, who say they alone are people, claim they invented war and refer to 1914-1918 as the First World War, but eagle and Raven know differently. Unlike two-legged men, the winged and the four-legged people gave it up the first time.)

Bat is a strange bird-animal. His disposition is different from any other person's. He sometimes walks on two legs and flies at other times. It matters little what he eats so long as he does. He eats without conscience. His one great love is himself. He watched the conflict between the people heat up. Interesting. He was sure it had nothing to do with him. The birds converged in their great number upon the animals, consuming their flesh and letting much blood flow. Bat flew about cheering them on, sometimes partaking in the carnage. The animals' wits sharpened by the attack, they stalked bird nests and slew the young. Bat joined them too, walking about, stalking bird nests and laying to rest their young.

An odd joy filled the bat. He was proud of his ability to walk and fly with equal comfort. The war intensified, each side polarizing, growing experienced, becoming more and more sophisticated in the business of war. No one called it art then, as some men do today. Carnage, strategizing and greater carnage abounded. Blood filled the mountain, covered the earth, and the smell of death filled the air. Animals learned to climb trees and destroy nests; birds ferreted out the newborn animals whose parents had gone to the water's edge to quiet their thirst. And bat, unnoticed, joined whichever side was winning the war.

Old eagle watched the war, wept with pity at the antics of bat and was bothered by the scent of death which contaminated their home, but she was not so faint of heart as to be saddened beyond living, as SHE had been. Eagle had not experienced love of mate in the same way. *No mate should ever pull the character from out of your soul — love or no love.* Eagle remembered her old mate and chuckled at the memory. She saw him tucking his old white head beneath his wing and worrying the down underneath it. She had had, at the time of his death, a funny desire to go first. Now she thought it was just as well it had gone the other way; the ridiculous picture of their grandchildren participating in the death below would have been too much for the old man. (In those days gentleness was not a trait of only one sex.)

Raven perched herself just below eagle. *How does Raven always know when I am lost in deep thought?* old eagle wondered, but didn't say. She whistled out a bored "Hello, and how are you?" Raven's voice annoyed eagle, but she had the redeeming quality of subverting the annoying stridence of her voice by always coming to the point and talking little. Eagle liked that. "We have to stop the war." Eagle knew Raven meant she should think of something Raven could do to stop it.

"What we need is a screaming wind, a tornado, to bring them to hysteria. We need to have wind sing a lamenting song of their lost ones. We need them to hear their lost ones wail sobs of recrimination at their grandchildren," eagle said.

"That will mean the old ones will have to do all the work of bringing conscience to their grandchildren, perhaps just a windsong to counsel them to meet and do the right thing. You could speak, eagle, and I will bring the wind and gather them together," was Raven's response.

"Sounds all right to me," eagle said, shrugging diplomatically. Raven drew the wind and the voices of the lost ones to the ears of the living.

Under the hysteria of the wind and the song of the ancients, the carnage stopped. Animal and bird people gathered, each forming a half circle that met the half circle of the other. The smallness of the numbers in the circle stunned them; the magnitude of death caused by war shamed them.

Now, eagle is no idealist. Practical reality had changed them; she knew they could not return to the old ways. The mash had been destroyed by fire sparked by the burn-and-destroy policy of the people at one stage of the war; neither could they negate the new feeling of territory which now filled each animal and bird. What they could do was come to an agreement on the law of survival which would govern the people.

Eagle recounted the history of the war, how it came to be, the numbers of dead, and determined the course to be taken should they all agree. She calculated how much meat each animal, bird and bat would need to guarantee survival. They listened. She spoke of survival of the plant world, who should eat plants, who should eat meat and how many births each race should have so that no population should overrun the others. She postulated that birds should have dominion over the skies and animals dominion over the land, but neither should rule the place of their dominion. Should birds need rest, trees should provide them with a home. Large animals should not rob nests. Each animal and bird was given a prey, food which would challenge their strength and yet assure their survival. No one would have any more than the bare necessities. Eagle restricted her own movement to gliding on the wind currents, and all were well-satisfied, except Raven. Raven was sure all things were not taken care of. There was bat, so confused about his identity and the nature of the gathering that he strutted about and flew by turns. Raven leapt into the air, wings beating furiously, and plucked the vision from bat's eyes. Eagle banished bat to fly only at night, never to be part of either race of people. A general commotion arose, but in the end bird and animal people all agreed to ostracize bat. But in order to protect against arbitrary judgement, the people exacted a promise from eagle and Raven that no ostracism should ever take place again without the consent of all the people. Raven and eagle agreed.

Content, eagle continued to live for some time after. She watched the water recede as the earth shed fewer tears for her children. Quietly, death came. It filled her bones with the need to rest for all eternity and bestirred memories of her mate worrying his wing. She smiled a soft grin of one musing over old familiar things and fell from her perch.

* * * * *

LEE MARACLE is a member of the Stoh:lo Nation of British Columbia. She currently works as a partner in Native Futures Group, where she integrates her traditional Indigenous teachings with her European education to create culturally appropriate processes of healing for Native people. She has been employed by various First Nations groups and governments to teach general health seminars from a traditional perspective and to reclaim culture, sociology, law and government through language, creative writing and counselling. She is the Aboriginal "Mentor in Residence" at University of Toronto, an award-winning teacher and the Traditional Cultural Director at the Centre for Indigenous Theatre.

One of the leading First Nations writers in North America, Lee Maracle is also the author of *I Am Woman: A Native Perspective on Sociology and Feminism, Bobbi Lee: Indian Rebel* (autobiography) and *Ravensong* (a novel). She is the co-editor of *Telling It: Women and Language Across Cultures* and her work has appeared in many anthologies, including the 1999 Before Columbus American Book Award winner *First Fish, First People: Salmon Tales of the Pacific Northwest* (Judith Roche, Meg Hutchinson, eds.). Lee is working on a new novel, tentatively titled *Eagle Whistling*, to be released by Press Gang Publishers in 2000. She is also publishing a collection of poetry, *Bent Box*, with Theytus Books in 2000.